To J.
M.
B.
C.
J.
S.
Without any of whom,
there would have been no book.

Extraordinary Rendition: a term used by US intelligence and military personnel in reference to the abduction, transporting and detention of enemy combatants for interrogation purposes.

It will have blood, they say; blood will have blood.
                                                    Macbeth

PROLOGUE

PROLOGUE

OUTSKIRTS OF RABAT, MOROCCO, NINE MONTHS AGO

'No, Daddy, don't go!'

It's this one line – four simple words spoken by his six-year-old daughter – that he hears now. It places him back in his home, in Paddington. He could still smell the dinner of roasted lamb that lingered in the air. The air that carried the sounds of central London going to sleep outside, hushed as if aware that his daughter was now past her bedtime, yet she always had that uncanny knack of knowing when he had to leave the house – often at any hour, at any time. Being an investigative journalist was like that, particularly for one who specialised in the Middle East.

Michael Rollins tried hard to keep the image of his family in his mind's eye. His wife's smile. The taste of her lipstick. That goodbye. Even the look that came when she noticed he had packed a Kevlar vest in his carry-all. Especially that look. It showed in every line of concern on her face, formed a map of her love for him. The contours of the life they had created. He looked back, from inside the black cab, and waved a final goodbye.

There are tears in his eyes now and the image blurs. It dissolves. Dissolves into a blinding white light. He wants to cry out but he can't. Wants to cry but he won't.

He strains to replay this memory.

The sounds that had come in through the open front door bounce around him. His daughter shuffling down the stairs. She is caught up in the arms of her mother on the landing. Each scene holds for no more than a second. The house. The door. The cab. Their faces. They both look at him – this was the goodbye. This is the image that is held in his mind. Burned into his memory. Forever. Was that forever? Or five seconds? It's – what? It's gone. Wait, how long was that? Where is it – where did it go? Come back. Come back. Come back . . .

He's there again, at home. His back was to the door. He felt a presence there behind him. His wife. He turned – his wife? No. There was nothing to see. He looked for his wife and daughter – they had not moved. They were right there, just inside his home. But he cannot move. He looks down to his feet but can't see them. Everything around him begins to spin out of focus. He sees his family through a tunnel of blurred vision. They're disappearing. Who will look after them? He wills himself to go to them and feels that if he can just make it back through the door . . . Go through it again, make a different choice. Don't leave.

He can't even turn around now. Can't move at all.

His last moments of time are caught in the eyes of the two women in his life. Then it's all . . . it's all gone.

Gone . . .

'My daughter . . . my wife . . .'

'Good, Michael.' The interrogator spoke close to him. If Michael could feel, he'd feel the man's breath as he spoke. If he could smell, he'd smell coffee. 'Your daughter, your wife. Do you want to see them again? Do you want to hold them?'

'My daughter . . . my wife . . .'

'That's right,' the interrogator said.

'My daughter . . .'

The CIA man nodded to his counterpart. They left the small concrete room with the man shackled to a steel chair. The xenon lights in the ceiling came ablaze, the room as indistinguishable as anywhere could be. This could be the surface of the Sun or the Moon or Mars. Anywhere unreal, unearthly. The sounds started up again. It might be music but it's too loud to tell.

Michael Rollins had worn a surgical mask, a black hood, orange overalls, shackles. Just the overalls and shackles remained now. He had moved but did not know how. He never felt the tranquilliser that entered his back four days ago. The plane flight strapped to a chair, the cabin chatter, all a blur, not even worthy of a memory. He just moved where herded, not the way a man moved but the way an eighty-kilo mass shifted from one position to another. His ears were ringing and his eyes saw spots of colour among the black and white. He remembered that his mouth was dry. It was dry. A memory. It was . . .

He'd been shackled to a metal chair, in this room, white on white. Blinding. He tries to close his eyes and wonders why he can't. They're taped open. So simple. But he cannot comprehend that. Why think about reasons.

A smell lingers. The last thing he could make out as a smell. It's gone – it's there again. Familiar. Piss? He could smell his own piss and then taste the acrid air. Taste!

It's through this and the dullest sense of pain from his crushed hands that he knows he is still alive.

He clings tight to these senses. Breathes them in, the short, shallow breaths of an asthmatic. Moves his hands so that they continue to crack and bleed at the puffy, broken joints. He almost laughs at the distant feeling – then it stops. It all stops.

It stops.

It is gone.

Gone.

He is not sure if he still moves his hands, if his nostrils flare to take in the smells. He is trying to feel, isn't he? Taste? How do you smell? It's all gone now.

Tears stream down his face, although he doesn't know it.

How? This final question is gone with as much alacrity as everything else. How? How? How ...

Rollins gives out a croak, a long, soft, guttural cry that fades to a shimmering whisper. It is a defeated sound, a sign that he has just lost the last of what he had.

Michael Rollins is broken.

AFGHANISTAN,
SIX MONTHS AGO

If it wasn't for the loaded pistol pressed hard against his head, Lachlan Fox might have enjoyed this morning. He was kneeling in the loose gravel of an airstrip in Afghanistan. A vast open pasture surrounded him, as far as the eye could see, to rugged mountains and rocky outcrops topped with snow. Nothing but blues and greys. Lonely. The sun was just starting to rise. Cold mist hung over the whole valley. Clouds crept down the mountains like slow-moving fingers. There was something ethereal in the vastness of this place that made Fox feel as though he were a pilgrim kneeling in the cathedral. A slight breeze blew through wild poppy fields that rolled to the west, all reds, yellows and oranges moving like a sea. A nice place to be, until an insurgent held him at gunpoint.

'More money, five million,' the armed man said, holding out a satellite phone for Fox to place the call on. The guy, Afghani or Uzbek by his accent, was entrepreneurial enough to know an opportunity to make money when he saw one. He'd seen the million dollars in used US bills, the shiny new Gulfstream G650 private jet parked on the side of the airstrip, and decided that he could make more money out of this transaction.

Fox took the offered satellite phone.

'Al,' Fox said. 'What's the number again?'

To his left, also on his knees, was his friend Alister Gammaldi. The two journalists were unarmed, as were the two pilots in the Gulfstream. Another insurgent, this one armed with an AK-47, covered the pilots, both of whom had their hands pressed up against the inside of the windscreen.

'Ah, let's see,' Gammaldi said. 'It's – no, wait for it –'

'The number!' The insurgent cracked the pistol against the side of Gammaldi's head as if it would rattle the information out. 'Make the call! Five million dollars, US, or you all die here today!'

'All right,' Gammaldi said, getting his balance back. He looked up at the man. 'I remember now. It's one-eight-hundred, kiss – my – ass.'

Fox could sense the man moving the pistol to Gammaldi again and then heard what sounded like a loud, heavy-handed slap. The left side of Gammaldi's face was covered with blood and gore. The insurgent fell to the ground between Fox and Gammaldi, half his head blown away.

By the Gulfstream, the gunman hadn't seen what had happened to his comrade when he succumbed to the same fate. The pilots cringed as the man's head seemed to vaporise.

Fox was to his feet and looked towards the two remaining insurgents. The one in the open, armed with an Uzi, stared uncomprehendingly at his fallen comrades. The other, behind the wheel of the old Land Cruiser, was panicked. Fox heard the engine start up and he pointed at the driver – a second later, just as the vehicle began to move, the windscreen shattered and was painted on the inside with blood.

The last man dropped his Uzi, turned and ran from the scene – he didn't make it more than five paces.

The hum of the car engine was the only sound for miles as Fox helped Gammaldi to his feet.

'Well, that was the second most disgusting thing I've ever seen,' Gammaldi said, dusting himself down and wiping off the collateral gore that had resulted from being close to a high-calibre head shot. 'Did she have to do that?'

Some six hundred metres away to the west, a woman emerged from the cover of the poppies, a silenced Accuracy International sniper's rifle in her hands. A man with a spotting scope followed her towards the airstrip. Both wore the camouflage uniforms of US military.

Fox opened the rear door of the idling Land Cruiser and helped a man out. Dressed in faded orange overalls, hands tied in front of him, Michael Rollins emerged from the car wide-eyed. Fox untied his hands and the Englishman embraced him.

'Lachlan – thank you,' Rollins managed to say. There were tears in his eyes and he started to weep. 'How long have I been . . .'

'Three months,' Fox said. 'Come on, we're taking you home, to your family.'

He led Rollins slowly towards the Gulfstream. *GLOBAL SYNDICATE OF REPORTERS* was stencilled down the fuselage. Fox and Gammaldi helped the weak Rollins up the stairs and the jet engines started up. The two GSR security members were the last aboard. Rollins shook their hands, shaky but smiling, as introductions were made.

'Thank you, Alister, thank you, Emma, thank you, Richard,' Rollins said. Exhausted, he settled back into a chair and drank from a bottle of water.

As the passengers strapped in, the aircraft turned and took off at full thrust.

'What the hell happened last week?' Fox asked Rollins.

The Englishman shook his head, summoning back the memories. He wiped a hand over his beard and through his hair.

'They broke us out,' he said, pointing back at those at the airfield. 'Attacked the camp. Killed a couple of CIA guys, put us in a truck. Later that night I convinced them I was worth more alive.'

'So you told them to call us?' Fox asked. 'It was your idea to do a cash trade?'

'Yes,' Rollins said. He peered out the window at the country-side that grew smaller below them. Fox looked out the window too and they all settled into post-adrenaline sombreness. A squadron of coalition fighter jets soared off to the edge of the sky, only their slipstreams visible.

Rollins said quietly, almost to himself, 'Sometimes, it's hard to know who you can trust.'

PART ONE

1

PORT HARCOURT, NIGERIA, PRESENT DAY

Pre-dawn in the oil strip. Clouds began to be lit from below and behind, shades of grey gilded in the reds that preceded the sun's first rays. Birdlife from the delta chorused their morning song. The two-million-plus population were awakening.

In the white Ford courier van Musa Onouarah was on his way to make sure the entire city heard his wake-up call. The van rode low on its axles, a thousand kilos of ANFO explosives in the load area. Battle-scarred hands steered the vehicle through the checkpoints. He waved to the soldiers who stood sentry behind Jersey barriers; they nodded and motioned him on as if he were their boss. Today, at least, he was.

He drove up to the main Western oil company building. A big blue glass structure that reflected the sky, twenty storeys high. Shiny steel mullions held the glass curtain that wrapped around a steel and concrete frame. It was dark within – too early for most staff. Only a handful of fluorescent office lights were on. Too late for anyone who happened to be in there.

Onouarah parked at the front entrance, shut the diesel engine off and set the handbrake. He looked out at the street – a small sedan motored by. A couple of white men jogged through the grassed park opposite. Onouarah snapped the key off in the ignition, got out the door, locked it by hand and shut it again.

He walked back down the road, went across the street, stood behind the glass-fronted corner of a convenience store. He scanned the oil building and its surrounds – all the CCTV brackets were empty.

In his hand, a radio control. A small black plastic box, two buttons and an antenna. He braced himself, just clear of the shop window, and pressed the detonator.

Half a second later the van was a fireball, its sheet-metal rupturing and being swallowed by the exploding mass. Flames ate at each other as it grew and grew, the destruction radiating. The thunderclap that rang off the buildings in the neighbour-hood was deafening. Windows absorbed the shockwave and shattered, showering the street with glass.

The shop-front laminated glass that Onouarah was behind cobwebbed but held. He went around the corner to see what was left of the building. The entire facade, gone. The concrete floors, crumbling. Pieces of rock and dust and paper and glass and insulation filled the air.

A gas main erupted in a secondary explosion, blowing him flat on his ass as it snaked under the road and sent manhole covers clear into the sky. The steel discs flew like coins at a toss, landing half a foot into solid pavement and road.

His work done, Onouarah got up, dusted himself off, and left the scene of the crime.

2

COLUMBIA UNIVERSITY, NEW YORK CITY

'I'm honoured to accept this award on behalf of the editorial team of our online magazine at gsrnews.com,' Lachlan Fox said. He held the Ellie award and looked out to the crowd, the flashing of bulbs in his eyes.

'Our content has grown to meet the demands of this inter-active environment of online publication and our front-line reportage continues to set the bar. In a time where many other media outlets have been cutting back their investigative reporting, I am proud to say that the Global Syndicate of Reporters is growing stronger every day.'

The black-tie crowd at the American Society of Magazine Editors' awards night were silent. Listening to this, another of many acceptance speeches.

'I'd like to take a few minutes, if I may, to dedicate this moment of time to the memory of some very special people.

People who should be with us, in this room, tonight. But they've been taken from us. They've been killed. All those unique voices that will no longer be read or be heard, those faces no longer seen, those thoughts and insights that will no longer be part of our public discourse.'

The room continued to reside in silence as they followed the cadence of Fox's speech.

'In 1904 Joseph Pulitzer said that this Republic and its press will rise or fall together. He said that the power to mould the future of the Republic will be in the hands of the journalists of future generations. I'm reminded by the work that is done by reporters out there on the front lines that makes this as true a statement now as it was back then. We are the shapers of more than just public opinion. What we do through our work is to keep alive the very societies whose freedoms we enjoy every day.

'And it's in light of that, that I remind you of the friends we have lost. In 2007, sixty-four journalists were killed in direct connection to their work. Thirty-one of those in Iraq alone. And about a similar number of support workers, security staff, drivers and translators, were also killed.'

'Last week, in Kabul, twelve of our colleagues left us too early. Two of my GSR staff, along with three from CNN, two from the BBC, one from Reuters, and four local support workers were killed by a terrorist bomb at a planned political rally. They were there early, setting up for coverage, and their families never got to say goodbye. They did not seek nor did they provoke the violent end that met them. We are working in dangerous places and live in dangerous times and we too may leave without having that chance of saying goodbye. But when we lose our friends, part of them lives on in us, and let's remember, as we stand here, that they shine down from the stars tonight. While we stand here, remember that there are seekers of truth out there on the front lines, where they'll be in the morning, where they'll be next week. Well may we never forget what any of our friends died doing.

'Thank you.'

'Well done, those men,' Wallace said. He clinked glasses with Fox and Gammaldi. 'Don't know if I can afford to let you award-winning reporters off the front line for a while. And here I was, considering if either of you wanted to go to work in Washington next year.'

'Doing?' Fox asked.

'We're getting a seat in the Press Room.'

'I'll go,' Gammaldi said.

'Why, so you can hit on Dana Perino?' Fox said.

'Who?'

'Never mind,' Fox said. He noticed Wallace check his watch. 'You have to be somewhere?'

'I'm going to The Met,' Wallace said, checking his watch again. 'Should be leaving now. I'll see you at the office tomorrow.'

'What you seeing?' Gammaldi asked.

'*Nabucco*. James Levine has come back to conduct it,' Wallace said. He'd already started to move away. 'We've got some tickets to each performance, if you want to see it?'

'Yeah, I might,' Fox said, deliberately stalling Wallace. 'I haven't been to The Met yet, and I do like Verdi.'

'Well, I'll let you know what it's like,' Wallace replied, about to turn and leave.

'Wait a second,' Fox said, protracting his boss's getaway. Tas Wallace, founder of GSR, had a highly profitable news business at his fingertips. By providing content rather than end product, the company turned massive profits from every major outlet of news media across the globe. It meant they were well-placed to take advantage of new media opportunities – their website gsrnews.com was one of the most trafficked news sites on the net.

He had noted the fifty-five-year-old bachelor was dressed especially sharp. He'd seen him attired for the opera before, but this was something else. 'Who are you seeing the opera with?'

'A friend,' Wallace said. 'Just a friend.'

'Come on,' Fox persisted, 'spill it. You've got a date, haven't you?'

Wallace looked around, and a woman about Fox's age approached. She shook Wallace's hand and he made the introductions.

'Lachlan, Alister, this is Jane Clay, of *The New Yorker*,' Wallace said.

'G'day,' Gammaldi said.

'Hi,' said Fox. She was attractive – he gave Gammaldi a look that said *Wallace has done well here*.

'Jane is writing a piece on us, starting with you and your department,' Wallace said to Fox. 'I'd better go, not polite to keep a lady waiting.'

Fox and Gammaldi shared a quick look – *Jane wasn't their boss's date*.

No way was Fox going to let him off the hook.

'Tas?' Fox said as his boss was heading off.

Wallace turned around, came back and spoke quietly: 'Maureen Dowd, okay?'

He left with a grin and a flick of his white scarf over his shoulder.

'I knew it,' Fox said, watching his boss weave through the crowd. 'He likes the redheads.'

'Most guys do,' Jane put in, still standing beside them.

Fox took a second to appraise her in more detail. Early thirties, dark hair, five six or so, a slim build typical of the type of journalist more fuelled by coffee and deadlines than yoga and serenity. Despite New York having just had a hot summer and the fact they were into the middle of a dry fall season, her skin wore the tan of a computer screen. Alabaster had more colour.

'Hell, I'd chase after Dowd if I was twenty years older,' Gammaldi added.

'Al, who are you kidding?' Fox said. 'You'd date her in a heartbeat.'

'Yeah, you're right – but only because of her beautiful mind and way with words. I'm gonna get us another drink,' Gammaldi announced, hightailing off after a waiter with a tray of hors d'oeuvres.

'So, what's your piece on, specifically?' Fox asked Jane. Her dark brown eyes were almost black, the kind you could get lost in.

'You.' Jane drank the last of her champagne.

'Tas said –'

'Yeah, he wanted me to take a tactful approach,' she said. 'Something I'm not very fond of.'

'Lachlan!' Graydon Carter came up and took Fox's offered hand in both of his. The *Vanity Fair* editor's hair was characteristically coiffed, his smile beaming. 'Wonderful speech.'

'Thanks,' Fox said, looking from Carter to Jane. 'Have you two met?'

'Yes we have. Jane is a protégé of Tina Brown, no less. How are you, dear?' he asked, giving her a kiss on the cheek. 'Lachlan, I want you to come over and meet the Pulitzer committee. They're already buzzing about the Indian water crisis articles you're doing for us for next year . . .'

'Sure,' Fox said, scanning around for Gammaldi.

'I'll wait here for Alister,' Jane said. She had a wicked smile. 'You go and reserve your medal.'

3

THE
WHITE HOUSE

'Good morning, Mr President,' Bill McCorkell said as he entered the Oval Office. The chief resident doctor was taking the President's blood pressure and unfastened the sphygmomanometer's Velcro strap.

'Pretty good, Mr President, one-thirty over eighty-five,' the physician said. 'Be sure to keep up the meds after your op on Saturday, and keep up the cardio work.'

'You should check Bill's blood pressure,' the President said, rolling his sleeve back down. 'Sure, he runs and rows and does God knows whatever other lame excuse for exercise, but I suspect he's one global crisis away from a triple bypass. It's the French blood in him.'

'His heart rate puts mine to shame, Mr President,' the physician said, a colonel five years younger than both the men there.

'I just cut out coffee too,' McCorkell said, pouring himself a tea.

'Mr President, I'll be travelling with you to Washington Hospital Center on the way to your op,' the physician said. 'Don't forget to follow the anaesthetist's instructions for the night before.'

The President grumbled his reply and the physician left the room.

'First up is Iraq: two Marines of the fifteenth MEU killed overnight in Baghdad,' McCorkell said. The 8 am meeting was the President's Daily Brief. A half-hour rundown of national security issues. McCorkell handed over the PDB folder and took a seat opposite the President. 'IED went off at a security checkpoint.'

The President sighed.

'Have their families scheduled in for a phone call tonight,' he said.

'Will do,' McCorkell replied, skimming down the notes. 'Still in that area, the Iraqi government's interior minister survived an assassination attempt, one of his bodyguards turned but he was taken down quickly. And Britain pulled out the last of their forces in the Basra province.'

'Their new force in Afghanistan?'

'Arrived overnight our time,' McCorkell said. 'Canadians and Aussies are each committing a company-sized infantry force to Kabul, in country by the end of the month. Denmark just announced they'll send a military police outfit, about a hundred guys.'

'We need more boots in there,' the President said. 'Thousands, not hundreds. Body count is rising too damned fast.'

'We've got a NATO military leadership meeting a fortnight from now, Vanzet will get the boots the Afghan government has asked for,' McCorkell said. 'And the CIA has just deployed a new squadron of Reaper UAVs, they're all armed hunter-killers, to the north. They're working with some Task Force Orange boys to clean out the mountains, village by village, house by house.'

'Congress are still pushing for a timeline for the next Iraqi troop withdrawal,' the President said. 'Attached it to the latest appropriations bill.'

'I saw that,' McCorkell said. 'You going to veto?'

'Have to,' the President said. 'They've made their point again, and round and round we go.'

'And we go out with the staged withdrawal based on security goals being met,' McCorkell said. 'It's the only interim option. We broke that country, and sure, we can't fix it in a hurry, but we can keep the civil conflicts from getting out of hand.'

'You don't call this out of hand?' The President tapped the headline of the *Washington Post* on his desk.

'Mr President, can you imagine what it would be like without our force in there? The country would split apart real fast, and it would be real messy. We're gonna need a big chunk of our own guys to remain there, at the very least inside Baghdad, for decades.'

'You don't think that if we announce withdrawal dates the insurgents will just hide under rocks until we bug out and then kick up hell again?'

'They can't pretend to stop the sectarian fights, it's in them, they'll do it until they wipe each other out,' McCorkell said.

'Or, hopefully, until their spiritual, political and community leaders can spread the peace.'

'So your security goals most likely won't be met. Congress will see right through that,' the President said.

'Like we see through their troop withdrawal add-ons to bills that pass through.'

'Round and round we go.'

'You got it, Mr President,' McCorkell said. He tapped his finger on his PDB folder. 'It's all we can do until we get the UN to move on putting blue helmets in there. Sure, we'll still have to foot the bill, but it will get the Hill to stop hassling us on this one. A force under a UN flag has the best chance of working.'

The President nodded.

'What's next?'

'Bomb went off overnight in Port Harcourt, Nigeria,' McCorkell said. 'Target was an oil company building, a couple of confirmed casualties and more to come, probably around twenty.'

'What's it mean for us?'

'Too early to say, but it's not a good sign for oil prices, they jumped a full ten cents in the past twenty-four hours.'

'The Middle East?'

'The terrorist attack in Qatar is hurting the markets bad,' McCorkell said. 'The fire at the *Knock Nevis* is out. They're moving quicker than we expected, a good half a million barrels of production coming back on tomorrow. Should have production back to capacity within eight, nine days tops.'

'NYSE, Dow Jones, NASDAQ, NYMEX –'

'Yeah, I know –'

'They don't share your optimism on this, Bill.'

'The markets are at their worst while being reactive to shock events, they'll rebound on this once the Qatari good news hits the stands tomorrow,' McCorkell said. 'Saudis will remain the real kicker on current oil prices though.'

'We'll go over that with the NSC this morning,' the President said. He made notes in the margin of the PDB for National Security Council discussion. 'You attending the eleven o'clock with the Saudi ambassador?'

'Wouldn't miss it,' McCorkell said. 'I think that this highlights the need for us to move faster on increasing the holding capacity of the SPR.'

'What's capacity now, close on a billion barrels?'

'Give or take, but bear in mind we've only got just over seventy per cent stored away in crude stocks.'

The President chewed it over.

'They done their feasibility on a gas storage?'

'Due tomorrow,' McCorkell said. 'Refined fuels don't have the shelf life of crude. A bigger buffer of crude will be our best measure of help, and it means we can use it more frequently as a driver of price, if not globally then at least here at the gas pumps at home.'

'Good. That all?'

McCorkell nodded, got up and made for the door.

'Bill?'

'Mr President?' McCorkell turned around to face his Commander-in-Chief.

'You all right with him? With Tom?' The President pointed to the side door that led out of his office, through his small kitchenette and into the Chief of Staff's office.

McCorkell walked back and stood behind the chair at the side of the Resolute Desk.

'Since you're asking, I think his time's up,' McCorkell said. 'Fullop's had three and a half years as Chief of Staff, that's pretty standard. It's a tough office, he should bow out while his record is still in good shape.'

'You'd have me not having a Chief of Staff, like Kennedy?'

'No, sir, the world's too busy nowadays. Was too busy even back then,' McCorkell said. 'And you and I know Fullop is good at getting things done below the agenda of Secretary level. He's a damn good political operator.'

'But what?' the President asked. 'You think too good?'

McCorkell paused to think about his answer. To word the truth just so.

'We don't see eye-to-eye very often, which I can deal with,' McCorkell explained. 'And I understand that you need varied voices of advice. I think he's got issues with the friendship you and I have, but that doesn't mean much either.'

'I've known him almost as long as I've known you,' the President said. 'And going into this, I did offer you your choice of jobs.'

'I know. And I know he's probably the most organised guy in this town, he could be CEO anywhere,' McCorkell said. 'Hell, he's been on enough boards as it is. It's – it's his political agenda lately. Fullop's been too focused on the next election, and it's blatantly driving the policy decisions out of his office.'

'Better he spends his time worrying about running for a second term than me,' the President said over the steam of his coffee. 'As it is, I've got the general chairman of my committee to re-elect on my back twenty-four seven. And I don't need them both to remind me, although they've done so often enough already, that we're less than two months out from the election and we're just next week announcing to the public that I have colon cancer. That's something that's going to weigh in on a lot of decision making around here from hereon in – you know that.'

'Yeah, I know that,' McCorkell said. This was the third president he'd worked for in this office, and he'd seen seven chiefs of staff come and go during that time.

'But what?' the President asked. He took his reading glasses off, looked at his National Security Advisor. 'What's he doing wrong?'

McCorkell met the President's gaze. He wasn't going to lie to the guy he'd known since undergrad days at Notre Dame.

'He's operating too much like a co-president,' McCorkell said.

'What – is this about the Veep thing?' the President asked, using the common West Wing jargon for the Vice-President's title. He leaned back in his chair, considered McCorkell while chewing on the arm of his reading glasses. 'That was your tipping point with him?'

McCorkell nodded.

'He cleaned out the Vice President's office and put his own deputy in charge as Chief of Staff,' McCorkell said. 'Put all his own guys in there, from aides to assistants. Poached over a dozen senior staff from the EOB and Secretary's offices and cherry-picked enough congressional aides that they've got jokes being made about it over on the Hill.'

''Bout time they developed a sense of humour,' the President said. 'What kind of jokes?'

'Vice President Jackson could be perceived as an instru-ment of your Chief of Staff.'

'I knew what you were getting at,' the President said. 'See, that was some humour on my part.'

'I'm with the three hundred million Americans who don't really get your sense of humour.'

'Jackson's office had an intel leak,' the President said. 'That stuff on Iran hurt us bad and every poll and commentator in the country called for a change of Vice President. Besides, I asked Tom to keep a close rein on him and his staff, he knows what damage another leak would do to this administration.'

'And Tom went in there with a scythe and a torch, slashing and burning everyone who he'd come up against over the years. He's got unrivalled influence in there now. And, well, I don't like coincidences. Don't believe in them.'

The President continued to chew over the info. He got up, put his glasses in his shirt pocket, and stood facing the south lawn with his hands in his pockets.

'You think the Vice President is gonna run this year – against me?'

'They put a poll out last Friday,' McCorkell said.

'I know about that.'

'Jackson's seen as a serious contender for this office.'

'The party is with me.'

'They see him as a viable alternative.'

'And he'll get his chance in four years, god damn it!'

McCorkell leaned on the back of the chair. 'Unpledged delegates on the Hill are being lined up,' he said, his voice calming. 'Back-channel word is he's going to nominate against you for Iowa. A party hasn't done that to a sitting president since Carter –'

'You can spare me the history lesson, Bill.'

'You selected Jackson as a running mate to appease the party hardliners in the first place,' McCorkell said, some exasperation seeping through. 'Look, I couldn't care less about the politics of this, I really couldn't. I'm working here because I believe in you. Jackson's a reliable operator, he's great in the West and somehow both California and Texas love him. He knows the country well, served as a damn good governor. But he ain't you. He's not a contender. He certainly doesn't belong on the world stage as a shaper of global history.'

'Bill, we've had a lot of party splitting over Iraq, you know that,' the President said. 'But I've spoken to Jackson. He's loyal. He's by my side, and he'll run in four years with my support and the full party backing, that's the deal we struck and I have his word.'

McCorkell nodded. He knew the deal. He didn't like it. Didn't like the Veep or Chief of Staff for the very reasons he'd just aired. But with POTUS's cancer . . .

'Mr President, with Jackson's appointment it was like Tom Fullop has been handed a co-presidency. This has gone beyond a red state or blue state issue. Next week the American public will want to know that you have control over the power of this office and they know it's now more in the hands of Fullop. Fair enough he takes on more of the daily tasks of government to help you through what you've got ahead of you – but, well, he's not the one who was elected, co-presidency of his office be damned. People elected you to lead, for you to decide on the policy and direction of this administration. If Fullop gets more of the driving seat, well . . .'

'Tom's got good morals,' the President said. 'Likeable or not, he's got his convictions. I was comfortable with him helping make decisions in this administration when we started here, and I still am.'

McCorkell rolled that one around. Yeah, Tom Fullop had conviction, but he also wanted to ensure that his political party stayed in office for the next term. Be that under this president, or, as McCorkell suspected, under a President Jackson.

'I'm not saying that I think you two have to play nice,' the President said, putting his coffee down and picking up his daily timesheet. 'It's just I want it out of view from the rest of the senior staff. I need him, I need you, and I need all my guys including Jackson playing their A Game. This office is only as strong as the team around me.'

McCorkell nodded.

'I'll speak to Tom some more about all this after my op,' the President said. 'Now, why don't you ask me the question that's really on your mind.'

The President knew him as well as anyone, so it didn't surprise McCorkell that his Commander-in-Chief knew there was an underlying uncertainty to all this.

'Next Monday you're announcing to the American people, two days after your operation, that you have cancer,' McCorkell said. 'You'll keep them informed of your health and it's up to them come the next election what they choose. I get all that. But I – I want to know, what if it's not an easy ride? What if this becomes – what if your health turns for the worse?'

He didn't have to say: *What if we're left with Jackson as President.*

'You don't think I've thought about that?' the President said. 'You don't think I've had that discussion with my wife and kids?'

'I'm sure you have, Mr President,' McCorkell said. 'Sooner or later, you'll have to have an answer ready for the rest of us.'

He didn't need to go on. The President knew what McCorkell was talking about. His staff, the American people, would want to know what their President would do if faced with ongoing treatment. The same worries had surrounded Reagan's prostate cancer in eighty-seven. They would all need to know what would happen with the executive office if things got worse.

'You'll be the first to know,' the President said. A small measure of a smile showed in his eyes. 'You remember when we were freshmen? The debating club?'

'Yeah,' McCorkell said. Both men shared a smile. 'Kicked some Ivy League butt in our time. We did good.'

'Me, I did okay. You did good,' the President said, taking his seat again. 'You're a natural. Smart as they come, except on sports, but that's not what I'm talking about here. You're good on your feet. Good in a crisis. You should have run for senate. It should have been you on this side of the desk.'

4

NEW YORK
CITY

Lachlan Fox jogged across the grey granite plaza at 375 Park Avenue, between 52nd and 53rd streets. The place was packed with morning commuters, moving fast in every direction.

The Mies van der Rohe designed Seagram Building towered as an example of the best modernist architecture of the twentieth century. Morning sun glinted a brilliant orange off the amber glass, making the bronze column monolith seem alive.

Gammaldi arrived twenty seconds behind Fox, panting, puffing, sweating – they'd been working hard.

'Getting slow, old man,' Fox jibed.

'Who you calling old?' Gammaldi said. 'Plus, I ran to your place from Park Slope.'

'And still you could only do the one circuit through the park. Anyway, you're six months older than me,' Fox said, punching his mate on the arm, and started walking for the entry. 'And I owe you thirty-one more of those.'

'What?'

'Your birthday, dumb ass,' Fox said. He led them into the entry foyer and waved at the guards on the desk. 'Don't try telling me that your momma didn't call you this morning.'

'Yeah, she did,' Gammaldi said through a smile. 'Woke me up at four, still can't work out the time difference from Sydney.'

Fox walked past the elevators and made for the fire door, holding it open for the birthday boy.

'Really?' Gammaldi said, walking past his friend. Both their offices were on the thirty-seventh floor of the thirty-eight-storey building.

'Come on, fat boy, or we'll be late for senior staff,' Fox said, dashing past him and running up the stairs.

'There'd better be cake,' Gammaldi said, his shorter legs taking two stairs at a time to Fox's three.

The morning senior staff meeting ended at 9.30 am. Each of the nine bureau heads had outlined the activities of their sections. Investigations were discussed, collaborations were made, ideas spitballed and fleshed out. More often than not, investigative reports were halted when those in charge of them were informed by someone else present that it was an area being covered by someone at another news agency or outlet. As individual investigative reporters, these staff were good. The team they formed was even better.

As the others filed out, Gammaldi stayed behind in the room, eating what was left of his birthday box of Krispy Kremes.

'Sounds like the magazine awards was a good night,' Faith Williams said.

'It was all right, as far as award things go,' Fox replied. 'Although our boss here lampooned me with a writer, she's wanting to do a profile piece on me for *The New Yorker*.'

'Actually, you can blame me for that,' Faith said.

'It's true, she sold you out for the sake of the company,' Wallace called over his shoulder as he led the way up the single flight of stairs to his top-floor office. He put on a mock J.Jonah Jameson voice: '*Aussie reporter becomes superstar!*'

'It will do you good to have more of a public profile,' Faith said, taking the stairs in her Manolo Blahniks like she was born in stiletto heels. It was company speculation that the GSR Chief of Staff had a black belt in shopping. 'I think you should do it.'

'And when you say do *me* good having more of a public profile, you mean GSR?' Fox asked, going through the doorway that Wallace held open.

'Something like that,' Faith replied.

'Can't you pimp out Al instead?'

'You wrote the rendition stuff that's getting all the traction,' Faith said, taking a seat opposite Wallace in his office. 'I thought you'd enjoy the moment in the spotlight.'

'It's not something I'm after. Besides, my work wouldn't have been possible without having Al always stuffing his face in the background,' Fox said. He sat in the chair next to Faith and could see this meant a lot to her. 'All right, I'll talk to this Jane Clay some more about it, see if she can get it over with quick.'

'That's the spirit,' Wallace said. 'So, where are you headed first for your OPEC pieces?'

'Nigeria,' Fox said. 'They literally just had a bombing in Port Harcourt and that's the final nail in the coffin for a lot of foreign oil workers. All their airport departure lounges are full of passengers with one-way tickets.'

'If you're headed there I want you to take some of our security team with you,' Faith said. 'I'm serious. And you have to be cleared by the psych—'

'Yeah, I'm seeing him today,' Fox cut in. He had no intention of taking any of GSR's security team with him, but that was an argument they could have over the phone when he was safely in Nigeria.

'Anyone claimed the bombing?' Wallace asked.

'It happened overnight our time, which is like a second in Nigerian time,' Fox said. 'No groups have claimed it but the Nigerian government immediately pointed the finger at a couple of local militant groups.'

'And you don't think it was them?'

'They're a grass-roots militia force and not in the business of killing their own civilians to get their message across,' Fox said. 'They just want a better deal. I'm trying every avenue I can to get access to the area to check out the bombing site and then to speak with government and militant leaders.'

'Seems I've had calls on this,' Wallace said, checking the messages piled on his desk. 'The *Post*, *Times*, *Guardian*, CNN – none of them can get access to Port Harcourt right now.'

'That was predictable,' Fox said. 'I'll get in the country and get access.'

'What's your plan?' Faith asked.

'I think we need to go straight to the top,' Fox explained. 'Contact the Nigerian President and senior ministers to offer to do a major international profile piece on them, a *Time* cover, man of the year or some such bullshit, and then when I'm in their face I squeeze them for access to Port Harcourt.'

'Squeeze them how?'

'We pick someone known for corruption,' Fox said. 'The energy minister, Brutus Achebe, would be my first choice, he's in charge of all the oil business.'

'It's worth a try,' Wallace said. 'I'll see what I can do to get you access to the ministers, get some arms twisted by Bill McCorkell.'

'Thanks,' Fox said. 'And I know how to get access to some militant leadership too.'

'How's that?' Faith asked. 'They've been burned by Western media before, they turned us down a couple of months back for an *Esquire* piece.'

'Michael Rollins spent a few years in Nigeria,' Fox said. 'I know he has good contacts there. I was thinking you could twist his arm to do a quick intro for me? I've spoken to him about it but he's a bit hesitant, and that was before this bombing.'

'I don't think he'd be up to it,' Faith said. 'And I don't blame him. The guy should stay home.'

'In and out, twenty-four hours,' Fox said. 'Won't do Rollins much good to stay holed-up in his house forever. He needs to get his mind outside his head for a bit.'

'I'll make a call and speak to him about it,' Wallace said. 'Let's meet about this again this afternoon. Faith, can you brief the security team, get them ready to go to Nigeria?'

'I'll be fine,' Fox said. 'I'll take my lucky charm in Al. Won't take me more than a few days to get what I need.'

Wallace weighed it up.

'What's it like on the ground?'

'Nowhere near as tough as our crew in the Middle East and East Africa are getting it,' Fox explained. 'Leave the security guys with them.'

There was a final weigh-up. Fox wasn't GSR's average reporter, he could handle himself.

'All right, see if you can get some local help,' Wallace said, making notes. 'Driver, bodyguards, whatever it takes to make sure you guys are safe. I don't ever want to lose another reporter in the field.'

5

THE
WHITE HOUSE

McCorkell picked up his internal phone.

'Yeah, I'm watching it,' he said to his deputy NSA for African Affairs. One of his office television screens showed BBC coverage, not from the bombing site but archive footage of the building and some file footage of balaclava-wearing militants. The anchor crossed to a crew on the ground in Lagos where the energy minister had held a press conference. 'We got anything to add to this . . . ? No threats out there . . . ? Government's blaming MEND . . . ? Seems knee-jerk to me too.'

McCorkell tapped his fingers on his desk.

'All right, call me when anything decent comes up. Run it through State, AFRICOM, the agencies. Someone must have heard something,' McCorkell said, about to hang up, but then he added an afterthought: 'Hey, CIA are almost done doing a new National Intelligence Estimate on Nigeria . . . Good, let me know.'

He hung up the phone. Picked up his blue rubber squeeze ball. Absently worked it in his hand to relieve the arthritis.

He scanned Intellipedia; more links were being created by the minute. He clicked the *National Intelligence Estimate* tab, scanned through the headlining links, the Nigerian page still very light on info. Just the country demographic and political details, economic briefings and indicators, key personnel files on the major political players, military capabilities and ongoing security operations.

His personal secretary entered and passed over some notes to read prior to the meeting with the National Security Council. A thick file in which the Department of Defense had mapped out some contingencies to intervention forces in the affected OPEC countries. That would take more NSC meeting time to go through. He checked his watch – the meeting with the Saudi ambassador would be straight after the NSC. Prep time was now.

He picked up his phone; the White House operator answered.

'Put me through to CIA,' McCorkell said. 'Langley, Saudi Arabia desk.'

6

SOKOTO CITY, NORTHERN NIGERIA

Brutus Achebe went about the afternoon prayer as the Iqama prompted. His uncle knelt next to him, his cousin on the other side. They were but a few among the many faithful amassed in the Shehu Mosque. The afternoon sun spilled through the open archways, across the brick floor, illuminating the faces of the front row of dignitaries. Behind them were devoted followers, not only of the ideals of Sunni Islam but of his uncle, the Sultan. Soon, when he was President of Nigeria, they would be loyally devoted followers of his, too.

When the prayer was over, Achebe followed his uncle out to an office in the annex to the mosque.

'You are looking well,' his uncle said to him. 'But you're eating too much. Too much good life.'

'Allah has been good to me,' Achebe said. 'And you, you look well.'

'Do not lie to me, Brutus, not here, not in this life,' the Sultan said. The old man shifted with stiffness. His own son came into the room, along with Achebe's advisor, Steve Mendes.

'Soon, your cousin will have to take my place,' the Sultan said. 'And he, with you, will lead Nigeria in its next phase. You two will find peace in your time. You will bring a better life to our people.'

His cousin nodded. He had that same smile that spoke to Achebe of a life he would never enjoy. Yes, he'd obtained much material wealth, he had his own following of supporters, but he would never know what it was like to have that following of *true believers*. There was a massive leap in the difference of the public support he and his cousin were destined to have. They'd grown up in its influence under the shadow of their fathers, and now their destinies were close to being realised – the Nigerian presidency for Achebe, and the position of Sultan of Sokoto for his cousin. Achebe found no familial friendship in this smile of his cousin. In fact, when in his presence, he could still taste the blood in his mouth from a lesson his bigger cousin had once taught him the hard way. It was a long time from that incident, more than thirty years, but Achebe still thought of it whenever he saw the heir to the Sultanate. He was sure his cousin was reminded of it too. That lesson given through fists when Achebe had argued that his own father, a state governor, was more powerful than his uncle. Of the power of religion over politics. Of his place in the family.

'Of course, Uncle. Of course.'

•

Steve Mendes rode in the back of the Chevy Suburban next to Achebe. He turned the air-conditioning up, and instinctively checked the other vehicles. Two Suburbans were ahead of them, two Toyota pick-ups trailed behind. The convoy wove its way back to Abuja, another monthly pilgrimage to the holy city could be cleared from their calendar. Ordinarily the American would also have an armed helicopter for added security, but they were being readied for use in the delta.

'He looks unwell, your uncle,' Mendes said, his gaze out the window not taking the slightest interest in the civilians who flashed past.

'My cousin will carry on his work,' Achebe said. 'Their house will continue their strong rule.'

Mendes looked across at him. The forty-three-year-old minister was dressed in a grey three-piece London suit. Surreal in the chaos of colourful poverty that flashed by the window like a time-delay photo.

'Why not you?' Mendes said.

Achebe faced his vizier.

'You are a natural leader, Brutus,' Mendes said. 'A born leader. Gifted.'

'I wish to be president,' Achebe said. He turned his attention forward. The driver and bodyguard were preoccupied with the way ahead. 'Only the president has more power than the Sultan. Maybe it is not seen like that here in the north, but in the south, over the oil, the president is like a god. That's the power I want.'

'Yes, and you will be a good president,' Mendes said. He turned to look out his own window again, shifted a little in his seat as his H&K UCP pistol dug in at the holster in the small of his back. When he spoke again, it was soft, as if feigning indif-ference. As if just putting the thought out there, to linger in the air. As if it were something that the minister would later think back on as his own idea. 'There's no reason you can't be both.'

Mendes let it hang in the air for a while, then said: 'President, *and* leader of the Muslim faith.'

'My cousin is to become Sultan.'

'True,' Mendes said, facing him. Meeting his eyes and holding them in his stare. 'But why be Sultan, when you can be the Caliph.'

'It – it cannot be so,' Achebe said. His eyes showed his mind was thinking it over, searching for an answer that would be otherwise.

'Look at what happened in Port Harcourt this morning,' Mendes said.

'Another bombing.'

'Another bombing,' Mendes said. 'And who led the country in prayer for that?'

'I did.'

'That's right. It was you. You belong in that position as head of a Caliphate, based here in Nigeria. You are the one who deserves to have conversations with god. Be the guiding light for the nation. For your people.'

Mendes could see Achebe rolling over all that he must in order to come to terms with this proposal. Nearly two years in the making, Steve Mendes had just delivered his punch-line. In the film script of this story, he'd just voiced the major plot path for this Achebe character to launch himself on. Now, to make sure he followed the right path.

'Have we found the militants, the bombers?' Achebe was so innocent sometimes. So foolish it was priceless. The right path was presenting itself as the only path. Beautifully.

'Militants, of course,' Mendes said. 'It comes as the world oil price is escalating and several oil contracts are coming up, it will force the hands of some oil companies. They will definitely move out now. It means we can have the new blood move in, companies that will pay us more, give you more, that we can have more control over. This could not have happened at a more opportune time.'

'That's right . . .'

'See, your God is guiding you,' Mendes said. 'You, Brutus Achebe. You are on the right path. You must follow it. Fulfil your destiny.'

7

NEW YORK CITY

'I seriously don't have time for this,' Fox said, fidgeting in the chair.

'The door's there,' Dr Galen said. He closed the folder, his capped fountain pen resting on the mahogany desk. 'Why don't you go through it and take a little holiday? Come back and see me when you have more time.'

Fox was silent. He looked from Galen's face to the desk. Bare but for his thin plastic file, a lamp, the pen, and a clear clock that faced the shrink. Third time in here and Fox knew the guy kept a close eye on that clock. A habit from what, thirty years in practice?

'I can help you, Lachlan. But it's gotta go my way. You have Post Traumatic Stress Disorder. You're a workaholic and a borderline alcoholic. None of that's gonna fix itself in a hurry.'

Fox shot him a look. A little self-loathing smile. Realisation. He was right.

'That all?' Dr Galen asked. Fox showed him his upturned palms in surrender. The psychiatrist opened the file. 'Okay. How'd the awards night go?'

'Good, it was fine,' Fox said. He knew what Galen was referring to.

Galen flicked through the file from the previous meeting's notes, and the referral details he'd received from the GSR psychiatrist.

'You been doing drugs since I saw you last?'

Fox shook his head.

'Not used any cocaine?'

'No,' Fox said. He hadn't touched it for over a week. He stopped his hands tapping on the arms of the chair, conscious of the body language he was putting out. He sat a little straighter.

'That's good. How many drinks a day?'

'About the same.'

'About five or six?'

'Five, six, whatever's in front of me.'

'You have anything you want to talk about today?'

'Not really. You know the shit that's been troubling me.'

There was a long pause between them both. Galen looked back through fifteen pages of handwritten notes in the blue plastic folder.

'We started with – Kate, didn't we?'

Fox nodded.

'Talked about her, what you shared with her,' Galen said, looking down his nose through his glasses as he read. 'She meant a lot to you, and could have been something special. Her death was very traumatic for you, understandably.'

Fox bit his lip, nodded.

'I just – I keep thinking about that night,' Fox said. 'It's like she was just snatched from me. I mean, I'd known her for such a short time but – it's weird, and I think I said this last week, it sometimes feels like she's still out there.'

Galen made notes and flicked forward through the pages.

'You told me about your time in Timor. And Venice. And last week,' Galen recalled, 'we began talking about your military posting in the Middle East. You touched on your first posting, in Iraq. Can we pick it up from there?'

Fox fidgeted in his chair; chewed on the inside of his cheek.

'Lachlan, I've treated many servicemen from Iraq. What you're going through is not abnormal. Hell, it's not abnormal for any young person who *hasn't* seen war. Many incidents within any house in any neighbourhood here in the States can trigger what you've been feeling. On top of that, there are pressures on you to perform. Expectations. Exaltations. And all this is amplified by the extreme circumstances you've lived through.'

Fox looked at the prints on the walls, soft pastel renderings of water lilies framed behind glass.

'There were one hundred and twenty-one US Army soldiers who took their lives last year,' Galen said. 'More than two thousand who either attempted suicide or deliberately hurt themselves. They're the highest rates since records began. I've worked at Walter Reed, I've seen the worst, Lachlan.'

There were two other clocks in the room, a few old reference books housed in a timber and glass cabinet, a couple of armchairs, a lounge suite and a coffee table. Catalogue sparse.

'Lachlan, would you rather you just had an eight-hundred number to call, like those poor kids coming home from Iraq and Afghanistan? Or would you rather talk about this with me?'

All the furniture looked new, although styled in some kind of post-colonial way. Evidence that nothing was built like it used to be.

'Your central nervous system needs help, it's crying out,' Dr Galen said. 'How many hours of work are you doing per day?'

'Depends,' Fox said. 'Now? I don't know, ten, twelve?'

'Schedule?'

'Going back to Africa the day after tomorrow,' Fox said. The shrink made notes, looking at Fox while he wrote. His glasses made his eyes seem a little smaller. Gold frames. A lot of gold plating in here.

'How long for?'

'What – Nigeria? A few days or a week, maybe more. Whatever it takes.'

'What are you working on there? The extraordinary rendition stuff?'

'No, that's over with for now,' Fox said. He was glad, too. 'I'm going to Nigeria to cover the bombing of the oil building in Port Harcourt. Part of an ongoing series I'm developing on security and stability in OPEC countries. Should be a nice, quiet job.'

Galen put his pen down. His chair was a good ten centimetres higher than Fox's, and he sat back and straightened his tie. The spots and colours clashed with his striped shirt and chequered suit.

'There's something about these places – Africa, the Middle East, war-torn places – that defies all logic in how I feel. It's like part of me is itching to get in the fight.'

Fox unconsciously rubbed his hands together, as if rinsing them with water.

'That's a bit like self-imposed exposure therapy,' Galen said. 'It can be helpful to be in situations that bring on your PTSD, but I'm concerned by how out of control it is. You may think you can operate there effectively but you're probably running at half speed.'

'I feel fine when I'm there, it's more the downtime here that gets to me,' Fox said. 'Give me a street in Baghdad and I walk tall. Give me an errand to run on Fifth Avenue and I just want to head home and hole up.'

Notes were checked.

'Last week I told you to take some time out each day and do something that you enjoy.'

That brought Fox back to the present.

'I've been exercising more, getting back up to speed since having my arm out of the sling just a month ago,' Fox said, alert, thinking about it. 'I watched a few films, although that was a mistake –'

'Why's that?'

'Watched my favourite Heath Ledger films over a couple of bottles of red – made me sad that I'll never see that talent on screen again.'

'At least you're aware of how that made you feel. It seems you're becoming a bit more aware, wouldn't you agree?'

'Yeah, maybe,' Fox said. 'I read a couple of books too. Going to the opera.'

'That's good, all good.'

'I'm trying to be a bit more social, but, I don't know. Just people from work, Al, a few other reporters.' Fox crossed his arms. Uncrossed them again. 'I don't know. Trying to have a laugh again, I guess.'

'Good. You make that list? Ten things you enjoy?'

He hadn't. He'd thought about it, but hadn't put pen to paper. It was a harder task than you'd think. Especially when there was work to be done. There was always work to be done.

'Not yet. Working on it.'

'Good.' More notes. 'It's important. Might sound simple but it will help. How's your sleep?'

'Shit. Two, maybe three hours a night, if I'm lucky.'

'You're still taking something for that?'

'Yeah, maybe one or two pills a night,' Fox said. 'I don't know, though – it's been what, two weeks? I think they're making me more nervy, anxious.'

'All right, I can prescribe you something else. Want some Valium in the meantime, to settle your nerves?'

'No, I hate the stuff,' Fox said. He shifted in his seat. There was silence for a while and then Fox's eyes came up to meet Galen's.

'About Iraq,' Fox said. 'I unpacked some stuff at my new place, and this morning I found a letter.' He shifted in his seat again, ran fingers through his short brown hair. Let out a breath. It wasn't like he'd thought about this much until the letter. And now – it was like a weight in his gut. Wrenching. Surprising. He felt he should be stronger than this.

'What was it?'

'A letter. A note. From about two years ago.' Fox bit his lip, scratched at the stubble on his chin. Galen's pen was down again. 'It marked an anniversary back in Iraq.'

Galen was listening. Still.

'When I was – I was first in Iraq for a few months in late '03,' Fox said. 'I was a lieutenant in the Navy. This – it isn't something that I've dwelled on over the years. I mean, so much has happened between then and now. But this letter. Man, it has brought it back, you know . . .'

The psychiatrist had leaned back in his chair, his legs crossed at the ankles showing leather soles of shoes that didn't see life outside a carpeted office. Fox shook his mind back on track.

'From an Iraqi woman – the letter was from an Iraqi woman. She –' Fox sat up straight, to full attention. Spoke with his hands as if wrestling the words out. 'Her husband was our team's interpreter. He was great, one of a – he got hit while we were on patrol. He just – he didn't make it.'

Galen let Fox have some silence. Fox took a few seconds to get it together.

'Sorry, Doc, I'm all over the place, aren't I?'

'No, you're fine,' Galen said. His voice was quieter than before, coaxing. 'What did it say?'

'The letter? Not much . . .' Fox said. 'Brought back memories is all. All that, back then.'

More notes, more silence. Fox felt he could swim in it.

'What kind of memories?'

Fox nodded. Resolved within himself.

'Images that I saw in Iraq. The constant sounds of war. The look on Iraqis' faces – they, these civilians, were the ones who'd been shocked and awed. You imagine what it was like for them when the bombs and missiles started raining in?'

Galen shook his head.

'And, specifically, since reading this letter I've been thinking about the day he died. All day today, at work, I've been practically useless because of it.'

'Can you tell me about that?' Galen waited patiently. 'Talk about it some. Share it with me.'

'It was just after dawn. Our patrol was in a shipping dock area in southern Iraq. There was armour and grunts farther afield, air cover all over the place – we felt pretty damn safe. Four of us special-ops guys and the Iraqi. We called him AB.' Fox smiled, remembered the laughs they'd shared with this man for what, six weeks? His smile vanished. 'I remember his wife's reaction when my CO and I went to her home to deliver the news. It was the least we could do for a friend. My CO did the talking, I'd never done anything like that before. It's something they don't teach you in training, it's just handed down through the ranks once you're in the field. I've had to do it myself a couple of times since; it never gets any easier. This woman's tears and those of her kids and her parents and AB's own mother . . . I just fell apart, right in front of them.'

Silence. Fox stared off into the middle-distance, summoning up the remainders of the day.

'He – Abdallo, AB – he was the first person I'd seen killed up close. Same for all of us in the team. We'd seen our share of dead people before but this was real-time. This shit was *real*, in our *faces*. We tripped an IED. He never had a chance.' Fox, through all his experience and for all he'd seen, could remember the sunset of that day as clearly as if he were looking at it now. Could still taste the copper of warm flowing blood.

'I brought his wife back a container of sand. Instead of her husband, I brought her back sand. Red. Soaked in his blood. There was almost nothing left. Just blood and bits of his – his uniform remained in bigger pieces than he did.'

Fox's eyes were wet.

'It was a monster IED. Rigged out of an old fifteen-hundred-pound bomb. A US bomb, mind you, probably a dud that crash-landed in the first Gulf War.'

Fox looked up and met Galen's eyes. The pen was in the doctor's hand but he wasn't making notes.

'We were all kids. AB was twenty-five. He had a face that spoke of the surface truths of faith in the liberty and justice that were being bandied about by us coalition forces. A look that lacked the depth that had yet to be bestowed on such an innocent. In just six short weeks he'd become like a brother to us, had got us out of trouble almost every other day. We drank tea with him. Laughed with him.'

Silence. Fox exhaled.

'Did you have a ceremony?' Galen asked. 'Did you have a chance to say goodbye?'

Fox nodded. Chewed his bottom lip.

'Yeah. My team wrote a message, put it in a bottle full of the sand, had one of the US ships toss it over the side in the middle of the Persian Gulf. It was a little thing, from Orwell:

'But the one thing I saw in your face
No power can disinherit

No bomb that ever burst
Shatters the crystal spirit.'

Fox gave full attention to the smallest details right now. He could almost taste the air in the room.

'At his home, we'd all chipped in and left behind whatever we could. Money, MREs, blankets, fuel. Seems stupid now. His family were all in too much shock to turn it down. It's like we said that was all he was worth. Some surplus gear. But what we left behind in Iraq was something so much more . . .

'We left our innocence behind.' Fox exhaled loudly, letting it out. 'His family all took it in turns to scatter some sand in the back garden, said some words in a memorial service that stretched through the afternoon. My CO had left by then, but I stayed on a bit.'

'So with his family, in front of his wife, his kids, what did you say when it was your turn to scatter the sand?'

Fox looked Galen in the eyes.

'Your son, my lord, has paid a soldier's debt;
He only lived but till he was a man;
The which no sooner had his prowess confirm'd
In the unshrinking station where he fought
But like a man he died.'

Galen made a clicking sound in his throat.
'*Macbeth*?'
Fox nodded. Continued:

'Your cause of sorrow
Must not be measured by his worth, for then
It hath no end.'

Fox was close to something now, the nub of the pain.

'Why is it I find this so insurmountable? How is it this sticks in me, stays with me, lives within me still?' Fox was full of sadness but there was some anger now too. Anger at being too slow at the time, anger at where he had placed his men that day, anger at the result. He was still fighting the result, he was battling demons that lived on within that voice in his head that would not let go.

'What am I without this? Can I forget and live on?'

'You're not religious, are you?'

'No. My parents were raised Catholic but were never strictly practising,' Fox said, looking down at his open palms. 'I can count on two hands how many times I've been to Mass.'

'But you sometimes go to church?'

'Rarely. Sometimes, to remember the dead. Light a few candles.'

Fox paused to consider his search for meaning.

'Do you think atheists, because of . . . I don't know . . . their lack of restraining faith? – are they more susceptible to evil?' Fox asked. 'Is that what's clouding me now, what's weighing so heavily? That I have some inherent evil that drives me, something faith could absolve?'

'I wouldn't think so, but it's hard to say. We know faith can bring with it as many problems as it solves. We must all find what works for us.'

Fox nodded.

'When I made to leave, AB's wife spoke to me for the first time that day. After she had got her anger out on my CO and prayed what she needed to pray in the backyard, she finally spoke to me.' Fox's eyes narrowed, recalling it all in clarity.

'She asked me to do something for her. *Get them*, she said. *Kill them*. And there, in her house, I promised her that I would.'

Fox pinched the bridge of his nose, fidgeted with a hand through his hair.

'I made a promise, on a life, that I knew I couldn't keep.' Fox looked at Galen with a hollow stare that showed something of realisation. 'That's what she asked me in that letter. She wished me peace, happiness. She wished me all kinds of divine protection. Blessed my loyalty.

'And then, finally, she asked me if I kept my promise.'

8

THE
WHITE HOUSE

The Saudi ambassador, himself a prince of the House of Saud, sat back in the armchair to the side of the President. McCorkell was to the President's other side, opposite the ambassador.

The clock in McCorkell's eye-line over the ambassador's left shoulder had just clicked over to 11.06. Greetings had taken less than a minute, business had been gotten down to, and the meeting could almost be considered as over. Not bad for six minutes in the Oval Office. Pity things had not gone their way. Yet. There was still a chance.

Fullop was there, as well as the Secretary of State, Adam Baker. The four Americans waited for their guest to answer the question.

'No, thank you,' the prince said. His body language and tone told them his heels were dug in hard.

Fullop raised his eyebrows. Adam Baker played his usual stoic role as Secretary of State when acting shotgun to the President's lead. McCorkell squinted ever so slightly into harder focus at the Saudi.

This prince had only been in the post for six months. He was on a par with his predecessor, which wasn't saying that much. The benchmark had been set with the guy before that. He had been in his post for almost thirty years, his career spanning alongside Secretaries of State Kissinger all the way through to Rice. He had been the only ambassador from any country who had a genuine personal friendship – going off to smoke cigars and drink un-Islamic beverages – with successive US presidents. Now, he was back in Riyadh as the head of the Saudi National Security Council. He was Bill McCorkell's counterpart over there, and remained a trusted friend – they'd had a day of meetings just last July at Camp David. This current ambassador, McCorkell knew, didn't like that his revered predecessor was still seen to carry far more weight than the office that he had left. A classic case of big shoes to fill. McCorkell could go over this prince's head but it wasn't that easy. The Saudi politics and family issues that surrounded ambassadorial postings was a mind-fuck of an ego minefield.

'Mr Ambassador, our FBI investigators are the best in the world,' McCorkell said. 'If anyone can find the perpetrators of the attacks on your oil infrastructure, they can.'

The prince's face was passive. He was silent, then turned to the President.

'These were not foreign terrorist attacks,' the ambassador said. 'And we are not expecting any more attacks. It was an isolated incident by a local criminal element and we are rounding up suspects as we speak.'

'And their actions are hurting us as much as you,' the President said. 'We would like our law enforcement specialists to help you. This was an attack on the global economy, with nothing to gain for the perpetrators involved other than seeing your royal family, and us as your friends, hurt.'

'Don't underestimate our own investigators,' the prince said. 'They will find those responsible for the planning of the attack. We will have justice.'

'Forgive us if we are not holding our breath for your police investigators,' the President said.

'It was Saudi workers who died in the attack,' the prince said. 'This is an internal matter.'

'Six Pakistanis were also killed,' Fullop added.

'We'll see their families receive justice too,' the prince said. His face remained impassive, despite McCorkell knowing the man had the propensity to show his feelings with little heed of the poker face that came with international diplomacy.

There was silence as the room considered the gravity of that statement. McCorkell knew the matter-of-fact tone of the prince's comments meant that those responsible, when caught, wouldn't see the inside of a courthouse. Just the swift justice of American-supplied munitions.

'Mr Ambassador, you know why we want to help,' McCorkell said. 'You've been in this room many times. You know you are among friends here.'

'Of course,' the prince said. 'And I know why you want to help. It's oil. It's always oil.'

A look was shared between McCorkell and the President. Baker spoke up for the first time.

'With all respect, this is about more than oil,' the Secretary of State said. 'It's our entire economy that suffers.'

'I am sorry for your economy,' the prince said.

'This attack directly affects us as the biggest consumer of your oil,' McCorkell said. 'Whatever we can do to bring that supply back on to the market, we will do. We've had the Qatari attack, and now Nigeria overnight – the markets are getting killed.'

'I don't want oil prices to rise any more than you do,' the prince said. He smiled. 'When it becomes more expensive than alternative fuel sources, we all lose.'

McCorkell nodded almost imperceptibly to the President. The signal to ask the real question, the reason why the prince had been called in.

'But you're not releasing any of your reserve capacity?' the President said. 'You're almost three million barrels per day down – and you have reserve refining capacity that you can bring on to the market to fill that shortfall.'

'Which would leave us totally exposed in the advent of another catastrophe,' the prince said, shaking his head. 'I say again, I do not want oil prices to soar too high. But for our own national security reasons we cannot do anything about that right now.'

'And yet you know these prices are making it easier for our alternative fuel industries to take a bigger market share,' Fullop said. 'All of a sudden a million acres of ethanol crops doesn't look too expensive to harvest. More individual consumers and company fleets switch to hybrids. Or, worse still, Canada and

Venezuela with their oil sands become the new Saudi Arabias of the world.'

'With respect, your alternative fuel industry seems to be growing quite fast as it is,' the prince said. 'Mr President, we are on track to repair the pumping site and resume production to the previous capacity within three weeks.'

There was an awkward beat for the Americans. Another look between the President and McCorkell. That was twice the time frame that the State Department had previously been assured of. The Saudi oil workers drilled for this type of catastrophe all the time. These oil guys did things one way: *fast*. In the Saudi oil machine, *nothing* took three weeks.

'Three weeks?' McCorkell asked. 'Is the damage worse than we've been informed?'

'Mr McCorkell, thirty-six of my countrymen died in this terrorist attack,' the prince said. 'We are moving forward as fast as the attack site will allow.'

'And you know we in the Executive branch are getting a battering on this from our congress and senate?' the President said. 'They can halt us on military supplies.'

'I am sorry for your internal affairs, Mr President, really I am,' the Ambassador said. 'If your politicians want to get career mileage out of this terrorist attack on my country, so be it. My hopes and prayers are that you do not have any other issues that arise to compound these pressures.'

'What do you think their idea of "justice" is? Eye for an eye, limb for limb?' Fullop said.

Baker had shown the prince out, and the three men in the Oval Office were more uncomfortable than they'd been fifteen minutes before.

'That and more,' McCorkell said. 'Saudi police and military are busting some asses over this. The royal family want to use it to bolster their image as being tough on crime and criticism, a way of proving legitimacy to the way they rule.'

'Bill, you know that governing bodies, including us, use catastrophes for their own agenda all the time,' Fullop said. 'From disaster economics to regime shift, significant events like a terrorist attack are ripe fodder for change. It's the way of the world, and the Saudis are no exception.'

'You think the Kingdom is gonna change in a hurry?'

'Mr President, their royal family might want this to be seen as their nine-eleven, to show the world that they have teeth,' Fullop said. 'What do you suggest we do, Bill? Hold up some military hardware until they budge on letting us lend a helping hand?'

'Too long-term – they can hold out on receiving more tanks and aircraft for far longer than the three weeks we've just been promised,' McCorkell said. 'We need something more immediate. I want to go to the press on this.'

'What's the angle?' the President asked.

'Saudis don't like bad press, particularly if we paint the picture that the royal family are refusing the help of the best investigators in the world. That they're sticking to their old-fashioned ways of getting things done.'

'Do I need to remind you we have a presidential election around the corner?' Fullop said, his cheeks flushed. 'We make this a bigger story than it already is and it shows that we don't have influence with these guys. Our opponents will make this spin that our administration is weak in the Middle East.'

'Saudi Arabia, Qatar, and now Nigeria, we've got ourselves a trifecta of bad news,' McCorkell said. 'The Press Secretary is getting hammered in the press room right now, every question from reporters who want to know what we're doing to alleviate the price pressures at the gas pump. And the entire press corp know that the prince's motorcade just pulled out of the White House gates.'

'So we tell them our help's been turned down?' the President asked.

'It's then an opportunity to make it our story. To own it,' McCorkell said. 'The Kingdom wants stability in their relationships here – we're their biggest customer, and they're a decent-sized consumer. They don't like bad press any more than we do. This will make our case go before all the finance guys, all the industry guys that have influence over there. We can bypass the prince and have dozens of big American companies applying all sorts of fiscal pressure over in the Kingdom.'

'How far do we go?' the President asked.

'I think this is a bad idea,' Fullop said. He stood and paced by the window.

'We issue travel warnings to Saudi Arabia,' McCorkell said. 'There's a legitimate threat there, so let's say it's of the highest terror threat level. No one in, all non-essential Americans out. Let it leak that not only is there another threat but that the Saudis are dragging their feet in the investigation. The Press Secretary will get the question as to why we haven't sent the FBI in . . .'

'Our response is that we have a team locked and loaded on the tarmac waiting for the Kingdom's green light.'

McCorkell nodded at the President's reasoning.

'We've been hitting a brick wall with that prince since he got here,' McCorkell said. 'I've been in the room with him and his uncle before; his family have been waiting for an excuse to replace him as ambassador. This means that they save admitting to the mistake of putting him in the job in the first place.'

'He still has the confidence of a big portion of their family,' Fullop said.

'Yeah, the portion that wants to see us hurt,' McCorkell replied. 'The moderate Saudi players will go around him and let our investigators in. Nothing surer.'

'And, more importantly, get the oil pumping again,' the President said. 'Bill, get it out with the press, make it happen.'

9

NEW YORK
CITY

Fox waited outside the Lincoln Center, hands in his pockets. He wore a black one-button Paul Smith suit, white linen shirt, black silk tie. Metropolitan Opera attire. His collar button was undone, his tie knot loose a couple of fingers at the neck. Under the fall of his trousers' hem his black RM Williams boots passed as dress shoes, their high-gloss military shine reflecting the lights of traffic.

He checked his Skagen watch. Al was late. Bastard had probably forgotten about it, too busy sitting at home watching sport on his birthday.

The bells chimed with the final call for patrons to enter and be seated.

'Come on, Al . . .' Fox said, and got out his iPhone to dial . . .

'Hey there, sailor,' Jane Clay said. Little black dress. Hair up. More make-up on than when he'd last seen her – smoky eye-shadow, heavy black mascara, red lips. A faint smell of spring perfume – Kenzo?

'Hey Jane,' Fox said. He turned his attention back to scroll through his iPhone. When he looked up again, Jane was right in his face. He was about to offer a handshake but she leaned in and kissed him on the cheek.

'Al's not coming, is he?'

'He gave me a call, something about watching the Windies play the Aussies? Anyway – I'm your date,' Jane said. 'Unless you prefer men?'

The final bell sounded.

Fox, still with his iPhone in his hand, raised his eyebrows. Smiled, and pocketed the phone.

'Come on,' he said, and crooked his arm for her to link her hand through.

They walked through the door, saying a couple of brief hellos to society. Fox was popular there, recognised by other reporters and some socialites who might have seen him interviewed or in a discussion on television. He was uncomfortable with it, and led the way to their seats. Centre stage, eight rows back. Several more people recognised him along the way.

'Well, aren't you Mr Popular,' Jane said, beaming. More at home with the attention than he was.

They settled in to their seats. The conductor turned to the audience, bowed to applause. Jane leaned close to Fox.

'You didn't call me,' she said.

'I didn't know we were at that stage,' Fox replied, smiling.

'I want to write your story,' she said. 'I have an agent, in Hollywood, at UTA, reps my stuff for film rights. She wants to sell your life rights, make it into a movie.'

Fox looked at her: *Really?*

'What, to have Jake Gyllenhaal and Reese Witherspoon dramatise my life? I'll give you your article,' Fox said quietly. The curtain came up, revealing the opening scene. He whispered into Jane's ear, 'But I'm not ready to tell you my life story, if that's what you're after.'

She nodded, her attention towards the opera. Fox's gaze hung on her for a moment. There wasn't any coltishness about her. She certainly didn't look like the sort of girl who had just got off the bus from Wisconsin. She'd lived life, and radiated a sense of – what? She turned to him, motioned with her expression that he should be watching the scene. Her smile held the answer Fox was searching for, and he himself smiled, and settled in to hear the opera.

Fox sat opposite Jane in Barcibo Enoteca, a small Italian wine-bar and restaurant near the Lincoln Center on Broadway and 69th. The interior was all blasted brick and timber shelves lined with wine. The dim hanging lighting and small glass cups with tea candles created a late-night atmosphere easily lost in. Their portion of the long white marble table was lined with wine glasses as they tasted their way through the Italian reds on offer.

'Why opera?' Jane asked over the rim of a glass of Tuscan Brunello di Montalcino. The aged red left sticky fingers of wine down the inside of the glass.

'Excuse me?'

'What's your interest in opera?'

'You have something against opera?'

'No – it's not the most popular of arts is all. Particularly in your demographic.'

'Well, for me . . . it's hard to articulate,' Fox said. 'I guess it ultimately comes down to a love of words.'

'Words? Not the music, the performance?'

'Well, yeah, opera has all the drama and storytelling to go with it, but it's the transition of words to music that really gets to me,' Fox said. 'The rhythm, pitch, timbre, volume, all the properties of music that have the ability to move us in ways beyond literal meanings. A great opera singer can deliver all this imbued with their life's journey. And there's something magical about the delivery of a great opera aria that just . . .'

'Moves us.'

'Touches the very core of us,' Fox said. He took the final sip from his glass and poured another for them both, finishing the bottle. The wine swirled around as it filled the empty space.

'You're going to Africa soon for your OPEC security pieces?'

'Day after tomorrow,' Fox said. 'There was a bombing in Nigeria, so I'm starting things off there.'

They were silent for a moment. It was the first time in the past hour and a half that neither of them had not spontaneously filled with words.

'This a favourite place of yours?'

'First time,' Fox said. Small talk could be revealing and he remained wary that this could well be material for her profile piece. 'You got a favourite bar in town?'

Jane took her time to answer and had a sip of wine, licking a drop from her bottom lip.

'Not really in Manhattan,' she replied. 'I grew up in New Jersey.'

'I would have picked your accent as Texan, somewhere in the panhandle?'

'Yeah, I was born in Amarillo, we moved over here for most of my childhood, then I went back there for my undergrad.'

'Cool – sorry, I just have a thing for that accent,' Fox said, smiling. 'Can pick it out across a crowded bar packed above fire code. But okay, New Jersey . . .'

'New Jersey, right. I remember sometimes going with my dad to a place called McGovern's Tavern. Went in there again recently, it's still much the same. The same murals of Irish scenes still look down on the same large, open room, and the walls are hung with the same old photos. There are still a couple of his old cop buddies, drinking at the same place, while the next generation comes in and goes through the same motions.'

Fox knew the type of place. Knew those kind of men that were the same the world over. Replicating some kind of ritualistic nostalgia their fathers had done.

'I got a couple places like that, back home in Australia. In Melbourne.' Fox stopped to consider the memories as a kid, the stale beer smell of old pubs still lingering in the back of his mind. Cricket on the television, vinyl music in the relic of a jukebox, smoke in the air.

'And you got a favourite now?'

'Went to a nice place on Lake Constance once, that was a pretty hard setting to top,' Fox said. 'But here in Manhattan, not really any favourites. There's a place at the bottom of the building where I work, the Four Seasons.'

'I know of it but I've never been there.'

'How about tomorrow afternoon?' Fox asked. He finished his drink; motioned to the barman for the bill. 'We can get a start on your profile piece in nice surroundings. Then there's something on for Al's birthday, so you can come along to that too.'

'I don't know if I can back up tonight with more drinks tomorrow – I'm really not much of a drinker,' Jane said.

'Well, you fooled me,' Fox replied as he signed off the bar tab and left a cash tip.

They got up and went outside. Fox hailed a cab.

'So you'll do the interview, my profile piece?'

'Yep,' Fox said. 'But I don't want it getting too big. Definitely no movie stuff. I'm not interested in talking to anybody else about it, I don't want producers taking me to lunch, I don't even want to be a story consultant on 24. I don't want anything out of this other than creating public discussion.'

'Movies are a big part of the public discussion,' Jane said, one foot in the cab. 'You want to share a cab – you're in SoHo, right?'

'All the same, I'm gonna walk,' Fox said. He guided her into the back of the cab.

'That's a long walk,' Jane replied. She scooted over in the back seat, patted the space next to her.

Fox shook his head.

'See you tomorrow, Jane.'

10

PORT HARCOURT, NIGERIA

'I don't like having all these Russians around,' Achebe said. 'They make me nervous. Throwing their wealth around, talking about having so many thousands more of their security guys in the country. It's like they're – they're moving in.'

Mendes was finding it increasingly easy to manipulate Achebe. The Nigerian's reactions were predictable.

'We need them,' Mendes said. 'It's the only way to get you in to power, to have their backing, their money.'

'But I don't trust them, not like the Americans.'

The meeting was in an old decaying dock on the harbour. Seven-thirty in the morning and the Russian oil representatives had arrived punctually. They travelled with a platoon of heavy-set guys, from a couple of big boats out on the harbour. The kind of flashy monsters with helipads and jet-skis and swimming pools. The oil guys were walking away, back down to the end of the pier. Conversation had lasted ten minutes, deals had been struck with handshakes and a few signatures, and the Russians saluted with vodka. Their helicopters lifted off the end of the dock and Mendes and Achebe were left alone, just their protective detail waiting by their vehicle convoy.

'We need oil contractors with money outside of the Americans,' Mendes said. They started moving towards the cars. 'You'd rather it was the Chinese?'

Achebe shook his head.

'Good, it's far too late in the game to switch sides now. Besides, I know these guys, I know how to work them. There are simple ways to deal with these people, once you know how they think,' Mendes said. 'And number one, don't let yourself get pushed around. They would have offered another fifty million for the exploration rights in Bayelsa state alone.'

Achebe's expression was hurt.

'It's all right, Brutus, I'll make sure we get that money out of them in other ways,' Mendes said. He made a circular hand motion to his driver to get things moving. Security contractors with submachine guns moved to their vehicles.

Mendes whistled to Boris, one of his private security couriers. He handed over a briefcase with the signed oil contracts in it, among other correspondence. The Russian took it and then went to his own three-car convoy, which peeled away with haste.

Mendes noticed Achebe's look at that action.

'Armed courier service,' he said by way of explanation as they got into the back of the SUV. 'Much safer way of moving sensitive information around than using phones, faxes or email. It will go to our compound in Abuja, it's the safest place for them.'

'You trust human couriers over modern telecommunications?' Achebe asked. 'We have encrypted gear.'

'When we are dealing with American spies, there is no way of encrypting communications,' Mendes said. 'You forget I am ex-CIA. I learned that the hard way, fighting in Afghanistan and the Middle East. The enemy that was able to stay off the Net was my enemy for another day. As soon as they spoke over a phone or a radio, sent a fax or an email, we had them.'

Mendes clapped his hands together loud. 'A missile right up their ass!'

Achebe laughed with his American friend.

'It's good to see you laughing again,' Mendes said. Their convoy was on the move, bumping down fast along the old timber pier. 'Your people are going to love having a leader with your passion for life.'

'Yes,' Achebe said through his big toothy smile. 'Thank you again. This is your hard work and contacts making this happen.'

Mendes held up a self-deprecating hand.

'I believe in you, Brutus,' he said. 'President Achebe . . .'

The Nigerian laughed.

'*Caliph* Achebe . . .'

The laugh petered out to a serious expression.

'The bombing here in Port Harcourt, it was an omen, don't you think?'

'Yes, an omen,' Achebe said. 'It meant we could sell those extra licences now.'

'Exactly,' Mendes said. 'And the terrorist attacks in Saudi Arabia and Qatar, they have pushed oil prices nice and high for us.'

'Things continue to work out our way.'

'They sure do,' Mendes said. 'Now, today, hold your next press conference at the ministry here in Port Harcourt. Tell them that this country is entering a new phase. Show that you are strong, that you are standing tall in the face of these terrorist activities.'

'And that our president has dragged his feet on real progress for too long.'

'Exactly,' Mendes said. 'Shift the world's focus from the president to you. You are the one speaking out about this bombing while he is busy elsewhere. Say it to everyone who will listen. And say that you, Brutus Achebe, with your uncle the Sultan, have led the prayers for this country, for a better life for everyone.'

'Yes, I have, I will.'

'You *own* the north. Lagos is there and waiting to be *taken*; make it the seat of the Achebe government, be a saviour to your people.'

Achebe nodded. This had been a discussion point of theirs for the past two years – reseating the federal government where it belonged.

'This is simple disaster economics doctrine,' Mendes said. 'The country is in a state of disrepair, the people are desperate. It has been this way for too long. Nigeria is crying out to be great again – only this time it's like fire-farming, we have to completely get rid of the past attempts at reform and start totally afresh. And, as the first step: all new oil contracts. We take advantage of the oil companies moving out and the Russians will take over the wells. I have more contacts waiting for the go-ahead. Then we sell off everything. Privatise the schools, the roads, all the infrastructure – power, water, you name it.

We build up the security, get fifty thousand private contractors in to guard the oil, headed by my own hand-picked men,
of course. This frees up your military to handle the populace,
the unrest that will soon be put to rest once the people see
what you have done for them. It's a model that my old countrymen have tried to follow in Iraq but have failed to do so
abysmally – because they have gone about it in a half-measured
way. This type of reform is all or nothing. You know that.'

Achebe nodded. Mendes' advice had gotten them this far,
and the picture he painted now was so simple that it seemed
like it could be implemented tomorrow.

'Selling all this will make the government small in its assets
but incredibly rich – beyond anything you could imagine,'
Mendes said. 'You will make billions. The country, hundreds
of billions. Use the money to do more exploration. We know
there's even more oil out there, we've hardly looked beyond
the surface, we could easily be the next Saudi Arabia. Not to
mention other resource wealth. This country is a gold mine,
you know that. It just needs the right people to bring out its
full potential.'

'If the government will be so small, why would I want to
run it? Why be president of such a small office?'

'Because you will be like the CEO of a major company,'
Mendes said. 'The biggest company in the land – and you will
still make the laws that govern all. You will be at the helm of
the mightiest country in Africa. Besides which, there's more
power for you to hold beyond the office of the president.'

Achebe's face showed he knew that too.

'You can lead your country into a spiritual revolution,' Mendes said. 'Think about it. With such wealth, such political and economic reform, you can be the leader of the Muslim world.'

'I should reinstate the Caliphate,' Achebe said. 'Be the head of my faith. Be in charge, drive it forward to its rightful place. Live my destiny . . .'

'Your country needs you. Your people need you.'

Achebe smiled. The possibilities of it glowed in his eyes. Then they reached the logical speed bump.

'But,' Achebe said, 'what of my uncle? I – I love my uncle, he should lead such a Caliphate.'

'The Sultan is wise, and I know you care for him,' Mendes said. He put a hand on Achebe's shoulder, leaned close like his truest friend and confidant. 'Brutus, I wouldn't worry about him. You know he is frail.'

Mendes noticed the tears in Achebe's eyes.

'He has been a great man, your uncle. He will know what to do to make your destiny fulfilled. He knows that when he passes to the afterlife he will be well-rewarded for his sacrifice.'

'You talk as though he must give up more than his position,' Achebe said.

'Brutus, don't worry about that now. It's time to make the future. Be the saviour that this country, your country, needs.'

11

WASHINGTON

Wallace and McCorkell sat at an outdoor table with the morning sun brightening the white linen.

'I just read the piece about Robert Boxcell,' Wallace said. The news today had carried with it speculation behind the sudden death of the former CIA Director.

'Yeah,' McCorkell said, and leaned in closer. 'Killed himself. Indictments were being built as long as your arm.'

'He's being buried later today?'

'Yeah, I'm going this afternoon,' McCorkell said, eating some of his heart-healthy omelette. 'Busy times, Tas. With the attacks in Qatar and Saudi, you're gonna see gas prices at the pump rise fifty per cent by the weekend.'

'Jesus,' Wallace said.

'Treasury and SEC are going nuts.'

'Saudis admit it was terrorists?'

'Not yet, but they should come around today,' McCorkell said. 'You keep pushing that stuff I sent through yesterday. Gonna force them to ask for our help.'

'I've got a team running it, already syndicated to over a hundred media outlets. *The New York Times* and Fox News are all over it.'

'And it'll grow – it'll take a couple of days to gather momentum,' McCorkell said. 'By early next week we should see the FBI team off, and by the end of next week we should see Saudi's production deficit back online.'

McCorkell picked around the goat's cheese and peppers in his omelette.

'I need a bit of help with something myself,' Wallace said, draining his coffee and motioning to a waiter for a refill. 'One of my reporters is heading to Nigeria tomorrow to cover the Port Harcourt bombing story. I need some political pressure to get him access to the energy minister, Brutus Achebe.'

'Nigeria,' McCorkell said. 'That's a can of worms. And they've got their hands full of their own problems right now.'

'This bombing in Port Harcourt aside, things could be worse in that country. We want in, there's a big story there.'

'All right. I'll have State try to push for access for you.'

'We tried that, nothing out of it,' Wallace said. His coffee was filled. 'Thanks. Yeah, we tried the State Department, the US Mission in Abuja, some UN and OPEC heavyweights, but Achebe ain't buying. He's got his walls up.'

'I doubt he's going to let anyone force him to the table, it just won't work. We need him more than he needs us especially right now with the attacks in Qatar and Saudi. Achebe's got the Russians, Chinese, Indians all lined up to buy Nigerian oil. He calls the shots with the oil companies and they're so far in his pockets that when he reaches in there to scratch his balls he scratches theirs.'

'We just need an in,' Wallace said. 'The cover story is a puff profile piece. The guy's got a big ego. Get Lachlan Fox in a room with him. Once in there, he can work him for access to the bombing story.'

'Lachlan Fox, hey,' McCorkell said. He made some notes in his diary. 'I could use that guy on my staff. Good man to have on the ground.'

'You couldn't afford him,' Wallace said. 'I've made sure of that.'

'Never seemed like a money man to me.'

'No, truth be told he isn't,' Wallace admitted. 'But I know that he'd never work for a government again. He's done his time as a soldier and intel officer and he's grown well outside of that life now. He's not a Jack Ryan or a James Bond-type character. He has too much disdain for the government line, all the bullshit that comes with being an instrument of an administration.'

'Present company excluded, of course.'

The old friends laughed.

'All right, I'll give Achebe a shot,' McCorkell said. 'Our Navy's got some good relationships forming, been supplying and training their delta water forces for a while now. I'll see if we can get them to have the Nigerian Navy commander lean on their president. He can go to the minister with the truth as he knows it: access for Achebe to the Western press. Let's just hope his ego's as big as you say it is.'

'Good press for Nigeria, bad press for the Saudis,' Wallace said. They shared grins. They'd been friends since post-grad studies at Oxford – Wallace had been lucky enough to have parents who could afford it; McCorkell smart enough to obtain a Rhodes scholarship. 'We missing anyone here?'

12

NEW YORK CITY

Fox wasn't used to being on the receiving end of a press interview. He knew the ins and outs of being the interviewer, the tricks of the trade, the cadence and familiarity used to coax information out of an interview subject. Pity that knowledge and awareness never quite translated when the shoe was on the other foot.

They sat in the Four Seasons bar at the base of the Seagram Building. One martini in and fresh ones just arriving. The friendly staff knew Fox, he was like a piece of furniture in this place. They knew his drink, shared in friendly banter. It created a sense that he was likeable, but Fox was becoming aware that it had a double meaning that might come across in the interview – he comes here too often, drinks too much. He let it fly.

'And that led you to investigate the extraordinary rendition program?'

'Yeah. It wasn't getting the press coverage it deserved here in the States,' Fox said. 'It touches something in us all: *what if* it was *your* husband who was taken off the street and detained without trial?'

'I'm not married any more,' Jane said. She fingered the gold wedding band. 'Actually, I'd quite like it if my ex-husband was picked up off the street and taken to Guantanamo Bay.'

'But you know what I mean,' Fox said. 'If it was your father, brother, friend, whatever. Taken aside at an airport, detained, flown around the world to countries where he can be interrogated in ways that US laws would not permit, held without any legally binding reason, unreachable. And they won't let him do zip – no calls, no legal representation, nothing. They might release him in a year, maybe five. No apology or compensation if it's a case of mistaken identity. No, "Sorry – thought you were a terrorist." Nothing. They just label it a case of *erroneous rendition* and move on.'

'You spoke to some of those wrongly apprehended?' Jane asked. Fox nodded. 'Like Michael Rollins. What had it done to them, to him?'

'You can only imagine,' Fox said. 'They're fucked up. They've been treated in ways you wouldn't wish on your enemies –'

'Do you really think that?' Jane asked. Her well-manicured hand held a Mont Blanc pen over a pad. 'You wouldn't want Osama or any of the September eleventh terrorists to be subjected to this treatment? Strap him up and squeeze information out of him to prevent attacks that might be on the drawing-board?'

'It's that kind of lynch-mob mentality that has taken us down this road,' Fox said. He took a sip of his drink, composing himself in an area of conversation that he could so easily get animated over. 'That's the argument I tried to counter in my reporting. Yes, we need to catch criminals. But they are just that – they've committed crimes. Mass murders. They should be subject to laws. It's laws that make societies and that's the very thing that these guys are attacking and trying to break down.'

'Don't fight them on their terms?'

'I like to think that we're better than that,' Fox said. 'You do that, and they've won. You fight like that, you're playing to their rule book, their game – and they're better at it.'

'So you wouldn't agree with the secretary-general of Reporters Without Borders when he said –'

'What Robert Ménard said was in response to the killing of *Washington Post* journalist Daniel Pearl, and he related his answer to how he would feel in the situation –'

'By saying that if it were his daughter . . .'

'That if it were his daughter who was kidnapped then there would be no limit on the torture. That's – when there are kids involved, that's when it really hits home.'

'So, you agree with his sentiments? That it's okay to go along with that if you're directly affected?'

'Like I said before, I hope that there's never an excuse for that,' Fox said. He thought about it. 'There is certainly a part of me that thinks that if, to save an innocent life, you have to squeeze some information out of a *known* criminal, I can see something there. But this is exactly why I wrote my pieces on this issue. To generate this kind of debate. To explore answers to questions like this, because right now, even with all the hours and days and weeks I've spent thinking about this, I still don't have a good answer.'

'Why not just say, *Well, if we know they are terrorists beyond reasonable doubt, then the gloves are off*? Surely we're pretty good at all this – we've got all the money and resources –'

'And what is that proof beyond reasonable doubt? DNA? Or are you talking about admissions? Oh, by the way, how do we get the terrorists to admit to their crimes?'

'By dubious methods,' Jane said.

'And when it comes to this kind of asymmetric warfare we're fighting in places like Iraq and Afghanistan, it's a case of all or nothing,' Fox said. 'You fight the way you've been taught and trained and within the law, or you fight like the insurgents. If you fight like them, you have to be prepared to throw out the rule book completely. Our guys in Iraq and Afghanistan are engaging an enemy who thinks nothing about the collat- eral damage of roadside bombs. You go down the path you suggested, sure, we've got all the gear and training to play like that and win. Can't find that target in a neighbourhood? Wipe the whole city from the map. Can't find the fighters hiding in the hills among the villagers and tribesmen? Remove the entire mountain. Hell, nuke the whole Middle East – we have weapons that can do that and leave the infrastructure intact. Take out every living thing there.'

'Well, I think we'd all agree that that's about ten steps too far.'

'Well, to me it's a case of all or nothing and something not really worth thinking too much about. It's that clear-cut. *You play by the rules or you don't.* What are we fighting for, our way of life? Yeah, some say oil, but let's just look at the prin- ciples here. What are they fighting us for? To erode our way of life? To get us out of their homes? Well, they're winning a lot of the battles.'

'Is it too late then? Have we gone too far?'

'I don't think we have, but we have to acknowledge what we've done. Admit we've made mistakes, admit that at times we got suckered into fighting at their level. Only then can we set the standard. Only then can we fight on our own terms and have peace in sight.'

Fox leaned across the table. He'd thought about this at some length; it felt good to articulate it all.

'If we live like we do and then have this double-edged playbook? It comes back to bite us in the ass,' he said. 'The lives that we are affecting by creating all these orphans, all those shattered families that are left behind, come back to haunt us bad. We're saying it's okay to fight like that, to torture when we have to. We take a guy off the street and water-board him and deprive him of all his rights; they pick a journalist off the street in Baghdad or Karachi and cut his head off – making sure to film it for all the world to see.'

Silence. Fox was getting agitated, and fought it back.

'You asked me what it was like for guys like Michael Rollins,' Fox said. He fidgeted with his hands, had a drink. 'The only time I've come across someone with the same kind of trauma is from the world wars.'

'Did any of your family serve?'

'My great-grandfather, Clarry, fought in the First World War with his two brothers. He was just sixteen. His brothers didn't return, but he did. He died when I was about seven . . .' Fox trailed off, lost in thought for a moment. 'But I remember all these little things.'

'Did he ever talk about it?'

'The war? Not really. He'd talk about the campaign in Gallipoli, because it's an entrenched part of Australia's history and identity. But he'd never talk about the Western Front in France. His daughter, my grandmother, would tell me some stories she'd heard him tell her own mother, many years earlier. Climbing over mountains of bodies; the mud that sucked you down. Even though he escaped the shells, he was destroyed by the war.'

Fox paused for a beat.

'That's what I saw in Rollins. That same hollowed-out sense of someone who'd been through too much. That same sense I've gotten out of veterans of the Second World War and Vietnam, guys all fucked up from being tortured. In many ways Michael Rollins is one of the few people I can really talk to. In many ways, I'll owe him more than he'll ever know.'

Jane stopped her tape-recorder, closed her notebook and put down her pen. She smiled and had a sip of her martini.

'Can we make another time to chat with some follow-up questions after you get back from Nigeria?'

'Sure, I'll let you know as soon as I'm back,' he said. He finished off his drink and motioned for the waiter to bring another.

'They like you here.'

'It's my local,' Fox said. He noticed the look. 'Yeah, I spend too much time here.'

'I'm not judging,' she said. 'God knows I've drunk myself to sleep some nights since being home alone.'

'How long were you married for?'

'Why don't you tell me, you're the perceptive one.'

'Married about five years, I'd say.'

'Close.'

'Divorced – what, three? But it seems you haven't quite moved on . . .'

Jane gave a mysterious shrug.

'Or not divorced . . . you're separated.'

A nod.

'What was it, Catholic guilt?'

Nothing – then a sparkle in her eye.

'You won't give him the divorce then.' Fox sipped his beer. 'He's moved on, maybe even while he was still in the marriage, and you won't give him the divorce.'

'Wow,' Jane said through a mocking smile. 'You know so much.'

'I know he was an idiot to cheat on you.'

'Okay, now you're on the right track,' Jane agreed, laughing. She had a sip of her drink. 'Tell me more about The Idiot.'

'He works in the industry – an editor, maybe, or likely now he's a news producer on TV, some B-grade cable station. You fell in love with him for the same reasons as the next woman – his charm, power, influence. Sadly, it wasn't until later that you realised he only liked house music.'

Jane laughed hard.

'If that wasn't enough, he only liked Hollywood blockbuster films, Michael Bay-type shit. He presented himself as a serious highbrow media player, but secretly he only wanted to live the life of a superhero and have all that that entails, especially the female interest.'

'Okay, that's him,' Jane said, smiling. 'I came home one night to an email in my inbox. It said he wouldn't be coming home and his lawyer would call first thing in the morning.'

'Ouch,' Fox said, drinking. 'Via email? The guy has class.'

Jane was serious for a moment. Fox had missed something, or trodden too far with this little game.

'I'm sorry . . .' Fox said.

'Don't be sorry,' she replied, then put her hand on his and left it there. She looked up to his eyes. 'I just wish he'd said that. Just two simple words, nothing more, and it would have been some kind of closure or acceptance on his part. But I guess I wouldn't have believed it anyway.' Jane's face was friendly in the permanent fine smile lines of her cheeks, her dark eyes soft, singing of emotions learned the hard, hurtful way. 'So much for death do us part.'

Fox had a look of his own, and took his hand away from under hers.

'Some promises are too hard to keep.'

13

ARLINGTON NATIONAL CEMETERY, WASHINGTON DC

McCorkell stood among a throng of black-clad officialdom. The coffin was draped with the flag in a military custom that had begun during the Napoleonic Wars. Back then, the dead that were carried from the field of battle on a caisson were covered with a flag. When the US flag covered a casket, it was placed so the union blue field was at the head and over the left shoulder. It was not placed in the grave, nor was it allowed to touch the ground. This flag was folded and a military chaplain handed it over to the widow as the casket was lowered into the ground. McCorkell had a hard time reconciling that they were giving this man military honours.

A guy that had spent his life serving his country – fine, fair enough. A guy who in the last act of his life had been expelled from his office as the corrupt head of the CIA . . . that was harder.

Robert Boxcell had left a mess that still required cleaning up. Would the situations in Nigeria and the Middle-East have developed like it had if there had been stable leadership in the agency? Maybe. Probably. They might have seen some signposts earlier in the piece, though.

McCorkell looked around. There were a couple of press close by, a helicopter buzzing high overhead, long-lensed paparazzi out the side door. The President had had second thoughts about being here. It had kicked off a discussion in a senior staff meeting that had taken under a minute to conclude: McCorkell would be the only representative of the administration to attend. McCorkell was the right guy in the right place – senior but without a high degree of public visibility. It showed they cared enough not to have cleaned their hands of a guy who had done a lifetime's good work, albeit that he'd gone out in disgrace, which the public didn't know the half of.

And so Boxcell had taken his own life. At sixty, leaving a wife and three adult kids to think about what their husband and father had really been. A traitor? Perhaps a traitor within the ranks, but not of treasonous proportions. He'd had his own measure of what he was doing, attempting to shift the balance of power within the intelligence community. But then, wasn't everyone driven by the path they thought they should be on?

The casket was lowered and the Navy pall-bearers gave a final salute and marched off. Those young men and women knew the deceased had been a decorated Vietnam Vet, a career intelligence man, the head of their leading intelligence agency who'd resigned and abruptly died. McCorkell guessed that they would speculate that the man must have known about a medical condition. The press had hardly touched on it, though. They'd allowed his family the dignity of grieving in relative peace.

But McCorkell, and a couple of the senators present who served on the United States Senate Select Committee on Intelligence, knew differently. They knew Boxcell had schemed to new proportions against his sister agency the NSA. They were still not playing nice, despite being more unified since 9/11. Maybe there was more hope of unity on the horizon, as for the first time in a long time uniformed men were at each agency's directorial posts.

The seven Navy riflemen shot a volley into the air. McCorkell stiffened at the report that was part of a ceremony that dated back to halting the battle to remove the dead. Once each army had cleared its dead, they would fire three volleys into the air to signify that the fighting could begin again. The act of firing your gun empty, therefore being unarmed, signified respect to the dead.

The last volley was fired. In the White House, the Pentagon, on the front lines in Iraq and Afghanistan, and in so many other places in the world at this very moment in time, it was back to business. But of course, those places never halted, never paused to take stock of what had been lost.

McCorkell's gaze had been drawn to the involuntary flinching of Boxcell's wife at the sound of the final volley. She stood there, veiled, on the opposite side of the hole in the ground that her husband had just been lowered into. He realised she had probably been at home when the former DCIA had sent a 9 mm slug through the roof of his mouth.

The rifles fell silent. The chaplain said his final words, and the gathered said their goodbyes. Dirt was tossed, roses fell.

McCorkell made his way between solemn nods of greeting and respect to the widow. Her punch-drunk gaze was still on the high-gloss mahogany. He winced at having to do this. His posture spoke of the short straw that he'd drawn.

'Mrs Boxcell,' McCorkell began. 'On behalf of the President, our deepest –'

'Tell him –' Her eyes, redder than the roses that she bore, met McCorkell's. There was more vengeance there than remembrance. She pulled a folded piece of paper from her clutch. 'Just give him this. I would have done it myself, if he were here.'

McCorkell took the offered note and left the grief behind at the grave. It had been less than fifteen minutes at the gravesite, and he could see the next procession arriving. Two other marching units were close by. Burial peak hour. Death was having a busy time here.

The fall sunshine glinted off the afternoon green of the grass, as a Secret Service agent opened the car door for his principal. McCorkell got into the back of the shiny black town-car and rested against the plush leather. The door slammed shut behind him, the tinted windows offering a bleak outlook. The agent got into the passenger seat and the driver set off.

McCorkell took in the note in his hand. Dog-eared lined paper, folded in four. '*Mr President*,' written in red ink. Well opened and closed in the four days since Boxcell's death. He opened it.

Boxcell's suicide note? Impersonal. Maybe there was a family one too. The words were familiar, from another time and place when written and performed, and McCorkell remembered when he himself had discovered these words as a freshman. It was part of a poem from Sophocles' tragedy *Ajax*. McCorkell read it aloud, softly, just for himself to hear. His mouth moved around the words as he spoke, ever present and mindful of the gravity not just of Boxcell's action but of the symbology behind it.

Thy son is in a foreign clime
Where Ida feeds her countless flocks,
Far from thy dear, remembered rocks,
Worn by the waste of time –
Comfortless, nameless, hopeless save
In the dark prospect of the yawning grave . . .
Better to die, and sleep
The never-waking sleep, than linger on
And dare to live, when the soul's life is gone;
But thou shalt weep,
Thou wretched father, for thy dearest son,
The best beloved, by inward Furies torn,
The deepest, bitterest curse, thine ancient house hath borne!

In his mind, McCorkell could still hear the Navy bugler playing *Taps*.

14

NEW YORK CITY

Fox leaned on the bar in the downstairs room of Eight Mile Creek. On Mulberry Street between Prince and King, it was a little slice of Australia in lower Manhattan. The basement was dark, just a small bar and standing area at the back and along one side, a seating and live music area at the front.

A young woman strummed at an acoustic guitar and sang in a soft, smoky folk voice in the mezzo range. There were two guys with her, one on a keyboard and bass guitar, the other with a small drum kit, a snare and a few cymbals. They started with some Australian stuff; James Reyne's 'Reckless' had half the crowd singing along as she picked away at the six-string guitar. It ended to much applause; there were maybe sixty people down there, which was pretty packed for the space. A familiar song started up, just her picking away. Powderfinger.

'This song is called "Nobody Sees",' the singer announced. More applause, then the crowd grew quiet to listen attentively. Conversations were whispers now, laughter more physical than vocal, movements were made to the rhythmic, haunting sounds.

Fox watched Gammaldi from across the room, his friend sitting at a table with some of the GSR staff. Emma Gibbs, a member of the security team, and Gammaldi were real close. Whispers were being traded close to ears, toothy smiles were shared and their laughter was contagious. A hand touch here, a brush of lips there, a look just so. Good one, Al.

'Can you send some more drinks over to that table?' Fox asked the barman. His Amex was behind the bar and he handed over a twenty for the guy's troubles. The barman nodded, and refreshed Fox's beer first. There were Aussie beers here; Fox was enjoying Coopers Pale Ale out of the bottle.

'So you're the lucky one buying tonight, huh?' a barmaid asked, filling up a tray of drinks to take over.

'Yep,' Fox said. She would not have been out of place on the set of *Coyote Ugly*. 'It's a belated birthday party for my best friend – ah, here's the man now.'

Gammaldi came over, a couple of lipstick marks on his cheeks.

'What are you having, mate? Bud Light?'

'Hey, it's my birthday, I'm not drinking lights,' Gammaldi said, deadpan.

'It was your birthday yesterday.'

'Well, okay, but it's my party.' Gammaldi turned to the barmaid: 'Bourbon and Coke, please.'

'Better make that Diet Coke,' Fox added, earning himself a punch in the arm from Al when the barmaid turned her back to mix his drink.

Fox looked at Gammaldi, all dressed up for his party – pressed slacks and short-sleeve shirt exposing his huge biceps. There was something different about his appearance that Fox had been trying to figure out for the past hour – and he had just spotted it.

'Jesus, Al – you pluck your eyebrow?' Fox said, a Cheshire grin on his face as he tried to grab at one, his mate lunging back out of arm's reach. 'Look at you – you have two eyebrows now! They're a bit on the thin side, though . . . shit, dude, now you're looking more like Nic Kidman than Matt LeBlanc.'

Gammaldi was far too drunk to be offended.

'Yeah, at least I don't look like Jake Gyllenhaal,' Gammaldi said.

'That's the best comeback you've got?' Fox sipped his beer, appraising the work of a beautician somewhere. 'Seriously, why the grooming? You seeing someone?'

'Maybe,' Gammaldi said.

'Maybe?' Fox repeated, pretending to nearly choke on his beer. 'I was kidding. You seriously seeing someone? Who? Is it a woman? Or a guy? Not that there's anything wrong with that.'

The music changed. It came from the jukebox now, and Fox knew Gammaldi had banked it up with INXS, Powderfinger, AC-DC, Eskimo Joe, Silverchair . . . every Aussie song in there was set to play at least once. Gammaldi had already fleeced Fox of all the dollar bills he had to feed the machine.

'I have a girlfriend now,' Gammaldi said, and Gibbs came up and put her arms over his shoulders.

'Come and dance!' she said, pulling at him.

Gammaldi raised both eyebrows and went where he was directed, bourbon steady in his hand.

'Hey there,' Faith Williams said, joining Fox, a glass of red in her hand. She was still in her corporate-wear, a form-fitting navy pinstripe suit with a lacy top peeking through the collar.

'Hey Faith,' Fox said, receiving her kiss on his cheek. Her smell was all too familiar.

'You all right? Haven't spoken to me much lately,' she said. Flaming red trusses of hair fell over her shoulders and down her back as she leaned on the bar next to him.

'I'm good,' Fox said, looking at her closely. Her expression and the intensity of her attention were as if she were here just for him. He fidgeted with the collar of his powder-blue shirt that was open a few buttons, the sleeves rolled up over his tanned forearms. 'Been busy is all. To tell you the truth I'm not really looking forward to heading back to Africa again.'

The expression in Faith's green eyes changed slightly. The playfulness was gone, there was real concern there.

'You don't have to go,' she said, putting her hand on his arm. She left it there, soft, still. 'Why don't you leave this to someone else? Run it from your office for once. Let some others go in there, we've got a lot of good front-line operators on the books.'

'The best of them are on assignments already,' Fox said. That wasn't gonna fly with the GSR chief of staff. There were others who could do this job and they both well knew it. 'I do actually like it, being on the ground. The rush of going out. The unknown. Seeing it for myself. Feeling it.'

'Dr Galen spoke to me this afternoon,' Faith said. They both knew this was in reference to him seeing the specialist after the company psychiatrist couldn't do enough for him.

'And?'

'And he said you're fifty–fifty,' Faith said. 'He's concerned that –'

'I can do this –'

'This is a business that's bigger than just you, Lachlan. What you do out there has repercussions for all of us,' Faith said. 'Look, I'll trust your judgement on this. You sure you feel ready?'

'Yeah.' Fox drained his beer, and motioned for another one. 'I've just been thinking about it a bit too much lately. Look, I really do love that part of the job. It's – if I think too much about it, like right now, then it gets the better of me. But when I'm there, on the ground, it's all good. It feels like I can do anything. I know I can do it, it's all second nature, instinctual.'

'You're a natural at it, a born leader,' Faith said. She was in work mode now but it was tainted by her feelings for him. Their affair had ended almost as quickly as it had begun. A few weeks of comfortable, carefree abandon, of exploring carnal knowledge. 'But sometimes it's best to delegate.'

'I know,' Fox said, sipping his fresh beer, putting the walls up. He felt a little light-headed – how many drinks had he had since this afternoon? He'd started with the martinis with Jane, then beers here. At least a dozen by now. He should have eaten something.

'There's – it's a journey.'

'A journey?' Faith asked, fully focused on him.

'Every step I take out there in another land, it's all so *new*,' Fox said. 'Yeah, I know I'm about to go and see the same travesties occurring, the same mistakes being made, the same violations of a civilian population. The ramifications of violence that I know will linger for generations. But . . .'

He fought hard to articulate it. A mix of being drunk and close to voicing this revelation, this meaning, made it almost too hard.

'I'm constantly enthralled by every step I take out there,' Fox said. 'It makes this not just a job. I see the world for what it is – it makes me notice things again. The blue sky, the songs of birds, the stars, trees, people, rivers . . . they're always there but it's like I'm discovering them for the first time, every time I turn around.'

Fox now noticed Faith differently too. Their relationship had been a convenience thing – not that they had used each other, but it was an attraction that occasionally spilled over into a passionate affair. They kept it quiet, even between the two of them. It was not a relationship with commitments but it certainly had its share of comfort. There was the temptation to go back there, but he knew now that those nostalgic thoughts were better left behind like so many other happy summer memories.

'I'm glad it makes you feel like that,' Faith said, brushing her hand over his arm again. 'You should take some time out for yourself, though. Live a little. Let someone in. I'm not saying me, but someone.'

'I'm not ready for anything yet.'

'Lachlan, you can't be human in isolation. You are human only in relationships. Don't forget to give yourself time to enjoy life, or one day you'll stop to take a breath and wonder where it all went.'

'Thanks, Faith. And for the record –'

'Looks like you've got company,' Faith said, giving a glance over Fox's shoulder. She squeezed his arm. 'You take care of yourself.'

Faith left to join the others on the dance floor, looking none too impressed but not too disappointed either.

Fox turned to see Jane Clay, newly arrived, with her handbag on the bar. She had changed clothes since their interview that afternoon, and was now wearing a shapely summer cocktail dress, black satin with bright swirls of colour. Her hair was still up but different now, designed to be messy.

'Not interrupting anything, I hope?' Jane asked.

'That? No.' Fox picked at his beer label. 'We're close friends.'

'Looks like she wants a little more than that,' Jane said. She dragged a barstool over and sat next to Fox.

'Drink?'

'Something soft for me, thanks,' she said. 'I'm still feeling those two martinis.'

Fox smiled the smile of two martinis backed up by a dozen beers and a couple of Jagerbombs.

'An old friend used to tell me that two martinis were exactly what was needed to jump into the night,' Fox said. 'Three martinis and you jumped right over it.'

'Um, yeah, but we had them in the afternoon on empty stomachs,' Jane said with a laugh, taking a sip of plain soda water.

'True,' Fox said. Smiled, drank his beer. Looked to the dance floor, where Gammaldi and Gibbs were mirroring each other's actions. He couldn't help but chuckle.

'Your friend Alister has some moves,' Jane observed.

'Yeah, it's thanks to his low centre of gravity,' Fox said over the music.

Jane laughed with Fox, and he considered the scene more closely.

'I think he's doing a bit too much of the dice thing,' Fox said. 'And what's that action – he feeding chickens or something?'

They laughed again, and for the first time Fox looked to Jane. There was something there in the look. A moment of knowing; of being aware that there's some mutual measuring-up taking place. He checked himself, a little too late. Looked to his beer. Picked at the label.

'You all right?'

Fox laughed as another drink was placed in front of him.

'If I had a dollar for every time I've been asked that tonight . . .' he said.

There was an awkward pause on his part. He blinked off the blurred lines of alcohol.

'Seems a lot of people care about you,' Jane said.

Fox rubbed his face with his free hand. 'Yeah,' he replied. He ran his hand around his neck, irritated. Drank more beer.

Jane shifted her hand and rested it on his leg.

'A lot of people like you too,' she said. 'And you're getting a profile. More and more people are going to want a piece of you.'

'Like you?' Fox said, a little too sharply. Her hand went away.

'Sorry. I'm –' Fox couldn't finish the thought. He just let out a deep breath, like he'd been waiting to exhale. He didn't want to give too much away to this reporter. On the other hand, he hadn't spoken to someone like this aside from his shrink in God knew how long. How long had it been? A couple of months. Since Kate, Fox thought. Their first night together, on a train in St Petersburg. That sweaty summer night on his old houseboat. That goodbye. Kate . . .

'You ever feel . . . that it's not easy?' Fox asked.

'What's not easy?'

'I – I don't know . . .' Fox thought about it. He was leaning forward with both his arms crossed on the bar. 'I guess I mean that – I don't know . . . like it's not easy to be me. Yourself. You ever get that?'

'I think I know what you mean,' Jane said. She patted her hand on his leg, a little squeeze. She wore her smile in her eyes. 'And you'll be fine. You're a survivor. Look at you. You've done so much in such a short time. And you're a writer – you know how the world works as well as anyone. How people work. Your story is hot property right now, but it's a story that's not a fad. The rendition stuff you've reported on, the places that you've served in – it's understandable that people want to hear what you have to say. Not to mention that you're cute and marketable . . .'

'Ha. The last thing I want is to join the ranks of the disposable celebrities,' Fox said. On this he was adamant. 'It seems a pretty fine line if I go down this path of being a commentator appearing on all sorts of media. I'm happy to report – but just to be there, giving my point of view. To write a movie script on extraordinary rendition? On my time in Iraq? Dramatising the stuff I've been through? Please . . .'

'Then don't do it,' Jane said.

Fox looked at her, taking it in. It felt good to have another voice of reason.

'No one's making you do anything,' she continued. 'Well, okay, maybe Tas has twisted your arm to do my interview for *The New Yorker.*'

They both laughed at that but Fox held back. He was uncomfortable with things, felt they were getting out of his control.

His life was getting out of control. He drained his beer, asked the barmaid for Bison Grass vodka – the bottle, and two glasses.

'I don't think I could,' Jane said, looking at the clear fluid.

'Well I'm not one to stand on ceremony,' Fox replied, downing a glassful.

He felt her watching him. He paused before refilling, did it despite his better judgement, which was moving further and further into the background of noise in his mind as the evening wore on.

'My brother served in Iraq,' Jane said. 'Just the one tour, bugged out of his Guard unit when he returned.'

'He all right?'

'He's – no, not really,' Jane said. She took her shot of the vodka. Downed it. Winced. 'When he first shipped over, he left all gung-ho, wanting to avenge or something.'

'For September eleven?'

'Yeah,' Jane said. A faraway smile on her face. 'He, like me and so many people in this town, had friends in the towers. I remember reading pieces like those *The New York Times* published on the fifth anniversary of the attacks and – and I just wonder – I'm just angry. I lost friends that morning and half of them have never been identified, and it's like they're still out there, as landfill in Staten Island, or maybe there're parts of them on the roofs of city buildings or under manholes in the city – you know they're still finding remains?'

Fox nodded.

'It's just this hole in my heart, and it's like we've not moved on, as a city, as a nation, as people.' Jane had tears in her eyes. 'It's like we had a chance to do something special and we blew it by going to war. We went ahead and took what should have

been that last option available. Yet can I accept why we do extraordinary rendition? Can I better understand why soldiers and
agents of my government are out there on the front lines themselves wondering why they were ever there in the first place?
Not much makes sense to me any more, so little surprises me . . .'

The pair sat in silence for a while. Jane had retreated into
herself; Fox didn't touch more alcohol. Another Powderfinger
song played on the jukebox.

'This song . . .' Jane said. She put her hand on Fox's,
squeezed. The smallest hint of a smile appeared. 'It's beautiful.'

'It is,' Fox said. 'It's called "The Metre". They're a good
band. I'll have to buy you some of their CDs, or make you a
mixed compilation from iTunes.'

'Aw, shucks, a mixed tape. People still do that?'

'That's romance, hey?' Fox said. 'Okay, it's not like I saw
you on the crowded number-five train to Brooklyn and used
the good people of New York to track you down via a webpage
– but it's a start.'

They were both laughing now. Jane squeezed his hand, her
eyes still wet but shaped in that happy way he'd known them.

'Let's get drunk.'

15

OUTSKIRTS OF PORT HARCOURT, NIGERIA

A nondescript four-wheel-drive with blacked-out windows sped along the road from Lagos, heading for Port Harcourt, led by a Toyota pick-up with a mounted 7.62 mm machine gun on the roll bar, two guys in the cab and another two sitting in the tray. Spotlights on the big chunky steel bumper bar – this pick-up was a mean machine, part of an armed courier convoy. Everyone was smart enough to give them a wide berth. They knew this vehicle's purpose. Protection. An insurance policy to ensure the safe transit of whatever or whoever was in the chase car. They knew that the convoy would not stop, and they knew that the drivers and shooters would drive and shoot their way through whatever happened to be in their path.

The driver of the Toyota pick-up never reacted to the attack. As he neared an old VW van parked on the shoulder of the road, he and his passenger were shattered in the blast of a massive car bomb. The pick-up's rear tray separated from the chassis before being swallowed up in the growing fireball. The two guys in the tray simply disappeared, eaten up in the blast.

The four-wheel-drive passed through the destruction that occurred not twenty metres ahead of it. Its tyres were ablaze as it came to a stop in the middle of the road, all the windows and most of the duco riddled with shrapnel. Almost lifeless inside – the faintest sign of movement in the back seat – a rear door opened. Smoke escaped the interior. The bloodied occupant almost emerged, but there was a smattering of rifle fire and his position was turned into bloody explosions of flesh and gore.

From the open rear door, his lifeless arm spilled out. His grip was released on the handle of a black briefcase that clattered to the road. A militant emerged from the trees and ran towards the fire. Cowering from the heat, he scooped up the briefcase and ran into the trees with it. Gone in sixty seconds.

16

NEW YORK
CITY

Electrical storms in New York were really something to behold, thought Fox. The energy in the pre-dawn air made the hairs on his arms stand straight up. The rolling blanket of clouds that marshmallowed around buildings like packing material flashed with bolts of lightning. The sound of the thunder surrounded him and waved through the canyons of Manhattan, as though JDAM bombs were striking down.

He checked his watch – he'd slept maybe three hours. That was about standard for the past couple of months. He hadn't had any sleeping drugs last night, either.

Fox sat in a chair by the window of the tenth-floor apartment in Stuy Town, the locals' name for the Stuyvesant Town, a large collection of postwar apartment buildings near the East Village. He watched as fat droplets of rain shot from the sky and smashed on impact. He was dressed just in his boxers, his clothes over the back of the couch where he'd slept. In the reflection of the glass he saw the creases in his face. There was more there than the life he had led. He saw the faces of the dead in his reflection. In the year that he had lived in New York he was still haunted by all this. Still heard and saw all the shit that he'd been working through. It was like he had only scratched the surface of what was bothering him. He looked at a reflection that he hardly recognised any more.

What the hell was he doing? This wasn't him. All this fucking drinking, drugs, losing his physical edge. Losing so much of what he used to be. Who was he becoming? This guy, this guy right at this second, it was not someone he wanted to be. Not a hero, not someone who'd saved lives. Changed lives. Or was it? Was this the path he had to go down? Was this the pain of redemption? For all those lives he'd taken along the way. They were people too. They were fucking people too . . . Visions in his mind's eye went from those he'd lost to those he'd killed. Who the fuck was he to kill anyone? Was he as bad as them? Worse? Did they sit like this, thinking through all this shit –

He turned at sensing a presence next to him – a little girl, no more than five. She stood there next to him, watching the storm, a little hand resting on the arm of his chair. Her bed hair was tussled with the sweat that came with nightmares, her red flannelette pyjamas a size too big, hanging over her hands and feet. An oatmeal-coloured teddy bear had been dragged along by one of his big rabbit-like ears.

She looked up at him. Her eyes awake, more than Fox's. There was so much innocence and truth in there, written all over this little face.

'Are you an angel?' she asked.

Fox smiled with his eyes, then his mouth.

'Why, should I be?' he asked.

'It would be nice,' she said. She turned her attention back to the storm and they watched in silence for a couple of minutes, the only sounds those of the rain and thunder and the wind in the trees in the oval below.

'I'd like to be an angel,' she said. 'I'd like to fly.'

'Then one day you will,' Fox said. Considered it. Smiled. 'I'd like it, too.'

Fox saw, in the reflection of the glass in the window, Jane standing in the open doorway behind him. The dim light spilled out of the hallway and back-lit her outline. She walked over.

'Come back to bed, little miss, or you'll fall asleep in school today,' she said, scooping her daughter up into her arms.

'Bye,' the child said.

'Bye, angel,' Fox replied. He shook the bear's paw. Watched them leave the room. He was left there in solace, the thunder moving off, the rain still belting down and whipping into the open window now. Fox felt the water, more wet than cold, spray his skin and run down his legs to pool on the parquetry timber floor.

Jane was back beside him. She sat on the arm of the chair and put a hand on his shoulder.

'You okay?' she asked.

'Yeah,' Fox said. He looked up at her. 'I slept for a couple of hours. I'm sorry if I got too drunk last night.'

'I have friends sleep on my couch all the time,' she said. 'Gabriella thinks they're all here for her to talk to when she can't sleep.'

'Gabriella. That's a sweet name,' Fox said. He put his hand on Jane's. There was a familiarity in touching her that went far beyond the few days they'd known each other.

'Sorry – I can't even remember how I got here,' Fox said. 'Last I remember we were at Eight Mile . . .'

'You don't remember going to Sing Sing?'

'Oh God, no,' Fox said. 'Tell me I didn't do karaoke.'

'You and Gammaldi sang some INXS song, and said that anyone Australian could join in and that everyone else could fuck off.'

'Shit,' Fox said, his forehead on his hand. 'I seriously can't remember doing that.'

'You were very drunk, yet somehow you almost managed to sing in key,' she said. 'We left when the rest kicked on to The Box.'

'Jesus.'

'And in the cab ride here, you said I could help you.'

'Help me what?'

'Help you through whatever you need. You don't need to do this alone – I can be there for you. I want to help you through whatever you're going through.'

'I can manage just fine, thanks –'

'Lachlan.' Jane put her hand on his shoulder. Looked steadily at his eyes. 'Let me in.'

'Look, I'm really sorry, I shouldn't have come back here.'

'But you did. You don't have to be alone. If you want help, I can be there for you.'

'Jane,' Fox said, looking into her eyes. 'I can't –'

'You've got so much going for you – you're hot, you're smart –'

'I can't do this now,' Fox said. 'Who I am now, what I'm doing, all this drinking, the no sleep, being irrational, erratic – this isn't me.'

'I can see that,' Jane said, 'and that's why I want to help. You don't deserve to go through this alone.'

'I'm big enough to look after myself.'

Jane got up. Fox watched as she sat on his lap side-saddle. It broke the tension and he let himself relax, resting his head on her.

Fox noticed a much-loved and dog-eared Bible open on the side table next to the sofa where he'd slept.

'You been reading the Bible?'

'A little,' Jane said. 'Reading some to Gabriella. My mother used to read it to me.'

'Does it help?'

She leaned her head onto his. Thunder broke the sky close by. No wonder he'd dreamed he was in Iraq again. They watched and listened to the storm.

'Some of the time.'

17

THE FLORIDA
KEYS

The Afghan arrived at the door right on time. He travelled light. Just a small backpack over his shoulder and a briefcase in his hand. He greeted his old friend in Pashto, and for a moment it took them back to their younger years.

'Where's Tahir?' he asked his friend as he entered the house.

'Mr Massoud is in Washington, waiting for us,' he replied. 'You and I will drive up there tomorrow, we have a safe house there.'

'What is Tahir still doing up there?' He looked at the three other men who were there. He'd not met them before, but knew of them, knew their families. They all waved – timid, slow movements, as if they were now conserving whatever energy they had left in this life for their travel to the next. He knew two of them were to be martyrs soon, piloting speed-boats into the next life. The other was there for support and back-up, his fate less certain, but there were many options for him. Guns were stacked against a wall, the dining table covered in bomb-making material. 'Is something holding him up?'

'I am not sure, but as it involves the infidel's president, he has not been using the telephone,' his friend replied. 'Don't worry, old friend. We are ready to strike on Saturday, when the country will be weakest.'

The Afghan nodded. He'd been a hero in the war against the Soviets; trained many of his countrymen in the fine art of precision mortar fire. He knew exactly what lengths Tahir had had to go to, to get the information for the timing of this Saturday's attack. The Afghan was, after all, the leader of this cell. His Saudi brother-in-arms in Washington was merely a tool at his disposal, much like these men here before him. Their unifying force was more than mutual hatred for this nation. This was jihad. Funded by friends in unlikely places, friends who shared in their vision of seeing this nation hurt.

He walked through to the kitchen, motioned for his friend to make tea. Opened the briefcase to reveal detailed blueprints of an elaborate and vast structure. Photographs of what seemed to be a steel maze, points highlighted where the two speedboats were to strike. The immense scale of the thing had him wondering if they'd arranged for enough explosives. But it had all been planned, by engineers, back in Saudi Arabia. Men used to such structures, men who knew the weakness and strength of all that steel and concrete and whatever else.

He turned to the men in the lounge room, and studied them as they sat there silently watching the television. The volume was low but it was still an affront to his ears. They watched the show in detached interest, sometimes with expressions tinged with vehemence.

Yes. Finally, they were all ready.

18

SOUTH KENT, CONNECTICUT

It was mid-morning and the earth was damp underfoot as Fox ran. Dressed in shorts and a T-shirt, mud flicked up the back of his legs as he pushed himself in a final sprint.

Fox ran on a well-worn path that formed a ring just inside the dry-stone wall that bordered Wallace's five hundred acres of rolling green fields in Litchfield County. Unlike when he ran or rode alone in NYC, he didn't run with his iPod here. Instead, he freed himself in the quiet that surrounded him.

He checked his watch. Forty minutes, at least ten k's. He stopped and stretched against the waist-height stone wall. His skin bore the scarred marks of an outdoorsman combined with those of a war veteran. Two quarter-sized scars on his right elbow dimpled an entry and exit point of a gunshot wound. A reminder of peacekeeping duty in East Timor. Some ominous scars bore memories of torture; other, lighter ones spoke of the sports he'd played over the years. One wound was still sore, over his left collarbone, still stiff from the rehab he was just getting through. More than once he'd wondered why he couldn't have Indiana Jones's ability to take the blows, show he felt them in some macho way, then move on, ever able to deliver shotgun-sounding punches.

The distinctive *pop-pop-pop* of 9 mm pistol fire brought him out of his stretching routine.

He stilled himself and listened closely. There – more shots, echoing up from the low point on the property. Controlled three-round bursts. Someone from the GSR security team? He couldn't make out the figure at the firing range, and not for the first time thought that maybe he should get his eyes checked. It was the sort of distance he used to be able to see with precise clarity. Now, he noticed that leaves on trees were more a mass of colour rather than individual forms. He knew that each leaf had its own hue, shape, texture, but it was something he hadn't seen for some time.

Jogging back along the path, Fox lost his footing where it closed on the shallow creek. He went down hard and fast, sliding into the frigid water and collecting a side full of mud along the way. The rain runoff from the storm acted like a rising tide, almost knocking him down as he stood knee-deep. It was coloured with the nutrients from the soil and waste runoff from the livestock on nearby farms. Filtered through the earth but carrying so much with it. His Sox cap moved with the current, spun in an eddy around some smooth rocks and floated away, conforming to the inevitability carried in the force of water.

The gunfire stopped; some birds squawked their return to the lone peppercorn tree across the other side of the creek. Its sad curtain of leaves dipped into the water as flashes of red signalled the birds' presence. A group of Red Crossbills.

'A crookedness of Crossbills,' Tas Wallace said, giving Fox a start. 'Birds have such wonderful collective nouns.'

'That they do,' Fox said, washing the mud off his hands and arms. He clambered over the slippery creek-bed, took the offered hand of Wallace and let his boss help haul him out of the water. Thanks didn't need to be spoken, and Fox had little doubt his boss, a reformed alcoholic, could smell the alcohol on his breath. 'I saw a bald eagle when I was here last, about a month ago.'

'Yeah?' Wallace said. Poured himself a coffee from a thermos, his black retriever, Molly, close by his leg. 'Haven't seen one of them around here for years.'

'Pity. Beautiful creatures.' Fox took an offered cup and waited for coffee to be poured. 'Was that you shooting?'

'Me? You kidding?' Wallace said. 'Haven't fired a gun since I shot a fox with Dad's under-over shotgun. It had been attacking our family's chickens for weeks. I would have been about fourteen, I suppose. Got up at dawn every day for two weeks to try and catch him in the act. Well, I did, and the image of its head blown away gave me nightmares for months.'

'A fox, hey,' Fox said, with a wry smile.

'Sorry, hope he wasn't related,' Wallace replied, taking a sip of coffee. The older man's eyes narrowed. 'You're drinking too much, aren't you?'

Fox dug his heel into the soft earth underfoot.

'This is a messy business we're in,' Wallace said. 'Lousy hours, hard, stressful work. Particularly the area of responsibility you have.'

'When did you give up?'

'I would have been about your age,' Wallace said. 'I was working at the *Washington Post* then. I think I was the only guy who didn't get plastered over lunch.'

'And why'd you do it?'

Wallace turned, paused to reflect.

'I was in my late twenties,' he said. 'Just broken up with my fiancée, and she didn't want to know me. I was a workaholic. I was stressed, confused, overwhelmed. Didn't take long for the self-medication through booze to turn me into an alcoholic. Eventually got to a point where I was about to lose everything, and it took a friend to point out that most of my problems came from the bottle.'

They stood there as the truth washed over them.

'Go clean for a while,' Wallace said. 'It'll hurt, but you won't regret it. And forget the twelve steps, just do it, mind over matter, and you'll be that much stronger. It's a life-changing action. Gives you back control.'

Fox nodded slowly. It sounded like a sensible move but he knew it was harder than that. There were good reasons why he drank. Weren't there?

'So, you haven't drunk in fifty years, hey?' Fox jibed.

'I'm not that bloody old,' Wallace said. 'About twenty-five years, I guess. Only lapsed the once.'

Fox caught himself before asking *When?* Wallace had lost his daughter less than a year ago, surely something that would drive you to drink.

'Come on, back to business,' Wallace said, with a slap on the back for Fox. 'I've come through with some gold for you. You're gonna owe me.'

'And what's that?'

'I'm going to London to collect Michael Rollins, he's agreed to meet you in Nigeria the day after tomorrow,' Wallace said. 'He'll set up some interviews for you with the militants, in and out within twenty-four hours. I'll be dropping him off personally, if you can meet us on the ground?'

'Will do,' Fox said. He drained half his brew, watching the steam rise and through it the flowing ripples of the creek water.

'You'll be all right with this? You don't have to go, we can outsource it,' Wallace said. Not known as an emotional man, he did possess qualities that his staff sometimes took refuge in. Half priest, half father.

'Yeah,' Fox said. He shook his cup dry onto the ground. 'It's just been one hell of a year.'

'The year of the Fox,' Wallace said. He slapped Fox on the back as they got up and headed back to the farmhouse.

'I hope next year will be my year of sleep,' Fox replied.

'I head back to New York in an hour,' Fox said. 'Think you can get me back up to speed?'

Fox stood at a roofed timber bench that served as a shooting position. Down the hundred-metre range was a series of targets spaced across his line of vision and set at ten-metre intervals. Sandbagged walls marked the edges and ends of the range.

'I doubt it,' Richard Sefreid, GSR's head of security, said. 'You taking a pistol to Nigeria?'

'There's only so far I'm willing to rely on body armour,' Fox replied. He sighted the first target and squeezed the trigger twice in quick succession. The Heckler & Koch Mk23 CT pistol was smaller and lighter than the old H&K SOCOM he was used to. He fired again and emptied the clip at the target, the compact .45 remaining steady in his hands. Relatively steady – his hands weren't what they used to be. He put the pistol down, squeezed his hands tight, released them, then repeated this a dozen or more times. 'Damned if I'm going to allow myself to be picked off on the street like so many other journalists around the world.'

'That's what we're here for,' Sefreid reassured him.

'I'll be right,' Fox said. He replaced the H&K with an FN Five-seveN. It immediately felt right in his hand. Well weighted, the fit snug in his grip. He looked down the sights at the twenty-metre target. Crack-crack-crack. Three holes in the centre of the silhouette's head. He looked down the sights, lined up the three-dot sights and let rip with a few double taps. Ten, twenty, thirty metres. All tight groupings, certainly better than the .45 at the thirty-metre mark.

'Nice grouping,' Sefreid commented. 'Try further down the range.'

'Less recoil in this one,' Fox said. He brought his left arm up to steady for a two-handed shot, and fired off the remainder of his twenty-round clip. All the rounds had found home, any one of them would at least incapacitate a live target. His left shoulder ached under the stress, and he pushed through the pain by ejecting the spent magazine onto the floor and ramming in a fresh one.

'Kill house?' Sefried asked.

'You know it,' Fox said. He safetied the pistol and they ran over to a big timber barn. Inside was a full-sized pre-fab house, set up to train the security team in close-quarter scenarios.

'One hostage inside, unknown enemy agents,' Sefreid said as they kitted up. Overalls went on, helmets, clear face masks, vests with neck protection. Special pistols armed, they went in through the front door.

Clearing room by room, Fox took down three plywood targets in as many seconds. Smoke was pouring in through holes in the floor and it was dark; no outside light made it to the hallway, which doglegged through the floor plan.

Fox inched into a room – noticed the target with the yellow mark that signified it as the hostage. Took a step inside, turned to clear –

Hit in the back. Turned around, another shot to his chest. Bright red paint.

Emma Gibbs was there, crouched on the ground behind the door.

'I think that means you're dead,' she said.

'I thought you only took head shots,' Fox replied as he helped her to her feet.

'Occupational health and safety,' she said, tapping her clear plastic visor.

Sefreid was in the hall, and saw Fox and Gibbs file out of the room.

'Come on,' Fox said, leading the way to where they cleaned and loaded their paint-ball pistols. 'Have the targets moved around and let's do this again.'

19

LAGOS,
NIGERIA

The afternoon sun spilled into the gymnasium above the garage. The sound of running shoes on a treadmill at full speed filled the room.

Mendes was running flat out. Dressed just in shorts and gym shoes, sweat pouring off his body. He was never out of shape, and although he didn't have the body of a long-distance runner he had that of a sprinter. Big, powerful muscles built for speed and brute strength. He'd programmed the treadmill to sprint for two hundred metres, slow to a jog, sprint again. Each time the interval between sprints would lessen, so that by the time he'd run six kilometres he was at the breaking point of exhaustion.

Off the machine he caught his breath, stretched out against the wall. He went into the bathroom, a big room decked out in marble and gold fittings. He took a piss in the toilet, looking through the open window at boats cruising down the waterway outside. This waterfront double-storey house reminded him of the Spanish-style mansions of LA. Whitewashed walls and terracotta-tiled roof and floors. This was his favourite of their safe houses in Lagos; this would definitely be his exclusive residence when they settled into power. Yeah, he could run things out of this location real good. It was close to the CBD and all the oil contacts that he'd soon be running the economy with.

In the basin he washed the sweat off his hands, then dried them off and zipped open a leather satchel. He pulled out a vial of human growth hormone. Inserted a sterile syringe into the rubber top, filled it, tapped out the air bubbles. He didn't need a tourniquet, his veins were thick cords that wrapped around his muscles. He injected, tossed the spent syringe, took a big drink of water from a glass, then left the bathroom with a towel over his shoulders, heading downstairs.

He was almost at ground level when his maid opened the front door. It was Boris, already cleared through the security gate. He had an awkward Russian name that started with a B and had mostly consonants in it, so Mendes went with *Boris* to piss him off. The arrogance this Russian wore with his pimped-out eighties suits was a joke.

'Mr Mendes,' Boris said, extending a hand.

Mendes bypassed the offered hand, and walked into his ground-floor study.

'Shut the door, Boris.'

The stupid Russian closed the study door behind him.

'Mr Mendes –'

'Save it, you fucking useless Russian,' Mendes said. He

towelled the sweat off his face, and sat in the leather chair behind the big old desk. 'You lost a courier.'

'Yes, we –'

'No fucking *we* about this, you ignorant fucking pig!' Mendes said.

The Russian's face turned as if he were going to start raging, but he had the sense not to.

'What security did you have on the courier?'

The Russian looked to his feet.

'That's right, you stupid fuck.' Mendes was cool. 'You've made a lot of cheddar out of me, and you cut corners to make even more. You are fucking useless. Five years in the FSB? You have no idea what it means to be a professional. You don't belong in this brotherhood of mine.'

'I will –'

'Spare me,' Mendes said. 'You'd better hope the tracking still works on that case. Locate it. Bring it back. It's embarrassing to me if you don't. You hear me, Boris?'

'Yes, boss.'

'Take all your guys, get it back for me,' Mendes said. He leaned down to reach under his desk, nice and slow. Boris's eyes went wide. Mendes produced a bottle of water from a bar-fridge. Started drinking it. 'Helicopters, boats, whatever it takes. Track it, get it back. And in future, if your two-million-dollar-a-month courier service gets compromised, it's back to Kazakhstan, or wherever the fuck a piece of shit like you has come from.'

Boris was about to fire back, but before he could blink Mendes was over the desk and had him pinned up against the bookcase, Boris's own pistol pushed up hard under the Russian's chin.

'This is just business, my Russian friend,' Mendes said. He took the pistol's aim down, inspected the gun. 'This is a good gun. Beretta ninety-two – 9 mm. Served my country's armed forces well. I want you to be like this gun, Boris. Reliable. Simple, not flashy, there to do a job and do it well. That's what I need from you, okay?'

Boris nodded.

'Good,' Mendes said. He released the Russian, safetied the pistol and put it back into Boris's holster. 'Otherwise, I have no use for you. No bloody use for you. I will not have this conversation again.'

20

NEW YORK CITY

Gammaldi sat at the island bench in the kitchen of Fox's apartment, reading the *New York Post*.

'How'd you get there and back already?' It was lunchtime but Gammaldi was munching away at a breakfast burrito.

'GSR helicopter with Tas,' Fox said. 'Where'd you get that? Looks like road kill.'

'Street vendor,' Gammaldi said, finishing off his food. 'You did all that and I just woke up? You packed for tonight's flight?'

'Yep, I'll meet you at the airport,' Fox said. 'I'm gonna get in a bit of Parkour before I leave.'

He ground some coffee beans. Noticed his hands shaking as he set out two cups.

'So this is what nearly twenty grand a month gets you in SoHo,' Gammaldi said. 'About five thousand square feet of empty, boring space.'

'And three bedrooms, two bathrooms, fifteen-foot-high loft ceilings, a fireplace, a private balcony, central air, polished timber floors and a laundry room,' Fox said.

'And you need three bedrooms because . . .' Gammaldi said.

'Not to mention the ornate pressed-metal ceiling, exposed beams, columns –'

'And you need columns for . . .'

Gammaldi dumped his soggy burrito wrapper in the bin; hesitated at the sight of pills and bottles of booze there. He and Fox looked at each other and not a word needed to be spoken. Gammaldi respected what Fox had just done, and he would give him his full support. Period.

'You should put a half-pipe in here, you got the room,' Gammaldi said, turning the topic like he always managed to do so well. He took a seat back at the island bench, flicked through the *Post* and waited for his coffee.

'I don't skateboard,' Fox said, working the espresso machine. The little Gaggia had travelled around the world with him over the past couple of years. It was his one constant piece of furniture.

'You slay at Tony Hawk on the PS3. I reckon some of those skills would translate,' Gammaldi said, sage-like. He noticed some kitchen appliance catalogues on the island bench.

'Over-easy, and don't scrimp on the bacon,' Gammaldi said, flicking through the appliance catalogue.

'Dude, you know the stove's out of action,' Fox countered. He put a couple of boxes of cereal and a carton of milk in front of his friend.

'A Smeg oven, really?' Gammaldi said, still flicking through the kitchen brochure. 'You should go Miele. Those things go from zero to four hundred in, like, ten seconds. And they have a rotisserie, you can fit a whole lamb in there.'

'How have I ever survived without a rotisserie?' Fox said. He passed over Gammaldi's coffee, then put out a bowl of fruit salad.

Gammaldi set into a bowl of cereal and milk, spilling milk all over the countertop in the process. He totally bypassed the fruit.

'You need bigger bowls,' Gammaldi said around a mouthful of Fruit Loops.

'Why don't you slow down there a little, Augustus Gloop, or you might get sucked up into a pipe,' Fox said. He sat at the bench and settled into *The New York Times*. 'Seriously, dude, one day you're gonna end up in a fructose coma.'

Gammaldi just looked puzzled and kept eating. Fox ate his fruit and drank coffee.

'How about them Sox, huh?' Gammaldi said. 'Curse of the Bambino.'

Fox looked up from his paper to eye his friend sceptically.

'Do you even know what you're saying?' Fox waited, but his beefy friend just went back to eating. 'Did the Celtics win last night?'

'No, they got totally smashed.'

''Kay, when I say "Did they win?" you can just say yes or no.'

'They got pretty well smashed.'

'What the hell is with you today?'

'Read that your rendition story is gonna be a movie,' Gammaldi said, through more crunching of cereal. 'Hugh Jackman to play you.'

'And Nicole Kidman to play you and your eyebrows,' Fox said, not the least bit interested. 'Where'd you read that crap, Perez?'

'Nikki Finke's *Deadline Hollywood* –'

'Shit,' Fox said. 'I was joking, I thought at least you had a decent source, douche bag.'

Fox went back to his paper.

'What about that girl from *The New Yorker*?' Gammaldi asked. 'Judy? Jemima?'

'Jane.'

'Yeah, that's it. Jane. Plain Jane.'

'What about her?'

'Well, she seems nice.'

'I don't have time for girls right now.'

'What, are you dead?'

'I've been kinda busy.'

'Too busy for women?'

'We're a generation of men raised by women,' Fox said. 'I'm wondering if another woman is really the answer I need right now.'

Gammaldi surrendered his attention back to his food.

'Movie would be cool, though . . .'

'Jesus, Al,' Fox said. He folded the paper and went to the Gaggia to make a couple more coffees. Beans were grinding. 'I'm so not interested in that. I'm on a fucking journey, I'm on a walkabout. A lot of people think ambition or success, and they think dollars. You, you think of movies made of my life. My measure of success is to get underneath all that.'

'Says the guy with a Jasper Johns and a Casimir Malevich hanging in his office,' Gammaldi said. 'Not to mention this big empty apartment.'

'They're from Wallace's collection,' Fox said. 'You've got one of his Lichtensteins hanging.'

'I ain't the one being all high and mighty,' Gammaldi said. 'And I ain't the one renouncing women. This is New York, man, live a little.'

Fox handed over a fresh coffee.

'All right,' Fox said. 'All I'm saying is that all this, it doesn't define me. It's what I'm doing with myself every day. That's why I've decided no more booze, no more drugs. This is it, I'm gonna see what I can do at full speed. Make a difference to something, somewhere, however small. At the end of the fucking day, that's the only thing you're going to carry with you when you die.'

Fox dedicated the afternoon to getting some more exercise in, to clear his mind, sharpen his movements.

He'd first come across Parkour when Gammaldi had shown him a YouTube video of a Parkour game of tag. Two young guys in Russia, chasing one another over and through abandoned buildings. Fox looked into the art further, watching some of Parkour founder David Belle's achievements. It was out of this world. The guy moved around city buildings like he was a monkey, leaping from one to the other, free-climbing walls with unbelievable speed, moving with grace and agility like he was a cross between a gymnast and a ballerina. Belle's aim was simple: to show Parkour to the world and make people understand what it is to really *move*.

So, Fox investigated the NY scene, and sure enough there were several clubs around Manhattan and the surrounds. He'd still been living in DUMBO when he joined up with the local chapter, and he continued to go there some three months later. He found that Parkour had changed the way he approached most things in life. As he trained to overcome what at first seemed almost insurmountable obstacles, so he applied that to his work. To tackle everything with that same ethos. To forge his own path. Make his own way. To show others the way.

He went to the big warehouse on Old Fulton Street in DUMBO. They leased the whole floor, some eight hundred square metres of space, obstacles everywhere. Obstacles like you'd never seen. This was a training room for the ultimate real-world obstacle course: a modern city. This was designed to work every major movement of Parkour, so that when confronted with the outside world you could surmount whatever lay before you. And you'd do it *fast*. Faster than an observer would think humanly possible.

Parkour, or *l'art du déplacement*, was exercise of a different kind. Cutting edge, yet primal. This was as hard and fun as movement could get, inside or outside of a building, an urban or rural environment. As such, Parkour was different for all participants. While there were many standard moves proven to be the most efficient, everyone in the world moved in a different way. And that was one of the beauties of Parkour. It was as individual as it was practical. But at the end of the day, one thing was always constant: Parkour was all about moving in the fastest and most efficient way *in an emergency situation*.

About ten guys and a couple of chicks were in the room. The guys were known as *traceurs*, the women as *traceuses*. All wore form-fitting gym gear, most were in bare feet. K-Swiss made special Parkour shoes. Fox stuck with the Geox's he had on. Light, flexible, good grip. Mats were assembled at varying heights, from on the floor to on top of wooden structures six feet from the floor. Gymnastics equipment, horses and bars, were being used like you'd never seen. *Traceurs* and *traceuses* were somersaulting off them and using the dismount momentum to then run up the walls, jumping, rolling, climbing their way around the room. They traversed a path that was judged in a snap decision at the time to be the best way through. Each time refining, improving, moving the route even *faster*.

'This is Parkour!' yelled Spike, the instructor. He was berating a couple of newbies who'd been showing off. Young punks who'd look more at home on skateboards. 'Every activity is designed to move you from point A to B and back again with the greatest efficiency and swiftness possible! You want to do Free Running, you want to show off, get the fuck out of my building! Get the fuck away from Parkour!'

'Hey, Spike,' Lachlan said. They shook hands, 'hood style.

'Lach,' Spike said. No one really knew much about Spike other than he lived Parkour. He was Polish-American, wiry, tough as nails. 'You believe these kids? They watch *Casino Royale* and think this is a sport where they can show off their air-time. *This isn't Free Running, you pieces of shit!*'

The kids hung their heads, sulked over to a corner.

'Shoulder strong?' Spike asked.

'Yep, all good,' Fox said, stretching out. The dull pain was still there, from the tissue around the pin that had held his collarbone while it had set. 'Nice new track.'

'Yeah – watch this *traceuse* go through the motions . . . see that *passement*?' Spike said, his eyes following a young woman somersaulting her way over some gymnastics horses, landing in a run, then turn-vaulting over a six-foot wall. 'Whoa! I think I will marry her.'

Fox was a natural at Parkour, with his tall, lean, muscular frame, his quick reflexes, good balance and sharp eye. He was a quick, clear thinker, and he had soon discovered that this extreme sport, this art form, cleared that thinking even further. It sharpened more than his reflexes and worked more than his muscles. It was a total mind and body experience. If you were not present and in the moment, you fell ten, twenty, thirty metres and busted limbs. Land on your head or neck or back and you're fucked. If you're not on your game, you fumble the easiest of gap jumps – say, pouncing from a static roof to land on a hand-rail of an overpass – you feel it. You miss that ten-centimetre landing zone of a hand-rail and catch it just with the tips of your shoes, you might lose your teeth on the way down. The rush that came with mastering a new movement equated to an excitement that made him feel like a kid again. This was so new and different as to be exciting even when doing the same motions over and over again, each time refining the details to move faster from point A to B and back again.

That's why this centre proved invaluable for Fox. He could make his mistakes in here, in a controlled environment, under constant observation and evaluation of instructors and his peers. There were many, in this city and around the world, who didn't agree with this side of Parkour. So-called *purists* who took it as nothing other than street art. But the pros knew that training made the difference. Work out the moves, then go outside, where the surfaces were slippery, dusty, greasy, unstable, unforgiving.

'You know what?' Spike said. He moved to tag Fox.

The game was on.

21

COOPERATIVE SECURITY LOCATION, DAKAR, SENEGAL

A CSL was the US military term for their forward facilities for contingency access to remote parts of the world, in this case a speck on the African continent. Made up of an airstrip and some fuel storages, CSL Dakar was one of several such 'lily pads' in western Africa. It was currently undergoing expansion construction by a Navy Seabee battalion to convert the location to a reinforced Forward Operating Site under the new entity of AFRICOM.

The ten V-22 Ospreys lined the side of the dusty airstrip. The fuel trucks had done their work, now mechanics followed the pilots around the aircraft in the final preparations before takeoff. Three massive C-17s were flying somewhere overhead, due in to land soon, carrying the rest of the squadron's gear as cargo.

Captain Garth Nix didn't like the Osprey, and he wasn't alone. His troop of the parent company – or squadron, as the cavalry referred to it – was a force of some one hundred and twenty-two men split into three platoons. They were designated 1st Squadron, 71st Cavalry Regiment, 1st Brigade Combat Team 'Warrior'. They were the lead element of 10th Mountain Division, which was to be inserted into Sudan over the next three days. They were an RSTA squadron, specialists in Reconnaissance, Surveillance and Target Acquisition. Good on the ground, at home when inserted deep in hostile territory and evading overwhelming odds. And, the fact was, they didn't like flying in Air Force aircraft that had so little operational mileage under its belt. They felt more at home in the Chinooks that these craft were destined to replace. Sure, the Osprey had greater range and speed, and in theory they were a better aircraft. But it was the newness of them. Nix had been in Operation Anaconda in the Shahikot Valley, where Chinooks had proved both sides of the air insertion argument – both as effective modes of transport, and as prime targets for enemy RPG and heavy machine-gun fire. The tilt-rotor Ospreys *looked* awesome, and the whole world had oohed and ahhed at them when they filled the screen in the 2006 *Transformers* movie. They were hybrids that bridged the gap between helicopters and fixed-wing aircraft. Yet still, in Nix's mind, they remained just that – good in theory – and it would be some time before they proved their effectiveness in operational circumstances. He knew that most of his troops, even the hard-nosed sergeants, prayed before takeoff and landing.

'As you just heard, Top and I will be leading first platoon onboard four V-22s into Nigeria,' Captain Nix said. As he spoke of locations he stood true to his usual teaching method of *wall-map studies 101 Nix-style* by using the laser light on his

M9 Beretta to point out locations. 'The rest of the troop will be flying the route to Al Fashir, Darfur, as planned, with the squadron CO and his HHT.' The squadron's CO, a pencil-thin, bookish major, nodded to his men. 'Spec Troop's Colonel Schuster is on the ground, he will assign tasks to establish the mission to prep for the rest of 1st BCT's arrival. Hooah?'

The assembled men replied as one: 'Hooah!'

'Sir, why the four aircraft for a platoon?' the lieutenant of second platoon asked.

'We'll be taking two Humvees as cargo,' Nix said. 'So the troops of your platoon that miss out on riding in those Ospreys get to have a comfy ride with the rest of the squadron's equipment in the C-17s. Means you have another five hours on the ground awaiting aircraft arrival, hooah?'

'Hooah.'

'All right,' Nix said. 'First Platoon, have your squads ready for a thirty-minute takeoff. I want two fire teams to accompany the Humvees, designated chalks one and two. Rest of the men with me on chalk three and Top on chalk four. Remainder of you will be bugging outta here as soon as the C-17s and V-22s are cleared by aircrew, under direction from the major's chalk five.'

Nix paused to take in the looks of the young battle-hardened faces before him. There was excitement mixed with the anxiety of the unknown. They'd all fought together, all served in Iraq at least once, all relished being in a conflict zone again. They trained for it, they lived for it. Some of their number had died doing it. He could tell this last-minute change to their planned deployment seemed like a bad omen for all concerned.

'I don't like splitting our team up any more than you. But we gotta make this detour to make sure another African country don't start fallin' apart like Som, or Chad, or Sudan.' Nix pointed with the laser to the countries of which he spoke. 'AFRICOM got enough shit to shovel on this continent already, hooah?'

'Hooah!'

'When Top and I finish in Nigeria and get to your location in Darfur, which should be in, oh, six months' time by the time we stop to refuel . . .'

The men in the tent laughed, and the mood lifted at the expense of the V-22's operational range when carrying cargo.

'Seriously, though, us and first platoon shouldn't be any longer than four to five days separate to you, until an MEU aboard the *Wasp* arrives off the Nigerian coast to relieve our post,' Nix said. He noticed some of his men making sideways comments about the Marines, laughs and smiles barely suppressed. Good to see 'em lightening the fuck up. 'Until then, I hear any of you boys been playing up, anyone gets hurt, anyone does stupid, my size thirteens are just a couple o' countries away.'

More laughter.

'Okay, go and get your squads sorted,' Nix said to his senior NCOs, a group of first and second lieutenants, E5 and E6 sergeants. He'd seen most of them come up through the ranks from private over the past six years. Knew they had his back. They knew that he had their trust and dedication under any circumstance. They were a young bunch, each of the sergeants in charge of his own squad, while his senior squadron NCO was a First Class rather than a Master Sergeant. That guy had just been promoted and rotated back to training at home in Fort Drum.

'Safe travels, hooah?'

'Hooah!'

The men left the op tent with a spring in their step. Beyond the next short refuel and piss stop, they were headed into action before the parent combat brigade rained in with their heavy gear aboard more C-17s. The 1st Brigade Special Troops Battalion had forward deployed two days ago, to set up the HQ element. A Ranger rifle company had been in the country two weeks previous to that, securing the airport and making sure it was clear for the arrival of the C-17s – the largest aircraft that the runway could accommodate. It would be the role of Nix's RSTA squadron to venture outside the airport, making contacts with local warlords and tribal chiefs, to forge a network of fighters to combat the militias that were terrorising the city and surrounds. The Ranger element were already due to rotate out and head back into 'Stan.

His E7 hung around: Sergeant First Class, nicknamed 'Top', the squadron's senior NCO and his most valued advisor. A big, hulking Arkansan to Nix's lanky Tennessee frame.

'Going into a country with unknown hostiles . . .' Top drawled, 'population about one-fifty mill . . .'

'I don't like it any more than you do, Top.' Captain Nix collected his gear from the table. 'But we gotta safeguard our nationals as they depart.'

'You know what we went into Iraq with? A country with twenty-five-mill population? Three hundred thousand. Backed with enough armour and ordnance to roll through to Russia. About a thousand aircraft, half our friggin' Navy . . .'

'Friggin'? What, you got yourself a new PG-13 rating on that potty mouth of yours, Top?' Nix patted his senior non-com on the shoulder. 'Relax. Command know what they're doin'. We get into Nigeria, and make sure the US Mission is secure until the Marines arrive to do the grunt work. Hooah?'

'Fuckin' hooah.'

'Now that's more like it,' Nix said, all grins. 'Now let's get the fuck outta this shit-hole airfield.'

22

JFK AIRPORT, NEW YORK CITY

Outside a private hangar at JFK International Airport, Fox and Gammaldi carried their backpacks up the stairs of a GSR Gulfstream. Next to them was GSR's latest acquisition, an Airbus A318 Elite.

'That sure is big,' Fox said, looking at the Airbus as he had to duck to enter the cabin door of the Gulfstream.

'That's what they tell me,' Gammaldi replied.

'Ah, you're hilarious,' Fox said. 'Glad you packed your sense of humour this time.'

They settled into the plush leather seats of the executive jet, and buckled up as the door was shut by the co-pilot and the engines began higher revolutions.

'You really need that?' Gammaldi said, on seeing Fox make sure that the Five-seveN pistol was not loaded with a round.

He put it in his backpack, next to some plastic cable ties and a canister of pepper spray.

'I hope not,' Fox said. He zipped up his bag and put it on the seat that faced him. Opened his camera case and made doubly sure his Nikon was loaded with the ten-gig memory card. Then he held the camera up to show his friend across the aisle. 'This is all I plan to shoot with.'

'Just make sure you get my good side,' Gammaldi replied.

'You have a good side?' Fox asked, snapping off a shot of Gammaldi pulling a face. The jet moved down the runway, the landscape of the airport moving outside in the afternoon light.

'Ah, my sides,' Gammaldi said, mimicking clinging to his sides from non-laughter. 'You obviously unloaded your sense of humour before boarding.'

Fox smiled, put the camera away and clipped his belt on.

'Heads up,' Fox said, and took a bottle of water from the stowage area to his right, tossing it over to Gammaldi. He popped one for himself too.

Fox noticed Gammaldi was looking at him as he drank.

'What's up?' Fox looked at his water bottle, then noticed his hand was shaking a bit. He was immediately frustrated, angry at himself.

'Nothin',' Gammaldi said, and looked out his window as the aircraft taxied along.

Fox tightened his belt, while Gammaldi put his chair back a little and closed his eyes to settle into sleep.

'Al?' Fox said.

Gammaldi opened just one eye, looked over at him. 'Wha—?'

'It's cool, okay?' Fox said. He held his hand flat and steady. It was still shaking a little.

'Okay,' Gammaldi said. 'I know you've given up booze, but am I meant to be confident that you've got my back over there?'

'The drink isn't the real problem. I've been the problem, up here.' Fox pointed to his head. 'Problem is I haven't done enough about it. I can see that now.'

Fox thought Al understood. They'd known each other since high school and had entered their military careers together. Gammaldi had followed Fox into hell and back on more than one occasion and never questioned his friend's judgement or doubted his ability. *Almost never*, Fox conceded.

23

THE
WHITE HOUSE

McCorkell only had a ten-minute window for lunch, and he was downstairs in the mess. He reached into the cooler for the last Waldorf salad and another hand touched the plastic tub at the same time as his. He looked over, and the young guy went red in the face with embarrassment.

'Sorry, you take it, sir,' he said.

'No, that's fine,' McCorkell replied. He picked up a Greek salad instead. 'This is healthier for me anyway. You're in the physician's office, aren't you?'

'Yes, sir, Jack McFarland, sir. Been a nurse here six months now.'

They shook hands. McCorkell paid the cashier for both meals.

'You take good care of our boss now,' McCorkell said. 'If you can figure out a way to put a supercharger in him while he's under, that'd be just great.'

The nurse laughed. 'Yes, sir,' he said, and went on his way.

'Hey, Bill?'

McCorkell turned around. Secret Service SAC O'Keeffe was there.

'Wanna pull up a pew?'

'Yeah, I got five, let's sit and eat,' McCorkell said.

They pulled out chairs and sat at a small round table.

'How you getting on with the Saudis?' O'Keeffe asked.

'All right, the press is working in our favour,' McCorkell said. 'Still haven't gone so far as to call their attack an act of terrorism, but the Feds have got a team heading over there now.'

'About time they let them in,' O'Keeffe replied. 'Give those sons of bitches a schooling in how to investigate.'

'Speaking of Feds,' McCorkell said through a mouthful of lettuce, 'I just heard about a close call with a parcel bomb?'

'Yeah, Bureau's Field Office in Burlington, Vermont, had a parcel bomb go off in their remote opening unit.'

'Casualties?'

'Just the million-dollar piece of equipment.'

'That just paid for itself.'

'Amen to that.'

'Anything on the sender?'

'We think it could have been sent from a mosque in Austin.'

That gave McCorkell something to chew over with his salad lunch.

'Why do you figure that location?'

'Feds have some wire taps in there under the auspices of the Patriot Act,' O'Keeffe said over his soup. McCorkell had never known the guy to have a lunch he couldn't drink in one way or another. 'One of their high-ranking members was picked up in a suspected DUI stop a few months back, and he had a trunk full of bomb-making equipment.'

'I remember, that was in Brentwood, right?'

'Yep. Well, they put in the bugs and we picked up chatter that something was being planned, references to sending a present to their friends in Vermont via the post.'

'So where are the Feds at on that?'

O'Keeffe checked his watch. 'In about ten minutes I'm gonna be briefed,' he said. 'They want blood, but the last thing we need is news footage of black-clad FBI SWAT teams kicking down mosque doors.'

'That's why they don't wear black any more,' McCorkell said. 'Pop your head in and brief the Press Secretary on this, would you, Seamus?'

'Was just on my way,' O'Keeffe said.

McCorkell pushed the last of his salad around in the container, then got up and tossed it in the nearby trash.

'Bill?' O'Keeffe said.

'Yeah?' McCorkell turned. O'Keeffe was standing now too, close to him. He could see the lawman was tired, worn out from too many years of chasing down bad guys. He had seen too many innocent lives taken, been through too many trials and security crashes of the White House. The crashes, almost monthly events since September eleven, were total security lock-downs of the House that managed to pretty well piss off every staffer while they sat confined to their offices. McCorkell could see this man wanted peace, needed it, like everyone else in this room, in this House, this city, country, planet.

'You think this is gonna end?' O'Keeffe asked. His eyes said this was a sincere question. 'In our lifetime? These constant terror threats? These jihads and Islamic fundamentalists?'

McCorkell mulled it over. Watched as the staff milled about the room. White, black, Hispanic, Christian, Jewish, Hindu, Islamic . . . Men and women sharing the same tables, the same discussions, the same rights.

'This has been going on a long time, long before we got here,' McCorkell said. 'Will it change? I can't see it happening, not in our lifetime.'

O'Keeffe nodded.

'But it don't worry me that much, because I see the best and the worst, every day,' McCorkell said. 'Look around this room, Seamus. Whaddya see?'

'People with eight different levels of security clearance,' O'Keeffe answered. They both chuckled.

'Yeah, well, I see the ultimate multicultural society,' McCorkell said.

'I was gonna say that,' O'Keeffe added.

'Abe Lincoln said that it was the ideas that make us Americans that are greater than anything else. The people in this room get that,' McCorkell said. 'They all believe in America. They're together in their belief in political democracy, religious freedom, capitalism, choice. We're tied together because we respect human life, and because we respect the rule of law. We're a plural society, Seamo, and these guys we're fightin' hate us for it. Why, because they're stuck with strict adherence to seventh-century beliefs. I think there's always going to be nutters out there, no matter what.'

'I just hope Joe Public still believes in America like these good people in here,' O'Keeffe said.

'Most of them do, Seamo,' McCorkell said. 'We're fightin' the good fight. Most of the successes we've had won't be public under FOI for fifty years. The stuff we stopped on the millennium? It'll be our kids and grandkids who'll look back from 2050 with pride at what we've done. The good work that's gone on behind the scenes? There's plenty of people in here and out there who thank us for it every day.'

'You really think they appreciate what we're doing? Forgive us the mistakes we've made, the lengths we've had to go to in order to get the jobs done?'

'I know for a fact that every day thousands of ordinary Americans thank us in prayer for the work that we're doing,' McCorkell said. 'Many more love us than despise us. So long as we stay a step ahead of the bad guys, I can sleep at night.'

24

LAGOS,
NIGERIA

The Press Club in Lagos was a building dating back to the first British colonialists in the city. It had been built by a cacao exporter as their Nigerian base and turned into a saloon during the nineteen-thirties. It was a whitewashed two-storey stone structure with towering arched windows and doors with pale blue shutters. A first-storey terrace opened out onto the palms that lined the street. Inside, little had changed since the set-up in the thirties. Dark wood panelling surrounded a bar and a raised dining area, green palms grew thick and fast like they were in a greenhouse, sunlight shone in through the shutters over the windows. It resembled Rick's from *Casablanca*, and the clientele looked like a cross between those of Rick's and of the bar scene in *Star Wars*.

Fox sat at the time-scarred wooden bar and Gammaldi followed suit. Both sipped the complimentary iced tea poured by a smiling waiter.

'No, this place doesn't feel scary at all,' Gammaldi said, trying hard not to stare at an eye-patched guy on the opposite side of the bar.

'Relax, Al, we've been in rougher bars in Brooklyn,' Fox said. He scanned the room – a couple of tables in the centre full of white reporters, the rest either local reporters or from other African countries. Ceiling fans did little to cool the place, more than anything they just moved the smoky air about. The two walls that were not made up of arched openings were covered in blue and white mosaic tiles and hanging rugs. Dark booths were overstuffed with rowdy patrons getting their morning drinks in.

The barman came around, and Fox gave him a twenty.

'We're looking for a local guide, someone with transport?' Fox said.

The barman took the money, smiled and disappeared.

'That was money well spent,' Gammaldi said, crunching on the ice-blocks from his drained glass. 'Oh yeah, another wise investment from the guy who's been making my hair grey over all these years.'

'You're not going grey, Al, it's just thinning out,' Fox said in between sips of iced tea. 'I think it could actually be that your head is growing up through your hair.'

'Okay, Mr Forehead,' Gammaldi said, still chewing hard on the ice-blocks. 'Recede much?'

'Easy, tubby,' Fox replied.

Gammaldi looked hurt.

A guy came up, dressed in a faded blue suit, sweat-stained shirt and cheap tie. He sat next to them like their best friend.

'You need a guide,' he stated with slick confidence. 'I can offer you much more. Whatever you need –'

'A driver to Port Harcourt and Abuja, that's all we need,' Fox said.

The guy's face sank, and he left them.

The barman came back and nodded to a white guy sitting at a table by himself, reading a newspaper. He appeared to be the other side of seventy, Leo McKern playing Horace Rumpole. Bulbous red nose and the ruddy cheeks of a professional drinker.

Fox led the way over and they stood by him, backpacks over their shoulders. Gammaldi pulled out one of the three empty chairs by the low table and sat down. Fox joined him, and they waited long enough for Gammaldi to cough in order to get the guy's attention.

'Help yourself to the water,' the man said in thick Scottish, more Sean Connery than Billy Connolly. His focus remained on his newspaper. 'Touch my martini jug and I'll take your arm off.'

Fox and Gammaldi shared a look, the latter man shrugging it off and pouring himself a water. He leaned back and sipped at it as if considering this fascinating creature.

Finally, the newspaper was closed, folded in half and dropped onto the table.

'Sir Alex Simpson the third,' he said, extending his hand.

'Lachlan Fox.'

'Alister Gammaldi the first.'

'Ah, Aussies!' Sir Alex said. 'It's been a while since I've seen any of you chaps here! Martini?'

'No, thanks,' Fox said.

'Here to talk about the '05 Ashes, I hope, what a series . . .'

'Actually, Alex –'

'Sir Alex. Forty years of service to the BBC no less.'

'Right. Er, Sir Alex, we're just after a driver to get us into Port Harcourt and Abuja,' Fox said. 'We're reporters out of New York, doing a story on the bombing of the oil building.'

'Hmmm . . .' Sir Alex pondered their request, his bushy grey eyebrows dancing as he sipped his martini. He drained the entire glass, then poured another from the jug that was resting in a bowl of ice. 'You need a driver.'

'Yes.'

'Nothing getting into Port Harcourt, I'm afraid,' Sir Alex said. 'The bombing, big security lock-down.'

'We know that flights have been suspended,' Fox said. 'We're after a car and a –'

'No, you don't understand me, Foxy boy,' Sir Alex said. He leaned his girth forward in the creaking old cane armchair. 'The roads are closed. Military and police are letting nothing in there that doesn't belong in there. That means no press, certainly no Western press.'

'Really?'

'Yes. I wouldn't say it otherwise,' Sir Alex said.

'When's it open again?'

Sir Alex paused as if considering it.

'I've been to Sydney once, didn't care for it,' he said.

Gammaldi gave Fox a look that would normally be accompanied by a finger twirling around his ear to signify they were in the presence of a crackpot.

'How about via the coast?' Fox persisted. 'In a boat?'

Sir Alex shook his head.

'CNN crew tried that yesterday. They were put on the first flight home this morning.' Sir Alex seemed to like being the one with information. 'It wasn't all their idea – those guys over there, by the corner of the bar? For a price they will pretty much get you whatever you want. Boats, information, access. Linked to what you might call a local mafia. Politicians and cops too, but that's much the same thing.'

'How about those guys in the cheap suits?' Fox asked.

'Couriers,' Sir Alex said. 'The old-fashioned way to get things communicated in this country. Different levels of service depending on the price: normally two guys – driver and an armed courier – to get documents around. The more you pay, the more guns and cars they send along. Oil companies use them all the time to transport not just documents but personnel too.'

'They any good?' Fox asked. The guys were drinking pretty hard to be anywhere near alert enough to be trustworthy with a life worth caring about.

'No, not really,' Sir Alex said. 'What you must realise is that this place is kind of like the Wild West. There's pretty much anything to be had, for a price of course. Access is about the only thing that's hard to come by, you need someone with direct contacts for that.'

Fox checked his watch. He wondered how Wallace was getting on, and whether the plan of getting Achebe to a table had worked.

'Excuse me,' Fox said, and got up. 'Back in a minute.'

He went upstairs and onto the decked balcony, then dialled Tas's cell phone.

Wallace picked it up before the second ring.

'How you getting on down there?'

'Still nothing getting into Port Harcourt,' Fox said. 'Any luck with Achebe?'

•

Five minutes later Fox was downstairs again.

'And you should only eat what you've seen cooked,' Sir Alex said. 'Otherwise you'll be shitting through the eye of a needle for weeks.'

'Thanks, that's good advice,' Gammaldi said, martini glass in hand, a plate of food in front of the two of them half-demolished already.

'Okay, Wallace has come through with our interview with the minister,' Fox said, taking a seat. 'We have to head for Abuja now. Then we make for Port Harcourt, where he'll meet us with Rollins.'

'I'm telling you, no planes in or out of Port Harcourt, except from the oil companies evacuating staff,' Sir Alex said while chewing on an olive.

'We'll get access,' Gammaldi said.

'On your say-so, little friend,' Sir Alex insisted. He raised his glass for Gammaldi to top up.

'So, can you help us with transport to Abuja?' Fox asked.

'That I can do. There's a good driver who can take you there, reliable chap. Used him once or twice myself, I'll see if I can find him for you,' Sir Alex said. 'It won't be cheap, though, I'm afraid.'

25

LONDON

Wallace was inside the home of the Rollins family. It was on a street of brick-fronted, double-storey houses with slate roofs and picket fences. Nothing to say of the front yard, just a few trained roses, white-painted timber sash windows – the whole street was the same. The only difference in appearance was in some of the front doors. The Rollins's was the scarlet red of British redcoat soldiers from a time long past.

Wallace sat in the lounge room, a cup of tea held on his knee. Penny Rollins was there, on the couch, sitting upright. Their six-year-old was standing by her mother, staring at Wallace.

'Sorry, she's obsessed with people who come to see her father,' Penny said.

'You know why I'm here?'

Penny nodded. Her daughter did the same, a little carbon copy of her mother.

There was an awkward moment between the two adults.

Wallace could hear the tone of Michael's voice coming from the study across the hall. He couldn't make out the words, despite his nicely trained BBC English.

'They call him all the time, the press,' Penny Rollins said. 'Wanting his story. Wanting a piece of him, as if what he went through was not real. To them, it's just a story. Words on a page that a reader somewhere in the world will scan over with detached interest. They talk to him wanting realistic detail that will never be properly appreciated.'

'Lachlan Fox's pieces got some traction,' Wallace said. 'And he won't just let this story disappear. He'll keep on it. As long as extraordinary rendition keeps happening, he'll do his best to keep the public aware.'

'If it were anyone else's investigation, I would insist he didn't go with you today,' she said. 'But I, we, like Lachlan. He's a good man.'

'That he is,' Wallace said.

Penny rubbed her stomach and looked a little off. She whispered in her daughter's ear and the little girl reluctantly left the room, trudging up the timber stairs.

'Those newspaper readers will never understand how my husband now sleeps,' Penny said. 'How he cries in the night. How he can't stand being alone in a room. He doesn't like bright light. He can't write with a pen for any longer than five minutes without having a fit of pain – have you seen how his hands have healed? His fingers – they are not fingers any more.'

They shared in a moment of silence. What answer could he give this man's partner? This man's companion, carer, the lover that saw into the darkest recesses of Michael's being, what could he possibly say to make any difference?

'The US Supreme Court still not moving?' Wallace asked eventually.

'They won't even hear his case.' She sipped her tea, her expression bitter. 'Too many official secrets involved, national security and all that rubbish.'

'I don't know what else I can do,' Wallace said.

'I know. You have done enough, Tas, thank you – sincerely, thank you,' she said, softening. 'I know Lachlan's reporting made some difference in Washington. Created some awareness back there in the US. I guess I cannot ask for more than that.'

'Michael will be safe in Nigeria, he doesn't have to leave his hotel room, and it's just for the twenty-four hours,' Wallace said.

She nodded, set down her tea. Put her hands in her lap and talked to him matter-of-factly.

'In and out, he told me that,' she said. Her eyes narrowed and she shifted forward in her chair. She leaned into Wallace's space, spoke so only he would hear. 'What was it that convinced him to work again? Hmm? The old *"You've never sat on the sidelines like this before"*?'

Wallace was still looking her in the eyes. She had every right to be angry, and in this moment he'd take it. All that she had to dish out, he was willing to wear it all. If not him, who else could she strike out at?

'What did it take?' she asked again. Shook her head in disgust.

Wallace didn't answer. It was between him and Michael.

'I'm not asking you to promise me his safety,' Penny said. 'I know Lachlan will look after him. I just want it to end. I don't want him going out there any more. And I *never* want to see you again, ever. Not here, not in the street, never. He does this for you and that's it, no more work. *This is the last time.*'

26

NIGERIA

Fox sat up front with the driver, the diesel Land Rover navigating a road that for all intents was not a road at all. They were two hours out of Lagos, heading for Abuja. Gammaldi was in the rear seat, attempting to take photos out of the window. Their driver, known only as Simon, drove at a speed on these roads that had them holding on to stop bouncing out of their seats.

'If you drive too slowly, they will stop you and you will not get through without paying a big price,' Simon said. 'So we drive fast.'

'Who will stop us?' Fox asked. 'These people on the sides of the road?'

'Yes. It's their little economy. It's all they have, there's no other option. They sell what they can, others wash windscreens, many beg, many more are armed and will rob you at gunpoint.'

Fox instinctively glanced at his backpack on the floor by his feet. His Five-seveN pistol was in there, within easy reach.

'This city we are entering, I grew up in,' Simon said. 'But that was a long time ago now.'

The outskirts were walled, mud fortifications that were probably at least a thousand years old. Here, like so many cities on this continent, the slums were among the worst imaginable. No running water, power, sewage, nothing. But it hadn't always been like this – there *were* power poles, some with greasy old unbroken lights, most stripped bare of anything made of metal that might have some value, others sawn off at their base as even the timber of the pole was put to use.

'What happened here?' Fox asked.

Simon didn't answer for a while as he leaned on the horn and shifted down gears to overtake a caravan of food trucks and open-topped cars full to the brim with armed guys in civilian clothing. Fox snapped some photos out of his window. Focused in on a young child looking at the trucks, her expression showing that she knew what was in the precious cargo that bypassed her.

'It fell apart,' Simon said. 'This was a major trading town for centuries. The government simply forgot about it, like so much of the country.'

'Societal breakdown . . .' Fox said. They rode in more silence for a while. 'This road, it doesn't bring much trade?'

'This highway was built on a major trade path, but that's long gone,' Simon said. 'It is still a major thoroughfare but that's all they have now, people flashing through as quick as they can. No one stops, and the government is likely to make a bypass around it soon. The people you see here, on the sides, they are the ones that are trading. That's as organised as it gets now, aside from the criminal gangs.'

Simon steered through a roundabout, the centre of which was a burned-out petrol tanker, a rusted skeleton long stripped by salvagers.

'There's nothing here any more . . .' Simon's words faded into oblivion. 'No more industry, barely enough agriculture to support the local population, yet they can't go anywhere. They have nowhere else to go that will be better for them.'

'Lagos is too full?'

'Yes, and too full of its own problems. No one wants these people – every town and city in this country has people like this. All of them, going nowhere. They live slowly and die young.'

Fox looked out of his window. Gammaldi was doing the same. Scenes of decay flashed by. Rusted tin houses. Decaying wrecks of cars and trucks. Dead trees. Shit ran in the gutters, accented here and there by the slick swirls of crude oil that spilled and gurgled. Repressed shells of people clung to life by threads. The broken road was lined with piles of useless litter. Down side-streets the garbage-heaped slums stretched for miles. Skinny dogs were the only animals they saw, and even they looked half-past-dead.

'There's oil here too?'

Simon nodded.

'People used to think that finding oil was a godsend,' Simon said. He surprised Fox and Gammaldi with a laugh, but it developed into a laugh that smacked of depression. A what-else-can-I-do laugh. 'They treated the oil explorers like God's own sons! They gave them everything, the land, their food. Their way of life; their means of survival. But then they realised the curse that it is. They realised, too late, that they gave away their soul for nothing in return. This is blood oil.'

'Can we stop here?' Fox asked. 'Talk to some of the people?'

Simon was silent for some time. There was just the rattle of the diesel engine and the rolling of the tyres on the cratered road full of potholes and ruts.

'Yes,' Simon said. 'I know somewhere we can stop.'

27

KEY WEST,
FLORIDA

'*De kuday pa aman*,' the Afghan and his friend said to the other three. '*Allahu Akbar.*'

Hands were clasped, hugs were shared, prayer beads were swapped. There were no tears shed among these men, just resolve, even a measure of pride.

A final phone call to Washington had been made, the goodbyes were over, and the Buick backed out of the driveway, turned left down the quiet suburban street, then left again onto Truman Avenue. US Route 1 lay ahead of them, a road that would take them all the way to their final destination of Washington DC. The car rode low on its rear axle, six twenty-five kilo sacks of ANFO in the trunk. The Ammonium Nitrate and Fuel Oil had been easier for the group to get hold of than they'd planned. Cheaper too. Some three billion kilos of it were exploded in this country annually, mostly in mining operations. Their purchase would not be missed from any inventories.

The Afghan was silent as his friend drove the first shift. It was the third time he'd been to this country. There was much he liked about it, although he didn't share that much with his friend. There were certainly worse places to die.

'Tomorrow is D-Day!' his friend said, breaking the silence the Afghan had been enjoying.

'Did he give you the address of his safe house in Washington?'

'No, we must meet him at a McDonald's,' he replied. 'That is what Mr Massoud said to me on the phone. He called it *D-Day*!'

'Tahir takes too much joy in what he does,' the Afghan said. 'Do not –'

He stopped himself. He knew his friend was excitable, knew he idolised the Saudi and what he stood for. He hadn't been a trained soldier like himself. He didn't understand that, with war, there was a certain solemnity to be respected.

'I'm sorry, my friend,' the Afghan said. 'Do what you like with your last moments here. Speak how you like, it is your life. But, for now, let us drive in peace so that we may think of our families.'

28

NIGERIA

They were parked by the bank of a river that, like all the rivers, creeks and tributaries in the south, fed into the massive Niger Delta. This would have to be among the most fertile places on earth. The water ran dark and fast, full of nutrients that were carried downstream and out to sea.

Fox had his backpack over one shoulder, his Nikon up and clicking away. Half-naked kids walked about, with not enough energy in their whippet bodies to play. Sullen adults milled around the riverbank, their bare feet caked in the rust-brown earth that baked underfoot in the humidity. At the river's edge, Fox took a shot of the water's surface – but the display showed that the camera could not pick up the full extent of the slick, oily image. Rotten, mauled fish carcasses bobbed by. Little boats lay upturned on the banks, the dust and dirt on them signalling when they'd last been used. Fox took a photo of several lined-up boats; the one in the foreground had grass growing through its hull. Fishing nets were melting into the ground.

'This way,' Simon called.

Fox followed him down a well-trodden path between rusted metal shacks. Coloured material was hung ahead, forming a curtain that Simon walked through, then Fox, then Gammaldi. He was silent, Gammaldi. More so than Fox could ever remember. He wore a look that reflected clearly what he felt, that this place was really getting to him.

They passed through a covered courtyard. Several men lay there in bandages, their gunshot wounds unmistakable. No doctors or nurses, just some local help that did little more than soothe them with company.

Simon paused to talk to one of the wounded men. They spoke quietly, slowly. Nods were shared and they continued onwards.

'What happened to them?' Fox asked.

'Reprisal attacks, yesterday and the day before,' Simon explained.

'Reprisal for what?'

'They were found selling black-market oil. They are considered oil poachers – they tap into the oil pipelines, siphon-off oil and sell it to the locals.'

'Was it a rival group that attacked them?'

'In a way, yes. It was the security men of oil companies, and government soldiers, Nigerian Mobile Police – MOPOL – and the like.'

The climate of fear in this part of Nigeria was palpable. It was on the faces they saw, in the air they shared, in the sounds that came. Fox knew that whatever loss and hardship he'd ever experienced was miniscule in comparison. Here was a place where the universe came together in a snapshot of compassion and cruelty. He knew that there was an uneasy truth here that must be told.

'Lachlan, Alister, this is my uncle, Solomon,' Simon said.

They shook hands. Sat inside at a timber bench cleared by Solomon's family, who now sat on a rug in the concrete cinder-block house. Five kids, from teens to five. No wife in sight.

Simon spoke quietly to his uncle, and handed over a few bank notes which at first were refused but then were taken, thanks being returned in a long, humble embrace.

Fox reached into his bag, and handed over an MRE. The man accepted it, and passed it to the eldest of his sons who took it away with the other children. Their quiet fascination would last for hours. Fox motioned to Solomon with a digital voice recorder. Simon translated; Solomon nodded his consent.

'They are offering tea, but I suggest we refuse – they don't have much drinking water to give away to us.'

Fox nodded.

'Why don't they have fresh water here?' Gammaldi asked. 'I know the river system is polluted but they get plenty of rain.'

'They cannot catch rainwater in this town any more,' Simon explained. 'It's like this in much of the southern states. And the more they rely on ground wells, the quicker they are drying up.'

'Why is that?' Fox asked. 'Why can't they catch the rainwater?'

Simon talked to his uncle, then thought about the answer – the translation of the broken English and local dialect.

'Here, they say that the water is poison,' Simon said. 'It makes them ill, kills children and the frail, makes babies deformed. It's from the gas flares and burn-offs in this area, it makes acid rain. So they rely on rations of water, often having to buy it from water farmers – men who have invested enough to drill the deepest of wells. Sometimes a little government aid arrives, but not more than three or four times a year.'

Fox took a handful of old faded colour photos from Solomon. 'What are these of?'

'Here – this place,' Solomon said in broken English. 'Three decades ago.'

Fox looked through the photos. They were well-loved, the edges faded and bent. A young Solomon was there, as a schoolboy, among a sea of happy school children's faces.

'That was on the first day of independence,' Simon narrated. His uncle pointed to the particular picture of his family dancing in the street. The hope they must have had. The photos changed formats – different camera or film, a later time. The classroom was a shattered wreck, books strewn on the floor. The school in ruins. Bodies in the street.

Fox's cell phone rang. He excused himself, went outside to get better reception.

'Tas?'

'Lachlan, I've got you a meeting this afternoon in Abuja.'

'With Brutus Achebe?'

'Yep, at two o'clock. And there's more,' Wallace said. 'You owe me big. Rollins will be there in Port Harcourt later this afternoon, to take you into the delta to meet with some militants. I want you to make sure he's safe –'

'We'll be fine.'

'Well, Rollins will have protection from a guy from the British embassy as well,' Wallace said. 'I'll fly him in on the

Airbus. Give me a call after your meeting with Achebe and I'll let you know which airport we're coming in to.'

Fox went back inside Solomon's house. The Nigerian was reading a part of the Bible to his nephew. Psalm 137. Words of revenge, connotations of displacement and rape. Desperation. Solomon's voice was scholarly and his Bible-reading English crisp and well-rehearsed. Fox had little doubt that this man could recite much of that book.

'Solomon, I have a meeting today with a government minister,' Fox said. 'Is there anything you want me to tell him?'

The Nigerian was silent as he searched the faces before him. He looked to his children, who continued to play outside. Their faces wore smiles that Fox knew this father did not see often enough.

'The only way that Nigeria can be fixed is if all the men in power, all of them, are killed.'

There was certainty in the man's tone as his eyes burned into Fox. His face told of the lives he was responsible for, that each of them hung by the tenuous grip of uncertainty that came with being on the downside of disadvantage. As if what he said was the collective consciousness of all the people of this city. 'That is the only way . . .'

29

WASHINGTON

'Tim – where are you going?' Jack McFarland asked, breaking the silence. It was the middle of the night and the White House nurse had been woken from his sleep. He had sleepily walked into the lounge room and now saw the bags packed by the door to his apartment.

'Out,' Tahir 'Tim' Massoud said, his face impassive.

McFarland looked at the bags again. Not just Massoud's overnighter, there was the big one with the wheels and the handle. Everything was packed. Everything. Tim had been living with him for a month or more. And now this?

'With all your stuff?' Jack's pain was on his face – he knew what this was. He stood there in just his underwear. Tears in his eyes. 'Were you going to say goodbye?'

'I cannot see you any more,' Massoud said. He looked away from the crying man. Picked up his carry-on bag from the floor.

The dam broke for McFarland and tears rolled down his cheeks.

'Why?' McFarland looked angry now. He got close to his lover, banged on his chest. 'Why!'

'Look – I will . . . I will speak to you later,' Massoud said. He moved around McFarland and made for the door.

The nurse was after him, fast. He grabbed Massoud's arm and spun him around.

'You can't do this to me!' McFarland said. 'I've done nothing wrong. I've looked after you for weeks! I love you!'

There was nothing telling in the man's eyes. Literally nothing. No emotions, none of the love and adoration that he'd bestowed on Jack all this time. He turned and made again for the door.

McFarland pulled him around again, and in the same fluid movement the man brought his hand up and slapped the nurse hard across the face.

'You don't love me,' Massoud said, his voice low, quiet. 'You don't even know me.'

McFarland was too shocked to make a sound. He stared at his lover and saw a new look in his eyes. Hatred? Revulsion?

Massoud turned his back, and McFarland jumped on him, using his full weight.

The Saudi stumbled forward a step but managed to keep his footing. McFarland's arms were wrapped tight around his neck, his legs around the man's body. Massoud charged backwards, into the adjoining kitchen, and slammed McFarland up onto the bench, where the nurse hit the back of his head against the top cupboards. He cried out in pain, and released his grip on the man, who turned and punched McFarland fast – in the face, then the stomach. McFarland was curled up on the bench, crying and sucking for air. His lover turned, picked up a heavy Le Creuset cast-iron frypan from the stovetop. Swung it towards McFarland's head in a big, arcing swing.

McFarland moved like a dancer. One fluid, graceful move and he'd uncurled off the bench and his fist was hard against Massoud's sternum. Massoud looked back at Jack wide-eyed. Dropped the pan. Stumbled backwards, and looked down to the handle of the big carving knife pushed up into his chest. Blood began to run over the hilt and down the handle.

McFarland's adrenaline came down enough to realise what he'd just done. Instant cold sweat. He was still perched on the bench as his lover collapsed to the ground. Massoud's throat made a gurgling sound, his eyes still locked in that look of surprise.

Despite the years of medical training and practice, it would be six hours before Jack McFarland got off the bench to feel for a pulse.

30

ABUJA,
NIGERIAN CAPITAL, NIGERIA

'The only way that Nigeria can be fixed is if all the men in power, all of them, are killed. That is the only way.'

Lachlan Fox pressed the stop button on his tape-recorder. He shifted in his seat, waiting for a reaction from the politician opposite him. Brutus Achebe, Energy Minister for Nigeria. Early forties, political pedigree – read corruption – since Nigeria's independence in the sixties. He had the universal appearance of a bureaucrat – could be a politician anywhere. A face used to false smiles and far too much hubris.

'Such things are said in this country all the time,' Achebe said. Spoken like one who conformed to whatever it was that drove him. Money, most likely. That was the common driver around here. Nonetheless, he now appeared annoyed – this had gotten on to a different track than he'd imagined. This was no puff reporting piece. This reporter was out for blood.

'Then I'm sorry for your country,' Fox said. 'I have dozens more interviews like this, it's painting quite the picture.'

'Where have you been interviewing?' Achebe asked.

'Places your oil policies have affected,' Fox said. 'They're educated, smart, capable people. They've had their family displaced from the Niger Delta and seen first-hand the brutality that federal and state troops have dished out; your out-of-control security contractors. These people are living off nothing and have little to hope for.'

Achebe waved his hand in the air. 'Whatever. Let them speak. I agree that things must change, and they will.' He offered Fox a cigar – Fox turned him down. 'I am from the northern states, Mr Fox. My uncle is the Sultan of Sokoto, a very learned man. The spiritual leader for more than seventy-five million Muslims in this country.'

Fox watched and listened as the politician shifted into gear.

'I know my country has had a chequered past, but we have a bright future. We have gone a long way to stamp out the endemic corruption at every level of government. Through the sound economic management that I am applying to the economy, Nigeria will move forward. We will soon be the jewel of Africa, and a beacon of the –'

'The . . . ?' Fox waited, but, oddly, this conversation had halted. This guy was just getting on message and suddenly stopped himself, mid-sentence.

'I think you have your statement now,' Achebe said.

Fox let the moment hang, gave him the room to press on and fill the silence. Achebe leaned back and puffed smoke up to the ceiling.

'In the north we have Sharia Law. Officially, it has been that way since 1999. And you know what, it works!' Achebe sat straighter in his chair, looked at Fox. 'I hope that the rest of Nigeria can some day embrace such laws nationwide. With nearly one hundred and fifty million people under such law, finally we will see an end to the violence you speak of.'

'Mr Achebe,' Fox spoke slowly, 'if you have nothing more to add about the bombing, I'd at least wish to have access to the site.'

Achebe returned a hard, measuring stare.

'I would like access to the Port Harcourt bombing site,' Fox stated, clarifying his request, third time lucky.

'We are not letting press in the area – it is still too dangerous,' Achebe said.

'I'll take my chances,' Fox replied, resolute. 'It's been three days and no Western press have had access. I need only an hour, to get a feel for the site.'

'No press have had access,' Achebe repeated. He leaned back and considered Fox. 'This is why you're here – you are not doing a profile piece on me. You want me to grant you access to the bombing site.'

'Yes.' Fox looked at Achebe with an unflinching gaze topped with ten tons of defiance and a sledgehammer as back-up. He'd tried the soft approach enough, hadn't he? Yeah.

'I can run a profile piece on you, sure,' Fox began. 'Brutus Achebe: cabinet minister for seven years, in his current office for four. In control of the energy resources of a country that's the world's eighth largest producer of oil. A country where the poor are getting poorer. You have your own companies and charities who have received over ninety million dollars in oil money since you've been in office. You have a house in London, worth some four million pounds. You travel there twice a year with the younger of your two wives, not that it stops you from indulging in the company of several prostitutes.'

'Lies.' Achebe's face was flushed. Good.

'I have the paperwork to back this up,' Fox said. 'This won't be something that runs in the local papers. This will be syndicated to *The New York Times*, the *Guardian*, the *International Herald Tribune*. This is above-the-fold stuff – you know, just under the masthead?'

No reaction. Next card:

'In 2006 you had a meeting in Northern Nigeria with some of the FBI's most wanted terrorists.'

That sentence got a reaction. Fox locked eyes with Achebe. A stare down. Fox wasn't bluffing. Much. Achebe couldn't risk it and Fox knew it.

'That's not "World News section" stuff,' Fox said. 'That's above that fold in the paper that stares up from first-world news-stands and the front porches of families about to drive to work in their gas-guzzling SUVs. Headlining the nightly news. Running along through the ticker of the world's biggest news outlets on every television and computer screen in the West.' Fox let it hang in the air. Couldn't help the faintest of smiles, the not-so-involuntary raise of one corner of his mouth. 'That's career-ending stuff, even here in Nigeria.'

'What do you want?'

'Access.' Fox added a little shake of his head as if he'd finally gotten through with chiding a delinquent child. 'Port Harcourt is *locked down*. Three days ago four Dutch oil workers, seven Nigerians, two Italians and two Englishmen were killed in the bombing. I want to see the site. I want to walk it and feel it. To enter the Westerners' residential compound. To interview witnesses. To have access to your investigators on this. A sit rep on where they're at.'

'An hour at the site?' Achebe tapped the ash from his cigar, sat a little straighter as if being observed, despite the fact that it was just the two of them present.

'An hour at the site,' Fox agreed.

'Okay,' Achebe said. 'I'll give you access, but not to the police investigators. This is a sensitive issue and we are still in the middle of things.'

'I want access to the investigators,' Fox said. 'I want to speak to the team, see what they've got.'

'An hour on site, Mr Fox. And I will give you the first look at the investigators' findings.'

Fox nodded. A small concession. Considering his lack of hard proof of some of the allegations he'd just aired, it was a decent compromise.

'I can't promise your security in transit,' Achebe said. 'If I give you government troops, then everyone expects them. We cannot spare –'

'That's fine, I can take care of myself,' Fox said.

'I am sure you can, Mr Fox,' Achebe replied. 'I am sure you can.'

In the adjoining office in the Energy Ministry building, Steve Mendes looked at the monitor. Video and audio feed from a concealed device in the ceiling of Achebe's office gave Mendes a crystal-clear view of what was going on inside.

Mendes was making notes on Fox, building a profile from what he heard and saw.

The fax machine next to him buzzed to life, whirring out pages. Details on Lachlan Fox, the header showing this was from the Department of Homeland Security: *'Unclassified Report on Australian national Lachlan Clancy Fox. Age thirty-one, dual US/Aus citizen, department head of New York-based Global Syndicate of Reporters. Height six-two, weight ninety kilos, brown hair, blue eyes,'* blah, blah, blah. Mendes looked at the file photo of Fox – the type of eyes that missed nothing. He looked like he could handle himself. *'Ex military'*, Mendes read. *'Australian Navy officer, Intelligence analyst then leader of Special Forces diving team. Discharged in 2005, following the death of a soldier under his command – the result of an un-authorised mission into West Timor . . .'*

And here he was chasing this story at a time when Mendes would rather he didn't – but then the ex-CIA operator was used to having to turn things his way. In fact, this was fast becoming a task he relished, the rush that came with playing the game at which he excelled. He had a major operation underway, and this little intrusion was about to hit a dead-end.

He picked up a radio, pressed talk:

'This is Mendes. Make sure our guest doesn't make it back to –'

He paused, turned up the volume on the monitor. Lachlan Fox stated to Achebe that he was heading back to Port Harcourt. He listened closely to the way Fox pressed Achebe into allowing the one hour at the bombing site. They set a time for Fox to be there, tonight. Fox then mentioned that he would be going to interview some militia accused of the bombing . . . *perfect*.

'Say again, sir,' crackled over his mike.

'Change that,' Mendes said into the radio mouthpiece. Smiling at how it had all come together. 'He's headed to Port Harcourt. Follow him when he leaves the bombing site. Make sure he's swept up in tonight's raid in the delta.'

Mendes closed the file on Fox. The hand-held Motorola crackled again:

'And the case?'

'You still have to get it back,' Mendes said. 'Bring me the case, and make sure Lachlan Fox is dead.'

PART TWO

31

THE
WHITE HOUSE

At 7 am five staff assistants exited the office of the Deputy Chief of Staff on a delivery errand. Each staffer had a wad of Xeroxed letters to deliver to all senior staff in the West Wing and the Executive Offices Building next door.

Mary Swanson did the rounds of the first floor of the West Wing, efficiently knocking on doors or speaking to personal secretaries for the handover. She was typical of the junior assistants: fresh out of grad school, working over seventy hours per week for thirty K per year just to say she worked at the White House. It was more than a stepping stone to big places. Sure, employers nationwide respected the dedication it took to work in the team of the executive branch of government. But she, like all staffers in this building and next door, knew that she was a part of something bigger. Working within the executive branch of government was more than a job, it was to be a part of history.

She walked through the deserted Roosevelt Room and gave a copy to the Press Secretary, who thanked her and tucked the letter under her chin as she opened her office door with both hands full. Through a corridor and beyond the lobby the staffer passed a copy to the smiling secretary to the Vice President – a woman who looked *way* too perky for this hour of a Saturday morning.

A few paces down the corridor Mary came to the last drop on this level. She tapped on the closed door, reading the stencilled title *Assistant to the President for National Security Affairs*, and she was not surprised to find the room occupied.

'Enter,' Bill McCorkell said, looking up from his computer screen.

'Good morning, sir,' she said, passing over a copy of the letter.

'Thank you,' Bill McCorkell replied, taking the note. 'What's your name?'

'Me – my – Mary, sir. Mary Swanson,' the junior staff assistant replied, going red in the face.

'New here, Ms Mary Swanson?' McCorkell asked.

She nodded, as if words were almost too much.

'What department are you working in?'

'Communications.'

'Ah, Aaron's crew. Listen to him, learn from him – he's as smart as they get,' McCorkell said. He looked over the typed note, the letterhead and the President's distinctive signature showing its origin from the Oval Office. 'You read this?'

'No – yes, I mean –'

'That's all right, I'd do the same,' McCorkell said with a smile. 'This is a copy of a letter that would have just been faxed and hand-delivered to the President Pro Tempore of the Senate. The Speaker of the House and all senior executive staff are just getting a copy now. You understand what it means?'

She nodded.

'Good. Read it to me.'

'Yes, sir,' Mary said. She read from the stack of undelivered letters still in her hands:

Dear Mr President,

As my staff have previously communicated to you, this morning I will undergo a medical procedure involving surgery and requiring sedation. In view of present circumstances, I have determined to transfer temporarily my Constitutional powers and duties to the Vice President during the brief period of the procedure and recovery – expected to be no more than 48 hours.

Accordingly, in accordance with the provisions of Section 3 of the Twenty-Fifth Amendment to the United States Constitution, this letter shall constitute my written declaration that I am unable to discharge the Constitutional powers and duties of the office of President of the United States. Pursuant to Section 3, the Vice President shall discharge those powers and duties as Acting President until I transmit to you a written declaration that I am able to resume the discharge of those powers and duties.

Sincerely . . .

'"*The President of the United States*",' McCorkell finished for her. 'What do you suppose the line "*In view of present circumstances*" means?'

'It could be because of the War on Terror – I mean, we're at war, we need a Commander-in-Chief who is totally capable,' Mary replied.

'That's right. So by the President invoking the Twenty-Fifth it means that the Veep is in charge for a day or so,' McCorkell said. 'And that, my dear Mary Swanson, is another example of our great democratic republic at work.'

'Yes, sir,' she said. She hesitated by the door before departing. 'He'll be all right, won't he, sir?'

'The President? He's as tough as they come, don't you worry. He has a lot of work he wants to get done before his first term ends, let alone when he gets to his second one,' McCorkell said. 'Good luck with your job here – I'd say don't let Aaron work you too hard, but I know that's asking the impossible.'

'Thank you.' And with that she was on her way.

McCorkell had a sip of tea from his Oxford University mug and went back to scanning Intellipedia. The intelligence community's version of Wikipedia, it was accessed over the SIPRNet – the Secret Internet Protocol Router Network – the intelligence community's secure version of the internet. It allowed users the world over to log in and edit data in real-time, to have discussions and even to rate the quality of the content. That latter point was proving a valuable new tool to a rapidly changing face of the intelligence, military and security of the nation. Accountability was becoming real-time, sharing data a priority, ownership of opinions paramount. McCorkell could now see a time not too far off where the millions of reports created by government departments and officials would become a much more interactive and accountable product. None too soon.

He heard the unmistakable sound of Marine One flying overhead on its way to the south lawn. The massive power of the three General Electric engines that powered the VH-71 Kestrel vibrated the heavy double-glazed windows of his north-west-corner office. In less than an hour the President would be at Washington Hospital Center, undergoing surgery for the removal of cancerous polyps from his colon.

McCorkell checked his online diary: a Cabinet meeting at 9 am; an update from his Middle East assistant who'd headed up a joint task force to monitor events and analyse the attacks in Qatar and Saudi Arabia; and the final of the draft of five African country National Intelligence Estimates round-tables to get the heads-up on any details prior to their publication to the intelligence community on Monday. Hopefully, out by five to enjoy a day and a half outside the West Wing.

He clicked on the 'nation briefings' tab and scanned the headline activities in African hot spots that were covered in the upcoming NIEs – Sudan, Chad, Nigeria, Libya, Angola. Each country had dozens of links that led to more detailed information.

A widget caught his eye on the screen and he winced at the price of oil that flashed with a new rise. NYMEX had sky-rocketed this past week. Three terrorist attacks were to blame for a reduction of global production, worsened by the fact that there was already a shortfall of supply. It was through a wide-angle lens that McCorkell viewed the world. Oil, the world's most fungible commodity, was the lifeblood of not only America's economy but its national security. Still, his ethos this morning was the same as any other morning: every day he went to work trusting that the work he would do that day would be better than anyone else could do in his place. Time would tell.

32

OUTSKIRTS OF ABUJA

Fox rode in the back seat of the early eighties Land Rover, built desert tough. Next to him, Gammaldi was in the process of destroying an MRE.

'You know, those things are meant to keep a soldier in the field going for twenty-four hours,' Fox said. 'And now you're eating your way through your second.'

'The first one was vegetarian,' Gammaldi said. 'And vanilla pudding in a tube? Is that even food? I mean, come on . . .'

'You ate it all, though.'

Gammaldi just grunted and continued looking out of his side window and mashing away at a muesli bar. His bulky five-four frame seemed always in motion, even while sitting there in the back seat – and he was constantly eating to make up for the energy expenditure. *Energy in, energy out*, he'd say often enough. Fox could hardly argue with him about it. With just on nine per cent body fat, Fox had nearly a foot and ten kilos on him, yet he couldn't bench twice what Gammaldi could pump out in sets of ten.

Fox looked up ahead as the road abruptly ended its relatively smooth bitumen for potholed gravel.

'This is where the federal road ends,' Simon called over his shoulder. The teeth-rattling corrugations on the gravel road accentuated the point. Outside, mud-brick and fibreboard shanty towns flashed by in their wake of dust.

'Why are these people situated so far out of Abuja?' Fox asked, taking photos out of his side window with his Nikon D40x. A woman washing children's clothes in a bucket. A man standing on a roof, reaching his radio to the sky for reception. Kids with sticks, herding chickens. A group of old men smoking rolled cigarettes, their open faces passive as vehicles rumbled past.

'They have been moved out here for the past couple of years,' Simon explained. 'The government bulldozed their homes in Abuja – despite them purchasing their land legally, the government back-flipped and is sticking to the course of making Abuja a designed city, as it was originally planned. No civilians can afford the new houses they are building, only senior bureaucrats, foreign diplomats, and contractors.'

They came to a halt behind some petrol tankers returning to the oil fields in the delta region.

'This another toll point?'

'I don't think so – they don't dare toll petrol tankers, the government makes sure of that,' the driver said. He inched the Land Rover forward to see if he could look further ahead. Having made a career as a driver based out of Nigeria's main seaside city of Lagos, Simon knew well when to be wary. His reach was never far away from an old revolver holstered to the inside of his door.

'I'll check it out,' Fox said. He reached for his backpack on the seat next to him – his own pistol was in there. But he thought better of it, and took his camera only.

'Stay in the car, Al,' Fox said, and headed out into the noisy street.

The traffic jam was made up of twelve petrol tankers. Their drivers were honking their horns in tandem. Still, this stall was not enough to get them outside their air-conditioned cabs. He passed one driver shouting into his radio, either checking with the lead truck in the convoy what the hold-up was or calling it in.

As Fox neared the front of the convoy he came to a crowd where the traffic jam started. Chaos. Shouting, arguing, screaming. As he neared he could make out crying too – a woman, sobbing inconsolably. Men were pounding on the cab of the lead truck, and the action quickly spread through the crowd of fifty or more who began to rock the eighteen-wheel rig with their bare hands. Fox snapped off shots as he moved and bumped his way forward through the ever-swelling mass of people.

Fox tumbled into the hollow at the eye of the crowd, by the driver's door just behind the front wheel of the truck. A mother sat there – she was the source of the crying. She was growing quieter, sobbing and praying, while rocking back and forth with a small child in her arms, as if trying to get this little girl to sleep.

It was horrific. Where the child's legs should have been was just bloodied pulp. She was well past dead, a little lifeless rag doll torn in half by the truck.

Fox snapped shots of the scene. The driver yelling into his radio set. The crowd with their rocks smashing against the cab. The spider-web of the windscreen as it shattered.

Automatic gunfire filled the air, AK-47s. The crack of pistol shots. The crowd moved back but their hum remained, the shouting and blaming and mourning.

Fox watched as a Toyota pick-up skidded to the side of the road ahead, members of the black-shirted MOPOL filing out. They were threatening the crowd, pushing them back, more shots filling the air. Fox knew these guys were paramilitary, that their main objective was to protect the nation's oil assets and the staff and infrastructure of companies that owned them. They had to keep the system going at full pace, and in this case it meant getting these trucks moving asap.

The crowd was pressed back against the houses on either side of the dirt road. Fox was still taking photos as a cop came over and grabbed the dead girl by the arm, dragged her away from her screaming mother and tossed her to the side of the road. The mother got to her feet, and ran to the cop as he motioned the petrol tankers to continue on.

Fox couldn't believe it – they were just letting this guy motor on without a single word uttered. He noticed that these cops had the same oil company logo on their shirt-sleeves that was sprayed onto the sides of the trucks – a federal police force for hire. Fox was still snapping off shots, the Nikon clicking away automatically at two pics per second as he held the button down.

The mother had moved again, and stood up holding her lifeless child in her arms once more. She was yelling at the senior cop, something in the local Hausa language. The cop's eyes squinted into hard focus as he drew his 9 mm and popped her twice in the head. There was little left atop her shoulders. The bark of the pistol rang in Fox's ears and he had a flash of an image he'd seen before – of a coalition soldier executing a Taliban member in Afghanistan. Only this time it was a defenceless, innocent woman.

For the first time the crowd was silent as the trucks rumbled onwards – the cops on one side, the civilians on the other. The stand-off was uneasy, each side like a coiled spring about to jump free.

Fox's eyes were locked with those of the senior cop's – he caught glimpses of him in-between the tankers as they rumbled past. It was clear this guy was not pleased with Fox's presence. As if the camera was as much a threat to him as his 9 mm pistol was to Fox.

A honk and Fox looked to his left – the Land Rover pulled to a stop in a cloud of red dust and before Fox could get in the cop was standing in front of it, the traffic stopped once again. His pistol was raised at Simon's head – then arced slowly across to Fox. His aim was steady. Fox's heart was beating through his chest.

Fox looked into the back seat, saw Gammaldi glance down to the bag containing the pistol – and gave him a look that said *no*.

'The camera!' the cop yelled, holding his hand out for Fox to pass the camera over.

'We're press,' Fox answered, holding his ground.

'You have five seconds, Mr Press,' the cop said.

Fox held for another moment, then walked over, passed the camera to the cop. Then he turned on his heel, walked back to the Land Rover and climbed into the back seat.

The cops waved them on. The senior cop, holding the camera by his side, watched Fox the whole time as they passed.

'Once we're out of sight, drive as fast as you can,' Fox said.

Simon minced through the gears, the turbo diesel whining into action. Fox was shaking slightly – adrenaline, ready for a fight, nerves a bit out of control.

'What's the rush?' Gammaldi asked, looking over at his friend.

'This,' Fox said. He held up the camera's memory card.

33

THE
WHITE HOUSE

At 9.05 am Bill McCorkell had the floor of the meeting in the Cabinet Room. The Cabinet were assembled to discuss releasing some of the Strategic Petroleum Reserve to alleviate oil prices, their daily discussion for the past ten days.

Given the President's absence, McCorkell was providing his usual rundown of global hot spots designated the PDB to the Vice President and the Cabinet as one. This had been prearranged prior to the President's surgery, not as a sign of distrust in Vice President Jackson, but as a way of including the wider executive in the heightened circumstances. Simply, the ramifications of three major terrorist attacks against global oil infrastructure proved the necessity of Cabinet involvement as they had greatly affected the US supply of imported oil. The domestic economy was taking a beating at a larger rate than the global one.

McCorkell pointed to a satellite image on a large LCD screen and was on the fly: 'Following the explosion at the Saudi Aramco oil terminal of Ras Tanura, the Kingdom are still running four million barrels per day below usual production,' McCorkell said. 'To put that shortfall on supply in perspective, this alone has equated to the price of petrol at the pump being seventy cents higher per gallon than it was two weeks ago.'

'Aramco are still refusing to release any reserve refining capacity?' the Secretary of Transport asked.

'That's right. We're getting no make-up refining from them at this stage, but we're working at it from every angle,' McCorkell said. 'How much are you hurting?'

'Updated figures went to press this morning,' she said. 'Put simply, seventy per cent of the oil this nation uses is in transport. It's hurting bad and it's only getting worse. Prices on everything are going up as a result. We haven't seen this sort of inflationary pressure in a long time, not since the early eighties.'

'I have a meeting with Prince Fahid today,' Adam Baker, the Secretary of State, said. 'They've got a number of demands on the table, from procurement of F-22s to our halting of a push for democracy in the Kingdom.'

'And they'll be getting nowhere on both. The Kingdom's enjoying seeing us hurt, and the higher global fuel prices are boosting their coffers,' Tom Fullop said. The Chief of Staff spoke louder than necessary, a custom in Cabinet meetings that McCorkell assumed was to make up for his physical stature. 'They're in a high position and they know it. Nigeria's the key here: we get them back up to their peak production, we have room to manoeuvre with the Saudis.'

'Need me in the meeting with the Prince?' Peter Larter, Secretary of Defense, asked.

'State, the VP and I have got it covered, but thanks, Peter,' Fullop said. 'Like I said, we won't be bending over for them today.'

McCorkell noticed Jackson smile. He could sense the Veep was about to go on the attack.

'I was thinking something more along the lines of having our Navy board every vessel to leave their ports,' the Veep said. 'See how they like the logjam that would create in their oil exports.'

Most of the table laughed with the Vice President, while Fullop look bemused.

'Are they still denying it was a terrorist attack?'

'For the moment, yes,' McCorkell said. 'The 2004 attack at their processing facility in Abqaiq became a "terrorist incident" only after Al Qaeda laid claim to it on the Net. I suspect much the same this time around.'

'And no group has claimed this attack?'

'Nothing yet,' McCorkell said. 'So, on the one hand we have the Saudis still refusing to admit the explosion as a terrorist attack; while just a stone's throw away, in Qatar, they've not only stated that their attack was the result of a terrorist cell, they're also stating that this Saudi attack is linked.' McCorkell switched images on the screen. 'This is the *Knock Nevis*. The world's biggest ship, a floating oil refinery in Qatar's Al Shaheen oil field, and it's been a smouldering wreck all week. They got the fires under control today, and with back-up links they have managed to bring refining capacity back to near pre-explosion levels, currently losing just on four hundred thousand barrels per day. Good under the circumstances and within six days of their attack. This is fast-moving for Qatar standards.'

'What's the ETA on full production?' the Secretary of the Treasury asked, making notes.

'Back up to capacity by Wednesday when two other refining ships get to port – but we've yet to feel the effects of their loss due to the immediate release of their reserve stocks,' McCorkell said.

'The Qatari government has welcomed our FBI agents with open arms,' the Attorney General added. 'They're doing everything they can to make the investigation work. I'd call it two more days until our team on the ground give the oil companies the all-clear to work from the site again.'

'Pity the Kingdom doesn't share their spirit,' the VP said.

'Qatar is playing nice because CENTCOM just made their JSOC forward-operating base there a permanent facility,' McCorkell said. 'Qatari military got a new airport out of the deal, and two squadrons of our retired F-18s.'

'Pity the Kingdom's already got fourth-gen fighter jets,' Fullop said.

'So where does this leave us on the issue of SPR draw-downs?' the Secretary of the Treasury asked. 'We've had a halt on filling the SPR since the first of these attacks to alleviate the prices at the pump. When do we start dipping in?'

'This puts the talk of draw-downs on the SPR and fuel rationing on the back-burner for the time being,' Fullop said. 'There's global supply out there that's not far off coming back online, we just have to ride this out.'

'As we touched on before, Nigeria is the linchpin here,' McCorkell added. 'They've come back on with a million barrels this past week, still down two million from their peak capacity two months ago due to militant unrest in the delta. National political stability is an issue and we've got a small element of 10th Mountain heading in to ensure the interim security of our US Mission in Abuja.'

'And their energy minister announced yesterday that they can have a new offshore rig adding a couple of million to their cap within two months,' Baker said. 'That'll be a big help all round.'

McCorkell nodded, and checked his notes.

'The bombing in Port Harcourt no doubt set them back,' McCorkell said. 'Shell have evacuated all personnel and it doesn't look like they're heading back in a hurry. Several other companies are following their lead.'

'LUKOIL is close to securing Shell's rights to their Nigerian oil infrastructure,' Baker said. 'This could well be the nail in the coffin for the Anglo-Dutch company's presence in that part of the world.'

'They're freeing more of their capital to buy into Canada?' Jackson asked.

'Yes, sir,' McCorkell said. 'These latest incidents have ensured that the price of crude is well over what it needs to be to make Canada's Athabasca Oil Sands deposit more than just a viable option. With over 1.7 trillion barrels and counting, Canada has more heavy oil reserves than the rest of the world's conventional proven reserves combined. Lucky break for us, so we'd better cut back on the wisecracks about our neighbours.'

The room laughed.

'Venezuela may have a shot at that heavy-weight title,' Fullop said. 'Their Orinoco Tar Sands keeps getting bigger the more they explore. They're calling it 1.8 trillion barrels and rising.'

'And while China's already pouring their cash into there, it's a drop in the ocean compared to where our northern cousins are at,' McCorkell said. 'Canada's infrastructure is decades ahead of Venezuela's, not to mention the political volatility in and around the latter region. We're not going to see oil companies fight over themselves to pour the tens of billions of dollars it will cost to get at and refine that nation's heavy crude until the government is secure and their South American neighbours promise to play nice.'

'Won't happen in a hurry.'

'Exactly, that's something we've all learned the hard way, not only from conflicts in the Middle East, but in Nigeria as well,' McCorkell said. He made sure he had the full attention of the table. 'Look, we can't get around the fact that Nigeria is still currently our fifth-largest importer of oil and they will be for at least a decade until Canada's output can take over. Make no mistake, we need the Nigerians to be exporting to us, and dealing with Russian oil companies will be a very different proposition.'

'I'm not so sure,' Fullop said. 'With the price of oil right now they'll be looking to sell to whoever is willing to pay premium.'

'Which will further inflate prices,' McCorkell said. 'We need oil today, same as we did yesterday. So does China, India, Western Europe . . .'

'Has anyone bothered to crunch the numbers to see if we're higher than 1980 at our current price?'

'Press has been doing that for days,' Fullop said. 'They've got a shotgun-spread of data – some say it's not even close, others say it's gone over.'

'But do we actually know?' Larter asked, turning to the Energy Secretary. 'Where's it at?'

'At the pump?' she said. 'It's pretty much on a par to what it was then.'

'That's right,' McCorkell said. 'When looked at as a proportion of spending based on comparative income, it's still slightly cheaper as it stands now. We can thank vehicle fuel-efficiency standards and low mortgage rates for that one.'

'And if something pushes us past where we are now?'

'We've got a fair amount of known production that should come back online within the short term,' McCorkell said, checking his notes. 'Overall right now, global capacity is running at around ninety-two per cent of some ninety-five million barrels per day, while our imports are down just over eight per cent –'

McCorkell stopped himself as he noticed the Secret Service agent at the door to his left move his hand to his ear.

The door to the Cabinet Room burst open, and an Air Force Major entered, slightly short of breath. Phones and pagers in the room started ringing and beeping.

'Sir – we have a situation at the Louisiana Offshore Oil Port in the Gulf of Mexico.'

'Go on.'

'Still putting it together, but it appears a water vessel has struck the LOOP –'

'Was it an accident?' Fullop asked.

'We got another one,' the Secret Service agent said, listening to the radio feed into his earpiece. A member of the White House security detail was downstairs in the Situation Room at all times, their radio system currently playing the role of instant messenger.

The internal phone on the wall rang, and McCorkell listened to the five-second brief from the Situation Room. His world seemed to halt for a moment as he watched the clock strike 9.17 am.

'We're under attack,' McCorkell said as he hung up the handset. He was back in the moment, and nodded to the Secretary of Defense. 'Two separate craft hit the LOOP, damage reported as massive.'

'The Vice President and Cabinet have to follow me to the Executive Briefing Room,' the Secret Service agent said, moving the bodies he was sworn to protect. Located under the East Wing, it was about as secure as a site could be before being locked away in the vault that was the adjacent Presidential Emergency Operations Center.

The Secretary of Homeland Security was already conferring with his aide at one side of the room.

McCorkell instinctively scanned the Cabinet.

'Who's not here?'

'Sec Agriculture's in California,' the Secret Service agent said, ushering bodies out of the room. 'Let's move, people, leave your things here in the room.'

'Sec Ag is now the Designated Survivor,' McCorkell said to the agent. 'And get word to the Hill.'

'Copy that.' The agent started talking into his sleeve mike.

In the span of ten seconds McCorkell had ensured government would survive in the advent of a terrorist attack upon the capital. The Presidential Line of Succession beyond the members of Cabinet present were now being moved to secret, secure locations until further notice.

34

PORT HARCOURT, NIGERIA

Fox and Gammaldi waited on the tarmac of Port Harcourt International Airport. They sat on the hood of the Land Rover while their driver took a nap. There was hardly any outgoing commercial traffic but the place was busy with private flights evacuating oil-company executives.

The climate was markedly different here compared to Abuja. The dry and blustery conditions farther north had been replaced by a low sun, piercing through storm clouds that rolled down across the coastal plains and out over the delta with each wet season. The waters flushed through the Niger River and flowed out into the Gulf of Guinea.

'Here she is,' Gammaldi said, his airman's eyes picking out the Airbus A318 Elite as it banked into a landing approach.

The sun's rays disappeared again, and steam started rising

from the blacktop as fat, warm drops of water slowly rained down. It actually made the humidity more comfortable.

'You missing flying?' Fox asked Gammaldi. It was a year since the former aviator had left the Australian Navy, a chosen departure, unlike Fox's earlier exit from the service.

'Nah – Wallace says I can have a fly any time I want,' Gammaldi replied. 'He's just bought a new helo too.'

'I didn't think he had enough toys,' Fox said, drinking from his bottled water.

'You miss diving?'

Fox thought about it as the Airbus touched down at the end of the runway. It was a shorter version of the A318 commercial airliner but with extended intercontinental range. The sun glinted off the silver writing down the white fuselage: *GLOBAL SYNDICATE OF REPORTERS*. Sixty million bucks worth of private aeroplane.

'Yeah, I do actually,' Fox said, getting off the hood of the Land Rover and tossing the empty water bottle into the open back window. He slicked back his wet hair as the rain shower paused again. 'I go for a swim in a pool a couple of times a week but that ain't the same as the ocean – and no, New York harbour isn't the kind of waterway I'd choose to swim or dive in.'

The Airbus taxied down the runway towards them and came to a halt at the causeway. Immediately the cabin door opened and Tas Wallace emerged, followed by a slight, middle-aged man. Wallace's six-foot bulk and thick mane of white hair were a stark contrast to the other man's small build and thinning buzz-cut as they walked down the stair-car and across the tarmac.

'Michael,' Fox said, shaking hands. 'Thanks so much for coming here.'

He took measure of the guy. It was just over six months since Rollins had been through the extraordinary rendition ordeal. Three months of hell. It was a testament to his family that he'd pulled through this well. Mid-forties, his well-creased face had seen its share of laughs and far too much anguish and stress. His piercing light blue eyes reminded Fox of a Siberian husky. His ancestral heritage of Wirral peninsular in north-west England was visible in his Viking features. Wallace had arranged that Rollins would receive a decent pay-out for an early retirement, although any recouping of that money would not be forthcoming from the US government. It didn't hurt Wallace's GSR any. Rollins, a specialist reporter in Middle East and African areas, had headed up GSR's bureaus there for much of the nineties.

'You hear about Louisiana?' Wallace asked.

'No, what happened?' Fox said.

'Terrorist attack at an offshore oil repository – a few oil crew dead, big hit to the US economy,' Rollins replied.

'Jesus,' Gammaldi exclaimed.

'Anyone claimed it?' Fox asked.

'Nothing's gone public yet,' Wallace said.

'Linked to the Qatar attack?' Fox asked.

'Could be, sounds like a similar MO,' Rollins said. 'Qatar authorities have come out confirming that their attack was perpetrated by a sympathetic Al Qaeda group, the IMU. They've got some DNA evidence found at the scene to link it back to some known terrorists that the Pakistanis let loose a couple of years back.'

'That was sharp work,' Fox said. He'd been in Nigeria for twenty-four hours and felt as though he'd been on another planet. It seemed the press here paid as much attention to the American trash media headlines as international events – he'd read what Brad and Angelina had done yesterday, but no updates on the oil crisis. And it wasn't for a shortage of some decent newspapers in the country, nor ballsy reporters. There was a seemingly inexplicable absence of coverage on the oil attacks, both in Qatar and Saudi Arabia.

'CNN ran it eight hours ago,' Wallace said, checking his watch and waving to the pilots in the waiting Airbus. The engines started picking up revs again.

Fox turned his attention as another vehicle pulled into the private taxi-way. Its movement seemed to rumble the earth – this SUV was a monster, the latest model Range Rover Sport, black on black, the windows as dark as the duco. The single occupant got out, bearing a slight but compact no-nonsense pose. Ex-military, Fox thought. The doors on the Range Rover were thick – like those on the US President's limo. This thing was armoured to the max, a tank in disguise.

Rollins shook the guy's hand double-handed, the school-yard style of best friends, and made the introductions.

'Lachlan Fox, Al Gammaldi and Tas Wallace,' Rollins said. 'This is Stephen Javens of the British High Commission.'

That sealed it. The guy was MI6, probably ex-SAS. Definitely a door-kicker disguised as a paper-pusher.

'I'll be your tour guide,' Javens said. 'Take you boys from here to the delta and on to Lagos.'

There were nods all round, then he and Gammaldi went about moving the GSR men's gear from the Land Rover into the new vehicle.

'There will be a G5 waiting for you on the tarmac in Lagos

in twenty-four hours,' Wallace said, already moving off towards his waiting aircraft. 'I have to get back to a thing in London.'

'See ya,' Gammaldi said.

'You guys go get your story,' their boss called over his shoulder.

'Will do,' Rollins said.

Fox turned from the others and went after Wallace.

'Tas,' he said.

'Yeah?' Wallace turned around.

Fox reached into his shirt pocket and passed over his camera's memory card.

'What's on here?'

'Pics I shot coming out of Abuja,' Fox said. 'Some shots of the MOPOL officers executing an innocent civilian.'

Wallace took it and squeezed Fox on the shoulder, searching his eyes, a measuring look for any signs he wasn't running at full capability.

'You got this, right?'

'Yeah, I'm fine,' Fox said. 'Gammaldi has my back.'

'Don't let this place get to you,' Wallace said, fatherly advice from the older man. 'If it gets too much, if it gets out of hand, don't hesitate to bug out. You've had a hell of a year, I don't want you burning out on me – or worse.'

Fox nodded. He knew he was good to stay the course, no matter what. He knew when to keep his head down, when to run, when to shoot.

Wallace ascended the stair-car with the agility of someone half his age, despite the rain on the metal treads, and disappeared into the Airbus cabin.

Fox walked back to the team, to wave farewell to Simon, their Nigerian driver. He departed with a wave out the window.

Yeah, a busy year was an understatement. He'd raked up as many frequent flyer miles as the Secretary of State. He'd been shot at more than most guys in Iraq. He'd lost more than he cared to dwell on.

'Ready to motor?' the British agent said from behind the steering wheel, then gunned the engine, a big throaty V8 roar.

Fox climbed in the back seat next to Gammaldi. Inside it was smaller than it seemed from the outside due to all the armour – with Fox's six-two frame his head just passed under the ceiling. Up front, a pair of snub-nosed MP5Ks were slung in holsters on either side of the centre-console.

Fox grinned; the adventure lay ahead. 'Let's roll!'

35

THE
WHITE HOUSE

'What have we got?' McCorkell asked on entering the Situation Room. It still smelled of paint from the previous month's warp-speed refurb, after which the President, together with the Prime Minister of England, had held a ceremonial opening and briefed their commanders in Afghanistan over the new LCD video-conferencing screens. The work area of the main conference room was now twice the size of its predecessor. All the technical components were updated, new communications gear installed, more space for the specialists who worked in there and monitored global hot spots.

The chairs around the boardroom table were vacant, all personnel were either working the phones or punching away at computer screens along the walls. Organised chaos among the security staff.

'Two small civilian watercraft struck the LOOP,' Admiral Donald Vanzet, Chairman of the Joint Chiefs of Staff, said. 'ID as yet unknown –'

'Make them to be thirty-foot speed-craft, sir,' the Air Force watch commander said. 'Screen two shows still images received from the CCTV cameras at the site before they went offline. Each craft is piloted by a single occupant, assumed KIA on impact.'

'Piloted,' McCorkell said. 'So these were definitely suicide attacks?'

No one in the room was game to call it yet.

'You got a usable image to ID these guys?' McCorkell asked, moving closer to a massive LCD screen recessed into the west wall.

'Partial facial shot from high alt, running double-time through DHS facial recognition.' The shot was indistinct on the screen and would need serious re-tooling to get something usable.

'Get the Europeans on it too. The Brits, Interpol,' McCorkell said as he moved back to Vanzet. The presence of the Navy veteran was, as usual, a welcome cool-head under fire.

'And the Israelis,' Vanzet added, picking up where McCorkell left off.

'Aye, sir,' the Navy intel officer said.

Vanzet continued his brief to McCorkell: 'The LOOP –'

'I've got real-time imaging from a Coast Guard helo,' the Air Force officer cut in, uploading the feed to the main screen at the end of the room. This thing was the size of most living-room walls and could be configured to be viewable as thirty-two separate split-screens. 'Main screen top right.'

'Jesus . . .' McCorkell said. The structure of the LOOP, a mass of steel structures linked by walkways and piping, was almost non-existent – a smouldering wreck of twisted steel at the waterline. 'What would it take to do that kind of damage to the LOOP structure?'

'She's designed to withstand a ten-knot bump from a super-tanker,' Vanzet said. 'You're looking at the results of high-explosive hits, damn big payload too.'

McCorkell's mind was racing. Two speedboats had hit the target, both deliberate hits. Waterborne suicide bombers. As much as they'd tried to take the fight to the terrorists at the front line in the Middle East, they'd just shown how devastating the enemy could be for the first time since 9/11. The US had been schooled in what it meant to have your home turf turned into a war zone. A painful lesson in asymmetric warfare.

'Don, Qatar?' McCorkell asked.

'FBI are getting all their evidence sent through to us asap,' Vanzet said. 'There were images captured of the attack in Qatar, but their Navy reported civilian-type speedboats breaching the security perimeter and striking the *Knock Nevis*. Fibreglass recovered confirms this, and the explosive residue was ammonium nitrate and nitromethane, at least five hundred kilos' worth, with a Tovex explosive for detonation. They even got some more recoverable DNA from the scene, at least three known terrorists involved in that op.'

McCorkell scanned the screens before him.

'We got overhead imagery to replay?' he asked. 'War-fighter, Landsat, Keyhole – anything with eyes?'

'Working through the grid with NRO, they're almost on hand,' a Homeland Security agent said, ear glued to a phone to his department's command centre at the Nebraska Avenue Complex. 'Two minutes out, sir.'

'I've got a possible hit from a DEA Predator,' the Air Force watch commander said, bringing up a replay of the UAV's fly-over.

McCorkell scrutinised the images. The two fast-moving civilian craft were the type favoured by drug-runners skimming the waves – those things were really moving it until they were gone, out of shot. The screen shot zoomed out, the ocean now a massive expanse with two dots leaving tracer-like wakes behind them akin to an aircraft's slipstream.

'What are those boats – are they custom-made? Get an ID on make, track it,' McCorkell said to the DHS agent before turning back to Air Force. 'Major, where and when was this feed?'

'Ten-hut!' the Marine in dress uniform at the door called, interrupting, as the Acting President entered with Fullop in tow. They joined McCorkell and Vanzet in viewing the big-screen footage.

'Gulf of Mex, two hundred nautical miles south-east of LOOP,' the Air Force Major said, reading from the operator's log on his computer screen. 'This DEA image is four hours old, targets flagged as "contacts of interest" and Coast Guard advised to pick up the chase . . . However, the local assets were too far out of the zone, responding to distress calls.'

'These two craft could have originated from the Keys?' McCorkell asked, checking their positioning on a map of the area.

'On it,' Vanzet said, moving over to get orders off to the Pentagon. Every pair of eyes the military and intelligence community had over the region would be back-played over the past twenty-four hours to track the movement of these two boats.

'If we can track to a point of origin . . .' McCorkell said, a million-mile stare at the smaller LCD screens that lined the south wall. CNN and Fox News were starting their broadcasts from the bombing scene. McCorkell watched the muted faces of the TV anchors intercutting with news helicopter feed. Behind his eyes the wheels began to turn . . .

'Okay, let's consider the timing of this attack,' McCorkell said to the room.

Jackson, Fullop and Vanzet were all ears.

'So soon after Qatar and the Kingdom?' Vanzet said. 'Part of the same group or copycats? Either way, targeting our economy where it hurts.'

'Worse than that, Don,' McCorkell said. 'Who knew the President was going under today?'

Fullop's expression read that he'd just been sucker-punched, and McCorkell turned to Seamus O'Keeffe, the Secret Service SAC, who'd been talking on the phone to his White House command centre the entire time.

'We've got the list at sixty-three,' O'Keeffe said. 'Informed of the POTUS surgery schedule five days ago.'

'Break it down,' McCorkell said.

'The list is being faxed here –'

'We've got secondary explosions!' Vanzet interjected.

McCorkell turned to the big screen at the end of the room. A real-time image of the Louisiana coast showed a massive flaring plume that kept rolling up in scale.

'Lost one of two shore-based pumping stations at Fourchon,' the DHS agent said. 'Shut off on the other is in place, as is the feed into the Clovelly Dome Storage Terminal . . . EMT and fire crews already on the scene at Fourchon – responding now.'

'Was that another strike? What was that?' McCorkell asked. Despite himself he felt a sweat break out under the back of his collar.

'Negative, sir, secondary explosions from the LOOP's damage,' the DHS agent said. 'Fire crews and paramedics calling in medevac now . . . We've got four – make that five – oil company fatalities, two litter-urgent med lifts . . .' The military term for the most serious of wounded for medevac hung in the air.

McCorkell looked to Vanzet and the Admiral conferred with the Air Force officer and received a nod and a look saying, *It's done.*

'Across the nation I've got fighter squadrons chewin' up the tarmac,' Vanzet said. 'We'll have two hundred fixed-wings over all major cities within ten minutes and I've got all US homeland bases operating under DEFCON Three.'

'DHS?' McCorkell asked.

'Homeland Security Advisory Level is at Red across all ports, airports and mass transit systems,' the Homeland Security agent said, one ear glued to a telephone handset. 'Coast Guard are waking up their rotation crews and calling up all personnel on leave.'

McCorkell nodded as he took in the information, the wheels moving faster now. O'Keeffe was in his face, the faxed sheet thrust into his hand.

'The list of people who knew POTUS would not be at the helm this morning,' O'Keeffe said.

McCorkell scanned the print-out. The Cabinet numbered fifteen . . . another seven cabinet-rank members such as himself, the Veep, the Chief of Staff ... and another three in senior executive staff. Then there was the First Lady ...

'Where are FLOTUS and the First family – where are they?' McCorkell asked O'Keeffe. 'Tell me you have them.'

'We have FLOTUS at the Washington Hospital Center,' O'Keeffe said, conferring over his radio with the SAC of the Presidential Protective Detail. He paused, held up his hand ...

'And you've got the kids?' McCorkell asked.

The Secret Service agent waited for the confirmation over his mike. Those within earshot were silent. McCorkell's heart skipped a beat – he'd never noticed how loud the air-conditioning system was down here.

'We have them secure. The kids are on the move. We have them, they're secure,' O'Keeffe said. The room breathed again.

The last names on the list in McCorkell's hand were the President's Secret Service detail, the twenty-one-member White House Medical Unit, and two surgeons and an anaesthetist at Washington Hospital Center.

'Where are you at with this list?' McCorkell asked O'Keeffe.

'We've got agents on it. Pulling in all the medicos, shaking trees and checking under rugs,' O'Keeffe said.

'NSA pulling in anything?' McCorkell asked a spectacled guy in civilian clothing.

'We have over three thousand Echelon hits on LOOP in the past month alone,' the National Security Agency agent announced to McCorkell, his phone headset glued on, his fingers a blur over the keys on his laptop. 'Over four hundred have mixed flags to the *Knock Nevis*, those are being followed up on – change that, that figure is now down to eighty-six, mostly via foreign ISPs and cell networks. We should have the numbers down again on those within the hour, transcripts of all communications and user data.'

'Work it. Take it back farther, too, six- and twelve-month blocks,' McCorkell said, pointing at the still image of the two boats on the open water. 'This attack was a long time in the planning.'

McCorkell was fully present, up to speed and taking in information like a sponge. A dozen military and intel aides worked computers and phones, getting every security apparatus in the nation ready to bring the noise if need be. Leave was being cancelled, National Guard Units were standing to, and every intel back-channel was being worked for information. In every theatre of operations around the globe, more than seven hundred US military bases were gearing up ready to roll out the thunder.

'The NSC is ten minutes out from being in the room,' Fullop said. 'I'll be over with the Cabinet and get the ball rolling on domestic actions.'

'The Sec Tres has to suspend trading,' McCorkell called after him.

'On it,' Fullop replied, before disappearing.

McCorkell looked to Vanzet. The shorn head of the Navy Admiral was a calming presence in any storm, and in all the years McCorkell had spent in executive office he'd never seen him lose his cool, no matter how shocking the crisis.

'Don, what's your feel on this?' McCorkell asked him.

'With the DNA on the Qatar bombers being from known terrorists, then I'd say this is more of the same,' Vanzet said. 'In a way the good news would be that this was the work of Al Qaeda. The scary version: we got ourselves another capable,

organised, well-coordinated terrorist outfit with intercontinental reach.'

'So much for our work in 'Stan,' McCorkell said. He turned
around to face O'Keeffe. Talked close to the Secret Service
agent, who still held the faxed list in his fist.

'Have every person of interest on this list brought to the
House,' McCorkell said. 'One of them has a big mouth, and
I wanna be there to hear it.'

36

PORT HARCOURT, NIGERIA

Fox watched the bustle of Port Harcourt flash by the window at warp speed. Javens was hammering the Range Rover, weaving the roads at one-sixty, one-eighty kilometres per hour. It seemed supersonic compared to the lumbering hulks they were speeding past.

'We're gonna take off at this rate,' Gammaldi jibed.

'We'll know if we're being followed,' Javens said by way of explanation.

Fox gave Gammaldi a half-smile and turned back to look out of his window. He was amazed how few cars there were on the street, and those mainly belonged to Westerners being chauffeured about, or the people that provided the goods and services they required. Petrol tankers were everywhere.

'A lot of these tankers are carrying pirated oil to be sold on the black market,' Javens explained. 'For a country so rich in the highest quality crude, petrol at the pump here is relatively expensive. With little other way to make a living, locals skim oil from the delta where pipes spill, while the more entrepreneurial tap into the pipes and siphon off tanker-loads.'

'That's how the militants raise money to buy arms?' Fox asked.

'The main way, although they have some money coming through grass-roots fund-raising,' Javens said. 'Amazing how those with nothing to give still manage to give so much.'

'They're desperate for change in this country, and through their desperation violence is seen as a viable way ahead,' Rollins added, turning around in the passenger seat to face Fox. 'There's money in this city, massive oil money. But the poverty divide is no better than anywhere else in Nigeria. If anything, here it's more apparent.'

'Do the oil workers live in secure compounds?' Fox asked.

'Yes, for the most part,' Rollins replied. 'Port Harcourt is kidnap central. The Westerners have their own secure suburbs, with malls, cinemas, cafes. The local oil workers have their cheaper versions. There's a big working class that scratch a living off the back of the oil industry, and then there are a million or so that are living out of what you'd consider brick and corrugated tin sheds. For them, they eek out a living any way they can.'

'How about the CBD?' Fox asked, the Range Rover taking a turn off the expressway and hammering down the off-ramp. *This guy should drive NASCAR.*

'We're entering it now,' Javens said, giving a few toots of the horn to clear a way through afternoon crowds heading home. 'Oil companies are mostly headquartered along a single road, with a permanent MOPOL police cordon and a visible military presence.'

'The MOPOL are the federal police force,' Rollins clarified. 'Paramilitary outfit, responsible for the security for the oil companies. Kill civilians with impunity.'

'Black shirts, khaki pants,' Fox said. 'We ran into some coming out of Abuja.'

'Don't let yourself get too bogged down with the smaller-scale stuff,' Rollins said to Fox. The reporter spoke with the experience built up from having seen more than his fair share of conflicts. 'It gets lost in the daily news cycle, I've filed it and seen it happen too many times. It didn't take me too long to figure out I was after the bigger fish, the wider story.'

The Range Rover slowed and entered through the Jersey barriers that cordoned off the oil companies' street. It was set up so that the concrete dividers made incoming vehicles do two slow turns to traverse through. Beyond that were two ageing Vickers Main Battle Tanks that had seen better days. The turret machine-gunners covered their entry, the 12.7 mm belt-fed cannons leaving little doubt this was an area where not many outsiders were welcomed. A platoon of soldiers milled about holding their rifles a little too relaxed, a little too high. Poorly trained, Fox noted.

Inside the security cordon, one side was lined with office buildings, a mix of sixties concrete structures and modern glass high-rises to twenty storeys. The other side was a green park, a few office workers enjoying a dry break in the weather.

'The oil building that was hit last week is just ... here,' Javens said, pulling the Range Rover up against the curb and shutting off the engine. They piled out, Gammaldi taking his pocket-sized digital camera. Debris blocked most of the road ahead, a nearby bulldozer having forged a single lane through the rubble with little heed for preserving a crime scene.

Fox looked up at the wreckage. It looked like a building as designed by Jackson Pollock. The entire facade was reduced to a pile of glass, concrete and twisted steel. Office furnishings and bits of paper and plastic were showered across the street and the park over the road.

'Reminds me of the images of Oklahoma City,' Gammaldi said, taking a couple of pictures.

'Similar construction to the Murrah Building,' Fox said. Broken concrete slab floors were exposed to the street, bent rods of steel reinforcement twisted at all angles. Scanning around he saw that not only had the dozer driven a traffic lane through the debris, but the area had been cleaned up too. He walked to the park and felt around in the wet grass – nothing but the finest debris remained.

'What is it?' Rollins asked as he joined him.

'Place has been cleaned up already,' Fox said. 'Where are the investigators?'

'This is Nigeria,' Javens said. 'They named the culprits minutes after the attack. Sent helicopter gunships into the delta to strike at militant targets.'

'Government did some token looking around but they don't see it as their problem,' Rollins added. 'Which has its pros and cons. They do a shit job – as you can see, they've got little idea in the way of investigative procedure. They've got nothing in the league of what the FBI or Scotland Yard has in the way of crime scene investigators. Their guys are beyond not being in the same ballpark, they're not even playing the same game.'

'Looks like I have my work cut out,' Fox said absently while he dusted his hands off on his pants. He scanned the area around them – something else wasn't right. 'If this was a car bomb then the crater would be under that rubble. And any evidence – explosive residue, detonator fragments . . .'

'They've got their culprits,' Rollins said. 'Textbook case for the cops and politicians – this was the work of delta militants. No witnesses otherwise. We're the only Western journalists to have access here. This site will be cleared of rubbish by next week and a new building built. They've got it down to a fine art around here.'

Fox was still scanning the streets. A couple of no-nonsense guys in mismatched fatigues approached Gammaldi and waved him away from the building. New Kevlar vests, Steyr TMP submachine guns, no visible ID.

'They oil company security?' Fox asked.

'Yeah, Blackwater types,' Javens said, returning the stare of one of them. 'Over five thousand of them in the delta regions, mostly out of control, beyond whatever laws there are to be upheld in this country.'

'Russians,' Gammaldi said as he joined his friends. 'It's always fucking Russians.'

'They're the latest crowd to Nigeria, following some new deals with Moscow over oil exploration,' Javens said. 'Their security forces are setting new standards when it comes to bad house guests. Shot up a platoon of state police in Lagos last week.'

Fox's mind was elsewhere, still looking around the street, searching for that something that just wasn't right. His scanning gaze fell across the other buildings – and it finally clicked.

222 • JAMES PHELAN

'You know, as reporters we're pretty good at taking notes of what we see,' Fox said, looking up and down the street. 'But my time in Special Forces taught me to take notice of something else: what we don't see.'

Fox turned to the three men, who listened intently.

'Like what is missing from a scene,' he said. 'Civilians in a town, normal behaviours among a population, that kind of thing.'

'Not many civilians here,' Rollins said. 'It's a Saturday, for starters.'

'And a lot of the Westerners are either hunkered down in their residential compounds or leaving the country,' Javens added.

'Take a look at the surrounding buildings, the street lamps and power poles on this side of the street,' Fox continued.

'And?' Gammaldi asked, scanning the area, trying to imagine what it was that he could not see.

'Cameras,' Fox said. 'No CCTV of the attack? No security cameras directed at the target building?'

'Nothing's been released, but there should be coverage from somewhere – every modern building here has to have them for insurance purposes,' Javens said, pointing to cameras on other buildings further down the road.

Fox inspected a building two down from the oil building. It was a perfect vantage point for camera surveillance. Sure enough, three metres up from street level there was a bare wire coming out of the wall and an empty mount. Another scene like this one across the road.

'Both cameras have been removed,' Fox said. 'Perhaps some time before the attack?'

'Now why would the militants go to those lengths to go undetected?' Gammaldi asked, as Rollins's cell phone chimed.

'Surely the act of removing those would be more noticeable than parking a van out the front of the building?'

'Al, contact the insurance company and see if they have anything,' Fox said.

Rollins listened to his cell phone and hung up within five seconds.

'We have to motor,' he said, and made towards the Range Rover as he spoke. 'Our meeting is on in twenty minutes, south delta region.'

37

SITUATION ROOM, THE WHITE HOUSE

'We've got the list down to eleven staff here at the White House med unit who knew about POTUS's condition from his last medical,' Secret Service SAC O'Keeffe said. 'That was just on two months ago – the longest lead time of all those who knew of his scheduled surgery.'

McCorkell and the rest of the National Security Council sat around the conference table. The wall-mounted screens showed several real-time images of the LOOP and the pumping stations at the shore, smoke rising from each.

'That's more than long enough to fix a timeline,' McCorkell said. He started nodding and tapped the table as if to help bring his thoughts out. 'That medical was scheduled for the day after the sub incident in New York. We had to push it back, postpone the medical, remember? Then they found the cancer . . .'

'Bill, could there be a connection to the New York thing?' the VP asked.

'The Euro power group?' McCorkell said. 'No, these oil prices are hurting them as much as us. This is a totally different story. This is someone who wants to harm the global economy as much as take a swipe at us. The past two weeks we have a similar MO in three attacks. Saudi, Qatar, and now here. This is a well-planned piece of terror.'

'So let's squeeze that medical team,' Peter Larter, Secretary of Defense, said to O'Keeffe. 'Phone records, bank accounts, travel, relationships, everything.'

'One of them might be talkative at home,' McCorkell added to Larter's comment. 'Maybe their place is bugged?'

'We're on to it,' O'Keeffe said. 'At this moment Secret Service and FBI agents are heading teams backed up by the DC police in knocking on or down doors of all White House medical staff.'

'Mr McCorkell, internal line two,' an aide said.

'Yep?' McCorkell said into the phone. His secretary reminded him of a meeting due now in the Roosevelt Room. It was the final draft of the African NIEs for his consideration prior to publication within the intel community and to the Hill.

'Thanks – tell them I'll have to reschedule for a couple of days' time.'

'I'm sorry – the NIE editor and Deputy Director of the CIA said they have some critical intel pertaining to a current situation.'

McCorkell instinctively looked to where the President usually sat at the table – currently occupied by Jackson. He winced slightly, then decided it was worth the five minutes it would take to figure out what was up.

'I'll be right up,' McCorkell said.

•

McCorkell raced up the stairs. Fifty-four this year, he was among the healthiest and fittest of men his age in Washington. He exercised every day and although his knees were running out of cartilage faster than he cared to think about he gritted his teeth through it. Tas Wallace was a long-standing training partner. It was a friendship that had weathered many international crises and bore mutual fruit from their labours. Wallace got access and scoops that only the best connected could get, and McCorkell had access to the information coming through Wallace's GSR reportage from the front lines, his own little quasi-intelligence unit.

The corridor of the ground floor led around to the Roosevelt Room. He entered through the main door, which stood opposite that of the Oval Office, to find the National Intelligence Estimate African editor and the Deputy Director of the Central Intelligence Agency both standing waiting for him. The latter was an unscheduled attendee for this meeting.

'Bill, thanks for coming,' the DDCIA said. 'I know things must be hell downstairs.'

'Ridley, you've got no idea,' McCorkell said, shaking hands with him and then the NIE editor, a senior analyst from the Director of National Intelligence's office. 'Tony.'

They all sat at one corner of the long conference table.

'What's up?' McCorkell asked. 'This on the NIEs?'

'Yes, Bill, and Tony here brought something to my attention. Nigeria,' Ridley said. Despite being the all-knowing DDCIA he had the look of being sucker-punched. Not a good look for someone of his position.

'You've got my full attention for five minutes,' McCorkell said. 'What have you got?'

'It's what we haven't got that's the problem. We've currently got nothing of worth in humint on the ground in Nigeria,' Ridley said. 'No NOCs, no doubles, nothing other than embassy staff.'

McCorkell took it in. No human intelligence operators – spies – on the ground in a country that supplied the US with a fifth of their oil.

'How can that be?' McCorkell said.

'As you know,' Tony began, 'this is one of our first NIEs done on Intellipedia –'

'Spare me,' McCorkell said.

'We got this via inter-agency users.' Ridley took over. 'Highly ranked on Intellipedia as top analysts and field ops. They've noticed, and now so have we, that over the past twelve months we've got a hole in Africa – a Nigeria-sized hole. We're just not getting the intel that we used to. It's dried up to . . . well, we've got *nothing*.'

McCorkell scanned the printed notes.

'Nothing? You needed the Port Harcourt bombing to flag this for you?'

'That, and, like I said, Intellipedia users all started ringing alarm bells at the same time.'

McCorkell shook his head. The most populous country in Africa, one of the United States's most vital oil suppliers, and they had *no* eyes and ears on the ground?

'Nigerian Energy Minister Brutus Achebe is offering an alternative to government . . .' McCorkell said, stopping at a page in the brief. 'He's gonna push for power?'

'He wants our support,' Ridley said. 'He wants to do this peacefully and has extended this olive branch for us to help them along. He says he can bring peace to the delta, and fast. Read that as secure oil production coming back online.'

'You know POTUS had the Nigerian President in the Oval Office a few months back; they shook hands on a defence pact,' McCorkell said. 'Greater oil exploration; more aid; military training. Hell, we are working on headquartering a Navy element of AFRICOM there.'

'That list goes on, I know,' Ridley said. 'This heads-up comes from an ex-agency asset, Steve Mendes. He's dealing on behalf of Achebe.'

'And that's why I'm hearing this from you rather than from the State Department?' McCorkell asked. 'He made contact via Langley?'

'Yep.'

'Steve Mendes. I vaguely know the name, I think,' McCorkell continued. 'You trust him?'

'I trust that he will do what he sets out to do. His pedigree is Grade-A. His dad got an agency star when killed in East Germany. A young Steve's first deployment was in Beirut, under the Non-Official Cover of a journalist.' Ridley pushed a personnel file across the timber table. 'He went on to work in Iran, came home and did a couple of years training new recruits at The Farm, then NCS operators at The Point. Several years in Afghanistan, then left the agency in '04 after helping ramp up our rendition program. Went on to the private sector heading security ops for Russian oil oligarchs and some military hardware guys in Uzbekistan.'

'And what is he to Achebe?'

'His principal advisor, been in the country for two years,' Ridley said. 'He's really shaking things up on the local scene, using his Russian security and business contacts to spearhead a new push for oil exploration and using their money to buy out the Western companies that are bugging out from the recent bloodshed.'

'So he's behind LUKOIL's bigger presence there?'

'Them, among many others.'

'Tony, what kind of time frame have you got on this transition to power?' McCorkell asked.

'Conservative guess, end of next week,' the NIE editor replied. 'The incumbent president has been losing ground domestically since the scandals around the last election. Achebe brings the twelve northern states that are under Sharia Law due to being the nephew of the Sultan of Sokoto, who's the highest religious leader of the some seventy-five-million Muslim population.'

'Where does that leave the seventy-odd-million Nigerian Christians?' McCorkell asked. It was a question neither intelligence man wanted to quickly voice an answer to.

'Where is the military power residing?' McCorkell continued.

'The President currently has command on the military where he served himself for twenty years. We put their number close on eighty thousand,' Tony said. 'There are a few brigades up north that would certainly be favourable to an Achebe government. And possibly a factional force in Lagos. These, with the paramilitary police force that is under Achebe's control in the protection of oil assets, are numbered at about twenty to twenty-five thousand. But they're the better-equipped force, better trained and hard-assed operators. Add to that an estimated force of fifty thousand well-armed Islamist militias from the northern states and external insurgents from Chad, Sudan, and probably some ICU terror cells out of Somalia, all hoping that a strong ally in Nigeria will help them in their own native areas of operations. All that, and not to mention five to seven thousand private security contractors in the country, mostly Eastern Bloc. Man for man that private force are worth twenty thousand regular Nigerian Army personnel.'

McCorkell rapped his fingers on the table, and got up and poured himself a tea from the service tray.

'Why haven't we heard of this sooner?'

'That's a tough one. Convoluted.'

'Spitball it.'

'I came to Ridley with this because it involved NOCs – this dry-up of humint was left out of the NIE that we're releasing,' the NIE editor said. 'But it won't go unnoticed now that it's a live online community of users. Already there are discussion threads from users in Africa, the Middle East and beyond, asking where the Nigerian intel is at.'

'And this slipped through the cracks until now . . .' McCorkell said. This was exactly the type of thing that Intellipedia was meant to be circumventing. It should have been picked up earlier, but that was another conversation for another day. 'If this leaks, we've got a bigger problem.'

'It won't leak, we're padding out the online intel from what what we can buy in from allied services,' Ridley replied.

McCorkell shared a look with him – he knew this seasoned operator was on to this, making the best he could out of the situation. He certainly wasn't after bad press for his agency, and the results that would lead to all over the world. The fact was, if bad people heard that the CIA had lost its greatest asset – spies in the field – they'd go about their business that much faster as they'd be working with less heed for being caught out.

'So the million dollar question here is *Why don't we have spooks in Nigeria?*' McCorkell asked the DDCIA. 'How could this happen?'

'Three entrenched networks of NOCs' – Ridley pronounced it as 'knocks' – 'were either made over the past four to six months, or killed. We've lost twenty-eight valued assets across levels of government, military, police, private sector and the press. Not to mention their networks of informants. All up we've probably lost a couple of hundred voices that we'll never get back. Starting up again takes years, the other side of ten to cast a net as big as we had.'

'And now all we've got to rely on is embassy staff on the ground . . .' McCorkell said, leaning forward with his forearms on the back of the chair.

Ridley nodded and Tony cringed.

'And what is your gut telling you?' McCorkell asked.

'It's – it goes against what you'd think.'

'Try me.'

'I think Mendes is behind this,' Ridley said. He looked McCorkell square in the eyes in a *this is certain beyond a shadow of a doubt* way. 'He's proved since leaving the fold that his primary motivation for employment is money. Who else but him would have such an insight to sell out our guys? It's a national problem, Nigeria only, we're not losing assets like this anywhere else on the African continent. Steve Mendes sold them out, had them killed or ejected from the country, for his own gain. He doesn't want us interfering in what will likely be a bloody power shift. Certainly doesn't want us looking into things too closely.'

McCorkell looked down at the personnel record again.

'You really think he'd go that far? That's a big step, from "all-American A-grade field op" to "sell-out gun for hire".'

'It's happened before, Bill.'

He didn't need to be told specifics. There were plenty of cases in the CIA's past that could be rolled out. Double agents. Agents who had sold national secrets. Agents who'd defected. Often enough these were Americans whose loyalty was beyond reproach until the benefit of hindsight played its hand.

'What are you basing this on?'

'His personnel file is only half the story,' Ridley said, pointing at the stock-standard agency folder on the table. 'He's got another file that is code-word protected from the DNI's office.'

'Kipling?' McCorkell said. The new Director of National Intelligence had only been in the office for three months, sworn in during the same week the President had asked for the Director of CIA's resignation. The intel community had gone through many shake-ups since 11 September 2001. There were more uniforms in directorial positions now. There was a new department – the Department of Director of National Intelligence – which headed up the updated command structure over the agencies. No longer was the Director of the CIA the head intelligence officer of the country. That fell to the DNI, and some things, well, while designed to maximise inter-agency synergy and minimise conflict, some things just slipped through the bureaucratic spider-web. It didn't matter how many extra billions they threw at it.

'It was our old director, Robert Boxcell, who closed the file,' Ridley said. 'And I'd like a look.'

Ridley sat firm. What he was asking for was access to that file to back his hunch. McCorkell had known Ridley for years, and respected his thoughts. This was a DCIA in the making, and not too far off from now.

'You need Kipling's okay to access it?'

Ridley nodded.

'All right. I'll speak to him,' McCorkell said. 'I'll call you back when I get another breather from downstairs.'

'Thanks,' Ridley said.

'What are the implications for us with such a shift in Nigeria?' McCorkell asked. 'How does it look if Achebe comes to power?'

Ridley looked to Tony, who'd spent the past couple of months heading a team working through hundreds of reports to prepare the National Intelligence Estimate on Nigeria.

'Sir, what do you know about the price of oil?'

38

PORT HARCOURT CITY LIMITS, THE NIGER DELTA

The setting sun pierced through the rolling overcast clouds, the light that special hue of orange unique to this time of day. Every now and then there was a flash of lightning deep within the clouds, the puffy grey marshmallow cumulus nimbus lit from within as thunder rumbled some way off.

'Left here,' Rollins said from the passenger seat, watching the streetscape intently. 'It's up here, park at the end of the street.'

Javens parked the Range Rover in a neighbourhood that wouldn't have looked out of place in the shanties of Mexico, Johannesburg or Cairo – anywhere with people on the downside of adversity, scratching a living from nothing. Most buildings were cinderblock, some rendered within colour palettes of yellow to red. Stray dogs sniffed at litter in the street, fighting over scraps. A few kids kicked a threadbare soccer ball against a wall.

Fox walked warily. His pistol was still in the Range Rover and a couple of armed men appeared from a building at the end of the dead-end street. Local militants. Rollins talked to them, each armed with old British L1A1 SLRs, and they nodded and stood sentry by the vehicle. Fox noted that they treated Rollins with respect – they'd met before.

'Through here,' Rollins said, leading the way. Fox walked at the rear as they entered a bakery. An old man sat behind a bread-laden counter; a near-empty cashbox that doubled as an ashtray. Gammaldi tossed him five dollars on the way through and picked up a loaf of bread. Fox pushed his back to keep him moving forward.

The rear of the building was a one-room apartment, and Rollins led them on through the beaded back doorway, into a walled courtyard where a baying goat was chained to a gnarled orange tree, and through to another building only accessible via this route.

Inside, it was a boathouse, two timber doors opening to a finger of water that was one of thousands where the Niger Delta fanned out to sea. An aluminium boat was tied up there, two militants waiting for them. Rollins greeted them, said a few words out of earshot of Fox and the others, and they were all waved aboard the craft by a man with two revolvers tucked into his belt, pirate-style.

'This looks like it will be a fun ride,' Fox said to Gammaldi out of the corner of his mouth. His mate grunted a reply through a mouthful of bread.

The second militant patted down the three arrivals although not Rollins. Fox and Gammaldi came up clean. They considered

Gammaldi's digital camera but Rollins told them it was okay. Javens's Walther P99 9 mm pistol was removed.

'I want that back later,' the Englishman said in protest as the outboard engine roared to life and they set off into the river system.

'How far?' Fox asked Rollins. They'd settled into the bench seats that ran up each side of the boat.

'Five minutes,' he replied. 'They keep moving their camps to avoid detection.'

'The baker?'

'You'll find all the locals are supportive of the militants' cause in any way that they can. They've all been adversely affected by the government and those in power in some way, through violence, neglect, poverty, appalling conditions. This place, this land, this history is their home, worth fighting for. This fight is their voice.'

'A war worth fighting,' Fox said.

'A just war, I would say,' Rollins responded. The two men shared a look that spoke of depths of understanding. 'This country has been broken for too many generations, and too many generations have paid the ultimate price in this war against colonialists in some form or other. It's so easy, though, as we know, for a just cause to be hijacked by thugs and men of opportunity.'

Fox thought about what Rollins said as he watched a few small fishing craft motor by, their occupants giving a wave to the two militants even with these Westerners in their boat. But although they traded in friendly gestures these people wore their pain and despair in the open, the looks on their faces haunted and hollow.

There were small shacks along the overgrown waterline, timber jetties where kids sat watching the world spin by. Steam rose from the water where the sun hit it, the whispers of the coming night rising as curtains of mist into the sky. Fox touched his hand into the water and rubbed the wetness between his thumb and forefinger – it left an oily residue.

'Pollution from the oil wells,' Rollins said, noting Fox's action. 'This is not a place where world's best practice in extracting oil occurs. Here, they get it out as quickly and cheaply as possible.'

Fox looked about as they went from one tributary to another. All the fishing craft were returning from out at sea, none were fishing the local water.

'The area is too polluted to fish?' Fox asked. Kids with toy guns carved from wood were firing at them from the end of a jetty.

'Yes.' Rollins looked ahead as they motored into darkness. A canopy of vegetation grew over the waterway here, and the militant steering the boat navigated by experience. The other, by the bow, signalled ahead with a torch. Three flashes came back in response.

'Michael?' Fox said.

The English reporter turned around, his face visible from patches of dying light that stole in through the canopy above, giving him the appearance of camouflage from the silhouettes of leaves.

'You're looking well . . . stronger. How have you been?'

'Much better since we last met,' Rollins said. 'You, on the other hand, are not looking so sharp, my friend.'

Fox was silent for a moment. 'I never thought to ask you . . . When you were taken – the rendition – what got you through?' he asked. 'Your family?'

The smile on Rollins's face came through in the dim light. It was the smile of a man who had worked it out. It was the content look of one who needed nothing else, of someone with nothing left to prove. A kind of half-smile that spoke of serenity, contentment, peace.

Rollins answered as the engine shut off and they bumped to shore at their destination. The others shuffled out, so only Fox heard him speak, and it touched his very core.

'I found God.'

39

WASHINGTON

'Subject is White House nurse Jack McFarland. According to the lead White House physician he hasn't answered any phone calls for two days,' O'Keeffe told the FBI agent over the cell phone. 'Called in sick and has not contacted anyone since. His landlord says he knows he's in his apartment but he won't answer the door. I have two agents in plain clothes at the scene, apartment has curtains drawn. They will wait for your all-clear to enter. Make it as soft as you can – we want to question this guy.'

'Thanks, we've got it. On scene in thirty seconds,' Duhamel said, and ended the call. An image of McFarland came onto the LCD screen in the car. He sat in the passenger seat of the lead Suburban, a DC police sedan clearing the way ahead as they wove through the Bethesda streets.

FBI Special Agent Jake Duhamel was a French-Canadian-born quarterback and grad student of law at North Dakota

State. The thirty-five-year-old was among the best marksmen in the world; he had a silver medal in shooting from the Sydney Olympics to prove it. He had joined up with the FBI like so many young men and women in the patriotic aftermath of 9/11, which saw a massive influx of recruits outside its normal base of lawyers, accountants and ex-cops. He was now the poster boy for the FBI and their elite Hostage Rescue Team. HRT, part of the Tactical Support Branch of the FBI's Critical Incident Response Group, were the lead unit to respond to the most urgent and complex FBI cases in the US and abroad. They were more than just another specialist counter-terrorist tactical team: in the world of paramilitary police units, these guys were rock stars. Duhamel looked around in the car – all his guys had their game faces on. Each of them were hands-on cops who could kick your ass with a look.

Duhamel certainly didn't pack a match-grade air pistol into the field. He cranked the cocking slide on his silenced Heckler & Koch MP-5, chambering a 9 mm Hydra-Shok round. He thumbed off the safety, switched on the laser pointer.

'Weapons hot!' he called in the Suburban. Two other men readied their MP5s, a fourth pumped a 'Master Key' slug into his H&K Super 90 shotgun. These were close-quarter weapons, high stopping power with low velocity to minimise the collateral damage of going through residential walls. The ammunition loaded had a simple purpose. It would make a real mess of whatever tissue it impacted with.

The four special agents filed out the doors as the SUV was still rocking on its shocks and they split into two-man fire teams to enter the three-storey apartment block. The sound of fighter jets above the nation's capital heightened their senses that this was a real op.

Duhamel followed 'Brick', his shotgun-wielding door-opener, up a flight of stairs and waited for the other two HRT agents to enter the corridor via the rear stairs.

A nod of his boss's helmeted head and Brick was through the front door with an ear-shattering boom from the shotgun. Duhamel was second through the door, splinters still in the air coating his clear goggles. Instantly he sensed things were wrong – he could smell death.

'Clear!' was called from the open-plan living area. 'Bedroom clear!'

'Body in bathroom, unknown deceased,' called a special agent.

In the kitchen Duhamel knelt down to the form of Jack McFarland. Brick hovered a few feet back, his shotgun hanging by his side and his Glock 22 side-arm trained on the nurse, red laser dot on the subject's head. Duhamel felt for a pulse – there but faint.

'Call in the bus,' Duhamel said. He checked McFarland's airway was clear, then looked over his body for anything telling – he didn't have any defensive wounds, just a slight bruise to one side of his face. The special agent stood and looked about the kitchen. Some pills were spilled on the floor – had the nurse tried to OD? The sink had a long knife in it that – yep, it was missing from the knife block. The blade was clean.

A siren announced the arrival of the paramedics, who had been on station around the corner.

Duhamel went to the bathroom. An agent hovered by the open door. The smell of death had come from here and had leaked into the rest of the apartment. A naked corpse of Middle

Eastern appearance lay in the tub, his arms and legs straight. Dead a good forty-eight hours, a single stab wound to the sternum. Wound had been cleaned, there was some congealed blood around the drain hole.

'Killed out there, dragged in here and cleaned up,' Duhamel said to himself as he heard the paramedics enter the apartment and shake out their fold-away trolley. He stood at the edge of the bath and snapped away with a small digital camera, taking a dozen high-res shots of the man's face.

'Question is, who are you?'

40

PORT HARCOURT CITY LIMITS, THE NIGER DELTA

'You will find no sympathisers for Al Qaeda here. Yes, some here may have their faith in common, but that is all. Do not make the mistake of labelling us terrorists. We are a mixed group with a single cause: we want a better life for our families.'

Fox shook hands with the militant commander, known as Godswill, and took a seat in the large military tent. These militants, most under the banner 'Movement for the Emancipation of the Niger Delta', were a motley crew. That said, they displayed every aspect of being as well-prepared, trained and staffed as they could be under the circumstances. Their motivation was immense and never-ending. Indeed, it was a perpetual state of growth – the more they struck at the government and private oil infrastructure, the more volunteers from the local populace came forward to join the fight. It was like throwing water on an oil fire.

Rollins was the last to greet Godswill. The Nigerian took off his sunglasses to reveal burn scars down his face and hands. They embraced like long-lost brothers, talking close and quietly. Fox thought nothing of it until Rollins handed over a thick envelope. There could be fifty grand in there.

'We actually have a righteous cause that we are pursuing,' Godswill said.

'I'm sure Al Qaeda feel their cause is pretty righteous,' Gammaldi replied as he took a seat.

'You see good in all people – a good quality to have,' Rollins said to Gammaldi.

'A quality that gets you killed, in my line of work,' Javens said.

'We're here to talk about the bombing of the oil building in Port Harcourt,' Fox said, getting back to the point and breaking the ice with a smile. He looked to Godswill. 'We need to know what you know.'

'It was not us,' Godswill said.

'The world thinks differently,' Fox replied. 'Every news cable and television outlet, every –'

'That came directly from the office of Brutus Achebe,' Godswill said. 'His advisor is responsible, the American.'

'Steve Mendes?' Fox asked.

Godswill nodded.

'We met him in Abuja,' Fox said. 'What's his involvement?'

The Nigerian laughed, then said to the two Englishmen: 'You want to tell him?'

Javens turned to Fox and Gammaldi.

'A little background on your American friend,' Javens said. 'Ex-CIA turned gun for hire. He was responsible for providing much of the info that led to Charlie Wilson and co. to up the US funding against the Soviets in Afghanistan.'

'Yeah, right, Operation Cyclone,' Fox said.

'He's one smooth operator,' Rollins said. 'He gets the job done, and it's the main reason why Achebe is seen as a contender for the Nigerian presidency. Steve Mendes is driving a revolution in the economy of this country; it will be the better for it.'

The MEND guy shook his head.

'You don't agree?' Rollins asked. 'He has been instrumental in reforming the oil industry here – he's kicking out the Western companies in favour of those who will put back into communities.'

'We've heard all this talk before, Michael,' Godswill said. 'It never changes. One man is as corrupt as the next. I didn't think you would sympathise with him.'

Rollins didn't respond.

'Well, if it weren't for nine-eleven,' Javens said, 'Mendes would still be a CIA poster boy.'

Fox could sense the Nigerian had more to say about this. Perhaps he didn't because the sympathetic ears he had been expecting from them were not evident.

'What's he done to put you off?' Fox asked.

'He has in his direct employ thousands of private security contractors. Russians,' Godswill said. 'They came with Russian oil money, all the new production areas and contracts are going to them. They planted this bomb, and then Achebe went before the media and pointed the finger at us minutes later. Yes, what Michael said has some truth – Mendes wants a revolution. But at what cost?'

Rollins was still silent.

'Do you have any proof of their involvement in the bombing? Anything that we can use as a source?' Fox asked. He noted for the first time that the smell of marijuana was faintly carried in the wet air.

'You have my word.'

There was a brief pause. Fox took measure of the man's pride. Palpable but frail.

'I'm sorry, but we need more than that,' Fox said. 'Sir, I appreciate your struggle. We need something that we can show the world, contrary to what they're reading and hearing. We need something to back up the truth, to tell your story.'

The man looked Fox in the eyes. He was Fox's age, living in a part of the world that should be as rich as Saudi Arabia, yet the wealth bypassed them all. Instead, they bore the worst that producing oil had to offer. They watched wealth literally being bled from the veins of their land and they were left with a rotting corpse.

'You will all follow me,' Godswill said, and stood, moving out the rear door of the tent.

Rollins led with Fox close behind, walking past a platoon of resting militants under netting.

'My men are active every night, policing the streets against soldiers' attacks and rogue militia groups,' Godswill said. 'We own the night in these delta states, like a community police force, and the people are thankful for it. We are provided with food and supplies from the locals, who see it as a small payment for the safety of their women and children at night. Violence, particularly against women and among young men, is – it's so high in this area.' That frailty was there again – it was a sense of hopelessness that he tried so hard to cover.

Fox and Gammaldi nodded in understanding. The group continued on and they entered another large mess tent. Here, it resembled a military hospital, smelling of disinfectant. Cots were littered with wounded militia, each covered with bandages soaked through with blood. Doctors and nurses in makeshift scrubs were attending them as best they could.

They walked through the tent, the moans of wounded men mixing with those of women and children: this was also a civilian hospital.

'We treat over a hundred people a day,' Godswill said. His face remained passive, as if emotion had left him a long time ago. This man had forgotten how to smile as much as he had learned to cope with violence and despair. 'More than half are from local communities, victims of police and soldiers. There is a civil war going on here, and it's not over religion like in the northern and middle states. Here, it's over the basic rights to live. What these people seek is no more than the most basic living conditions found in any Western country.'

Gammaldi signalled he wanted to take some photos. Godswill nodded his consent.

'Here, you have over a hundred people who will tell you where the evil lies in this country,' Godswill said. 'They will tell you who bombed that building.'

'This won't change anything abroad, I learned that long ago,' Rollins said to Fox. 'You have to go bigger in scope, something political. These small human stories get lost. Look at Sudan. Look at Somalia. Chad.'

'I will not let it get to that,' Godswill said. 'We are strong, and for every man who falls we have two more waiting to pick up his gun and carry on.'

'Sometimes one has to go that extra step, I understand,' Rollins said. His hand was on the MEND leader's shoulder in friendship and support. He looked at Fox. 'We all have to do what we can to make things right. Maybe for us that means that sometimes we have to go beyond reporting. Intervene, make the story something other than history. Shape it. Change it.'

Outside the tent they came to a small clearing in the overgrown canopy and the very last rays of sunlight licked through. The sound of birds here was astounding, the noise from the flocks that converged and darted at insects over the water.

A corrugated-tin roof covered about twenty people working around trestle tables. This was a production-line bomb-making unit. Fox counted dozens of IEDs being built. Improvised Explosive Devices, the weapon of choice in places like Iraq and Afghanistan. They evened out the odds somewhat for militia fighting an enemy in armoured vehicles. Old artillery shells were being wired with remote or timed detonators. Small quantities of off-white C4 were moulded into old food tins, in turn placed in large paint cans full of shrapnel. Wooden boxes held nuts, bolts, screws, nails, scraps of metal and short lengths of steel pipe. Firearms and machetes lay in disordered heaps.

Fox watched kids helping out too. Teenage boys hefted the tins of shrapnel their spindly arms could hardly carry. Younger kids loaded bullets into rifle magazines. There were women of all ages too, doing the most archetypal of tasks while cleaning down firearms and arranging uniforms for their husbands, fathers, brothers and sons to go into the fight. This was more than just family-run operations, more than neighbourhood protection, Fox thought. This was a people fighting over the right to life that their forefathers had enjoyed in this place for centuries. This was the last push for survival before their once-fertile delta region was lost out to pollution for good. These people didn't have to worry about climate change – they wouldn't have a habitat soon. It was the Alamo in an open expanse of waterways that stretched for hundreds of kilometres of coastline. Sheer back-to-the-wall desperation.

'We move this camp and others like it every few days,' Godswill said. He took in the scene as if seeing it for the first time like his four guests. 'These people are here because they want a better life.'

He went to a table and picked up a briefcase, handed it over to Rollins.

'This is what I spoke to you about over the phone,' Godswill said. 'It was taken from a Russian courier, one of the security contractors. Some of it's in Russian – maybe this will be all the evidence you need?'

Rollins nodded, tucked it under his arm.

At the end of this speech Fox noted the sunlight finally blinking out. Before anyone switched to the power-generated lights, the Adhan sounded from an amplified muezzin atop a mosque's minaret calling for the Maghrib. The fourth of the five daily salat and offered at sunset, about half the militants went to prayer. The remainder took a brief rest in waiting for their comrades.

'Why not the rest?' Fox asked Javens.

'Pretty good representation of this area,' Javens said. 'These people are about fifty–fifty Christian and Muslim. They work together, they live together, they fight together. And, as he said, this fight is not about religion. It's about basic standards of living. They want what any people would want and expect from a government.'

Rollins took an offered rug, then knelt into prayer position too. Fox and Gammaldi didn't react but Fox noticed that Javens was surprised. They watched and listened in silence. The MI6 agent looked to Rollins after he got up, a look that said *that's new.*

Before anyone said a word, and in the instant that the bare light-bulbs hanging from the tin roof and from tree branches came alight, gunfire ripped through the air. The deep staccato of heavy-calibre machine-guns.

Fox and the others ducked for cover as tracer rounds shredded into the compound, zapping laser-like through the tin roof. They punched through the tree canopy like hail. The thunder of two Eurocopter Super Puma helicopters raced close to the water straight towards them. In seconds they were overhead and the reverberation from the rotors thumped in Fox's chest.

41

THE
WHITE HOUSE

'A nurse?' McCorkell said, reading over the personnel record on his way down the stairs to the West Wing basement level. 'Jack McFarland. Jesus . . .'

'FBI took him to Bethesda Naval Hospital,' O'Keeffe said. 'He's still unconscious, apparent OD. Deceased has been IDed by the neighbours as his boyfriend. Single stab wound is the likely cause of death, looks like it could have been a domestic dispute.'

'And the deceased's ID?'

They entered the Situation Room and O'Keeffe pointed to one of the large OLED flat-panel screens on the western wall.

'He's our man,' O'Keeffe said. 'Part of an IMU cell we thought we saw the last of in Afghanistan.'

'What are the chances that Jack McFarland knew who his

boyfriend was?' McCorkell asked. 'Did he know he was telling a terrorist the health condition of POTUS?'

'It is possible. FBI and my guys are at Bethesda, ready to talk to him as soon as he comes to,' O'Keeffe said. 'But at this stage my cop gut is telling me that this was an open-shut domestic.'

'Lucky break for us,' McCorkell said. 'So who is he?'

'The deceased is Tahir Massoud,' O'Keeffe said. 'Saudi born. Suspected of the murder of five foreign aide workers and a BBC journalist in Afghanistan. Entered the US three months ago under a false name and Israeli passport.'

'He enter alone?' McCorkell asked.

'No,' O'Keeffe said, grim-faced. 'There were three other men travelling with the same nationality passports and work visas for a dead-end address in Atlanta.' The Secret Service agent got all four immigration photos up on the screens.

'Wait – what's that? That Al Jazeera?' McCorkell asked, indicating the news image displayed on a section of the massive screen at one end of the room. An aide worked the controls and the image and sound now took up half the space.

'Al Jazeera is running the story now!' the DHS agent replied. 'IMU cell have claimed the attack. Two men from Islamic Movement of Uzbekistan, names and pics, as pilots of the boats that struck the LOOP.'

'Run it through the facial –'

'That's them,' O'Keeffe said, pointing to two of the faces who had entered the US. 'I don't need facial rec to put this together – they are two of the guys Massoud entered the country with.'

McCorkell watched the footage. The image of the smouldering LOOP structure was shown in the background along with the names and photos of the two Afghani-born martyrs.

'Tell me the NSA is tracking that Al Jazeera tip-off,' McCorkell asked an agent on the phone – receiving a nod in the affirmative in reply.

'We're tilting the earth to find the fourth guy,' Mark Kipling, Director of National Intelligence, said. 'We're tracking names, faces –'

'We've got three of them kicked out of a Tampa strip-bar four nights ago,' the FBI agent said. 'Got a bit touchy-feely during amateur hour.'

'Looks like they wanted a sneak peek of what lay ahead for them in the afterlife. Someone get that shit to Al Jazeera and CNN, see how their sympathisers view their martyrs now,' McCorkell said. He turned to the FBI agent. 'Anyone see them arrive or leave the bar? Surveillance of the area, car park, door cams?'

'Working through it now,' the FBI agent said. He was the mouthpiece for the FBI in the room, a direct line of access for the White House to the massive workforce of the FBI's National Security Branch. 'Got a hit on the passport alias. Car rental company in Miami. Matches a vehicle that left the club in Tampa – yep, here's the image now, Ford Escape with four occupants, security footage from car park.'

McCorkell considered the grainy footage.

'I got a traffic camera which clocked that vehicle speeding later that night – make it early the next morning – on Highway One,' the FBI agent said. 'Southbound, just before the Keys' Overseas Highway.'

'Get FBI CT teams in the area, alert Miami SWAT, have anyone with serious firepower ready to move,' McCorkell said.

Fullop entered the Situation Room with the Acting President.

'SPR draw-downs?' McCorkell asked. The pair had come from the Cabinet meeting in the Executive Briefing Room under the East Wing.

'The Cabinet's with me. We're sitting firm for now,' Fullop said, taking a seat next to the Acting President.

'Mr Vice President, the LOOP will be out of action for days,' McCorkell said. 'That's a big disruption to a big percentage of our oil imports. I've just learned that the Nigerian political landscape may change real fast. If we don't release the Strategic Petroleum Reserve right now, we'll see gas prices at the pump rising a couple of dollars over the next few days.'

'We're staying put for now,' Jackson said. 'Let's not knee-jerk here. Now, what we got here – who're the Arabs on screen?'

McCorkell motioned for an aide to update them, then he led O'Keeffe outside the room.

'What's the status of POTUS?'

'Just out of recovery, doing fine. He's spending tonight at Washington Hospital Center, we got it locked down good,' O'Keeffe said, misreading McCorkell's concern. 'No one's getting near him.'

Bill McCorkell weighed up some options. The wheels were grinding again.

'Have a car ready to take me to see the President in –' McCorkell checked his watch, 'twenty minutes.'

O'Keeffe nodded and relayed the order into his sleeve mic. McCorkell entered the Situation Room again and moved to the Chairman of the Joint Chiefs.

'What's that squid gut of yours telling you, Don?' McCorkell asked the Admiral.

'We've had over eight groups claim the attack so far,' Vanzet said. 'Al Qaeda or ICU seem more legit. These IMU boys can't punch this hard and they're far from home without serious help.'

'Al Qaeda . . .' McCorkell said. 'Massoud's the right pedigree . . . The IMU may be a smokescreen to make it clear these guys weren't Saudi backed?'

Vanzet and O'Keeffe nodded. McCorkell turned to address the room:

'I want to know everything about these guys.' McCorkell pointed at the screen as he spoke. 'Where they sleep when they're not on our soil, where they eat, who wiped their asses when they were kids. Everything.'

'Agency rap sheets are here,' the CIA liaison said. He opened the computer files on a wall-mounted screen. 'Their known activities include every Islamist hot spot of the past fifteen years – Chechnya, 'Stan, Iraq, Pakistan, Somalia, Indonesia –'

'Massoud was not far out of the FBI's Most Wanted,' the FBI agent said. 'He has several documented travels in Indonesia, confirmed as having provided materiel support to Jemaah Islamiyah.'

'Might have met his Afghani play friends over there,' McCorkell said. 'Call up the agency team heading this –'

'On line three,' the CIA rep said.

'Have them put everything on these guys, press every humint asset they can to see if we can find out who they've been playing with.'

The agency rep motioned to speak.

'Yep?' McCorkell said.

'Last known IMU cell activity was Kabul '04, where their senior leadership was declared dead as killed by a missile strike from an Agency Predator UAV.'

'Whose op was that?' McCorkell asked. He waited a few seconds for the reply, then repeated himself to the clean-cut analyst in the light grey suit. 'Whose op, and who declared them dead?'

'CIA High Value Target hunting team called in the strike after a tip-off of location and confirmation by Grey Wolf operators. Lead agent was a Steve Mendes.'

'Steve Mendes?'

'He was a senior Agency NOC agent in –'

'Now freelance in Nigeria,' McCorkell said.

'That's right . . .' The young Agency guy looked surprised.

'Have everything you can get on Mendes sent through to my office, and cc in the DDCIA of Operations – sorry, of NCS,' McCorkell said. 'Mark, I'll need you to clear some locked files on Mendes from Boxcell's days and have them sent to me too.'

The DNI nodded and spoke to a staffer.

'Don,' McCorkell said, 'I'll be on the cell if you need me.'

'I got it,' Vanzet said. 'We hauling anything into Nigeria besides the *Wasp*?'

McCorkell looked to Jackson, the Chief of Staff whispering in his ear with running commentary.

'You're the acting Commander-in-Chief right now,' McCorkell said. 'As your National Security Advisor, I'm telling you this: we need security ready to roll to help stabilise the government in Nigeria.'

'They asked for our help?' Fullop queried, acting point-guard on his man.

'It's likely their president doesn't know how close the coup is,' McCorkell said. 'We can have the State Department send someone in to tell him.'

'A small element of the 10th Mountain's 1st Brigade Combat Team is already headed to Abuja to ensure the security of the US embassy there,' Vanzet said. 'The rest of their squadron is en route to Darfur. They're in V-22s and C-17s, the latter refuelling in Rota, Spain. They can re-route.'

'Direct them to the airport in Abuja?' McCorkell said. 'Send them in as a security force for the Nigerian President?'

'If this coup happens and there's trouble that could be a hot LZ,' Vanzet said. 'C-17s are big targets. I say wait and hear what the lead element in the V-22s report in.'

'The lead element of the 1st BCT is a single platoon from their reinforced RSTA squadron, designated chalks one through four,' the Air Force aide said. 'Current location over southern Algeria.'

'They can secure the airfield if need be?'

'We'll need to wait and see what the initial force report in,' Vanzet said. 'But make no mistake: a full 10th Mountain BCT could defend DC from the devil.'

McCorkell looked to Vanzet, who nodded his consent. He turned to Jackson who'd been taking it all in – military actions 101.

'Bill, Don,' Jackson said. 'This has to be done?'

'If you want to secure the government, yes, sir,' Vanzet said. 'And if this coup becomes a threat to our national security, it means we can have a more flexible military option available to us.'

McCorkell nodded.

'Sir,' Fullop said to the Vice President. 'I think if we are talking about sending in troops, we should talk about forces heading for the coastal areas. Wait for the two-thousand-strong Marine force aboard the *Wasp*; secure the delta region, that's where the oil's at.'

'Don, how many troops would it take to secure the Niger Delta?' McCorkell asked. They'd had this discussion before and it was the sort of thing that the Pentagon war-gamed at constantly.

'A hundred thousand, give or take,' Vanzet said. 'And that's just in the major cities. If we have to police a civil conflict in Nigeria as well as protect oil infrastructure, at least double that number.'

McCorkell looked at Peter Larter, Secretary of Defense, eyebrows raised: *You got that many shooters available?*

'Mr Vice President, a security force of that size can't be assembled inside a month,' Larter said. 'And even then, we'd be stretched. I'm talking we'd have to pull most of our boots out of South Korea and expand our stop-loss program.'

'If Nigeria goes down, our economy goes down,' McCorkell said, a last ditch at getting the men he knew were needed onto the ground. 'An attack on oil production there is an attack on the American way of life. Put it this way – if no oil gets to us from Nigeria, we'll lose those three million American jobs the Cabinet just heard about, and that's just the ramifications this week. We add this so soon on the back of the credit crisis, we're talking the deepest recession we've felt in our time.'

'Jesus . . .' Jackson said.

'No, not even He can help us – but you can,' Fullop said. 'I say, do a national broadcast, prime-time tonight, assuring the nation – and the markets – that following the attack at the LOOP we have everything under control. Ask for international help in calming political unrest in Nigeria.'

Jackson tapped his fingers on the table. The decision was close. McCorkell could see that Fullop's proposition of a TV spot was alluring to a man who wanted public perception to associate him with the Oval Office.

'How about the UN?' Jackson asked. 'Could they send in a force?'

'Give them twelve months, maybe,' McCorkell said.

'Having a few boots on the ground to safeguard the Nigerian presidency is not enough,' Fullop said. 'Oil flow can still be cut off and a stalemate for power will ensue for God knows how long. You want to secure it, wait for the power shift and support the new guy. Show him we mean business by a show of power. Lead with an MEU and carrier group, follow up with an armoured division, and have the entire airborne corps fall in from the sky. Shock and awe tactics, in and out, and leave no doubt that we can be back in hours. We can have the hundred-K boots there within a month and ensure the new government sees things our way.'

'We are stretched too thin to police their delta region,' Larter said. 'Nigeria has nearly ten times the population of Iraq. You really sure you want to put an occupying force into that? I know I don't.'

'Then we work on gaining command of their own army to police it,' Fullop said.

There was silence as the room considered all that had just been discussed, just the hum of air-conditioning and the aides tapping away at laptops.

'The Abuja airlift of 10th Mountain is a good first action, Mr Vice President,' McCorkell said. 'Within a day our boys will secure the elected Nigerian government. They will have air cover, and their transport will stay on the ground ready to bug them out if need be.'

Fullop looked down at the table and shook his head, a touch of drama.

'I'm not sure the President would agree about sending US forces so deep into a potentially hostile country,' he said, clutching at a last straw. 'And who knows, maybe this Achebe government *will* be better for us?'

'Well, right now I hold that office,' Jackson said. 'And this is the direction we're going in: Bill, Don, Pete – get your boys moving towards Abuja, whatever we've got spare that's close. Buy us more time. Give us options.'

'That's a green light to stabilise the government?' Bill McCorkell asked.

'Did he say that?' Fullop said, sensing a victory in this argument was still within his reach. 'I think you need –'

'Look,' the VP said. 'Move them to the area. Secure the elected government. Have the State Department let the Nigerian President know what's going down in his backyard. And I don't want us taking our eyes off the ball here at home. We've had an attack on American soil today that has taken innocent lives. Make no mistake: no one fucks with America tonight.'

42

PORT HARCOURT CITY LIMITS, THE NIGER DELTA

Fox had trained with the best military operators in the world. He'd seen action in Timor, Iraq, Afghanistan. He'd been shot at too many times to count, and hit twice, which was two times more than he would have liked. He also well knew that there is a sensation that comes with being under fire that one never gets used to. The sounds you can train yourself to cope with, to react the right way around. But it's the randomness that you can never escape. The unpredictable nature of an unknown enemy. The chaos of munitions exploding around you. It leaves the best-trained weary, the untrained behind.

Fox ushered Gammaldi across the ground, pushing him towards the riverbank. The militia were responding with fire now, the deep crack-crack-crack of 7.62 mm rounds from the L1A1s, the fast staccato of AK-47s peppering the air.

'Boats, twenty metres!' Fox called to Javens, who had Rollins pinned to the ground by the back of his shirt collar.

'Got it, move in five seconds,' Javens said, getting ready to move. He grabbed his Walther from Godswill, who looked about himself in the darkness. The whites of his eyes were alive but calm – he was used to this, this was his kind of warfare and it was about to be fought on his terms.

A militia soldier fell by Fox's feet and Fox took his L1A1 and passed Gammaldi a Browning High Power pistol.

'Let's move!' Fox said, leading the way to one of several tin boats with outboard motors. Militiamen were lined up on the riverbank, hunkered behind sandbag cover as they fired up at the helicopters that were now making another pass. Several RPGs whistled into the sky, the dark night swallowing them up.

Fox had the outboard going and powered away from the bank as the three climbed aboard. The Honda outboard was at full throttle; the bow rose into the air and twisted with the torque pressure. As they rounded a bend away from the camp, several attack boats came in from behind them, the militiamen pouring fire towards them.

'Contacts ahead – get your heads down!' Fox yelled over the battle sounds. Two big watercraft with wind turbines on the back, like the airboats you'd see in the swamps of the US, came fast at them, machine guns mounted on the sterns spitting out long arcs of 7.62 mm tracer rounds.

'They're militia!' Gammaldi said, as the two craft flashed by either side of theirs to go and join the fight in aid of their comrades under attack.

'Take this left –'

'I got it,' Fox said, rounding the bend. 'I'll take us back the way we came.'

It was eerie now. Fox's heart raced at one-eighty as he navigated the river bends, the other men equally on edge as they scanned for threats. The sounds of dozens of firearms intermingled with explosions from RPGs and grenades. Fires licked into the humid air and smoke punched into the heavens with each explosion, the mushroom tops floating into nothing.

'I can see the boathouse ahead,' Javens said.

'Got it, cover our approach,' Fox replied. Both Gammaldi and Javens were in stable firing positions at the prow, while Rollins kept himself in a tight ball in the middle of the boat, clutching the briefcase that Godswill had given him.

Inside the boathouse Fox killed the engine and held the boat to the timber jetty for the others to jump off. They retraced their path through the courtyard, the bakery, and into the street. The firefight was still within hearing range, and the two militants had long disappeared from their post guarding the Range Rover.

Javens opened it and they piled in, Fox up front in the passenger seat this time. He tossed the L1A1 to the ground, as it was far too long a rifle to use within the car. Climbing in, he unholstered the snub-nosed MP-5K strapped to his side of the console. Ejected the clip, checked it was full, rammed it back home and chambered a round.

No sooner was the last door shut than Javens had the black beast roaring down the gravel road. Only the under-bumper driving lights lit the way ahead as the MI6 man navigated the streets, with a couple of near misses as two vans loaded with militia raced past.

'Buckle up,' Fox called, doing up his own seatbelt.

They passed scores of locals running – men and women, old and young, kids even. Running towards the firefight. Almost all were unarmed.

'Why are they heading towards the trouble?' Gammaldi asked.

'They're going to help in any way that they can,' Rollins replied.

They rode in silence for a few blocks, watching the crowds race past them. Fox watched them move by as if in slow motion. The faces were those who had seen violence their entire lives, possessed of the type of psyche that has built up a tolerance to what most people could never fathom as bearable.

'Where're we headed?' Fox asked.

'Over land, the airport is too choked up with oil companies leaving, this is a city tearing itself apart,' Javens said. 'We'll make for the Deputy High Commission in Lagos, we've got regular airlifts out –'

'Helo just buzzed overhead!' Gammaldi said, the aviator craning to look out the side and back windows.

'He see us?'

'Don't think –'

Machine-gun fire tore up the road to their left and pounded a row of storefronts, concrete and glass disintegrating in showers of dust and debris that they drove through like a sandstorm.

Fox watched as the helo zipped overhead and made a banking manoeuvre – heading back, straight at them.

'You got anything else in this rig?'

'Two smoke grenades in the glove box,' Javens said, taking a hard right as two tracer streams tore up the road ahead like laser beams. Despite the low-profile tyres and super-low air suspension, the Range Rover threatened to roll in protest of taking a sharp corner at eighty clicks an hour. 'This baby is armoured, but anything heavier than rifle rounds and I'd rather not be in here.'

'You read my mind,' Fox said. He pulled out the smoke grenades, and passed one over his shoulder to Gammaldi. Normally used for signalling to aircraft, in this case they might provide some cover.

Javens noticed Fox contemplating the grenade.

'Sorry, old chap, but 007 beat me to the garage; he took the Rover that had the heat-seeking Stingers built into the roof.'

'Fucking Bond,' Fox said, smiling as a plan formed. 'Take a hard turn behind some buildings and come to a stop – we'll release the smoke and fire through it with the MP5s.'

'Got it,' Javens said, squinting ahead. 'Hard left, five seconds!'

Fox nodded to Gammaldi in the back and both men pressed 'down' on their windows. The thick bullet-proof glass slid away as they pulled the pins on the grenades.

'Now!' Fox yelled. He and Gammaldi tossed the grenades, the orange smoke billowing into the sky. In moments they were surrounded by it, the plumes twice as high as the two-storey buildings that made up the street canyon they were in. The Range Rover skidded to a stop under ABS – Fox leaned out of his open window and looked down the sights of the MP5K. He flipped the switch on the submachine gun, just forward of the pistol grip – FULL AUTO. He took a sniper's breath – measured, calm, steady. The sound of the helicopter thumped down on them, appeared for a brief moment – entering the space that Fox pre-sighted. Wild shots sprayed the buildings as the helicopter pilots juggled shooting with this new surprise ahead of them, as Fox let rip the entire clip perfectly. It was a couple of heartbeats before the helicopter was in the space he'd just fired into, and every bullet hit home, the left-side canopy becoming spider-webs as it shattered. Something bright red painted the interior while Gammaldi's MP5K clip hit home along the length of the fuselage as it passed close overhead, the sound like hail on a tin roof.

Javens planted his foot and spun the wheel, and they were out of there as he did a one-eighty on a dime. Fox and Gammaldi pulled themselves in and pressed the windows back up.

All occupants scanned the sky, even Javens as he navigated the streets. The massive supercharged engine was roaring.

They travelled ten blocks before anyone was game to call it.

'We've lost them,' Fox said. He turned in his seat and punched fists with Gammaldi.

'Victory!' Gammaldi mock-yelled like a Viking.

Javens settled to a more sedate driving style, more rally-driving through city streets rather than driving for the last few miles of the Dakar with another team on your tail.

'Clutching on to that briefcase pretty tight,' Fox said to Rollins. 'Checked it out yet?'

Rollins audibly exhaled, then loosened his grip and popped the clasps.

'I think –' Rollins was looking forward and his eyes went like saucers. Fox tensed at the look and spun around in the seat –

'Hard left!' Rollins yelled.

Two MOPOL police vans were ahead, and an unmarked Toyota Land Cruiser. A dozen guys with guns let fire, bullets sparking as they struck the Range Rover.

'RPG!' Fox yelled.

The world seemed to halt in Fox's point of view. The flaming rocket-propelled grenade corkscrewed its way straight at them.

Javens hit the brakes and yanked hard to the right but it was too late, the RPG struck the rear of the Range Rover and took out a back wheel and the rear-window. The interior filled with dark acrid smoke.

Fox looked out the back-window hole – their rear wheel was bouncing down the street. They were still travelling at sixty kilometres per hour on three wheels.

'Lost the brakes!' Javens said.

They were lame ducks in the long expanse of street ahead, with no turn-offs visible.

'Hold tight!' Javens said, taking another hard turn that took them straight through the glass front of a bookstore – and he kept the accelerator to the floor, the three wheels driving the three-tonne tank through stacks of shelves and right out through the back wall – all twelve airbags deployed – and into the next street where they T-boned into a row of parked cars and came to a smoking halt. Bricks and debris covered the windshield.

Fox and Javens were out in a flash, guns drawn, scanning for threats. There was banging from the inside of the car – Gammaldi on the glass of Rollins's side window.

'Door – open!'

Fox slung the strap of the MP5K across his shoulder as he placed a foot on the side of car and yanked on the door handle. It wasn't going anywhere, jammed tight.

'Climb through the front!' Fox yelled, as bullets tore up the road behind him.

Javens was at the back of the Range Rover for cover, firing from one knee at the approaching MOPOL sedan.

'Clip!' Fox yelled – and caught a fresh mag in one hand from Javens as he ejected with the other. He reloaded like a pro, military training coming back to him in the well-drilled precision that never leaves a Special Forces soldier.

The attacking sedan had a passenger and back-seat gunner, both with pistols. Javens and Fox let rip with two clips on full-auto – the interior looked like a bomb had gone off. The siren stopped but the remaining red light still swirled as the lifeless car passed them and continued on down the street, carried by inertia.

Javens ran across and checked for survivors. He reached in, retrieved something, came running back.

Rollins and Gammaldi were out of the Range Rover, and they scanned the scene. A few civilian cars had stopped farther up the street; the occupants had run from the mayhem when the bloodied police car ambled past.

'They're after you, all of you,' Javens said. He presented what he'd taken from the police car – photocopied pictures of the three of them. All taken from a long-lens camera.

'They're from the airport earlier today,' Rollins said. 'Why would they be after us?'

'Cars, let's move!' Fox said, and led the way to the deserted vehicles. It was a two-hundred-metre dash that felt like two kilometres by the time they got there.

'The Jag!' Javens said.

Bullets ricocheted off the bitumen at Fox's feet, a couple more disintegrating the side windows of the Jaguar. He drew his Five-seveN pistol from his backpack and fired two double taps at the approaching Land Cruiser – its driver swerved into a side street, the mortally wounded gunman almost falling out of his open passenger window.

It was decision time. Fox looked up and down the street. It was deserted for the moment, but not for long. Four empty cars still had their engines running. The Range Rover was now on fire down the road and the dead police car was stopped at about the same distance down the other end of the street, its light still slowly revolving. In an instant the heavens opened up and rain belted down on them in a wet-season downpour.

Fox moved to Javens. The intelligence man knew the plan. 'I'll head the chase off,' Fox said.

Javens shook his head. 'I'll do it. I'll take the Jag and lead the chase elsewhere,' he said. He ran a hand through his wet blond hair. 'Take the highway to Lagos, Rollins knows the route. I'll alert the Deputy High Commission that you're on your way.'

'You know the way better than me. I'll spread the chase around here,' Fox said. But he knew that the Englishman was right.

'I know these roads, and I know people around here. Take the others and get in that Golf and drive as fast as you can,' Javens said. He didn't bother with handshakes or goodbyes. He got in the Jaguar and gunned the old V12 engine. 'Besides, I work better alone.'

43

THE
WHITE HOUSE

McCorkell left the bathroom and walked into his office. He entered his password into his computer and scanned the emailed information on former CIA agent Steve Mendes. Within seconds he had his phone on his shoulder, waiting for the White House operator to connect him through.

'Ridley, Bill McCorkell.'

'Get the info on Mendes?' the DDCIA asked.

'Just reading it now,' McCorkell said, scrolling down the CIA personnel file on his screen. 'He left the agency in a mess. Suspension of duty, that's what was suppressed in his file?'

'That, as well as some deniable ops stuff in Iran and some erroneous rendition details. The previous director cleared his slate after a bargain: Mendes gave us a Taliban leadership cell and nearly got himself killed in the process. Evidently it worked in his favour too, as that cell was in opposition to the forces he had allied himself with in the north of Afghanistan. Seems he had two employers for a while at the end there.'

'The agency and who?'

'Whoever paid the highest,' Ridley said. 'I've got an FBI counter-espionage agent on my other line who has an ongoing investigation on Mendes, he seems to know this guy inside-out.'

'Patch him in,' McCorkell said.

'Andrew, you there?' Ridley asked.

'Yep,' the voice said. 'Mr McCorkell, Special Agent Andrew Hutchinson.'

'Ridley was just telling me that Mendes went gun for hire.'

'That's right,' Hutchinson said. 'Russia, Azerbaijan, Kazakhstan, Afghanistan –'

'Right, got it, all the "Stans",' McCorkell said. 'I suppose Uzbekistan is on that list?'

'Yep,' Hutchinson said. 'Worked with the richest guy there, I'm talking serious oil money, then helped him make a push for presidency.'

'What happened?'

'Two weeks before the polls he was assassinated by his own brother,' Hutchinson said. 'Poisoned.'

McCorkell chewed the info over for a moment.

'Mendes ever do anything to connect him to the IMU?'

'IMU were the eastern franchise of Al Qaeda at the time he was in the country. He was known to those guys, and they had a price on his head – probably still do,' Hutchinson said. 'He worked on their turf for a few years, hunting Al Qaeda mainly, then not long after the US invasion he called in a Predator strike against a known IMU leadership meeting with senior Taliban in northern Afghanistan.'

'Right, I got that one,' McCorkell said. He read over the file. 'He called them in as KIA from a Hellfire strike launched from an Agency Predator UAV. My problem is, Al Jazeera have just announced two of those listed as KIA as those responsible for the LOOP attack.'

'They what?' the FBI agent said.

'Al Jazeera called it not ten minutes ago,' McCorkell said, checking his watch. 'Look, both of you go over this stuff and get back to me with a total file on this guy, the short version. Ridley, get any and all assets you can into Nigeria –'

'Most people are headed back Stateside, the oil industry –'

'Just get assets in there.' McCorkell noticed another line still blinking on his phone. 'We got some DoD cavalry inbound to play, possibly to take Mendes and Achebe out if it comes to that.'

'Mr McCorkell,' Hutchinson said. 'Ever heard of a CIA operation called Magellan?'

'Yeah, the picking up of ex-KGB types after the Soviet Union folded,' McCorkell said. 'We and some NATO countries extended olive branches to many of the old spies, to make sure that we didn't have thousands of them becoming guns for hire.'

'And it nearly worked too,' Ridley said. 'We kept the numbers that went on to terrorist organisations pretty damn low.'

'But a lot of these guys slipped through, or got much better offers from Iran and Chechnya and the like,' McCorkell said. 'What's this got to do with Mendes?'

'These Russians formed quite the club,' Hutchinson said. 'Problem is, some of them formed their own club within the club. We think it's called Umbra.'

'That's CIA myth,' Ridley said.

'That's because they're good,' Hutchinson replied. 'Steve Mendes was one of the point guys for Magellan in picking up these Ruskies in the first place. He was a money man, a transporter, a recruiter.'

'And you're gonna tell me he recruited his own little team on the side?'

'You got it, Mr McCorkell,' Hutchinson said. 'Our good friend Robert Boxcell was the Moscow Station Chief at the time and had the green light on the spending budget for Magellan. Hell, we were throwing money at these ex-KGB guys to keep them from straying to the dark side.'

'What was Boxcell's connection with Mendes?'

'A few months back, Boxcell tried to get control of the NSA's Echelon system,' Hutchinson said. 'We've since got intel that that was his endgame. Having that communications intelligence capability, this Umbra brotherhood of ex spooks would have been flush with cash for eternity, through insider trading, blackmail, you name it. As it is, they're into every cash-cow business you could imagine. Oil in Nigeria and Venezuela, water projects in South America and the sub-continent, dozens of arms companies – mostly selling looted Soviet stuff and even some Iraqi gear has turned up in the arms bazaars being sold by these guys. Their businesses are legit, it's just the way that they go about their business that stinks. They make the mob look like schoolkids.'

'How far up the food chain is Mendes?'

'Close to the top,' Hutchinson said. 'Look, I've had a team of twelve guys on this round the clock for five months and we're just scratching the surface.'

'Need me to get you a bigger team?' Ridley offered. 'Inter-agency?'

'Nope, we're a closed unit here,' Hutchinson said.

'There's something else you've not told us,' McCorkell said. 'What's their objective?'

'We're working on that,' Hutchinson said, desperation in his voice. 'As far as we can tell, it's all about making profit for the members to share around and get even richer. I was serious about the mob reference. A few of my team are the Bureaus' finest, busted up mob outfits over the past three decades. This is much more organised than anything we've ever seen. And the scary version?'

'Yeah?'

'The Ruskies had a unit specialised at getting WMD out of conflict zones –'

'You think these guys got Iraq's?' Ridley asked.

'We've got some known ex-soldiers from that special Russian unit selling ex-Iraqi military hardware looted after the fall of Saddam,' Hutchinson said. 'You think those guys were in country and didn't take the good stuff while they were there?'

'Jesus. All right,' McCorkell said. 'Both of you, keep me posted on this. I'll let you know where we get with Mendes.'

'If I had any input, I'd say let the guy keep going at whatever he's doing,' Hutchinson said. 'I know that's not an easy thing to agree to, but another six months or so and I think we'll be on track to get to his level in the organisation. Maybe even those above him.'

'Keep me posted,' McCorkell repeated.

He hung up the connection with a finger and hit the other line that was blinking as his secretary came to the open door.

'Your ride to Washington Hospital is at the South Portico,' she said.

McCorkell nodded his thanks.

'I'm sorry – who is this?' He strained as he listened to his telephone, the crackling static of a bad cell line on the other end.

'Bill, it's Lachlan Fox! Can you hear me?'

44

LAGOS, NIGERIA

Fox had driven through the night, the old VW Golf running smoother since he'd stopped and filled the fuel tank, added a litre of oil to the engine and air into the bald tyres. He wiped the drowsiness and sweat from his eyes, the sweat that came in the early-morning humidity which even the sun's first rays seemed to produce. It was like a humidity switch, where this country instantly became a hot, sticky place to be. The interior of the car was almost all metal save the bead-covered seats. Twenty years of this environment had steamed the linings off the dull red frame.

'Still no cell network on either of our phones,' Rollins said, putting his cell phone away. He sat in the passenger seat, cradling the briefcase, the contents of which he was just now reading. The sound of the Adhan came through the open windows, marking the morning prayer time for the weary travellers.

'That normal here, the bad cell network coverage?' Fox asked. His last call, to McCorkell, had cut out after just a minute of conversation. Just long enough for McCorkell to tell Fox he needed him to stay put in Nigeria, to be his *man on the ground*.

'I haven't seen it this bad, they must be having problems,' Rollins replied. Pointed up ahead. 'You'll need to take this turn off to Victoria Island.'

Rollins began talking quietly, reciting along with the distant muezzin.

'*Allahu Akbar, Allahu Akbar, Allahu Akbar . . .*'

Fox found something infinitely comforting in the tone and phonetics of speech in the Englishman's prayers. Many of the cars on the road were pulled over, their occupants kneeling on well-worn rugs as they went about the Fajr. Other cars driven by the country's Christians continued on, their drivers and occupants as used to the ritual around them as the morning song of birds. Even those creatures seemed dulled in respect for a greater sound that filled the world right now.

It was the sound of awakening.

'That line . . .' Fox said, when Rollins had finished.

'*Aṣ-ṣalā tu khayru min an-na ū m.* I've not heard it before – what does it mean?'

'It's a line in the Sunni first daily prayer,' Rollins said. 'It translates to "Prayer is better than sleep".'

Gammaldi awoke with a snort on the back seat, making both men in the front laugh.

'Have you made the Hajj?' Fox asked. The pilgrimage to Mecca was another of the Five Pillars of Islam.

It took a while for Rollins to answer.

'I thought I had,' Rollins said. 'For a long time, I thought I had. But it was in my mind.'

'Tell me,' Fox said, in the tone of someone asking for explanation from someone who knew a secret. This man had been through the unimaginable and survived. He had an inner peace that Fox dreamed of obtaining. 'You said you found God when you were in detention. What did it do for you? How did . . .'

'It's funny, now,' Rollins said, with a distant look as he gazed through the windscreen. 'I was born in London, raised a Catholic. My father's mother was Kurdish and his father Iraqi, but he was raised an atheist in the UK from age ten and slowly became Christian through my mother, a Catholic Englishwoman. They taught me all the major religions, which got me into some trouble when I boarded at a Catholic high school.'

Fox geared down as he turned onto the ring road. He saw in the rear-view mirror that Gammaldi had sat upright, though his face and hair were of one still asleep.

'There's something in Islam that spoke to me when I wished for help,' Rollins said. 'After two months in detention they gave me a Qur'an. For the first day I just held it, didn't dare open it in case it was empty. It had all the hallmarks I'd known in the Bible and then took me to places that I wished to inhabit. Those pages really took me somewhere else. I was at school again.'

They drove along a wide road lined with towering coconut palms.

'Will you raise your daughter as a Muslim?' Fox asked.

'I think, like my parents, I will teach my children all religions, and let them find their own path,' Rollins said. 'In a way, I can understand if Nigeria is to come under Sharia Law. It will be a way to make many steps forward in one leap. Ah – this turn up here will take us on to Ahmadu Bello Way.'

Fox navigated the turn and traffic appeared up ahead. The road was lined with cars and hundreds of people queued up. Families, young and old; it was obvious they'd camped out all night and maybe more.

'They are Nigerians seeking visas into the UK,' Rollins said. 'It has been like this for years . . .'

'We there yet?' Gammaldi asked from the back seat.

Fox looked at Gammaldi in the mirror again, and beyond his dark tangle of Italian hair, down the street behind them, spotted the glimpse of a gun –

'Heads down!' Fox yelled. The rear window shattered from rifle fire. Fox geared down into third and weaved into the free oncoming lane as another salvo shredded their rear tyres.

'Deputy High Commission – on our left – turn left!' Rollins said, peering over the dash.

Fox pulled on the handbrake and the last of the rubber on the rear tyres tore off the steel rims. The front-wheel-drive surged left, sparks flying in their wake as Fox floored the accelerator.

In the rear seat Gammaldi emptied the clip from the Browning High Power towards the Land Cruiser that pursued them. A splash of red appeared on the side window as a bullet found its mark. The smell of black powder filled the VW.

'They're security contractors!' Gammaldi said. He took Fox's pistol from the backpack and fired double-handed, his hands resting on the rear shelf, the bullets blowing out the Toyota's radiator causing steam to erupt. The crowds that lined the street ducked and screamed as they sought cover.

'Hold on tight! Exit left doors, three seconds!' Fox said. The Deputy High Commission was dead ahead, its cyclone-wire outer fence already next to them. He drove up onto the hastily evacuated sidewalk, now driving between the fence and the parked cars on the road. Those vehicles provided relative cover as gunmen in the pursuing Land Cruiser let rip with submachine-gun fire that devastated the parked cars and sent splinters of steel and glass into the little red Golf.

'Now!' Fox said, stomping on the brakes. The car stalled and screeched to an agonisingly slow stop not ten metres from the entry gate. Two Royal Marines were there, L85A2 assault rifles shouldered at the approaching threat – they came under fire from the passing Land Cruiser, ducked instinctively for cover, and then moved to engage the vehicle.

Gammaldi and Rollins were out the left-side doors and moving close to the ground. Both Royal Marines in front of them were down; one ignored the blood pumping out of his leg and continued to return fire towards the Land Cruiser.

Fox climbed over the gear stick as more bullets tore into the Golf, shrapnel ricocheting and tearing through his shirt and turning his chest crimson. He ran ground-close and bumped into Gammaldi, who was kneeling beside Rollins.

'Let's move inside the compound!' Fox said.

Gammaldi shook his head, steadfast with Rollins.

Two bullet holes had drilled through the black leather briefcase – they'd found a home in Rollins's stomach. His legs were twitching involuntarily. Blood pumped out of his wounds, seemingly too fast to be fixed.

More Marines were at the gate now, firing with assault rifles and SIG pistols at the fleeing Land Cruiser, which fishtailed away down the street.

Fox looked from Rollins's wounds to Gammaldi. Amid the shouting and cries from the queued-up Nigerians the gunshots in the air fell silent. It was the quietest moment Fox could ever remember. He called to a Marine for help but he would never be sure if any sound came out. Even the distant thunderclap of a grenade sounded hollow, more of a bright orange flash and puff of smoke as the Nigerians crowded away from the embassy as fast as they could, Royal Marines taking cover and scanning for threats – screaming orders among themselves, guns raised and at hair-trigger.

Fox looked down at Rollins. The reporter's head was on Gammaldi's lap. Fox held his hands tight against the man's bleeding stomach. His blood was like the warmest water but it was a thick and visceral fluid that covered Fox's hands and stained the pavement.

'I'm sorry, Michael,' Fox said. The Englishman looked up to him. There wasn't any pain registering on his face. In fact, he had that same look on his face that he had worn earlier when they had been in the boat and he'd first spoken of God.

For Fox, the picture of another man was there in Michael Rollins's face. And it became someone else again. Rollins wore the many faces of the departed, of all those Fox wished were still here.

'Lachlan, do you hear?' Rollins said. There was hope and happiness and a look that was more prepared than Fox had ever thought possible. 'Do you see?'

Fox released the pressure to Rollins's stomach as the man

used the last of his strength to hold Fox's hands. Fox gripped hard through the blood on his hands to keep purchase.

'Listen . . .' Rollins said.

Through the shouting and footfalls of the fleeing Nigerians and the well-drilled clacking of military boots Fox heard what could have been the river. It sounded like all the voices around them, carrying the life of Africa and gracing the world as it spilled out here, giving life to the sea.

'I hear it,' Fox said. The older man smiled up at him, that same peaceful smile.

'I . . . I'm going there,' Rollins said. His face held a final frame that carried serenity in knowledge. 'I am going into . . . the unity of all things.'

Rain began to fall in a big warm curtain that advanced upon them, and as it hit the sticky, hot, blood-soaked pavement it immediately turned into vapour that whispered up into the air.

PART THREE

45

LONDON

Fox knocked a second time on the red door. A thick old thing, with a fresh coat of red high-gloss paint bordered with a white doorframe and set in the dark bricks that were uniform in the street. The door still had some masking tape on the dimpled glass panel, remnants of the Rollins family improving their home. Fox stood there in jeans, T-shirt, sports jacket. Aside from his boots, he'd bought all the clothes at Heathrow, dumping his blood-stained gear in the airport bathroom. He hadn't risked going back to the hotel in Lagos – he and Gammaldi had been ushered via helo from the Deputy High Commission to the airport and boarded a waiting BA flight evacuating British nationals out of the country. He looked down at his black boots, saw what might have been an imaginary blood stain on the leather, and buffed it off with his jacket sleeve.

He stood up and rapped on the door again. He turned around and looked back at his rental car, considered leaving. The death of Rollins was a lead weight in his gut. More than that. It twisted and rose in a wave of anxiety that came not just with the sudden death of someone close to you but with the implicit knowledge that came through knowing just how much the loss would affect particular people. To be this close to grief was to put your heart through hell. His heartbeat felt as uncontrollable as the sadness on his face.

From behind the door the sound of a key being turned, then there was a clunk as a dead-bolt slid across. It opened, and Penny Rollins was revealed through the doorway. Silhouetted from the bright window light at the far end of the hall, it was like she wasn't really there.

Fox hesitated before stepping over the threshold. There was no invitation to enter and there was certainly no friendly gesture in greeting. Just emptiness. Wallace had phoned earlier, had borne the first of the pain and shock and suffering. Anger and despair was sure to immediately remain. The loss, that would never fade.

Inside, Fox closed the door and followed Penny Rollins into the lounge room. He saw Scarlet sitting at the top of the stairs, as if waiting to run down them at the sight of her father. It seemed a place where she'd spent far too much of her precious time on earth.

Fox waited to sit, while Penny Rollins sat heavily in her chair.

'I'm –' Fox caught himself. The sight of Penny, the thousand-mile stare on her face. Distant, prone. Hands on her belly. Protective, comforting. A slight bump. Damn. That's the shit that smacks you upside the head and dumps you flat on your ass.

'I didn't realise . . .' he said, gesturing.

'It's a boy,' she said. For a half-second she almost smiled, but solemnity prevailed. 'Michael was so happy about it. The news was the first real step in his recovery. It brought him home in a way that I couldn't – I just couldn't do it on my own.'

Fox cringed. What was he supposed to do now? What was she supposed to do?

He started where he could; described the nature of Michael's death. The attack on the delta. Cheating death more than once. The photos of them found in the police car, that they'd been hunted. Driving through the night. Being so close to safety. His descriptions of her husband's last moments had made her even more disposed to weep, recognising, as she did, all that he so faithfully portrayed. The briefcase that he held onto at the end. Uncovering the truth behind the Port Harcourt bombing.

'What was in it?'

'The case?'

She nodded.

'Documents. Proof of corruption of the Nigerian leadership. Dirt files on them, all from the office of the oil minister, Brutus Achebe. Orders from his advisor Steve Mendes for security contractors. The very men that attacked us. Info on the bombing in Port Harcourt, what to do afterwards to reap the benefits of the oil companies moving out. Enough evidence for –'

'For what?' Penny asked. Animated. Agitated. 'Putting these guys before a court? How much are they worth? How well are they protected?'

Fox weighed the options before him. He knew all this. Mendes couldn't go to court, nor Achebe. Guys like them didn't get the usual kind of justice. Especially when they were from that part of the world, a place where everyone was covering each other's backs. These were the guys who made the law then embezzled enough cash to be beyond its reach.

'I don't know what to do,' Fox said. His eyes said otherwise – they were asking for permission. 'I thought I did, I thought I knew the way ahead. I thought it was clear . . .'

'I don't want you to forget what he died for.'

'I won't ever forget.'

'I want you to finish this.'

Fox noticed the change in her voice. Her eyes, still glazed over, locked on to his. He nodded as she spoke, assuring her that he agreed and would carry out what she said, as if she were speaking for them both and giving legitimacy to what Fox had considered a step too far.

'Finish this, Lachlan.' The remaining tears in her eyes refused to fall. 'Whatever it takes.'

'I'll get it done,' Fox said. Resolute. 'I'll do this.'

Penny Rollins nodded. Put a hand on Fox's arm. She was more matter-of-fact than pleading when she said:

'Finish it. Finish them.'

46

WASHINGTON HOSPITAL CENTER, WASHINGTON DC

The blocks surrounding Washington Hospital Center were being patrolled by no less than fifty DC police officers. The Secret Service counter-snipers on the roof were an unusual sight, as were the business-suited and uniformed agents who watched over entrances. The constant buzz overhead of two US Marine UH-60 Blackhawks on patrol left no one in doubt of who was currently a patient in the hospital. Farther out, two pairs of F-22 Raptor air superiority fighter jets flew in stand-off formations to enforce a no-fly zone.

McCorkell entered the President's suite in a hurry. He had walked double-time from the car and carried a sense of urgency in every inch of his appearance. The door was shut behind him by a Secret Service agent.

The President was sitting up in bed, resting with his eyes

closed as he listened to opera on a portable CD player at arm's reach.

'Mr President,' McCorkell started. He took a moment to compose himself. 'How are you feeling?'

'You my doctor now, Bill?' The President opened his eyes, could surely see the restlessness in McCorkell. 'I'm well rested. Best sleep I've had in years, you gotta try sleeping on whatever it was they gave me.'

'Sir, I need –'

'I was briefed on the LOOP attack,' the President said. 'There been another?'

'Another, Mr President?'

'Another attack?'

'No, there hasn't,' McCorkell said. He stood by the foot of the President's bed.

The President held up a hand to stop his National Security Advisor from going on.

'Then take a breather for just a moment, Bill. Listen to this piece of music. I was originally scheduled to be at the closing night of the Met. *Nabucco*.' The President held up a CD. 'They sent me this recording, though. You recognise this track?'

'Chorus of the Hebrew Slaves?' McCorkell answered.

'That's right. *Va', pensiero*. You heard it live, with a real opera chorus?'

'Once, would have been about twenty years ago,' McCorkell said. 'Covent Garden, I think.'

'I just love this track, it takes me back to – listen to this part . . .'

McCorkell listened. The CD player provided by the hospital or Secret Service didn't do the recording much justice. Tinny sound. Nothing on his Bang & Olufsen back at his apartment. Still, the Italian words filled the room.

> *O simile di Sòlima ai fati*
> *traggi un suono di crudo lamento,*
> *o t'ispiri il Signore un concento*
> *che ne infonda al patire virtù.*

'My Italian is a little rusty,' McCorkell said.

'Mindful of the fate of Jerusalem,' the President said, 'either give forth an air of sad lamentation, or else let the Lord imbue us with fortitude to bear our sufferings.'

'And so it became the unofficial national anthem for Italy,' McCorkell said. 'I remember going to a soccer game where the Italian supporters sang it instead of their official anthem.'

'*Il Canto degli Italiani* only became their official anthem in 2005,' the President said. 'Some sixty years *after* Italy became a republic. And it ain't got nothin' on Verdi. The man was a god with music, make no mistake.'

McCorkell nodded, not for the first time being put through one of the President's little history lessons.

'Mr President, we had a leak at the White House –'

'I know, the Secret Service told me,' the President said. 'The nurse's boyfriend. And that we are tracking the terrorists who struck the LOOP back to the Florida Keys?'

'Secret Service, FBI, DHS, they're all on it,' McCorkell said. 'I really think that, if you're up to it, you need to come back to The House. Sign yourself back in, take charge –'

'Bill, I'm waiting for the doctor's say-so, should be in a few minutes. Unless your Oxford PhD was in medicine? No, I didn't think so.' The President leaned over and pressed the back-track button, and the CD replayed the slave's chorus. 'So, in the meantime, we listen. This chorus piece of Verdi's *Nabucco*, do you know why it still resonates within us today, why it's so important to you and me right now?'

McCorkell shook his head. The President turned the volume down, so that the orchestra was playing softly in its lead-in.

'Verdi based it on a psalm,' the President explained. 'Psalm 137.'

'I didn't know that,' McCorkell said. 'And my Bible studies are about as fuzzy as my Italian.'

He took the moment the President allowed him to recall.

'That's the "Rivers of Babylon" one?' McCorkell ventured. 'The revenge psalm?'

'It's sometimes known as that,' the President said. 'What the displaced slaves are singing about here in the opera's third act is a longing for their homeland. The psalm, well, it's in that sadness of the Israelites, who, when asked to *sing the Lord's song in a foreign land*, they instead hang up their harps.'

'And they asked that if they forget Zion, may their right arm forget its skill,' McCorkell said, the fog of time over memory clearing. 'May their tongue stick to the roof of their mouth.'

The President nodded.

'And they speak of a revenge that we've all felt at times,' the President explained. 'A revenge, albeit they wished it delivered in different ways, nonetheless it's much the same as we feel today when it's our home that gets attacked.'

It was considered among the two of them. Seriously considered, by both men, in a silence akin to the serenity the two men shared while fishing from a boat in the middle of a lake.

'Revenge is a tough emotional place to reconcile, Mr President,' McCorkell finally said. 'Unless you're there, directly affected by it, have had your home and everyone and everything you've ever held dear raped and destroyed and taken from you – how could we ever really know that feeling of exacting such revenge.'

The President nodded, a reflective look on his face as he listened to the faint music play.

'At the end of the psalm,' McCorkell continued, remembering this passage as verbalised – had it been at Camp David last year? Yeah, by the visiting Israeli leadership. 'The slaves remember what their enemies did to their land. To their people.'

'Yes, and it's something that they will never forget,' the President said. 'All peoples have such lessons in their past. And it's how their leaders act in those times that makes the difference in how history treats them.'

The chief White House physician entered with the hospital's head of surgery. Medical charts and relieved faces showed that the prognosis was all good.

'I'll be outside waiting for you, Mr President,' McCorkell said.

'Bill?' The President stopped him as he was halfway through the door. 'The end of the psalm. Think about it. Why it's pertinent today, why we should remember its lessons.'

McCorkell looked at his Commander-in-Chief. His boss had the same look that he had when he beat him in their weekly chess match; that each mopping of the floor was a lesson for his friend.

'They say,' McCorkell said, summoning the words from somewhere deep in his memory banks – he recalled the notion behind it rather than the exact language but he knew that was all his friend was after – 'they bless those who will have the chance to exact their revenge. They say something to their captors along the lines of *fortunate is the man who will seize and dash your children upon the rocks.*'

The President nodded. Mouthed the word 'never' to McCorkell.

McCorkell shut the door, walked past the Secret Service agents, then took a seat on a plastic chair in the hallway and stared at the linoleum-covered floor.

Never, McCorkell thought. He'd been in the Oval Office when the President had said that very word to the Iraqi provisional Prime Minister, when the guest had asked after the President's directive to send more Marines into the Anbar province.

The Iraqi leader had asked the President, the presumed leader of the free world, *if he ever saw the hand of God in what he did?* All the President's men had been so quiet, McCorkell could hear his heart beat. The President had stood, extended his hand and shaken that of the Iraqi's, and wore the look of a father who'd lost his sons.

'Never.'

47

OXFORD STREET, WEST END, LONDON

Fox rechecked the map that came with the rental car. He'd spent the past two hours driving a circuit around his target, exploring all the entry lanes on the M4 expressway to Heathrow Airport and a couple of alternatives to outside tube stations. He now knew the streets surrounding his target, where the closest police station was, where good obstacles were, all to make sure he could navigate his hire car at high speed and without pausing to check the map. With each circuit he'd done passes of the house where his target lived. There was no visible security but he knew there was an armed bodyguard inside, around-the-clock protection. He would be ex-military and sharp, no fat security guard getting twenty bucks an hour here. Fox parked his hire car around the corner, walked the block in each direction – still no other security present. He knew his target was in there – he'd prank-called the house earlier, while the housemaid was still there. He'd watched her leave at eleven. It had just clicked past midnight. Now or never.

Fox made sure he had his essential gear on him: passport, wallet and car keys, all in his pockets.

He rapped on the door, a big old brass door-knocker that made echoes inside the house.

The neighbour's door next to him opened and Fox turned his back from view – heard it slam shut. Then he heard the click-clack of stilettos, the flick of a lighter.

He turned to look – a pretty young thing was walking down the house next door's steps in a leather mini. Clear plastic stilettos added a good six inches to her height.

She turned at the bottom of the stairs, put her lighter away, and puffed smoke up at Fox. She had big blue eyes with thick black eye-liner. Was twenty-five at the most. Sexy but sad.

'Lousy tipper?' Fox asked.

'Worse,' she said, with an Eastern Bloc accent. 'Lousy lay.'

Fox returned her sardonic smile with one of his own.

'He tell you where Osama is hiding?' Fox asked.

'Pardon?'

'Nothing.' Fox heard movement from behind his door. 'Have a good night.'

'Thanks,' she said, walking away with a practised sway of the hips that broke Fox's heart.

The door opened. A guy stood there, ex-military slab of beef in a dark suit. His former occupation was evident by the man's shoulders – the straight back and slope of the shoulder from the neck to arm giving away the combination of marching drills and lifting heavy weights. Maybe some jail time in there too. His eyes scanned Fox and then the street.

'Hi,' Fox said. 'My car just broke down – can you please call a cab for me?'

The guy didn't answer, just flapped open the left side of his suit jacket to display a holstered Glock.

'That meant to impress me?' Fox said.

'Fuck –' The guy couldn't finish his line. Fox took the two strides between them and feigned his left for the guard's gun. The beefcake leaned back and went to block with his left and draw with his right – leaving himself exposed and unbalanced. Fox's right uppercut laid the guy on his back.

Fox went inside and closed the door behind him.

The guy wasn't quite out, despite the nice *pock!* his head made against the tiled floor of the entrance hall and the instant swelling in Fox's knuckles. Fox was on him, holding a knee hard down onto the guy's sternum and relieving him of his Glock. He checked there was a round in the chamber, and pushed it hard into the beefcake's mouth.

For a few heartbeats Fox made sure no one was coming. Then looked back down.

'Turn over on your stomach,' Fox said quietly to the bodyguard. 'Make a sound, you lose your head.'

He lifted his weight off the man, still keeping the gun point-blank at the bodyguard's head as he rolled over. Fox pulled a few plastic cable ties from his jacket pocket, zipped them around the guy's wrists and through one another so that his arms were cuffed behind his back. He took a second and decided, given the man's size, that he'd double up with another pair. A soldier this guy's size that Fox used to serve with had once busted through a set for laughs.

Fox connected the man's ankles and put a hood over his head – it read 'British Airways'. Tight fit. It was the pillow cover from the flight he'd taken from Lagos that morning.

He knelt into the guy's back between his shoulders, put a hand at the guy's throat and pulled his hooded head up off the floor, whispering into his ear:

'Make one noise, it will be your last.'

Fox went down the hall silently, Glock in hand, his right index finger running down the length of the barrel just over the trigger-guard so as not to engage the Safe Action trigger system.

The first door to his left, a room that fronted the street, had the glow from a television coming from within.

Fox glanced in and saw an old man sitting by an unlit fire watching a movie. Hassan Ruma. Ex-president of Nigeria.

He went in, and put the gun in Ruma's face.

The old man stared up at him wide-eyed. Then settled a little, as if he knew the day would come when he had a gun pointed at his face. The armed guards only delayed that day, but no more. This was now, this was real.

'Anyone else in the house?' Fox said.

No answer.

The Glock pushed harder against Ruma's forehead.

'Anyone in the house?'

'No,' Ruma said.

Fox nodded, and put the Glock down on the mantle. Within his reach.

'I need some quick answers and I'll be on my way,' Fox said. 'Brutus Achebe. Steve Mendes. You know what they're up to?'

Hassan Ruma looked at Fox with interest now. It was clear that he was still unsure about Fox's intentions.

'I have intercepted some documents from Nigeria,' Fox said. 'Being couriered from Steve Mendes and Brutus Achebe to someone known as Musa.'

The old man's eyes showed that he knew the name and he shook his head.

'You know that name?' Fox asked.

'I know that name,' Ruma replied. 'Who are you? What do you want with him? With Achebe, with Mendes?'

'I'm someone concerned with what's going on in your country,' Fox said. 'As for what I want to do with this . . . I'll draw Mendes and Achebe out, then decide. Whatever the case, this is something that will come out in the press, eventually.'

Hassan Ruma nodded but there was doubt in his face. 'You can't get to them – they're well-protected,' he said. 'And their movements are made at the last minute. Achebe, maybe Mendes too, resides in safe houses all over the country. Unreachable.'

'But this Musa guy will know where to find them.'

'Most likely . . . but he's no ordinary man,' Hassan Ruma said. 'He was an assassin originally. Very dangerous.'

'I'll take my chances,' Fox said.

'What will you do when you find them?'

'I'll worry about that then,' Fox said. 'Right now, I need to find the sender of this.' He handed over the note. 'You know how I can get in touch with Musa Onouarah? His name came up in some references to you.'

Ruma looked down his nose through his bifocals. He looked almost grandfatherly now, like a fat, bald Morgan Freeman. He didn't look like someone who'd embezzled over five hundred million dollars. He nodded, handed back the note. Didn't say anything.

'Will you help me?' Fox asked, tapping the note. He considered glancing at the Glock but didn't. He felt the guy shifting of his own accord.

'You don't want to know this man,' Hassan Ruma said. 'He is one reason I have bodyguards.'

'One reason?'

'Those who control the oil, control the world,' Hassan Ruma said. 'I have many enemies, and not many friends left.'

Silence. Fox waited for him to go on – the raspy old guy had a sip of water.

'Musa Onouarah, yes, that is his name. He's what you'd call a crime boss. Gets things done, big and small. Runs the security in the Rivers State. Some federal ministers use him to fix election results at polling stations, oil companies pay him to ensure his thugs rule the areas around their assets. The populace don't look him in the eye. He rules a great deal of the coastal areas. Yet – he's like a phantom.'

'But you do know where I can find him?'

The old man weighed it up. He motioned for Fox to hand the piece of paper back to him, pulled a pen from the table next to him and wrote on the note. Handed it back with a Lagos address scrawled down.

'Thanks,' Fox said, and stood to leave. 'What's that?' he asked, a massive architectural model in the centre of the room.

'My penance. I'm dying,' Ruma said. He looked even greyer now, if that were possible. 'Cancer.'

Fox read the title – it was a new hospital for Lagos.

'You're trying to buy your way into heaven?'

'Biggest hospital in Africa,' he said. 'And it has mobile hospitals – a fleet of buses fitted out to go into rural areas . . .

And as for the afterlife, I know where I am headed, there's nothing that can change that.'

Fox considered it. 'You could do more,' he said.

'That will cost every cent that I am worth,' Ruma replied.

'You could go clean,' Fox said. 'Start something. For too long African leaders have protected one another. You don't need dirt files on corrupt leaders to bring them down. On former presidents and ministers to bring them to justice. Start with the press, then go to The Hague and come clean. Make a stand. Speak out against your peers. Go out on your own terms. Start something. Break the cycle.'

There was something, maybe a layer of honesty or truth, behind the old man's eyes that said just maybe he would.

Hassan Ruma checked his watch.

'You should go now, my friend.'

'What's that?' Fox asked. He went and looked out the front window through the curtain. A couple of cops wearing Kevlar vests were approaching the house – this wasn't a friendly house-call. 'You call it in?'

'I'm sorry,' Ruma said. 'I thought – I don't know who I thought you were. The grim reaper, perhaps? Now that I'm so close to making something up to my people . . .'

Fox looked down the hall – the security guy was still lying there. The rear of the house was dark – the kitchen was there, a glass door led into a courtyard.

'You got a car?'

'Garage is out the back.'

'Keys?'

'Kitchen bench,' Ruma said. 'I will stall them, my friend.'

There was a heavy knock on the door then a shout, 'Armed Police – open up!'

Fox, about to leave, turned on his heel.

'Come clean,' Fox said. 'You want to do something for your people, for Africa? Come clean. It's the greatest thing you can do.'

The old man nodded – maybe he understood.

Fox said before leaving: 'And I'm not your friend.'

48

LAGOS, NIGERIA

The Sultan's entourage took up the front twenty seats of the Nigerian Airways McDonnell Douglas DC9. The ageing airframe's interior had the stains and smells of cigarette smoke that continued to waft about the cabin. The passengers of Muslim faith looked on at the Sultan with reverence, feeling their flight was blessed. The Christians gave him respect, and they too felt their place was blessed by his presence. His bodyguards and staffers relaxed into their chairs for the flight home, enjoying the couple of hours' journey ahead. There was no anxiety aboard, only hope.

Two kilometres outside the airport, a cell phone beeped with a text message. The sender was Steve Mendes. Its message was clear, and was what he'd been waiting for all day.

NEXT PLANE.

Musa Onouarah put the cell phone down, got up from his armchair and switched off the small television set in front of him. He put on his hat and sunglasses, and walked to the side of the roof of his two-storey house. He cocked his head; he could hear the aircraft but not yet pick it out in the sky – there – light glinted off the silver sides of the fuselage. It headed towards him, north-by-northwest.

There was noise coming from his backyard. He looked down there: his young son was playing with his friends. Running around with toy guns, making noises with their mouths as they fired. He smiled. His attention went back to the aircraft, still far off. He watched its slow ascent.

By his feet was a Stinger missile launcher. He picked it up, stood back from the edge of the roof and steadied himself. He inserted the BCU into the hand-guard, heard the gasses move inside. The launcher chimed that it was activated and the missile armed. He shouldered the weapon, looked down the slender barrel through the eyepiece.

In use since the early 1980s, the Raytheon Missile Systems FIM-92E Stinger Missile was a tried and true surface-to-air weapon. This variant was its best incarnation yet. It had seen many successful actions, first in British hands in the Falklands, then from the Mujahideen in Afghanistan, to nearly all US operations since. Once fired, the infrared homing would take the missile up to speeds of Mach 2.2. Although only 70 mm in diameter, the Stinger packed an awesome punch. All but the best pilots in agile airframes would be doomed with this hunter on their tail.

Onouarah fired. The missile shot into the sky, so fast he had difficulty tracking it by eye. The pilot must have noticed the threat, either alerted by the initial flash of the launch or by the slender smoke trail as it streaked through the sky. The DC9 banked hard to port. The missile never lost its bead – this was fire and forget technology. This target was hardly a modern fighter jet with an A-Grade pilot in the cockpit, so there was no chance of escape. While most SAMs launched at aircraft were only successful if the pilot could not see the threat, there was little action that the DC9 pilot could do but add a second to the life of his passengers.

The missile struck the rear tail of the aircraft in the starboard engine. The three-kilogram warhead detonated on impact in an explosion that took both engines and the entire back section of the plane with it. The aircraft, now missing its propulsion and most avionics, settled into a rapid flat spin that saw it hurtling towards the ground six thousand feet below.

Onouarah was not a religious man. If he had been, maybe he would have said something to all the souls who had just departed the earth with a thunderclap of aircraft disintegrating against the neighbourhood it destroyed. Instead, he set down the Stinger launcher and went back to his television program.

49

WEST END, LONDON

Fox was out of the back door and rolled a heavy pot plant up against it. It wasn't much, but it would buy him maybe ten seconds.

He raced through the courtyard to the garage – the door was locked. He smashed the glass pane with his elbow; the plate glass tore at his jacket. He reached in and unlocked the door, went in, and locked it shut behind him. That bought another second or two.

He left the light off in the dark garage. Four shiny new cars were lined up: Land Rover Discovery, a Volvo and a couple of Jags.

Fox pressed the unlock button. His vehicle was the far one.

He scanned the workbench to his left, full of cleaning gear, waxes and polishes that the guy's chauffeurs no doubt had to apply after each use of a vehicle. He took a couple of four-litre bottles of motor oil, unscrewed the lids using both hands at the same time, grabbed the handles and walked backwards to the Jag, spilling the oil over the floor as fast as it would flow.

He dumped the empties at his car and jumped in. The Jaguar XKR's engine started up with a roar.

He looked about himself quickly – the garage roller door ahead was shut, there must be an opener somewhere . . . shit.

He heard the rear door of the house smashing against the pot plant.

There! He found the roller-door opener, pressed it hard. It cranked open agonisingly slowly.

Footfalls came down the brick-lined pathway. Torch beams flashed into the garage.

He put the car in drive, keeping the headlights off – the roller door was just clearing the windscreen. He released the handbrake – started moving forward, the bonnet was through the door . . .

The garage door behind him was smashed open. 'Armed Police!' He could hear the warning over the engine's throaty idle. He didn't see them slip but knew they had by the torch beam's erratic arcing through the dark night.

The roller door was at about roof level when Fox gunned the accelerator, the tyres burning rubber on the smooth concrete floor before surging forward, the edge of the roller door scraping along the roof of the XKR. He heard the sunroof shatter.

'That was close – shit!' Fox pulled the handbrake and spun the wheel to avoid a taxi that flashed by in front of him. He planted his foot and fishtailed the XKR onto Oxford Street, flicking the headlights on.

He slowed at the intersection, turned left, and eased up to his parked hire car – they wouldn't be looking for that, he could switch vehicles and make a getaway.

Too late.

A cop car turned its lights on, the sirens bursting through the air as he glanced across. A white BMW Five Series. At least a straight three-litre engine in there, likely a turbo V8. A seriously fast pursuit vehicle.

Fox planted the accelerator and hammered through a red light. A taxi clipped his rear bumper, nudging him slightly but sending the black cab into an out-of-control spin along the wet road. He checked his rear-view mirror: the cops had navigated the intersection and were on him, gaining fast. Very fast.

The next traffic lights were green. Fox slammed the car into second and applied the handbrake, skidding into the inter-secting road, slammed onto a straight path by sliding against the length of a red double-decker bus. Sparks flew along the passenger side and the curtain airbag deployed – gone as quickly as he noticed it, the interior filled with powdery gas.

In the rear-view mirror he saw the police BMW flash through the intersection – they didn't make the turn. Fox took another right, slowed to fit in with the light traffic rounding Cavendish Square, went down St George and crossed over Oxford Street again, two marked cop sedans speeding straight at him.

Fox pulled into the oncoming lane – down into second again, the supercharger screaming to redline the engine as he slammed the brakes and he saw the BMW in his peripheral vision. It had tried to T-bone him at the intersection and flashed past right in front of where he would have been. He floored the accelerator again, the car hitting eighty kilometres per hour in three seconds and the two cop sedans were now on his tail but melted back into the cars as he wove in and out of traffic. Another red light ahead – he moved into the oncoming lane again and a cop motorbike appeared straight ahead of him. It was split-second chicken time and the motorbike swerved at the last moment and flipped through the air, its rider tumbling across the road as his bike was sliding along the ground next to him in a shower of sparks.

Fox continued to push the Jag. The BMW was back in his mirrors. They'd have God knew how many vehicles closing in now and he'd never get anywhere in this car no matter how fast he drove. He had to ditch it.

He was hammering down Haymarket when he saw a chance ahead and powered towards Northumberland Avenue, where he was hit broadside by oncoming traffic on The Strand. A little Smart car pretty much bounced off his heavy XKR and flipped right over his car, hurtling end-over-end down the street. It went down the road like a basketball. The Jaguar XKR had a race-car low centre of gravity and stuck to the road like glue, continuing to spin in a complete three-sixty on the wet road as the tyres fought for traction. More airbags had gone off and were gone again, their limp white material filling the cockpit of the car like a bomb had gone off in there.

A siren announced the cop's BMW was close again. They came to a sliding halt right in front of him, and the passenger got out, drawing an automatic pistol.

Fox selected reverse and put the accelerator to the floor, the big twenty-inch wheels smoking up as he went backwards down Northumberland Avenue, cars bumping and scraping off the boot that forged a path ahead and cleared the way.

He was jolted forward as the BMW bumped his front – it didn't matter now, too late. The XKR cleared Victoria Embankment, while a car flashed by and took out the front of the BMW in a split-second mess of metal. Fox's car continued through a chain-link fence, bounced over a walkway, and soared into the air over the dark water of the Thames.

50

ABUJA,
NIGERIAN CAPITAL

The four CV-22B Ospreys came in hard and fast over the Abuja International Airport. Two of the tilt-rotor aircraft, those without external cargo, came in for a short landing approach.

Nix slung his pack over his shoulder and grabbed his M4 with underslung M320 40 mm grenade launcher, then led the way out onto the tarmac. This was his first area of combat operations outside of 'Stan and Iraq, and he went into the task with more trepidation than the previous two areas. Here, in Africa, it was more of an unknown. There was next to no intel of the current situation on the ground. Virtually no friendly voices, certainly far less US forces in the area. They'd be the biggest US Army force in country, next to the two squads of Marines that were garrisoned to protect the US Mission here in Abuja. For the next couple of days it would be him in charge of all US military operations in the area. Air strikes were en-route but were still several hours out.

At the load-ramp of his Osprey he looked up at one of their two vehicles that, for the immediate future, formed their biggest defensive hardware. A pair of up-armoured Humvees each with turret-mounted 7.62 mm machine guns. They would either prove to be a good addition, or bullet magnets. Probably both. Either way, his soldiers wouldn't be fighting each other to take a ride in one. All other firepower was to be what his men carried into the field, the biggest punch being provided by his 120 mm mortar team.

He watched as Top barked orders, his men fanning out in three-man fire teams. The North East Trade Wind whipped up more sand and dust than the massive rotor wash that the two hovering Ospreys created. Like the rest of his troops, Nix had his clear Oakley face goggles down. Every thirty seconds or so he had to wipe his gloved hand over the visor to clear his view.

The next two Ospreys hovered over the ground, each with the cargo of an up-armoured Humvee cabled ten metres under-neath. Ground teams unhooked the cables and the aircraft made to land down-wind from the troops.

The bulk of his BCT of 10th Mountain would be arriving in Djibouti about now, getting acclimatised for their next insertion, having skipped over the Atlantic with a pit-stop in Rota, Spain. They'd be in Sudan by the end of the week – and he'd likely still be here, babysitting the staff of the US Mission.

Captain Nix noticed the V-22's loadmaster motioning for him to plug in his helmet mic to the internal jack.

'Captain, you got chalk five on the line,' the flight officer called. On cue, Nix's Radio-Telephone Operator came running over, transceiver in hand.

'Thanks, I got it covered,' Nix said. He unhooked the flight jack and took the receiver from his RTO trooper. 'Chalk five, this is Nix of chalk one.'

'Copy that, Nix, chalk five. We got some new orders coming through,' his squadron's CO said over the radio. The Major was yelling to be heard over the sound of the C-17 engines as he rode with the Headquarters Troop. 'You are to take a land route to Lagos, that is three-point-four-zero long, by six-point-four-five lat. Copy that?'

'Copy that, chalk five. IPB on this, over?'

'Possible HVT acquisition for UAV take-out. Operational ID *True Target*, copy that?'

'Hooah, chalk five,' Nix said. Locating High Value Targets to call in for a missile-strike was likely boring work but it beat guarding an embassy. 'Operation True Target, Lagos, overland route, possible High Value Target acquisition.'

Top shook his head and pointed at a map in his hand. Nix followed his finger – they'd be driving halfway across the country. Around six hundred kilometres of open road; surface and travel speed unknown, hostility anybody's guess. 'That's a long distance to cover, chalk five. Request the use of Osprey insertion.'

There was a crackling of static over the line before the voice replied.

'Negative, Captain, all aircraft needed for possible urgent evac of Abuja Mission,' his CO said. 'I understand your concerns, chalk one, but True Target comes from beyond Drum, copy that.'

'Hooah, chalk five.'

Top's expression reflected what Nix felt. These orders had come from above their divisional command. That meant the Pentagon, probably the Joint Chiefs, and just as likely ordered from some suit from the CIA who had clout in the National Security Council.

'Chalk five, what's the Rules of Engagement on True Target?'

'Weapons hot, proceed to area at all costs. We are en route to Abuja as we speak, details to come.'

'Copy that,' Nix said. 'Details on target's location, chalk five?'

Moments passed as both Nix and Top could hear their commander's wheels turning. There was as much concern and frustration in the Major's tone as they each shared.

'Unknown at this stage, we're working on it, chalk one. Inbound EP-3 and Joint STARS aircraft combined with possible intel on the ground will lead you to target, you'll hear about all developments as I do.'

Nix and Top were not impressed.

'We got Close Air Support, chalk five?'

'Negative at this time. Be advised, we are doing everything we can and the stops are out. Likely F-22 coverage for CAS, minimum six hours out.'

Top kicked his boot against the Osprey's load-ramp.

'Any good news, chalk five?'

'Unmanned Aerial Vehicle for the HVT strike is on your station in two hours, approximately three hundred clicks north-west of Abuja, will intersect and cover your approach to target area.'

'Designation of UAV?'

'Make it a Reaper, chalk one,' the squadron CO said. 'Start rolling, Captain. Good hunting and godspeed, out.'

'Hooah, chalk five, chalk one is moving now. Chalk one out.'

Nix handed the handset back to his Radio Telephone Operator.

'Top, get the Humvees gassed up and fully loaded,' Nix said. 'Take the Grey Fox and an RTO fire team, one in each vehicle, ready to bounce in five.'

'Sir?'

'We're going on safari.'

'Who's leading it?' Top asked.

Nix squinted, looked around. The platoon CO, a twenty-one-year-old second lieutenant he'd gotten to know at Forward Operating Base Bernstein, south of Kirkuk, Iraq, was directing his men around through his squad sergeants. The kid's platoon was a well-oiled unit, his troopers alert, respectful, proud to be a page in the future history of 10th Mountain Division. Nix didn't know many soldiers outside those he served with right now who could match this kid's skills. They rolled hard and fast, punched pound for pound well above their weight.

'How about –'

'We got company!' a PFC on point defence yelled over the tactical radio.

The whole platoon of 10th Mountain stood to, ready to defend their positions and aircraft as Nigerian military vehicles approached – six open-topped Land Rovers, machine-gunners with weapons ready. Two Vickers tanks rumbled close behind, along with at least a company-sized unit of paramilitary. Nix's men suddenly had a good hundred and fifty barrels pointed their way, insults flying in the air as neither force knew what was unfolding.

The 10th Mountain stood with guns drawn and a shoot-out was about to go down.

'What's our ROE?!' was being called among the American troops.

'Stand down!' Nix ordered. 'Covert cover only!'

From the corner of his eye he noticed his sniper team were lying on the roof of the nearest V-22. Mortar team called in that they were prepped for close-in firing, another fire team had AT4s ready to take out the tanks.

Top was by his side, his M4 pointed down to the ground but ready for use within a second of action.

'These guys our enemy?' the sergeant asked out the side of his mouth.

'Not until they start shooting at us . . .' Nix replied.

A Nigerian officer approached Nix. He was a full colonel, airport detachment's CO. His side holster was empty – there was a nickel-plated pistol in his hand.

'Who are you?' the Nigerian asked. He was shaking – this fucker was ready to snap.

'US Army.'

'What are you doing here?'

Nix looked at Top, then at his RTO. The two faces that looked back said *What the fuck have we just landed in?* Nix considered calling it in to command to see if someone had overlooked giving these guys a heads-up. That would be a serious fucking mistake on someone's part.

'We were expected here,' Nix said. 'We are a security force to secure the US embassy.'

'No one told me,' the Nigerian colonel replied.

Shouting came from Nix's left.

'Point that fucking gun someplace else!' one of his men said to a Nigerian. Top motioned the trooper to calm down.

'Look, we don't want any trouble here,' Nix said. 'How about I get on the radio –'

'You must leave, now!' the Nigerian officer ordered. This was not a nice reception at all. 'Leave, now!'

Nix was thinking about a reply, things spiralling fast, when two Chevy Suburbans pulled up in a cloud of dust and sand, right in between the two forces of men. Out stepped a dozen members of the Nigerian President's personal security regiment. All smiles, oblivious to the Mexican stand-off. It was clear these guys were expecting the Americans, they just hadn't passed that information along.

The base commander and his force stepped back.

'Hello!' the new arrival said. Commanding officer of something, if all the gold and brass were anything to go by. Could be Mr T's brother. He pumped Nix's hand, then Top's. 'I love Americans! Uncle Sam! Denzel Washington!' He was still pumping hands with a big cheesy grin as his detachment all started snapping away with disposable cameras.

'What's with the cameras?' Nix asked him. Then he kind of got it. 'Where'd you get the camera?'

'Airport gift shop! You want one?'

Nix cringed. The 10th Mountain had almost been caught in an African firefight because of a stop-off at the gift shop.

'We love Americans!' Mr T was still beaming, posing for photos with the US force in the background, his men snapping away. 'Love cheeseburgers! Guns! Paris Hilton!'

Top stared at Nix, the sergeant's face cocked with a look: *What fuckin' planet did we just land on?*

'Small plane,' Mr T said. 'Can carry Abrams tanks? Where are your tanks?'

'No tanks,' Top replied. 'Just the Humvees.'

'No tanks? No helicopters?'

Top shook his head at the guy. Nix did the same.

'Sorry, bud,' Nix said. 'We're as good as it gets today.'

Mr T looked depressed. 'No tanks . . .'

51

WATERLOO STATION, LONDON

Fox was dripping wet as he walked along the tracks heading into Waterloo Station. There was a light London drizzle but it was the Thames that he wore on his clothes, his hair, his skin. He jumped up onto the end of a platform, to the much-startled stares of some late-evening commuters. He did his best to appear less conspicuous, if that were possible, walking slowly and milling into the main terminal building. He scanned for the least busy area, never stopping moving as he selected his course and entered a men's room.

In the mirror he looked like a drowned rat, much worse than he'd thought. His gaze lingered for just a few seconds and he was back in game-mode. He took his sodden passport and wallet from his pants pocket, and put them on the tiled shelf under the mirror.

Stripped down to his underwear, he put all his clothes in a basin with the tap on full. His actions were fast, he knew time was ticking. He let the clear water from the faucet run over his clothes and the dirty water stream away down the drain-hole. He lathered up his face and hands with the liquid soap and washed himself clean. Used paper towels to dry himself off, then wrung out his T-shirt and jeans. Gave up on the drenched sports jacket.

He was at the hand dryers now, drying out his jeans and T-shirt under two dryers at once. He checked his watch – Gammaldi would have arrived in Washington by now. The contents of the briefcase would no doubt be setting off alarm bells.

Behind him the door to the bathroom opened. Fox instinctively tensed. He looked over his shoulder – a Regular Joe. Startled, staring. Eyes fixed on Fox, stripped down to his socks and jocks drying his clothes under the hand dryer.

'It's really coming down out there,' Fox said.

The guy snapped out of it, just walked into a cubicle and locked the toilet door with a clunk.

Fox spent another five minutes drying out his passport, wallet and cell phone as best he could, and dumped his jacket in the waste bin on the way out.

All done, he looked in the mirror for a final moment. His hair was still damp, his clothes now looked slept-in, his boots were soaking. He knew they were wet with water but felt it could be blood. The blood of Michael Rollins. His final focused look in the mirror was not consciously at himself but it resolved something within him. He would do this, follow this path of retribution, whatever it took.

He walked out of the bathroom and joined the throng of people moving about the station. Then he headed outside and hailed a cab to the airport. For him, life rolled on. For others, it would soon end.

52

THE
WHITE HOUSE

The President entered the Situation Room with Bill McCorkell at his side.

All present stood up at the Commander-in-Chief's arrival, the military staff snapping to attention.

'Sit,' the President said, taking his place at the head of the table. 'Don, where are we at on the home front?'

'Sir, we have the nation as well-protected as possible,' Vanzet said. 'We've got no-fly zones over capitals and critical infra-structure. Every guard unit has been activated, and we've got the Coast Guard and Navy putting a wall of steel in every port and possible target.'

The President nodded.

McCorkell sat and looked across the table to Jackson and Fullop. Clearly the Chief of Staff was a little out of sorts with the premature arrival of the President.

'Mr President,' Fullop began, 'are you signed back in to office?'

'That I am, Tom,' the President said, without looking at the man. 'Where's the attack on the LOOP left oil price rises?'

'Jumped ten per cent a barrel,' McCorkell said. 'With the loss of the LOOP we've lost two million barrels per day of deep-water crude delivery, and five hundred thousand barrels of refining capacity.'

'SEC? Stock exchange and NYMEX?' the President asked his Chief of Staff.

'They're still –'

'Shut them down, Tom,' the President said.

Fullop looked from the President to the Veep. The man who was until moments ago the Acting President wasn't about to put his neck out.

'We thought that –'

'Tom, when this sort of attack occurs, we suspend trading, it's the 101 of a situation like this,' the President said. 'How much of the SPR have we started drawing down?'

McCorkell shook his head and looked to Fullop. The Chief of Staff was going red in the face as the whole room sat in silent consideration of him.

'We haven't released any of the SPR?' the President asked.

'Mr President, the Acting President and I felt that the Cabinet ought to start a ration–'

'I thought I asked you to do something just now, Tom?' the President interrupted.

Fullop looked dumbfounded.

The President's bottom lip hung low. McCorkell hadn't seen this kind of incredulous rage simmering on POTUS's face for – well, ever.

'Mr President,' began Fullop. 'Are you sure you're feeling –'

'God damn it, Tommy!' the President screamed, the palm of his hand slamming the point home onto the table. 'Leave the room, now.'

'Mr Pres—'

'Someone get him out of the room,' the President said.

McCorkell and Vanzet shared a look – both men would have taken this politician out of the room in a heartbeat. Two Marines in dress uniform outside the door entered and stood close to Fullop.

Fullop's gaze shifted to Jackson. The Vice President crossed his arms, resolute with the President.

Defeated, Fullop sucked it up and left the room.

'Bill, what's next?'

'Nigeria, Mr President. Platoon of 10th Mountain is on the ground. Rest of the 1st Brigade Combat Team will be in Abuja this time tomorrow,' McCorkell said. Back to business. 'The 24th MEU is steaming in from Rota, Spain, aboard the *Wasp*. On station in fifty-two hours.'

'The Nigerian President, where is he?'

'In his residence at Aso Rock, Abuja,' McCorkell said. 'That's his secure presidential compound.'

'And how secure is that?' the President asked. 'I don't want this to be like it got in Chad, with a president hunkered down and under constant attack.'

'It's a fortress, Mr President, and he's got a wall of armour and air power set up around Abuja,' Vanzet said. 'The 10th Mountain force in that city is ready to secure and possibly evacuate our Embassy, and another element is racing overland in a two-vehicle convoy in what we're calling Operation True Target.'

'That's to give us the option of taking down the coup leader?' the President asked.

'Yes, sir,' McCorkell said. The information was fresh as he'd had the conversation with the President on the way from where he'd met him at the steps of Marine One on the south lawn not fifteen minutes ago. 'The Army element will visually ID any target and the UAV missile strike will be ready to take immediate action. We're still working on exact targeting info.'

'Good,' the President said. 'And these sons of bitches in the Keys and the guy found dead here in Washington – that the end of this cell or are we gonna have terrorists turning up on the White House lawn?'

'We've got special ops teams in the Keys right now, Mr President,' McCorkell said. He checked a clock on the wall, the red digital numbers reminding him that the promised call from Lachlan Fox was way late. 'We'll comb the earth for remnants of this terror cell, Mr President. Rest assured, we've got agents and soldiers all over the world shaking down perps right now for anything that will lead to information. There won't be any gunmen saddling up to the White House lawn on our watch.'

53

LAGOS, NIGERIA

Fox walked into the Lagos Press Club, stepping from the brisk morning into the stuffy old architecture. Already the professional drinkers were hard at work. He looked among those downing their morning drinks, passed all the foreign correspondents who were still running their body-clocks on their home time zones, went beyond the local couriers and a few women and boys selling their bodies. Ceiling fans pushed around the humidity and the heat of the night, swirling cigar smoke around as well. Fox followed the haze to a smoky corner, thick, like it could have been a serious smouldering house fire. Under the shade of the rubber plant, behind the newspaper – there sat Sir Alex Simpson.

'Ah, my young Australian friend,' Sir Alex said. His reading glasses were down low on his bulbous sherry-red nose. 'What are you after this time?'

Fox took a seat opposite, and flicked a folded note across the table.

Sir Alex scanned it. No reaction.

'Well?' Fox asked. 'Can you get it?'

Sir Alex stared at Fox over the top of his reading glasses, weighing him up.

'It won't be cheap.'

'That's fine,' Fox said. 'I need a car too. Something fast but heavy. SUV heavy. And make it a non-loaner, it won't come back in one piece.'

Sir Alex took a few seconds to compute all this.

'I can get that too.'

'I need it all by this afternoon,' Fox said.

Raised bushy eyebrows said *that would be a bit of a stretch*. A smile formed that spoke of the money he could now charge. Or it could have been the excitement of it all. Perhaps a bit of both.

'That –'

'Won't be cheap, yeah, I got it,' Fox said. He looked around the smoky bar of the Press Club. No one cared in here, God only knew what other deals were going down.

'Have the Jeep parked out the back by four,' Fox added. He stood to leave. Dropped an envelope onto the table – ten grand in US bills.

Sir Alex looked down at the list again, then up to Fox.

'You're starting a war.'

'No,' Fox said. 'I'm going to end one.'

54

THE
WHITE HOUSE

'Thanks, Ed and Larry, I got it from here,' McCorkell said. 'Al, come on through.'

He ushered Gammaldi from the entrance hall across the Cross Hall and into the Red Room.

'You look worse than I do,' McCorkell said. 'You want a drink, something to eat?'

'No, I'm good,' Gammaldi said. He watched the orderly leave with what could have been read as either hunger pains or near-death agony.

'What's up?' McCorkell asked. 'And I haven't heard from Fox for a while, he was meant to call me.'

'Yeah, we hit some trouble in Nigeria,' Gammaldi said. He clung to a briefcase as he spoke. 'We got attacked in the delta.'

'I know that much from his last phone call from there,' McCorkell said. 'What's with the briefcase?'

Gammaldi put it on the low table between them. There were two bullet holes through the black leather. He popped it open, revealing some blood on the files inside.

McCorkell fingered a bullet hole. There was no mistaking what it was.

'What happened?'

'We got attacked in Lagos,' Gammaldi said. 'Right outside the British Deputy High Commission. Michael Rollins didn't make it. Fox just went to London to tell his wife.'

'Jesus,' McCorkell said, confused, as he looked at the files.

'They're that important,' Gammaldi said. 'Worth killing for. Rollins said that the militants got the case off some private security contractors acting as couriers.'

'Yeah, I'd heard they were communicating like that,' McCorkell said. He was silent a full two minutes while he scanned the contents. 'You guys running this as a story?'

Gammaldi shook his head.

'Fox wanted you to have it,' he said. 'Clearly, it's from Steve Mendes. A couple of places here in the US are mentioned. Brutus Achebe is named through a lot of the papers too, the stuff in English that I could read . . . I don't know, take it to the President, the UN, The Hague – wherever you need to take it. Fox would rather you took direct action than it being buried in the daily news cycle.'

'We've got some DoD guys on the ground in Nigeria,' McCorkell said. 'By now they've got the president and cabinet hunkered down in his palace to ensure the government is secure, but there's a coup going down. Achebe and Mendes are right in the middle of it . . .'

'This Steve Mendes was directly responsible for the death of Michael Rollins,' Gammaldi said.

'I can see that,' McCorkell replied. He read through the typed note giving instructions on preparing the Port Harcourt site for the bombing. Receipts for firearms, personnel lists of his security contractors in Nigeria. 'And I can see why he didn't want this to be read by the likes of me . . . There's dirt here on their president and most of the congress – election-fixing details. This is enough to support what we know – he's pushing Achebe for power. They've already split the government, and they're forming a provisional leadership majority as we speak. Only now we're realising at what cost . . .'

'Fox wanted to know if you're going in to get Mendes?' Gammaldi waited a bit while McCorkell continued to read. 'I'm heading straight back to Nigeria to meet up with him – if you have a message at all?'

McCorkell looked up from the files and met Gammaldi's look.

'We're working up options for dealing with Mendes and Achebe right now. Got another cell phone that I can contact you on?' McCorkell asked.

'Yeah, but the reception in Nigeria is deteriorating quicker than their political landscape,' Gammaldi said. 'I tried Fox just before, cut out every few seconds.'

'They're likely powering down their land-based relay towers to slow down possible military communications if their coup leads to an internal fight. We can loan you a military satellite handset –' McCorkell picked up his phone to place a call and stopped cold.

Beyond the oil contracts, the exploration rights, past the Russian documents, he saw Arabic. A couple of names of Saudi 'charities' – known fronts for terrorist fund-raising schemes. Then some names on a sheet entitled 'wedding guest list'. Twelve names. Two of them, the terrorists that had attacked the LOOP. Another was that of the terrorist found dead in Jack McFarland's apartment.

'They mean something to you?'

McCorkell considered it. It could have been written down as reported after the attacks. But why? There were no references to the places attacked . . .

'It – when did you say you got this case?'

'About twenty-four hours ago,' Gammaldi replied.

'Could have been after the event . . .' McCorkell said, more to himself. But all these other names . . . what's to bet some of them were responsible for the Saudi and Qatari attacks? And how many of them had got into America?

He looked at more of the papers in front of him. There were communication references here to cells in the Middle East. Addresses and contacts in Qatar and Saudi Arabia. The hairs on the back of his neck prickled to attention.

A 'medical asset' was mentioned, located in Washington.

Then – an address in the Florida Keys.

McCorkell picked up his phone and dialled the Situation Room.

'This is Bill. Bring everyone in asap, and put me through to the FBI.'

55

BRITISH DEPUTY HIGH COMMISSION, LAGOS

Fox paid the cab driver and walked across the road to the entrance of the Deputy High Commission's compound. The Nigerians formed a line down the streets, just as they had the last time he was here. Was it only a day ago? It was as if the firefight had never happened.

There was plenty of security visible. Nigerian Army troops lazed in the shade of the big palm trees that lined the street, leaning on their rifles and taking turns to scrutinise the vehicles that rumbled by.

There were a dozen Royal Marines at the gates, and Fox handed over his passport to a young corporal. The soldier recognised Fox, handed the passport back and waved him through. Before leaving the sidewalk, Fox couldn't help but look down to the ground. The blood stain was still there, despite the sand that had been laid over it. The corporal gave Fox a nod of respect – at least that's how Fox read it. Two of his colleagues had been wounded in the attack that Fox had brought to his doorstep; maybe the look was something else.

Inside the building Fox was ushered to wait in the dignitary waiting area, rather than the crowded main lobby with its bullet-proof reception desks and wary consular staff.

He didn't take a seat but filled a plastic cup from a water cooler and drained it twice.

Javens came out on crutches – hard plaster on his left leg all the way up to mid-thigh, just his toes poking out.

'Lachlan, I didn't think I'd see you again so soon,' Javens said.

'You're straight back to work,' Fox replied.

'Mind over matter,' Javens answered, propping the glass door open with his crutch. 'Come on through.'

Fox followed him in.

Javens's office was a cubby-hole with a small timber desk, a computer, a potted plant and a few photos on the wall – some with him dressed in military uniform. A small showing of his varied postings around the world – the ones that he could talk about.

Fox sat opposite the British agent. Javens passed over Fox's backpack, which he'd had to leave behind in the rapid evac to the airport following the shooting. Rollins's body had barely been put into an ambulance when Fox and Gammaldi had been thrown into a helicopter. His FN Five-seveN pistol was still in the bag, the can of pepper spray, a change of clothes.

'Thanks,' Fox said. 'So what happened?'

'Had a bit of a crash in the Jag,' Javens said, rapping his knuckles on the hard plaster. 'The old girl is not in driveable shape any more, I'm sorry to say. Still, she got me out of a jam.'

'I know how you feel,' Fox said with a smile. 'British engineering, who would have thought it.'

Javens laughed. Fox's smile faded, he leaned forward.

'I'm going back out there,' Fox said.

No-bullshit looks were traded.

Javens's look softened in respect.

'You did good, getting back here the other day,' Javens said. 'You made it to the five-yard line.'

'I know,' Fox answered. He couldn't shake the image of Rollins in his mind. The warmth of his blood. 'If I had just driven a little bit faster – reacted quicker . . .'

Javens held up his hand to signal *Stop it*.

'You're well trained enough to know what thinking like that will do to you,' Javens said. He reached for an orange plastic prescription bottle and shook out a couple of aspirin. 'Besides, Rollins well knew the dangers involved. I've known the guy for fifteen years. He went out on the front line one time too many. That's all it takes. We've both cheated death too many times. Sooner or later, for all of us, our number comes up.'

Fox nodded. He knew the deal as well as Javens did. You work in danger zones, there's the very real risk your work will get you killed. Training and caution just delayed it. Sometimes for years. For the lucky ones it was held at bay long enough to bug out and hang up their boots. To finally live a quiet life. To go out peacefully with the passing of time, not when time and life collided.

'What are you doing back here? What do you hope to achieve? Still after your story?'

'Those photos of us from the police car, they were *targeting us*,' Fox said. 'It was premeditated. Murder.'

'Yeah, I know.'

'Why would they do that?'

'Any number of reasons. They might have figured you were making headway in the Port Harcourt bombing? You might reveal something that they'd rather keep hidden?'

'They tried to kill us all. They wanted us dead, not just silenced or kicked out of the country. Dead.'

'And you know who "they" are?'

'Steve Mendes. Brutus Achebe,' Fox said.

'Yeah?' Javens was in more than mild shock. 'They're untouchable. No court will try them.'

'I don't want them to see a court,' Fox said. He passed over the note. Held Javens's stare.

'You won't find them,' Javens said, note in hand, yet to read it. 'Achebe has split the government as of yesterday afternoon. He's now in charge of the biggest coalition on the congress floor, and the bulk of the military is yet to decide which camp it stands in. So Achebe could be seen as leader of this country now, technically legal in their constitution or not. He and his people, including Steve Mendes, they're skipping across the country to safe houses while they push for power –'

He read the note and stopped mid-sentence, couldn't hide the shock. 'Where did you get this?'

'Does it matter?'

'Is it legit?'

'I'm going to find out later today.'

Javens handed it back. The note with the name *Musa Onouarah* and his address written on it. He shook his head.

'The judiciary have been after that guy for more than a decade. State police can't find him; MOPOL don't want to find him. And you waltz in with his address.'

Javens shook his head in disbelief. He pulled open a file drawer, flicked through the contents, then presented Fox with a photo and rap sheet on the guy.

'Have a read of that before you go in over your head.'

'Thanks,' Fox said. He scanned his eyes over Onouarah's photo, the list of crimes he was wanted for.

'I'm telling you,' Javens said. 'You don't want to know that man.'

'That's what people keep telling me.' Fox's look said it all. He was heading down this path, with Javens's help or without it.

'Give the address to the cops,' Javens said. 'There are some good ones on the state's payroll, guys I've worked with, guys who want justice just as badly as you.'

'This Musa guy knows where Mendes and Achebe are. Knows their movements, how to contact them.'

'Let this work itself out, Lachlan. You think this is the first political crisis this country has seen? This is Africa. It has its own rhythm, its own way of working things out. My country and many other European nations learned lessons the hard way on this continent. Learn from those mistakes. Turn around, get on a plane, and go back to New York.'

Fox passed the file back. Tucked the note back into his shirt pocket. Resolute. He was doing this no matter what Javens said. With or without.

'If you do make a house call on Musa Onouarah, there's not a chance in hell that he will tell you where Mendes and

Achebe are,' Javens said. 'Not a chance. And he'll put a bullet in the back of your head on your way out the door.'

Fox stood to leave and Javens held up his hand.

'Lachlan –'

'I'm doing this, Stephen,' Fox said. He traded stares with the MI6 agent. 'I'm not writing about this from the fucking sidelines. I'm making something right.'

'And you kill these guys and a couple more come up and take their place.'

'You really think that?' Fox asked. 'You really think another Steve Mendes, ex-CIA shooter turned political manipulator, is gonna pop up behind another puppet minister?'

'All right, sit down a sec,' Javens said quietly. 'Please.'

Fox leaned on the back of the chair, his hands flexed hard around the leather.

'They have to be stopped,' Fox said. 'Killed. It's the only way.'

Javens chewed it over.

'You realise what you're saying?'

'Steve Mendes is driving this Achebe train for all it's worth. He will see this plan through at any cost – he's already killed God knows how many people.'

'The chances of you –'

'I can do this. I've got the skills. I've got the gear. And, right now, I've certainly got the motivation.'

'You can't just –'

'Stephen, if you had one opportunity to square things, would you capture it?' Fox asked. 'Or just let it slip?'

Javens was silent. Chewed it over.

'And this is what you want?'

'It's justice, Africa style,' Fox said. 'Who else is going to do it? We've only got one shot. I'm it, right now, and I'm ready to move.'

Fox could see Javens weighing the worth of his career.

'What can I do to help?'

56

ENTERING CITY LIMITS, LAGOS

The convoy rolled fast. A MOPOL sedan led the way, clearing a path through the traffic. A Toyota pick-up before and after the VIP vehicle, the Toyotas driven and crewed with private security contractors. Achebe and Mendes rode between them in an armoured Mercedes G-Wagon. Everyone but Achebe packed firepower.

'It's confirmed,' Mendes said, closing his cell phone. 'The Sultan was killed on the plane.'

Achebe nodded. Tears in his eyes.

'Your cousin is dead too,' Mendes said. 'He and his family were aboard the same flight.'

Achebe shed his tears in silence.

'You knew it was coming,' Mendes said.

'I didn't want it to be like this! Why like this?'

Mendes considered it.

'You never wanted to know the details before,' he said. 'You wanted me to get you into power, and it's on your doorstep, right now. You want to take it?'

'I – I don't know now.'

'Take your place, as President of Nigeria and head of the Sultanate. Reinstate the caliphate.'

'You did this!' Achebe yelled. 'I should have you killed!'

Mendes's personal security guy in the front seat turned around. Achebe noticed it; Mendes waved his guy down.

'This is your destiny, Brutus,' Mendes soothed. 'You've known this, we've talked about it.'

'But if it is destiny then why did you act? You are not the hand of God!'

'We all do what we are destined to do, Brutus.'

There was silence for a beat. Achebe visibly weighed up the situation at hand.

'And meanwhile, the president is in his compound, and the military are still siding with him,' Brutus said, his voice becoming increasingly high-pitched. 'They certainly will not attack him.'

'Brutus, we have the generals meeting with us tomorrow night –'

'They are still loyal to him! You said that as soon –'

'Brutus,' Mendes spoke quietly, calmly, putting his hand up in the man's face. It was rare that he had to be this overtly controlling, but the Nigerian was getting too emotional. 'Brutus, this is it. You must be strong, right now. As a leader, if you let your emotions guide you in times of crisis, the results will be disastrous. Besides . . . we have another situation that needs our attention. An American force has landed in the capital.'

'US forces – in Abuja?' Achebe said. 'If they are – they are here to prop up the president!'

'Relax,' Mendes said. 'I told you this would happen. It's a small force to secure their embassy. It is a good sign, it means that we can open dialogue with Washington.'

'How many are there?'

'I will know soon, but do not worry about them,' Mendes said. 'They are not here to interfere. They will want to safeguard their nationals, as a first step. I will soon make contact with the American State Department. Make sure they're certain that they want to back the winning team. Us.'

57

LAGOS,
NIGERIA

Sir Alex handed over the keys to the four-wheel-drive with ceremony.

Fox looked, with a decent dose of scepticism, at the nineties-model Land Rover. It rode on big, fat, lairy rims. That's where the pimping of the ride ended. The bodywork was beaten to shit, it was missing a couple of windows that had been taped over with clear plastic, and there wasn't a panel not bent out of shape or painted in the same colours.

'So this is what ten grands' worth of car gets me in Nigeria,' Fox said, closing in for inspection. It certainly wasn't armoured like Javens's Range Rover was, but it would have to do.

'Start her up,' Sir Alex said.

Fox looked at him. Could tell something was up by the twinkle in the old man's eye. He put the key in the ignition, turned –

'Whoa!'

The unmistakable sweet hum of a big bore V8. A seriously huge, throaty thing, and perfectly in tune.

Fox popped the hood and considered the scene before him. Mercedes 5.5 litre V8, supercharged. It looked brand new, not even a speck of dust or oil.

'Some unsuspecting, undeserving soccer mum,' Sir Alex said, 'is now driving around town wondering why her two hundred thousand dollar SUV sounds like a tractor.'

'You've impressed me, Sir Alex,' Fox said. Man, would this sucker *move*. He slammed the hood shut, wiped his hands. 'You manage to get all the gear?'

'In the boot,' Sir Alex said.

Fox shook the man's hand, said goodbye, and tore off down the road. He saw the Lagos Press Club disappear in the rear-view mirror, Sir Alex waving goodbye, and couldn't help but wonder if he'd ever get to be such an age. As far as a grizzled old journalist went, Sir Alex's retirement was a pretty sweet gig.

Fox did two passes of the house of Musa Onouarah. He parked down the road, in the driveway of a house under construction. Waited. Watched as Onouarah entered his gated compound, followed by a chase car. No mistaking Onouarah as he shifted out of the SUV and entered the house: the fat fuck moved slowly.

Sitting in the car across the road, he waited a good thirty minutes to let Onouarah settle into whatever routine he might have. This was a better neighbourhood by far than any that Fox had seen before in Nigeria. All the houses had satellite dishes on the roofs, all looked to have power, water, and all the rest of the utilities the Western world took for granted but which were only available to the rich in this part of the world. Some places here even had grass lawns out front, surreal perfection of rolled-out green turf. The houses were all pretty much nondescript designs too, a development done all at once, each house conforming with the next like those in *The Truman Show*.

Fox got out and opened the boot. There lay another large chunk of his savings account. Ten grand bought a hell of a lot of firepower here in Africa. He sat there on the rear cargo area loading his two mags for the Five-seveN pistol. Sir Alex had charged him a small fortune for two boxes of a hundred shells, which was probably fair enough. Only two firearms used the Fabrique Nationale de Herstal's 5.7 mm x 28 mm rounds: the Five-seveN pistol and the P90 personal defence weapon. The only way that he could obtain the ammo in this circumstance was through purchasing a P90 too. Which wasn't too bad. It was a neat little submachine gun, as he'd worked out on the range back in Connecticut.

He strapped on a Kevlar vest over his T-shirt. Rapped his knuckles against it. This thing was near to useless – the civilian kind, stop a 9 mm if he was lucky. But it was better than no armour at all.

Back in the driver's seat, he waited. Tapped his fingers on the dash. A sedan pulled up – local Lagos cops, crooked, today under the employ of MI6 thanks to Javens. Here to make sure Fox's back was safe. They gave him a wave and drove down the street, then the four of them piled out, armed with automatic rifles. They moved casually, all in sunglasses, surreal. They could be young punks in any major city. They leaned against their car like it was another run-of-the-mill day. They'd screen who came in and out of the street. For Fox, it was go time.

He had one last check of the target building. Tall brick fence, metal gate, security cameras all over the place. He put the Land Rover in drive, did a loop out front, then stopped and selected reverse. He turned in his seat and looked over his shoulder as he planted the accelerator to the floor, backing the car through the wrought-iron gates. It smashed through them like they were made of plywood. Fox stopped the car there so that it was still ready to drive out in a hurry while blocking the driveway.

Four guys piled out of the house. All out the front door, all dressed in nondescript military fatigues. The two up front had AK-47s, the next two were drawing pistols.

They had no cover as they moved out of the door, still in the process of assessing the threat, as Fox let out a full fifty-round mag from the silenced P90. None of them stood a chance nor got a single shot off. He fired steadily, one knee in the plush green grass of the front lawn, partially shielded by a concrete fountain. He stayed in that position as he loaded a new mag into the P90. The silencer was smoking. The bodies were still bouncing down the stairs. The entryway looked like a grenade had gone off from the amount of blood and gore that spattered the cream-coloured facade. This submachine gun was that good.

Fox waited a few seconds, then scanned the windows and front door through the sights of the P90. No movement, no sound other than the thrum of the Land Rover's idling V8 behind him.

He stood and walked slowly, his weapon trained towards the possible target areas as he moved forward. He kicked each of the fallen guys as he went up the stairs to the front door.

He pulled lightly on the double-stage trigger, a single shot of the P90 sounding like the soft tap of a finger against a tin can as a bullet left the long sound suppressor. The guy's head exploded, the last twitch of life kicked out in his foot. Fox kept moving forward the whole time.

He was through the doorway now. Inside. Big glossy tiles that clicked under his footfall. He cringed, took it slow, lighter on his feet. Leather-soled boots did not a silent entry make – there was a good reason why special-ops crew the world over wore rubber.

He paused. Only his torso moved, scanning with the sway of the P90. There were noises coming from the kitchen. Pots and pans being cleaned up? Fox took a couple of steps forward and saw a reflection in a glass cabinet – a housemaid at work. Earphones pumped music that obviously drowned out the noise from his smash 'n' grab entry.

He scanned this ground floor – every room he could see into from this vantage point. Empty. He skulked past the kitchen. Down the hall. Looked into the lounge room. Saw a young boy, playing Halo 3 on a PS3. The surround-sound system blazed a cacophony of carnage. Sitting back in a leather couch, a bowl of crisps in his lap and empty cans of soft drink all around him – he was plugged in good.

Fox moved back to the entry foyer and looked up the stairs dead ahead – trained the P90's sights up there, waiting for movement. Nothing. Music was coming from up there, though, hardcore heavy metal, the kind of stuff troops would listen to before going into combat to get their psyche pumped.

Fox kept moving around the ground floor, making sure it was clear. Movement. Down the corridor, through the glass of the back door. An armed guard running in the backyard. As he ran past a side window Fox let rip with a few rounds. The guy splattered against the brick wall.

The sound of the windowpane shattering roused the maid out of the kitchen and she looked at Fox. She was fixed in his stare like a deer in headlights, her gloved hands raised. Soap suds fell to the floor.

'How many men with guns?'

'Five.'

Fox nodded. 'Musa Onouarah?'

She pointed upstairs.

'Alone?'

She shrugged. Didn't know.

'Take the boy,' Fox said. 'Go into the street. Walk to the police with your hands in the air.'

She nodded, and left in a heartbeat.

Fox moved up the stairs, the P90 raised to sight ahead of him, the stock nestled into his shoulder. Still no movement. The music was getting louder, though. He scanned outside through a window that faced the front yard, watched the maid drag the kid out into the street, her hands over his eyes so he wouldn't see what had happened to the guards.

Down the hall. The music was getting real loud. His boots were silent on the carpeted floor as he moved from room to room.

Six doors led off this hallway – all open. Fox stuck to the centre, walked steadily with head and aim scans side to side, pausing at each doorway to look and listen. Kid's bedroom. Toys everywhere. Bathroom. Couple more bedrooms. Main with en suite. Empty. The whole second storey: empty.

Where was this guy? And where was that fucking awful music coming from? Fox stood in the centre of the master bedroom, at what would be the foot of Musa's bed. It was a monster thing, must have been a couple of queen-sized put together. He looked about the place – en suite, behind the door the sound of running water, barely audible over the music.

Fox was tense. The door was almost shut. He listened – the water was still running. He inched closer, peered in, the dangerous end of the P90 leading the way. The door creaked.

He checked his back. Clear.

His attention was back at the bathroom door. He took a breath, flicked it open with the toe of his boot, and he was inside with gun drawn. Scanning fast.

Nothing.

The toilet was running.

Fuck.

He went back into the bedroom. The dressing table held a pile of papers overflowing from a stuffed briefcase which got his attention. On the top, the same long-lens photo of Rollins, Gammaldi and himself taken from the airfield outside Port Harcourt. Then some typed pages, correspondence from oil companies, Russian, Chinese. Seeking security contracts for their personnel. Short term, long term, this guy was getting set up for life with the sums of money mentioned here.

Fox looked around the room. He scanned the ceiling, looking for speakers. Dumbfounded when there was no visible source of the music at all.

There were two massive sliding doors to – what, a wardrobe? Fox gently slid one open. Bingo. The music was real loud now.

The wardrobe had a door recessed in the back. Another room beyond that. A safe room, maybe?

He tried the gold-plated handle – it turned, slowly. Clicked open. The music from within was almost deafening. There was something else too. Screaming? Crying?

Fox moved inside.

Musa Onouarah. Naked. On a bed, ripping into a young woman, still in her teens.

Two other girls were there, naked, holding on to each other inside a cage.

Sex slaves.

Fox slipped the P90's strap over his shoulder, pulled out his Five-seveN, and walked over fast. He used the pistol like a club, and whipped it against the side of Onouarah's sweaty head.

58

HIGH OVER THE ATLANTIC

'You really need that?' Gammaldi asked. He watched as his girlfriend field-stripped her sniper's rifle. Never before had he thought of guns as sexy, but seeing her hands move fast and efficiently over the gun metal . . .

'I hope not,' Emma Gibbs said. 'But you know your friend Lachlan, he has a knack for sticking his big boof-head into harm's way.'

'Yeah, you're right,' Gammaldi replied. He went back to the in-flight phone in the GSR's private A318, and tried Fox's cell number again. The aircraft looked like the civilian version on the outside, but inside was pure luxury. Configured with big leather recliner seating for thirty, it had a full kitchen, bar, lounge, dining area and conference room. There was an apartment up front, too, and if it weren't for Gibbs's boss being on the flight, Gammaldi would have taken her there for some sexy times.

'You want this?' Sefreid asked. He held up an FN Five-seveN pistol to Gammaldi.

Gammaldi shook his head. That certainly wasn't what he was after.

'I'll let you two do the shooting,' he said.

'Wallace said to bring Fox back in one piece,' Sefreid told him. 'We've already lost one reporter too many. I'll drag his ass back to the States if I have to.'

'Thanks for coming, guys,' Gammaldi said.

'You managed to get through to his cell yet?'

'Nah, I'll keep trying, though,' Gammaldi replied. His look turned hopeful but it was hollow and he knew it. 'Knowing Fox, he'll be lying on a beach somewhere.'

'That's not what I saw in him the last time I clocked him,' Sefreid said. The big ex-special-forces guy looked concerned over their friend. 'I just hope he doesn't come unhinged. I've seen guys do that before. In Iraq. 'Stan. Seen them do things they'll regret for the rest of their lives.'

'He knows what he's doing,' Gammaldi said. The two security operators didn't argue the point. Gammaldi watched the world pass by out the window, wondered how the time ahead would come to pass. Hoped his friend would stay in control. Hoped the death of Rollins would not take his friend with it. Time would soon tell.

59

LAGOS, NIGERIA

'I'm going to ask you questions,' Fox said. His voice resonated in the tiled en suite. 'Your answers must be the truth. You fuck around, you get this.'

Fox waved the canister of pepper spray in Onouarah's face. Tapped it against the guy's head. It made a hollow-sounding *tonk-tonk-tonk*.

'You waste my time? You lie to me? You get this.' Fox held his Five-seveN up close. 'Nod if you understand.'

The man's eyes were disbelieving but he nodded. He was still naked, on his knees; cable ties around his wrists held his arms behind his back.

Fox took his time before pulling out the hand-towel he'd gagged in the man's mouth. He picked up the canister of pepper spray. *FOX LABS* brand spray, he noted with raised eyebrows.

'The side of this canister says *over five million Scoville heat units*,' Fox said. 'I'm gonna guess that's pretty hot shit. You understand? I only want the truth.'

Fox's expression said that he expected another nod in affirmation. Onouarah did it, though still not as convincingly as Fox would have liked.

First up was a question that Fox knew the answer to from the courier documents.

'The attack on the Port Harcourt oil building,' Fox said matter-of-factly. 'Who did that?'

The guy's face looked disbelieving, as if asking, *You are doing this to me for that? That's all?*

'It was me.'

'It was you.' Fox nodded, was friendly on hearing the correct answer. 'Okay. It was you.'

He took out the photos of Rollins, Gammaldi and himself. 'Who took these photos?'

No answer. The man's eyes were searching Fox's face, probably looking for a reason. Fox held the photos in clear view, and flicked through them.

'This photo? This one? Who took them?'

There was no answer, but Onouarah's eyes looked back at the photos and there was recognition there. Fox picked up the canister of pepper spray. Held it close to the photo so he'd know what was coming to him real soon.

'I don't know – they were sent to me,' Onouarah said. His voice was higher pitched than Fox had expected. 'That's where my job started – I just sent them on.'

'You just sent them on,' Fox said. His tone said, *You just sent it on and got others to do your dirty work.*

'Yes. Yes.'

Fox nodded. 'Okay,' he said. 'Who'd you send them to?'

'Some of my guys, security contractors I know, MOPOL . . .'

'You sent them to the cops?'

'Yeah . . .'

Fox had a mental flash of Javens on the night they had fled the delta, when he'd reached in and taken the printed or Xeroxed photos of Fox, Gammaldi and Rollins from the MOPOL sedan.

'Why would you send it to the cops?'

'The cops – some MOPOL cops, they are my guys too.'

Fox nodded. He took the hand-towel, wiped some of the sweat from the guy's forehead to stop it from dripping down into his eyes. The fat fuck was shaking on his knees, probably hadn't had to hold his frame upright for this long in a while.

'Okay,' Fox said. He put the towel down and picked up the pepper spray again. 'Who sent the photos to you? Whose job was that? Who are you working for?'

Fox knew it was Mendes. But he didn't want to put that name out there. He wanted to hear it from the mouth of this greasy son of a bitch. He held a photo of Rollins closer to the guy's face and asked again, staccato. There was no mistaking his intention to get the answer.

'Who – sent – you – this – photo?'

Onouarah spat at Fox and then made as if to scream for help, but Fox had the hand-towel stuffed back down the guy's throat real fast. He followed up with the pepper spray, a good spurt right in the eyes. Now the guy was reeling. Gagging on the towel.

Fox leaned over and ran the bath, pushing the guy's face under the faucet. Then he pulled him around, and took the towel out.

'Who sent them to you?'

'Men— Mende—' Onouarah said, fighting for breath. 'It was his job.'

'Who?' Fox repeated. He put an ear closer to the guy. 'Say again.'

'Mendes! Steve Mendes.'

'Steve Mendes. Okay. Why did he want us killed?'

Onouarah shook his head.

'Sorry?'

'No – I don't know.'

Fox wiped his own face down with a wet towel, and blinked out some of the pepper spray that bit at his eyes in the confined space of the en suite.

'Where is Mendes?' Fox asked, close in the guy's face. 'Hmm? I know you have some way to contact him. Hmm? Where do you meet?'

Onouarah wouldn't look Fox in the eye. He just settled into a stubborn stare at the tiled floor.

Fox knocked him on the forehead with his knuckles. Knocked on his head repeatedly like rapping on a door.

'Where – are – Mendes – and – Achebe?'

Onouarah looked up at Fox and spat again. That would be his last act of defiance.

Fox considered the fat fuck in front of him. He had to remind himself that he'd not only had Rollins killed; that this guy had killed God only knew how many. He had those young girls in the other room. Fox wasn't there to cast judgement on the guy, that would be between him and God. But he would gladly hasten that meeting.

Fox had an idea. He scanned the bathroom – there, a plastic bag lined the trash basket. He emptied it and went back over to Onouarah. Put the plug in the bath, ran the faucet at full. The look on Onouarah's face, in his swollen red eyes, was one of not knowing. Maybe he was still dazed from the first blow to the head. Fox didn't give a shit. The bath was filling and it was crunch-time.

'You did this job for Steve Mendes and Brutus Achebe. Last chance. Where are they?'

The crime boss returned a glazed-over look.

Fox put the plastic bag over Onouarah's head. Dunk time. It felt like drowning but it was safer – Fox knew he could do this repeatedly without the guy actually inhaling water. He pushed Onouarah's head into the bath, held it under water as his body thrashed about. Pulled him out after about ten seconds, yanked the bag off. The guy was heaving for breath. His expression had changed, he was panicked.

'Where are they?'

'Who?'

Fox sat on the toilet seat, in close to Onouarah. His hands were bare, although the pepper spray and Five-seveN pistol were within easy reach. He sat there and gave Onouarah the look of a man who knew he had the upper hand. The look a cat gave a mouse that it caught and went on to play with, knowing that, in the end, there was only one outcome for the mouse.

'Where are Achebe and Mendes?'

'Fuck. You.'

Bag time. Back in the water. The tap was still running hard, the bath was nearly full. Water started splashing outside the bath now, spilling over the sides. Fox was using both hands to hold him down, until he felt Onouarah start to lessen his struggle. Then he pulled him out and took off the bag, letting him crash to the floor and fight for breath. Fox calmly turned off the tap and sat on the toilet seat, wiping his hands dry on a towel.

It took about a minute for Fox to get the pepper spray into view of Onouarah. His swollen eyes focused wide on the canister. He was panting for breath, trembling.

'What – do – you – want?'

'Achebe. Mendes.' Fox still had the canister up close. 'How do you contact them? Where do you meet them? Where are they?'

'Okay, I – I know how – how to – contact them.' He was heaving for air. Fox let him breathe for a minute. 'I am meeting him tonight, Mendes. Just before dusk.'

Fox listened to the guy and made him repeat the details three times. The location. The cars. The security. Same details each time.

'You're sure now?'

'Yes.' Onouarah's breathing was almost back to normal now.

'You're absolutely sure? This place, this pager number?'

'Yes. Please. Yes.'

Fox nodded. Okay. He believed him.

He put the bag back on, and shoved the man's head into the water before he could object. Held him down hard. His head was not under there for as long as before but it was almost too long. Fox pulled him back up. He was really heaving now, trembling, his face sucking in air, retching up bile. His eyes were frightened to shit.

'You want to change anything? Hmm?'

Onouarah shook his head.

Fox dragged him to his knees again.

'Okay,' Fox said. 'I believe you.'

'Yes.'

'I believe you.' Fox stood up and pocketed the pepper spray. He picked up the Five-seveN, his finger through the trigger-guard. Onouarah's expression said that he knew what was about to happen.

'No – no, my friend – I have money, in the drawers, the bedroom, fifty thousand –'

'It's off to the next life for you,' Fox said. Onouarah's eyes were wide, realising now that Fox could not be bought. The inevitable would roll on. 'But I promise you won't be lonely.'

Before Onouarah could speak Fox had put the bag over his head again, pushed him over the edge of the bath and applied enough pressure on the trigger of the Five-seveN to paint his brains into the bag and watch them pool into the water of the bath. His fat body shook for two seconds and then collapsed with the dead weight.

Fox turned, washed his hands in the basin, soaping them hard, scrubbing off blood, imagined and real. He looked up into the mirror. His blank stare finally focused on his reflection. He wasn't sure who the face in the mirror looking back at him was – didn't have time to consider it either – as he felt a presence at the door. He reached for the pistol but it was too late – the door was open.

The three young women were standing there. Each wearing shirts from the guy's wardrobe, swimming in them like oversized night-dresses. They clung to one another for security. Their eyes were wide and they settled on the lifeless form of Musa Onouarah. A curious if welcome sight for them.

'It's okay, he's gone,' Fox said. He didn't know what to say beyond that. He picked up the pistol, the P90 still slung over his shoulder. Their young eyes still didn't move from the corpse.

Fox went into the bedroom, took Onouarah's wallet from the dresser, and emptied out all the cash – about ten thousand Nigerian dollars and a grand in US bills. He rummaged through the drawers, finding thick wads of used US bills.

He handed all the money over to the girls. Then departed without a word.

60

CITY MARKETS, DOWNTOWN LAGOS

Steve Mendes cracked his knuckles, shifting his weight in the chair at the outdoor bar. The afternoon crowds of dockworkers were arriving to drink, and there were even a few tourists, by the look of them. He had a quick scan to make sure his six security guys remained alert. They were tough characters, all hand-picked by himself from a friend's private security firm in Moscow. Not the gun-shy suited types, these guys wore military pants, boots, Kevlars over T-shirts, submachine guns ready in their hands. All ex-para somethings, who would kill as soon as speak.

Mendes checked his watch, looked up and right on cue his guest arrived. Thirty-something American, sweat beading across his brow. This was the US Assistant Deputy Chief of Mission, the embassy's third-in-command, stationed to Lagos. A nothing-man with just enough seniority to be heard properly by his superiors. Lowly enough to be sure he'd turn up at this meeting with eleventh-hour notification.

Mendes waved the State Department guy to take a seat. He looked around himself like a startled animal, unsure of this habitat. He had a look that said *What the fuck have I got myself into here?*

The guy put a digital voice recorder on the table between himself and Mendes.

Mendes picked it up and passed it to his closest security guy who pocketed it for safe-keeping.

'You can make notes,' Mendes said.

'Okay.' The State Department guy was sweating hard. He looked like a guy who knew he was in over his head. He ran a hand through his prematurely grey hair. Knew he was just a messenger in this case. Hoped that would get him out of this meeting alive.

'You okay?' Mendes asked. He waved a waiter over. 'You want a drink?'

'Water.'

'Two bottled waters,' Mendes said. The waiter disappeared. Mendes shot the State Department guy a look that read *Calm the fuck down.*

'I'm the team you want to be behind. Brutus Achebe now has the backing of a clear majority in both houses. He will be forming a government and standing as interim president until the next election. I expect the US administration won't interfere with this internal political matter.'

'Yes – I'll pass all that on.' The man made notes.

'Good,' Mendes said. 'And make no mistake. You guys fuck us, we'll fuck you.'

'I'm – I'm not sure I –'

'If there's a US military presence in Nigeria that in any way opposes the Achebe government, there'll be no Nigerian oil powering the SUVs of soccer moms in Houston. No more Nigerian sweet crude to help power the US economy. That'll hurt. Feel me, champ?'

'Um – right.' More notes. His expression saying *Why the fuck can't the ambassador be here with a SEAL team behind him.*

'Relax, sport,' Mendes said with a smile as their waters arrived. He held his glass up in a toast, and the young State Department guy clinked glasses with an unsteady hand. 'The US is going to have a friend in Brutus Achebe. And you have got a friend in me. This is going to be a great opportunity for everyone. More oil will flow, more money will change hands, more security will be seen in the Delta.'

Mendes stood, and put a few bills on the table to cover the drinks.

'But how do we contact you?'

Mendes smiled. There was not a chance he was giving him a cell phone or pager number. He knew the targeting capabilities of the US intel agencies as well as anyone. Put your voice on the air, and be prepared to have a cruise missile come through your bedroom window at night.

'You don't. I'll contact you.'

He moved away with his bodyguards in tow.

As he got into his car, a big blacked-out Mercedes G-Wagon, his pager beeped.

Musa Onouarah. Meeting confirmed for this evening. Mendes checked his watch, and signalled to his guys to get the convoy on the move.

61

LAGOS, NIGERIA

Fox carefully planned his assault. He had just over an hour until Mendes would show up.

The meeting place was a gravelled lookout that turned off the main road. About the size of a basketball court. A good vantage point to see the sealed road leading up through the neighbourhood, and the road that continued out beyond and rounded the hill. A couple of gravel tracks led off from here too, back into the suburban jungle of cinderblock homes and corrugated-tin roofs.

Crouched down at the end of the lookout, Fox studied the landscape below. The convoy would be coming from Lagos city, which was via the major sealed road that led up through this outer neighbourhood. He'd place some IEDs to take the vehicles out down below this point, engage them in the narrow streets where there was no room to turn around in the canyon of cinderblock houses with messes of cars and trucks parked each side of the two-lane road.

He went to the back of the Land Rover. The tailgate was open, displaying a couple of plastic tubs of gear: a pair of 9 mm Glocks, plenty of spare mags, the P90, which was down to its last twenty rounds, and an M4 with underslung M203 grenade launcher. Two flash-bag grenades and two frag grenades. An AK-47 from the guys back at Musa's, one full mag spare. And the heavy firepower: an AT4-CS: a US-made rocket launcher specially designed for urban warfare. This version used a saltwater countermass in the rear of the launcher to absorb the back blast. It was a one-shot weapon, the tube being discarded once it was used. He'd leave it locked and loaded as a fall-back defence option

Then there was a timber box. Inside was something that Sir Alex's contacts had no doubt built rather than bought – a couple of remote-controlled IEDs. They were made out of sawn-off pieces of steel pipe, about seven centimetres in diameter and fifteen centimetres long. One end was a thick welded plate, the other, the blast cap, was a concave brass top glued into place. When the bomb went off, this would form a projectile that would pierce through heavy armour, adding to the lethality of the explosive blast itself.

This box he took out carefully. He strapped a black thigh holster on, inserted a Glock and two spare mags. Then he shut the tailgate, got in the Land Rover and tore off in a cloud of dust.

Fox drove down to where he had a good line of sight. From here, he had glimpses of the road as it turned around towards him, framed through gaps between buildings. He'd watched about twenty vehicles pass, and counted the travel time from between the gaps. He'd have a five-second window from seeing Mendes's vehicle to trigger the remote-controlled IEDs, which at this distance would have less than a second's delay in detonating. To be safe, he was going to place them a second's drive-time apart.

He backed the Land Rover into an alley off the main road, took the IEDs from the box and went out to the street. He looked up and down – deserted – then a bus came up the road. He walked away from it, to shield himself from the view of the passengers onboard. They'd just see the back of a guy walking. He waited until it left just a trail of diesel exhaust smoke behind. The only thing around now was dozens of birds sitting on a power line, backlit by the sun. They squawked and took off too.

He walked along the urban street, between apartments mostly two or three storeys tall. A few people ambled past, and a couple of cars went by that blew out black-blue clouds of smoke like they were running more on oil than petrol.

He went back to a spot where there was the wreckage of a three-tonne truck, placing an IED under the tray atop the carriage that would have held a spare wheel. The concave brass disc that formed the blast area faced out onto the road. He walked up the road ten metres and placed the other charge on the same side of the street, again the brass top facing in towards the traffic, this time among a pile of garbage. He made sure it was hidden from casual view, and secure in place. Then he put a sheet of cardboard over it to finish the job and went back to the Land Rover.

A noise startled him. Ringing – his cell phone, on the passenger seat. He reached in, answered it:

'Yeah?'

Static.

'Hello?'

'Lach – it's Al,' Gammaldi said.

'This is a bad line – I can hardly hear you.'

'I'm in the Airbus – we touch down in . . . minutes.'

'Say again, Al?'

'Touch down Lagos in forty minutes,' Gammaldi said. 'I got Sefreid and Gibbs with me. Where are you at?'

'North-west Lagos city,' Fox said.

'Wallace and McCorkell have been trying to reach you.'

'Been a little busy.'

'There are some US boys heading your way. Just a couple of Humvees. They want to know where Achebe and Mendes are at.'

'What for?'

'Don't . . . you'll have to . . . McCorkell.'

Fox thought about it. They wouldn't be going to go and arrest them. Could they be heading there to ensure the safety of Mendes and Achebe? Did they, the US government, want to back these guys? Had Mendes sucked them in?

'McCorkell? What do they want with Achebe and Mendes?'

'I'll . . . soon . . .'

'Al – you're breaking up. Al?' Fox shouted, a finger in his other ear as a truck rumbled by.

'Keep this line open,' Gammaldi said. 'Don't hang up the connection . . . track it . . .'

So they could track it?

'All right, Al, I'll leave it open.'

Fox put the phone in his Kevlar vest pocket, could still hear the faint crackle of static over the line. Much like the AT4 rocket launcher, having either Gammaldi or a US team closing on his location could prove useful in evening out the odds later on. He squinted up at the lookout. It was hard to make out details as the afternoon sun kept hiding behind dark clouds. Good conditions for hunting.

This neighbourhood was like a ghost town. An occasional car rumbled by but this was the tough outer limits of a big city like the worst you'd find in old-school South Central LA. There was even the occasional posse on foot or in cars wearing gang colours. Only the roots of many of those colours went further back than any US street gang. These were tribal colours, from all over the Niger Delta, come together to claim this cesspool of a location. It was one of those places you wouldn't go without serious firepower and back-up. Most streets that led off this main thoroughfare formed cul-de-sacs nestled among rundown cinderblock houses and apartment buildings. If it got to a street chase, there were far too many dangerous dead-ends to turn down.

An old Merc sedan pulled up hard next to Fox. Bald tyres squealed on the bitumen, leaving rubber tracks behind.

Five, six males were crammed in tight. Teenagers, twenty at the oldest. One rear occupant had an AK-47 in his lap, pointed the other way from Fox. It would be a hell of a thing to have to turn that assault rifle around in the confines of the car.

The kid gave Fox an unsettling mad-dog stare.

Fox was in a face-off with a carload of thugs. Before they

had a chance to get out of the car he'd pointed a Glock in the driver's face and aimed the Five-seveN into the back window.

He saw their minds ticking over. Should they reach for their pieces? Should they make a move on this guy?

One started to move.

'I wouldn't do it.' Fox's voice was monotone, matter-of-fact. These kids could see there was no bullshit here. This was big-dog work.

The driver nodded, a sign of peace. Fox took the pistols down and they drove away down the road. He watched them until they disappeared up the hill and around a corner. His heart rate was pumping fast, it felt like he'd just sprinted a couple of hundred metres.

He scanned around for any other threats. Some kids played in a bare dirt yard across the street. A rake-thin dog was chained to a tree. Women hung washing to a line that stretched between two apartment blocks. One old woman with a laundry basket looked at him oddly. He crossed the road, away from people.

He walked around the block, got into his Land Rover, drove up the hill and backed it into an alley. He could see, down below, the spot where he'd placed the IEDs. He had the radio transmitter to remote detonate, in his hand, ready to rock.

62

THE
WHITE HOUSE

'FBI Hostage Rescue Team is twenty minutes out of Naval Air Station Key West,' McCorkell said. 'They'll meet local teams on the ground for an assault on the house.'

'And they've got Navy and Coast Guard back-up, Mr President,' Vanzet said. 'Thermal imaging has confirmed that there's a target in the house. We will have real-time video feed from the raid.'

'And we're gonna take him alive,' McCorkell said. 'If he's got any playmates around the country, we'll get him talking.'

The President took it in. He was in the eye of the storm of National Security aides in the room.

'Where're we at with the price of oil?'

'Down almost ten dollars per barrel in the last hour and holding. EU and APEC countries are releasing their individual reserves, and all OPEC countries are coming to the table with some measure of ramped-up production,' McCorkell answered. 'It will relieve some price pressure and should see it dip back to pre-LOOP attack prices by tomorrow, and it will keep falling from there over the coming days as more production comes out of Qatar and the Kingdom.'

'And Nigeria, where're we at with the convoy?'

'True Target is on track to reach Lagos momentarily,' Vanzet said. 'But we still don't have a designated target location.'

'My guy got one of Mendes's security guys to take a tracking device,' Baker said. 'Hidden in a voice recorder.'

'We're working on that,' McCorkell said. 'We'll have something soon.'

'And if we strike against Achebe, where are we legally?' the President asked.

'All clear, Mr President,' the White House counsel said. 'Considering the data we've received, we know that both Mendes and Achebe were in materiel support of terrorist activities. They are designated enemy combatants, and can be treated as other precedents have set.'

'And who will do the strike?'

'There are a couple of options, Mr President, depending on when the targeting coordinates come through,' Vanzet said. 'We've got a Reaper UAV currently on-scene. It's armed with four Hellfire missiles, more than capable of doing the job – you've seen what they can do. In three hours we will have four F-22s within strike range, and we also have the *Wasp* steaming towards Lagos with a full MEU aboard, along with Harrier aircraft and strike helicopters.'

'And a couple of *Los Angeles* class subs with tomahawks in range by tomorrow too,' McCorkell said. 'This is not a matter of not having the firepower on hand, it's just a matter of getting a confirmed target, which we're working on.'

'And once we get the targeting coordinates,' the President said, 'and we take them out with a missile strike, what kind of civilian losses are we talking about?'

'Minimal if any, if we get our best-case scenario of striking at night, wherever they sleep,' Vanzet said. 'It's dark there in about an hour. If we have to strike in the daytime, whether at a Nigerian government installation or in a civilian neighbourhood, there'll be a lot more people moving around the target area.'

'How we gonna find him?'

'We've got the Nigerian President's security force working on the location,' McCorkell said. 'And our own local humint assets are working hard.'

'So I rely on their say-so to order a strike?' the President said.

'We'll get you an accurate ID,' McCorkell replied. At the back of his mind he was thinking of Lachlan Fox. He'd try contacting him or Gammaldi again from his office asap. 'Operation True Target, made up of US Army personnel, will laser designate any final target, so we are waiting on their visual confirmation from the field. Make no mistake, Mr President, when we give you the option to strike, we will have the target there in front of you.'

63

ON THE ROAD, NIGERIA

'Less than fifty clicks to Lagos,' Captain Nix said over their tactical radios. He rode in the passenger seat of the lead Humvee, an M4 always ready in his lap.

Already their travels had been epic. A stop to refuel had almost cost Top his life as someone took a pot-shot at him with a small-calibre rifle – the round was stuck in the side of his Kevlar helmet.

'We got two technicals ahead!' his driver announced. Muzzles flashed. 'Hostile, we're taking fire!'

Nix turned in his seat to talk to his RTO in the back. 'See if we got any CAS yet,' Nix ordered him. Then he spoke to his team over their radio headsets: 'Weapons free, engage targets at will!'

The M240B mounted machine guns started up, the belt-fed

7.62 mm rounds disintegrated the smoking linkages down into the cabin of the Humvee.

The hammer-like sounds striking their vehicle announced they were taking direct fire from the men in the two unmarked pick-ups ahead. The M1116 Humvee provided protection against 7.62 mm armour-piercing projectiles, 155 mm artillery air bursts and 6 kg anti-tank mine blasts. It could handle the fire it was receiving right now, but it still didn't feel good to be in there. The drivers kept them moving fast, ninety clicks an hour, a hundred, one-ten – one of the target vehicles exploded in fire as they raced past.

64

LAGOS,
NIGERIA

Onouarah's pager was on the passenger seat of the Land Rover next to Fox. He sat in the parked car atop the gravel lookout, pointed with the bonnet ahead ready to move, and kept the engine idling. The M4 with its underslung M203 was loaded, as was his Five-seveN on the dash and the Glock strapped to his thigh. He tightened the khaki Kevlar vest over his black T-shirt. He was as ready for war as he would get.

He looked through a Schmidt-Cassegrain spotting scope at the main road below. Seven-kilometre range, perfect clarity, this scope was much better quality than what he'd expected would be supplied by Sir Alex. He tracked the main road – and finally Mendes's convoy was approaching, on the open road that spanned a bridge over a tributary.

He would have engaged them down there, in the grassed expanse that flanked the bridge, but the open space was too big an area to attack a much larger force from. He planned to use the urban environment of these suburban streets to his tactical advantage. More places for cover, more opportunities to pen them in. Plus, the IEDs being placed within the enclosed canyons of the two- and three-storey concrete apartment blocks would add to the bomb blasts. More force would be redirected in towards the road, more debris and shrapnel would be created, more chaos would ensue.

He counted the beats in time until the three-vehicle convoy approached the hidden IEDs. The Mercedes G-Wagon with Mendes rode in the centre, a sedan front and back – big, heavy old BMWs. White occupants, military buzz-cuts – private security contractors. They were special-forces operatives – they wouldn't like this road, especially when they entered the suburban street that led up the hill. They'd be well-armed, wary, alert.

The vehicles passed through the last gap where he could see the road. He counted out the beats of their travel, matching the speed with the distance they still had to cover. The radio transceiver was in his hand, ready to thumb the detonator switch. Seconds away from the IEDs as –

A bus came over the pass behind him, and rumbled on down towards the kill zone.

Fox continued counting – watching as the bus thundered down the road, picking up speed. He willed it to slow and its airbrakes sounded –

He flicked the switch. Within a second both IEDs went off.

The dual thunderclap sounded and echoed around in the confines of the canyon-like street. The lead sedan was blown clear into the air, still flying as a flaming wreck as bits of bitumen and concrete and steel and glass showered down in front of the bus. Three seconds passed before the BMW crashed back down to earth and began melting into the road. The initial blast of fire and smoke that filled the air cleared enough for Fox to make out that Mendes's vehicle had been hit, the second IED having punched its shaped penetrator through the driver's door, leaving a fist-sized hole in the metal door panel. Beyond the shattered glass of the G-Wagon's windscreen Fox saw a lifeless body being pushed out of the driver's door, and he got a brief look at the new driver.

Steve Mendes.

The Mercedes G-Wagon reversed, the following BMW clearing the way with a handbrake turn as the two vehicles disappeared down an alley.

Fox put the Land Rover into gear and gunned the 5.5 litre supercharged engine. It leaped off the mark, the big off-road tyres spitting up streams of gravel as the vehicle roared forward, lifting clear off the ground as it soared from the lip of the lookout towards the dirt road that led down into the neighbourhood. The Land Rover's shock-absorbers protested as the heavy machine smacked back down to terra firma and screamed down the dirt and grass hill into the neighbourhood, ploughing through refuse and old tyres and timber fences of backyards. He kept his foot heavy on the gas as he bumped and grated the Land Rover down an alleyway, never slowing as –

SMASH!

He T-boned the BMW into the wall of a building. The front end of the Land Rover bent and the vehicle bounced back a metre. Fox's number plate was imprinted in what had been the side doors of the sedan. The old 7-series BMW was crushed in on both doors, pinned hard into the facade of a building, some of the car punched through the crumbling concrete cinderblocks.

Fox scanned to the right: the Merc G-Wagon kept on driving away as if oblivious to the carnage behind it.

The four BMW occupants were shell-shocked, sprawled about as if none of them had worn seatbelts. One managed to get a shot off at Fox, the pistol round going wide. Fox unclicked his belt and got out, the P90 nestled into his shoulder, then let loose the magazine with two sweeps left to right of the BMW's passenger compartment. Splinters of glass and steel and blood and bone replaced where solid mass had been just a moment ago. Spam in a can. Gunsmoke was still in the air as he tossed the P90, got in the Land Rover, manoeuvred around and went in pursuit of the G-Wagon that was rooster-tailing down the alley.

His foot was to the floor again, the roar of the engine in his ears, then he stomped the brakes and made a hard turn to skip around a truck, then a car that flashed through an intersection.

There, up ahead, taking a fast left, the G-Wagon.

Fox was on the gas again, engine and tyres fighting to hurtle the two-tonne SUV into fast pursuit.

Suddenly the window next to Fox's head disintegrated. Automatic gunfire peppered his Land Rover. Fox's back window shattered and he ducked under the dash as a full hail of bullets smashed through the back of his seat. Glass from the Land Rover's windows and the foam from his seat were still in the air as he sat up and kept on driving. There, in his rear-view mirror, were his attackers – a Toyota pick-up, one driver, a couple of armed guys in the back.

Fox kept his eyes ahead as he took a couple of sharp turns in pursuit of Mendes. With a long stretch of empty road ahead, he and Mendes left the Toyota pick-up behind. At a sweeping bend Fox flashed the Land Rover's high-beams as he weaved through the traffic of the four-lane black-top of a highway. There were no Jersey barriers to separate the oncoming lanes and he used those lanes as much as his own to gain on the G-Wagon. There was a MOPOL sedan in on the chase now too, back behind the Toyota pick-up.

The G-Wagon was only thirty metres ahead and Fox was closing fast. He swerved back into his lane and a truck blazed its horn as it flashed by where he had just been driving in the oncoming lane. Eighteen wheels raced by the window at warp speed.

Red lights ahead. The G-Wagon went straight through at a hundred kilometres per hour; two cars swerving to avoid the collision ended up smashed together and took out a power pole that crashed to earth right across Fox's lane. He hit the brakes, turned the wheel, the ABS fighting for grip as he let go of the brakes and stomped on the gas, the bonnet of the car lifting with the torque of the engine and the mass that had shifted onto the back axle as he navigated his way through the intersection. Ahead, the G-Wagon was purposefully bumping into cars to create chaos in its wake.

The Toyota pick-up was still behind him but a good fifty metres back now, and falling back faster as Fox gained on Mendes. The shooters standing braced in the back tray could not let go and fire effectively with the fast manoeuvres taking place. The MOPOL driver took the intersection carefully and the flash of a petrol tanker filled Fox's rear-view mirror as it took out the MOPOL sedan. He ignored that and concentrated ahead. The G-Wagon was there to be taken down.

Fox reached across the seat, had to lean right down and reach onto the passenger's floor, from where he took the M4 with underslung M203 launcher. His attention was back up to the road ahead, and he had to duck in and out of the oncoming lane to overtake a lumbering truck, the body roll of the Land Rover protesting as the top-heavy 4WD wobbled back onto a straight path.

Out of the side window he held the M4 by its mag, his index finger through the M203's trigger-guard. He steadied its weight on the side-mirror, then floored the accelerator as the G-Wagon took a chicane in the road that turned onto the main south-heading highway. A six-lane blacktop, Jersey barriers separating the oncoming lane.

The Land Rover bounced into the air as Fox hit the tyres onto the concrete guttering that lined the side of the chicane. He fought with the steering wheel to regain his drive-line and steady the car at eighty kilometres per hour, ninety, a hundred, one-ten . . . His hand holding the M4 steadied and he bumped two cars ahead of him out of the way and hit the gas full – the engine kicked down into third, then fourth – he was doing a hundred and fifty kilometres per hour and climbing fast.

He closed on the G-Wagon ahead, which continued to bump its way through cars that then spun out of control, and Fox had to weave his way through the chaos of the highway. A Subaru wagon was sent corkscrewing its way down the road, and for Fox it was a case of gritting his teeth and driving right through it. The Land Rover smashed through the Japanese car like it was a speed bump, the dazed driver left clinging to his steering wheel as he sat on a bare steel chassis, nothing but him and the engine left unscathed in the middle of the road.

The Toyota pick-up was still somewhere in his rear-view mirror, along with the distant blur of flashing red and blue lights.

Fox wove between two out-of-control cars – each scraping and bumping into the Land Rover as he entered a clearing in the traffic – both he and the G-Wagon hit one hundred and eighty as he fumbled with his hand on the M203's trigger, steady . . .

The launcher coughed out its grenade. The 40 mm high-explosive round struck the corner of the tailgate of the Mercedes G-Wagon.

What happened next seemed to occur in the same heartbeat. A massive explosion of fire, the tailgate was ripped off into the air and the back of the G-wagon was shredded open like someone had taken a can-opener to it. Fox slammed on his brakes as the G-Wagon slowed rapidly and began fishtailing wildly across the three lanes of the highway. Fox's chunky tyres were designed for off-road use, they were smoking up under the braking pressure, and he was still travelling at over a hundred k's per hour when he smashed into the rear of the Mercedes G-Wagon. His forward speed was instantly halved, and with both hands on the wheel he could not get control as the G-Wagon spun around in front of him like a spinning-top.

Fox and Mendes locked eyes. It was the first time Mendes had seen his attacker and it happened with four, five, six revolutions of the G-Wagon. Each time Mendes's expression changed: curiosity, surprise, shock, comprehension, hatred, venom.

Both their cars, each heavy SUVs still moving out of control down the highway, headed towards a truck that had jack-knifed ahead in a cloud of smoke, screeching and clearing its way down the three lanes of traffic in uncontrolled motion. The G-Wagon and Land Rover hit the oncoming flatbed semi-trailer hard, both vehicles becoming airborne. Fox's Land Rover flipped right over the G-Wagon, crashing upside down and spinning around on its roof down the freeway.

Mendes's G-Wagon was rolling over itself sideways, a violent tumble that flipped along like a washing-machine spin-cycle, bits of the car flying off with every impact with the asphalt. The 4WD got smaller and more crushed in on itself with every revolution, the black duco scraped back to silver metal.

Fox's world was a nauseating nightmare of motion. The Land Rover's roof held the weight of the vehicle as it continued to spin around. Forward momentum continued to take him down the highway and he finally stopped only as the Land Rover hit up against the steep grass embankment. As the spinning slowed he had an upside-down view of the world as it flashed by outside the windows. He was suspended in place by his seatbelt, his hands on the passenger compartment ceiling.

The G-Wagon came to rest on its side on the grass embankment just ahead of him. Fox had glimpses of it as his car continued spinning on its roof, each revolution a little slower than the last. He saw movement in the G-Wagon – Mendes, still alive.

Then there came the screeching of dozens of car brakes and tyres as all the lanes of traffic came to a halt before the two smashed-to-shit SUVs and the jack-knifed truck that completely blocked off the highway.

Fox's Land Rover had almost stopped its revolutions now. From the corner of his eye he saw Mendes, climbing out of the G-Wagon. He stood there, facing Fox, seemingly unscathed.

There were feet coming towards Fox. He turned his head to track them, to ID them – the three security contractors from the Toyota pick-up, guns aimed at him.

Bullets sprayed his Land Rover as he made to reach for his seatbelt clasp – the top of his leg erupted with blood as he looked down . . . on the ceiling of the Land Rover just a couple of hand spans from his head – the M4. He picked it up as another salvo of AK-47 fire came his way and he squinted through the exploding debris around him and pointed the M4 out of the window. He squeezed off a three-round burst, took out the closest guy's legs, reminding the others that the guy in this car was armed. They moved back as with the next revolution he let off three more bursts, and another gunman was down. The third man ran back to the cover of his car.

Fox struggled to undo his seatbelt. The Land Rover was on fire now and Mendes was getting away. He released the belt and fell onto the ceiling of the car, pulling himself out of the driver's window fast. He pulled his legs out as the Land Rover continued to slowly spin on its roof. He steadied himself to one knee, then squeezed off three rounds of the M4 – the remaining security contractor's chest erupted.

Fox turned, picked out Mendes, now at the top of the embankment. He was looking back down at him, from fifty metres away. They traded stares. Fox had the look of a hunter. Mendes was disbelieving, that this guy was still after him, after all this.

Mendes turned on a dime and ran.

65

ENTERING LAGOS CITY LIMITS, NIGERIA

There were two vehicles on the tail of Nix's Humvees, and up ahead they were racing fast towards a military roadblock where there were armoured vehicles. A few squads of men with assault rifles started firing hard.

'Is it mission critical, chalk one?'

The gunfire was constant. Bullets found homes against the metal armour of the Humvee, sounding like amplified hail on a tin roof. If he got out of this mission alive, Nix was never going to say a bad thing about a Humvee again.

'You hear that, you Air Force son-of-a-bitch!' Nix yelled into the radio handset. 'You tell me if it sounds critical!'

There was a pause for a couple of seconds.

'Negative, chalk one, I'm sorry. We've got five hours' Reaper flight time remaining, with HVTs as the only designation for

True Target. The road past these guys is clear – punch a hole through and proceed at haste. Do you copy, chalk one?'

Nix weighed it up. Looked back out the rear window at the second Humvee. Top was manning the turret gun, pounding the shit out of the couple of MOPOL vehicles in pursuit of them.

'Okay, we're good, Creech. Chalk one out.'

Nix passed the handset back to his RTO and yelled up to his turret-gunner:

'Sam, blast a way through the roadblock with an AT-4!'

His RTO passed the rocket launcher up into the hands of the turret-gunner.

Seconds later a rocket shot ahead of their position, and the armoured vehicles were engulfed in flames.

'Off-road! Go around them, punch it!' Nix ordered.

Both Humvees were travelling at over a hundred kilometres per hour as they raced around the wreckage of the roadblock.

66

CREECH AIR FORCE BASE, NEVADA

The aircrew were tense as they watched the Humvee convoy engage multiple technical targets. The colour image on the big monitor showed the massive explosion of a US-fired rocket, and the room full of Air Force cheered on their Army cousins as the Humvees broke through the roadblock and raced onwards, unopposed and unpursued.

Ask any American where the front line in the war on terror was being fought and most would have said Iraq, some would have responded Afghanistan, while others would have answered the Middle East in general or anywhere where there was an enemy to be engaged. They'd all be right answers. Some would have replied *wherever our armed forces are deployed*, and they'd be right too. Not many, though, would have considered an Air Force base in Nevada to be one of the busiest front-line forces of the Department of Defense. But, every day of the week, for the operators of 432nd Wing, to step into their air-conditioned offices and plug into their flight control panels was no different than if they were flying combat sorties over Iraq.

They were the first United States Air Force wing dedicated to unmanned aircraft systems. From here they piloted both the MQ-9 Reaper as well as MQ-1 Predator UAVs. They were the new breed of UAV operators. No more were they seen as remote pilots who provided aerial reconnaissance in airspace too dangerous for manned platforms. Their mission was force protection, fighter and close air support. They were an attack force, with the opportunity to quarterback the team on the ground to victory. Today, many ground troops didn't want to deploy without UAV cover, able to scout ahead, reporting on enemy positions around the next bend in the road or over a hill, ready to launch a missile in fire support.

The MQ-9 Reaper was a mean machine. Practically twice as good as the Predator in every respect, but make no mistake: both unmanned aircraft, when piloted by these crews, were among the most lethal hunters in the world. Unlike, say, an F-18 or F-22, there was no actual physical crew inside the aircraft that these Air Force operators controlled. That meant that each aircraft was not confined to the physical constraints of a human pilot, so they could direct it into dangerous missions that would be unthinkable to send even the best pilots into, and there was the ability to have a razor-sharp pilot at the controls twenty-four seven.

The Reaper that was being controlled as the HVT strike tool for Operation True Target was fitted with six stores pylons. The inner pylons carried their maximum load of two 680-kilogram external long-range fuel tanks. The midwing stores pylons each carried a pair of Longbow Hellfire missiles. The outer wing's pylons, usable for air-to-air missiles such as the Sidewinder, were empty. In this configuration the Reaper had a total of fifty-three hours' flight-time endurance.

Room Bravo at Creech contained a crew of fifty Air Force officers and non-coms, all with a specific task to do in order to control their UAV unit of four aircraft. Currently, one aircraft was on the ground in Djibouti for maintenance, two were flying recon over Darfur, and one, named *Swordfish*, was over Nigeria. For these men and women in uniform, in their air-conditioned office full of massive LCD screens and computer-game-style controls, this was as close to being at war as it was flying sorties over Baghdad. Or, in this case, the open roads of Nigeria.

Swordfish was currently being controlled via the Ku-band satellite data link. The Air Vehicle Operator who piloted the UAV was seated before a large flat screen, watching closely what the Reaper saw through its nose-mounted cameras. Three sensor operators were to his sides with their own control stations. The cruising speed, at around one hundred and thirty-five kilometres per hour, was on average forty clicks faster than that of the True Target convoy on the ground. He flew a track that intersected the Humvee's course every fifteen minutes.

To an enemy, the Reaper was like the unwanted guest who didn't want to leave. The gnat at a barbeque. To the allied forces on the ground, it was like having a guardian angel flying in the sky.

67

KEY WEST,
THE FLORIDA KEYS

Duhamel fast-roped onto the suburban street from a hovering Bell 412HP of the FBI's Tactical Helicopter Unit. The only Hostage Rescue Team member to accompany him was Brick, and he touched down on the bitumen next to the team leader and they gave the thumbs-up signal to the loadmaster above. The thick fast-ropes were released and fell to the ground and the helo pivoted and flew away from the target zone.

Duhamel rechecked his H&K MP5 submachine gun was still flicked to safe and was met on the ground by the lead agent of the North Miami Beach Field Office's Enhanced FBI SWAT team. Like Duhamel and Brick, these boys all wore the dark olive-coloured Nomex and Kevlar combat gear, ceramic helmets, clear anti-flash goggles, gloves and steel-capped boots. They had 'FBI – SWAT' stencilled in unmissable white lettering on their backs. Duhamel and Brick simply had 'HRT' on theirs.

Only their weapons, the webbing and Kevlar vests bristling with tactical assault gear, set them apart. The HRT members still had their close-quarters weapons. These Enhanced SWAT members carried serious firepower.

'Special Agent Shane Black,' the SWAT leader said.

'SA Jake Duhamel.'

Hands were shaken.

'Target still in the building?'

'Yes, sir,' Black said. 'We've got a fire-team in across the road that has him on thermal scope, and they've had a couple of tech guys listening in on him all morning.'

'What's he been saying? Who is he – he talking on a phone?'

'Nothin' but prayers,' Black said. 'We got a guy from the Field Office speaks Pashto. Talk'n' to himself, it seems. No phone or radio conversations, although he has placed six calls to a cell-phone number. No answer, cell is switched off and without a message service.'

'That phone got a location?' Duhamel asked. He knew the answer, otherwise it would have been the first thing that he would have heard from this SWAT agent.

'Nope. It's a clean cell number, never been used, prepaid variety purchased at a local convenience store with cash, seventeen days ago.'

'ID on the buyer from store surveillance?'

'One of the dead guys from the boat attack on the LOOP.'

'Quantico got a recording of his voice?'

'Yep, we're transmitting it through in real-time.'

'All right, good,' Duhamel said. The target's voice would be run through recognition software and a search done through DHS databases and those of the NSA and CIA. If this terrorist had ever spoken on a phone that had been intercepted by the US and her UKUSA allies, they'd have it on digital storage somewhere. That would then lead to more avenues to investigate.

'Where are the EMTs?' Duhamel asked. No ambulances were in sight.

'Round the corner with some black and whites. We doing this or what?'

'Yep, let's do this,' Duhamel said. He turned to address them all.

'Lethal force is a *last option*. Brick and I are first through the door,' he said. He chambered a round into his MP5, selected single-round fire, checked the sights. Brick loaded a bean-bag projectile into his shotgun. 'Okay, let's roll.'

'You heard the man, let's move,' Black said. He chambered a round in his M4. His nine SWAT boys all did the same, some with M4s and .45 H&K UMPs, others with Benelli M4 Super 90 Combat shotguns, a couple with CS grenade launchers. Black handed over two gas masks to Duhamel and Brick.

Black's team clung to the sides of two blacked-out armoured vans, ready to roll. It wasn't that these local feds couldn't take down the target. Hell, they would do that as soon as breathe, this terrorist being a member of a cell that had taken American lives in the Gulf of Mexico. Duhamel and Brick were there to ensure every chance was taken to take this guy in *alive*. Intel said there was one more known terrorist in the country, and they needed to know his whereabouts. So, for the purposes of today, for this op, this terrorist would be playing the role of hostage, and Duhamel and Brick were there to ensure that the job was done right. The FBI's Hostage Rescue Team didn't deploy from Quantico for anything but success. And success was measured by how they lived up to their motto: To Save Lives. In a sense, it was to be this bad guy's lucky day.

'Target's three streets to the north?' Duhamel asked. He and Brick readied to take stations next to Special Agent Black on the side of the van. The SWAT leader paused, and gave a vacant look towards the HRT agents.

'What – what is it?' Duhamel asked.

Special Agent Black held a hand to his radio earpiece. Listened hard.

'Target is animated – he may be preparing to move,' Black said.

'Okay, let's take him!' Duhamel said, climbing aboard the running rail of the van and banging on the metal side. 'Move out, now, now, now!'

68

LAGOS,
NIGERIA

Fox had the M4 slung over his head and shoulder, the black nylon strap angled across the front of his chest. It rattled against his back as he ran up the embankment after Mendes. His right thigh was throbbing, just below the holstered Glock, but his full attention was on the guy ahead of him. Steve Mendes was fast. Olympic fast.

Mendes was running flat out on the path that ran along the top of the embankment parallel to the highway. He half-stopped and looked over his shoulder – Fox was bearing down on him – then he disappeared to his right as he hauled himself up and over a chain-link fence.

Fox didn't stop. He wasn't a match for Mendes in a straight line, even if he had both legs pumping at full speed. But where there were fences, cars, buildings, any obstacle, he had a chance to gain on him. He'd trained his Parkour moves enough to tackle this stuff with his eyes shut.

Fox hit the chain-wire fence with his left foot connecting at waist height. He transferred the forward momentum upwards to push up the fence in a *passe muraille*, or pop vault. His right hand clasped the top rail and pivoted over it, landing on the other side three metres clear and exiting at the same speed he'd hit the fence. The manoeuvre didn't lose him a second – it had cost Mendes five.

Mendes was twenty metres ahead, and looked over his shoulder – his eyes wide at the closing gap. He surged forward again.

A car backed out of a driveway. Mendes managed to slide over the boot and continue on, which cost him another two seconds. The driver had jerked to a halt as she realised she'd hit something, and opened her door to get out as Fox took a step off the waist-height brick fence of the driver's house and another step off the roof of the car and over the driver's head, and he was back on the sidewalk, powering after Mendes who had crossed the next road.

The next main road had heavy traffic running southbound at about twenty k's per hour after pulling away from a red light. Mendes reached out and grabbed onto the side-door railing of a bus, pulled himself up and the toes of his Nikes were on the lip of the bottom stair that protruded under the door's rubber seal. He looked back at Fox.

Not once did Fox stop moving, with continual forward momentum as he merged with the traffic – it was clipping along a good five k's per hour quicker than he was sprinting. His arms and legs were like pistons as he gained just a little more speed and launched himself into the traffic, onto the bonnet of a taxi, both feet planted hard. He steadied like a surfer as the driver of the taxi, after two seconds of utter disbelief at the apparition of his new hood ornament, slammed on the brakes.

Fox anticipated this. He jumped at the same moment as the taxi's forward inertia was added to his speed and he was launched through the air, just far enough to make up the next five metres to land on the flatbed of a truck with a forward roll. Then he was on his feet again.

Fox stood there, steady, breathing in through his nose to calm his heart rate. He adjusted the M4's strap, made sure his Glock was still securely holstered, and looked ahead at Mendes. Just two cars separated them.

Steve Mendes turned his head, never letting go of the bus as it ambled along in the late-afternoon traffic. For the first time, his expression turned pale with total mouth-agape wonder: *this guy was chasing him down like a Terminator.*

Fox took a deep breath and exhaled in a gymnast's measured posture as he bounded up onto the cab of the truck, his foot on the edge of its bonnet. Again he used the forward momentum of the vehicle under heavy braking force as he launched himself onto the boot of the next car.

Mendes saw what was happening, knew Fox would be on him within three seconds, and turned around to check the way ahead.

Fox didn't stop as he sprinted over the first car, one foot on the roof, the other launching himself off the bonnet, and onto the boot of the next, then the roof –

Mendes let go of the bus, rolled across the pavement, picked himself up and ran flat out.

Fox jumped off the roof of the car. As his toes touched the pavement of the sidewalk he bent his knees as shock absorbers, and carried his momentum through a forward roll, favouring his turn away from the rigid M4, onto his feet and kept running. It had been one long, fluid movement from the back of that truck and he was still going for it.

Mendes checked back over his shoulder before he ran down a side-street.

69

THE SITUATION ROOM, THE WHITE HOUSE

'What was that?' the President asked.

'We're seeing what the FBI's Critical Incident Response Group are seeing in their HQ – this is the live feed from the suspect's house in Key West.'

'There's no sound – why's there no sound?'

'It's closed-circuit radio audio only, Mr President. The image is coming from a helmet cam.'

'We got their tactical radio feed available, patching it through –'

The sounds of 'clear!' were being yelled over the FBI team's comms gear.

'There, what's that?'

'They just called in the EMT,' O'Keeffe said. 'One agent down.'

'The terrorist?' McCorkell asked. 'He alive?'

Duhamel's MP5 was on the floor, the barrel still smoking. He had both hands on the terrorist's face, making sure he didn't pass out.

'Talk to me,' he said to the man. Slapped his face, made his eyes stay open. There was bright foamy blood on his lips from the two bullets he'd caught in the chest. An S&W auto was kicked away from the terrorist's hand. Brick was receiving first aid from another agent for a gunshot to his neck.

'Talk to me, you son of a bitch!'

'We got some info here,' Agent Black said. 'Washington – you getting this feed? You seeing this?'

His camera showed a dining table of documents. Fake passports. He went through them all.

'Okay, we got some IDs here,' he said. 'Count it as six individuals. Two new faces, you seeing this?'

He held the photos close and the faces of two other terrorists filled the massive screen of the Situation Room.

'Oh boy,' a voice said off-camera.

Black's camera turned to an agent at the other end of the table. He moved down there. Papers were strewn about.

'Be advised, we have maps of the DC area here,' Black said. 'That's maps of Washington DC, streets are highlighted in what looks like three different routes with 'stop sites' marked. They all lead to the White House. We got measurements too – looks like firing ranges, mortar-type ranges. Are you getting this feed?'

70

LAGOS, NIGERIA

Fox rounded the corner and followed Mendes down the street. The ex-CIA man was still pumping out a fast sprint, and Fox was falling behind as he heaved harder to suck in air and keep going at full pace. His hands had started to shake from the extreme exertion, they'd been flat out for close on fifteen minutes.

Mendes was sixty metres ahead and ran across a small bridge. Fox had his right hand down to the Glock – this was the longest straight stretch they'd travelled on for the entire chase. He fumbled with the Velcro strap holding it in but couldn't get a purchase on it or the pistol grip as his legs were pumping flat out. He put his arm up to the M4's telescopic butt-stock behind his shoulder, got a couple of fingers on it, started to drag the weapon around – but it was too late.

They were both over the bridge and Mendes turned down a street to the left that followed this part of the river around to where it spilled out to the sea. This was as ritzy as a neigh-bourhood got in Nigeria, real old-school colonial mansions from a time gone by.

Fox had the M4 pulled over his head now, had it in both hands ready to shoot, but couldn't get a good aim unless he stopped dead still – then Mendes disappeared again, down a street that darted to the right, and Fox was on his tail but dropping back. There was maybe a hundred metres between them now, and he just managed to catch sight of Mendes as he took two fast and immediate left turns – they were heading back to the street that lined the river. Fox's heart was beating hard in his chest, his breaths sounded loud in his head, he was really heaving for air. His right leg where the shrapnel had torn it up cramped at the quad and his pace finally failed him; his stride fell to a jog.

Mendes stopped at a walled compound. He was at a rear entry, punched in a code and disappeared through a door in the wall that quickly shut behind him. Fox arrived at the door five seconds later, his M4 spat out three rounds, and with help from his left boot he was through the thick timber door in the concrete-block wall.

This was the backyard of Mendes's and Achebe's current safe house. A big green lawn and garden, ponds and fountains and a quarter-acre swimming pool. The house was a two-storey forty-thousand-square-foot thing. Mendes was nowhere to be seen – the back door was open, still moving on its hinges.

Gunfire hit the ground behind Fox as he moved forward as fast as his legs would take him. He glanced up to see two figures on the flat roof firing down at him, cheap Eastern Bloc submachine-gun fire spraying the backyard all around him. He emptied the clip of the M4: one target went down, the other ducked for cover.

Fox moved sideways like a quarterback and headed for a door as two armed guys emerged from that very opening. Before they could fire he squeezed off the remaining grenade from the M4's underslung M203. It spanned the twenty-metre gap in a fraction of a second and hit the lintel above them, the high explosive reducing them to pulp and the back entry to the house to rubble as Fox crashed shoulder first through a timber door to his right.

He was in a garage. The empty M4 was tossed away, the Glock up and trained ahead as he double-tapped a security guy who had been taking a break. Coffee and cigarettes hung in the air as the man's chest was shredded; another shot and his head was half-vaporised by the Glock's 9 mm Hydra-Shok round.

The two garage roller-doors were closed, as was the one door to the side that led into the house. Four cars in here. Fox was at the body of the dead security guy, and reached down with his left hand – his Glock trained up at the side door – he took a handful of the guy's shirt, pulled it up and it ripped off him. He frisked the guy's pockets, pulled out a gas cigarette lighter. Then he ripped the shirt into two, opened the fuel caps of the two vehicles parked closest to the roller-doors and stuffed the ripped lengths of the shirt down them.

The door to the house opened. Fox fired three shots off and a guy rolled lifelessly through the open doorway. Pistol-fire spattered ineffectually into the garage as Fox lit the first petrol-soaked rag, then the other. The flames of each crept up towards the petrol tanks and threatened to enter into the gas tanks as Fox was on the move, firing the Glock as he ran into the house.

71

THE
WHITE HOUSE

O'Keeffe crashed the White House the second he heard that there was an imminent terrorist threat. Everyone had to stay where they were in the building, all staff, no matter who. Uniformed and plain-clothed Secret Service agents covered all exits.

The presidential detail locked down the NSC in the Situation Room and the remainder of the Cabinet were still in the emergency operations bunker under the East Wing.

The grounds of the White House were no exception. The Secret Service SWAT team were outside, all in their tactical gear and packing serious firepower.

Snipers on the roof flicked off safeties. Others shouldered rocket launchers, ready to take down any approaching vehicles that proved a threat. Pictures of the terrorists were handed out to all security staff – Xeroxed mug-shots that were taped to gun stocks, wrists, thighs, anywhere in easy view. The agents who patrolled the entry points at the gates were refusing all entry, and DC police were arriving en masse along Pennsylvania Avenue and surrounding streets.

News crews set up real fast. Those who were already on breaks from the Press Room had been ushered outside the gates as well. There were already over two dozen cameras set up.

'Seamus,' McCorkell called out. 'Find out how the press got here so fast.'

'On it,' O'Keeffe said. He looked at the security feed and picked up the internal line to the House's Secret Service command centre and started talking, rapid fire.

'How the hell they get here already?' he asked the agent in the Press Room. 'They told their news desks when? Right.'

He hung up.

'Fox News, CNN, BBC and others all got a tip-off four minutes ago to come and film the grounds,' O'Keeffe said. 'That was just before I ordered the security crash of the House.'

'The tip-off's from the terrorists,' McCorkell said. 'They want this seen. Whatever's coming, this is going to happen now.'

The agent only noticed the sedan as it clipped fenders with a DC police car and raced towards the north-east entrance. It slammed into the White House gate – pushed it up but got nowhere as it smashed against the massive steel crash-barrier and bounced back onto the road. Four Secret Service agents, two in uniform and two in assault gear, had weapons drawn at the single male occupant.

'Hands in the air!'

'Let me see 'em!'

'Don't move!'

•

Inside the car.

'*Allahu akbar . . .*' was repeated for the third time.

Both his hands were on the steering wheel. Fingers were pressed against a wire trigger taped there. The circuit closed, the current travelled to the detonator in the boot.

CLAP – BOOM!

The sheet-metal sides of the Buick ruptured, the explosion swallowing up the glass and steel gatehouse, although the barrier held true.

The four Secret Service guys were vaporised. People within forty metres were struck with flying shrapnel: bolts and nails courtesy of a US hardware store had become subsonic weapons of terror.

All Secret Service agents to the southern end of the White House grounds had their attention on the bomb blast. None noticed the other man scale the fence sixty metres away. Once onto the lawn, the Afghan ran. As Secret Service and emergency crews raced to help at the bombing scene, the lone terrorist ran towards the White House south portico.

EMT sirens and screams filled the air as he ran faster and faster, the distance to the House longer than it seemed from the other side of the fence. He was running like a quarter-back who'd just had his team-mate feign a pass to distract attention.

He'd made it over halfway to the House when he was spotted. A Secret Service agent on the lawn fifty metres to the east sprayed a full auto P90 clip his way – a round hit the terrorist's ankle and shattered the bone. He dropped to his knees.

Secret Service radio calls were going frantic. There was the *pop-pop* of pistol fire.

The Afghan steadied on his knees, wired detonator in hand that traced back down inside his sleeve and into a bomb vest.

'*Allahu –*'

His head snapped back with a sharp whack. Then again.

Two snipers on the roof called in their kill.

The terrorist's body somehow stayed upright, headless on his knees, in an image destined to be seen on news footage around the world countless times.

72

LAGOS,
NIGERIA

Fox was in a kitchen that was exploding around him in a shower of tiles and glass, but he pressed on, fired fast, a security contractor blown back through a glass door – then he heard automatic gunfire coming from outside, to the *front* of the compound. A real pot-pourri of small-arms fire. Then the explosion of a 40 mm grenade.

He ejected the spent mag from the Glock and rammed home a full one, cocked the slide and heard, in the briefest of silence between the mixed gunfire, a tiny voice.

Coming from his Kevlar vest's breast pocket – his cell phone. He lifted up the Velcro strap, looked at it. The battery symbol was flashing – it was down to its last bit of juice. The caller ID was GAMMALDI – the call from Al was still open, a good hour after they'd talked at the lookout.

'Al?'

•

'Lach! We're out front!' Gammaldi shouted, ducking down behind the wall of the compound as bits of stone showered down on him. The cell phone was in his hand, held tight to his ear.

To his right, Javens was hunkered down behind the engine block of an armoured Range Rover, all his weight on his unplastered leg. Gibbs and Sefreid were firing hard, with fast reloads.

To his left were the two battle-scarred Humvees of Captain Garth Nix. The Humvees had been through hell and back with stuff hanging off them everywhere: metal roofing, branches, fences; black burn marks from taking direct fire, windscreens too cracked to see into. The turret-gunners were both swaying the 7.62 mm M240Bs across the roof-line of the mansion.

'We're here with some US Army boys – is Achebe in there?'

'Not sure!' Fox yelled back. 'Mendes is, though. The garage, fire in the hole!'

'What?'

The two roller-doors of the garage that adjoined the house blew outwards and crashed against the stone wall to the front of the compound. Fire licked out as smaller secondary explosions kept rolling through the four cars inside.

Fox put the phone back in his pocket. He got up from behind the kitchen island bench and scanned the room down the sights of his Glock: no threats. The fire from the garage was starting to eat its way through the open doorway.

He went across the room, his damaged quad getting stiffer

with every moment of stillness. He tied a kitchen towel off over the wound, and moved to the door that led into the entry foyer.

Nix ran ground-close over to Gammaldi. His Humvee turret-gunner was reloading another box of belt-fed ammo into his M240B. Top was providing cover fire with his M16A4, sharp-shooting two targets through a pane-glass window of the first floor.

'Targets in there?'

'He's checking!' Gammaldi said, fumbling with his cell phone as he reacted to close gunfire hitting around him.

'RPG!' Top shouted.

Gammaldi cowered lower to the ground, while Nix held him down for protection.

The rocket-propelled grenade struck the ground to the side of the lead Humvee, making the vehicle rock on its axles and the gunner spray an uncontrolled stream of bullets across the entire battlefield, lucky not to cause any blue-on-blue casualties.

Nix got off Gammaldi, fired a full clip from his M4 then ducked back down. In the brief pause Gammaldi noticed the Army captain's decision-making process going on.

'Okay, I'm going in to confirm the targets,' Nix said into his helmet's tactical mic. 'Top, through the door with me. Sam, Jesse, cover-fire our approach with the 240s and call in the UAV's approach run.'

Top ran over to join Nix. He handed over four 40 mm CS gas grenades in a webbing belt. CS was a damn effective riot-control agent, non-lethal, good for evening out the odds. He handed a gas mask to Gammaldi.

'Ready to follow our lead?'

'Me?'

'You can ID your guy in there,' Nix said. 'I'd hate to put a round between his eyes. Tell him we're heading in with CS gas.'

'Targets – nine o'clock!' Gibbs yelled. 'Need help!'

Nix's Humvee gunner turned and engaged the four security-contractor vehicles racing towards them. One engine exploded under the fire, the hood soaring into the air. The other three vehicles pulled into cover and a good dozen guys raced to fire positions.

Nix and Top were fast on the defence, the captain launching a shell from his M4's underslung M320 grenade launcher. It was next-generation from the M203, more accurate, lighter, quicker on the reload. The HELLHOUND High Explosive Dual Purpose round was able to pierce through nine centimetres of solid steel and then create a lethal fragmentary radius of ten metres. The vehicle it hit seemed to vaporise, with five, six combatants down.

'Firing CS!' Nix said, loading the 40 mm grenade and firing just forward of the attacking force. It skipped across the ground and thudded into a tree, the white gas belching out. In less than three seconds the area was blanketed in a cloud. The enemy fire petered out, figures stumbling about holding their faces.

Gammaldi put the clear face mask on; his breathing sounded like Darth Vader.

'Give that back, change of plan,' Nix said. He took the gas mask and CS grenades and crawled over to Javens. The Brit was propped against the side of his Range Rover, an MP5 empty on the ground next to him, firing his Walther at the targets in the house a hundred metres ahead. His fire did little other than keep the gunmen's heads down. His leg prevented him from getting in a good cover-crouch.

'Take this,' Nix said. He passed over his M4 and the CS grenades and pointed down the road at the security-contractor force. 'Launch another grenade at them every sixty seconds.'

Javens nodded in reply. He shouldered the M4 and cracked off a few rounds towards the advancing guys.

'We got them engaged,' Sefreid said over a burst of his P90. He and Gibbs were going through the stack of ammo between them fast. 'Just get Fox the hell out of there!'

Nix was back over to Gammaldi. He said something into his mic that Gammaldi couldn't make out, then one of his soldiers tossed over an M4, which Nix caught in the air. It had an M26 shotgun mounted under the barrel.

Gammaldi was ready to move, crouched like a sprinter.

Nix yelled into his ear:

'You follow us through the door, okay?'

Gammaldi gave the thumbs-up.

Fox was at the upstairs landing.

Gunfire sounded from all the front rooms of the mansion; there must be at least a dozen guys up there.

He backed into an empty bathroom.

A security guy ran past the doorway, right where Fox had just been. Fox moved out to the landing and put two rounds into his back. He was carrying an RPG, the rocket in the launcher. Fox winced and took cover in the bathroom as the weapon clattered to the ground – but it didn't go off.

Fox reloaded the Glock with his last clip. He reached in his pocket for the cell phone – the battery was dead. He moved out and went down the hallway, his Glock double-handed leading the way. The screams of wounded men carried down the corridor. He stopped to listen carefully. The sound of – what? Kids crying?

Another target rushed in front of him. He fired two shots to the body. Blood splattered up the wall. Another shot to the head and he was out of the fight.

Fox took another step forward, an open door to his right. He turned to check – then back to the wall. Behind him, in the room, the click of a pistol cocking.

Click-clack. An assault rifle loaded now too.

Outgunned. Outnumbered.

Gammaldi was pressed up against the front wall near the door. The ground at his feet was exploding under rifle fire as gunners on the roof sprayed ammunition straight down. Nix and Top were on either side of the front door, ready to enter.

The facade of the old colonial was pounded to shit. The front door had taken two direct 40 mm Hellhound hits; it was now more a gaping, crumbling hole than a doorway.

BOOM! An RPG round went off close by, ringing in all their ears.

Gammaldi looked back towards the far Humvee – its turret was gone, the occupants of the vehicle tumbling out onto the street, smoke billowing out the open doors and a hole in the roof.

•

Brutus Achebe lay on the floor of his bedroom with his wife and two children next to him. The kids were crying. His wife was silent, too shocked to move. He held the heads of his children close into his stomach, hands over their ears. He rocked rhythmically as he prayed. The warmth of his breath caressed his children's skin. Their fresh smell filled his nostrils. Tears for their souls were worn in his eyes.

Fox dashed past the room behind him, turned to make sure the two targets in there hadn't seen him.

He was shot in the back and the Glock dropped from his hand. The force of the gunshot spun him around, wide-eyed in shock. There was instant, searing heat in his back under his Kevlar vest and T-shirt.

Mendes faced him, standing in the next doorway. Not two metres from him, a pistol pointed at Fox's chest.

Fox pounced forward, but Mendes was quick on the trigger. The ex-CIA operator fired point-blank into Fox's chest.

One, two shots in a second.

Then his pistol clicked empty.

Fox slammed up against Mendes, gripping both his wrists hard. He wrenched them back, squeezed. Both men were red in the face from the effort and Fox head-butted Mendes, connecting where Mendes's nose met his forehead. There was a crunch and Mendes's face erupted with warm blood.

Fox gave a final twist of the guy's wrists, with every ounce of his strength. The pistol clacked to the floor. He saw it fall, noticed with total clarity the make. H&K UCP. Armour-piercing.

•

Gammaldi stood directly behind Top as the bulky sergeant was at the foot of the stairs, engaged in a firefight with two targets. Both went down hard.

Nix bumped in close and stood by them.

'What are the chances that your guy has already killed our HVT's?' Nix asked Gammaldi.

'About 32.33 per cent,' Gammaldi said. 'Repeating, of course.'

'All right, funny man,' Nix said. 'Follow my lead. You ID your guy, I eyeball the targets, and we bug the hell out before the missiles rain in. Top, you stay here and cover the exit.'

'Hooah!'

Nix turned and ran up the stairs, Gammaldi close behind, the captain's shotgun booming 00 buckshot as he cleared a path upstairs. On the way through Gammaldi took the pistol out of Top's thigh holster, and ducked around the Sergeant who continued to fire, giving a guttural war-cry of his own as he charged up the stairs behind the Army captain.

Fox pushed Mendes through the open doorway, pinning him up against a wall. His forearm was up against his throat and he pushed with all his force. Mendes's hands were trying to pry the force off, he was coughing hard for breath.

'Why'd you do it?!' Fox yelled into his face.

Mendes repeatedly kneed Fox, sending him reeling back. He rushed Fox, who was doubled over, sunk elbows into his back followed by a knee to the head, which Fox caught with his hands, using the upwards momentum to raise himself and his own elbow, which clipped Mendes under the chin.

•

Gammaldi and Nix were lying on the floor of the bathroom Fox had been in. The tiles all around them had turned into clouds of porcelain dust as the room was shredded with machine-gun fire, a 5.56 mm SAW of some sort.

'Top, we need help!' Nix called into his mic.

Fox powered through his pain, mind over matter. He ducked under a computer monitor that Mendes launched at him – it crashed through a window. This room was at the front of the house, and now gunfire from the US Army peppered through the smashed-out window. Bits of books from the shelved walls exploded and rained throughout the room like confetti.

As he got up Fox reached behind himself onto the desk and picked up a stained-glass lamp. Mendes rushed at him and Fox brought the lamp up and smashed him across the face, slicing his cheek open.

They each took a step back, the smallest of breathers to gain a second of composure. Mendes's face was now all blood. Fox's breathing was laboured and he didn't stop to think about why.

Mendes stood with knees slightly bent, his shoulders hunched over and forward. Jujitsu stance. He spat out blood from the hole in his cheek, and launched himself at Fox, pushing him up against the old roll-top desk, head first, punching him repeatedly in his stomach, his sternum, his sides. He hammered away at the bullet wounds in Fox's chest.

Fox began convulsing under the pain. He couldn't react or respond to the attack that had him stuck up on the desk and taking hell. Finally, after what might have been fifteen seconds, when Mendes's assault was slowing, Fox's hand responded and he brushed it around on the desk that he sat pinned on – paper, pencil –

He picked up the wooden pencil in his tight fist, lanced it into Mendes's side, but it just snapped in his hand as it hit a rib. That spurred Mendes on, blood spraying from his mouth and cheek as he pummelled away at Fox.

Fox was down to his last. He blinked through the pain that waved within him. This was do or die. He could feel the bullet wounds in him now, like red-hot pokers pushing into him, two in the front, one in the back. On the desk, behind him to his right, he felt around. The papers, a plastic pen, something hard and cold. Metallic. A steel letter-opener? It felt like a fifteen-centimetre blade with a dull edge.

He pushed it around the tabletop, fumbled a purchase on the handle, but it kept slipping in his bloodied hand. He picked it up.

Then dropped it on the desk as Mendes started pressing his head against Fox's throat, never slowing the infighter boxing.

Fox had it in his grasp again, felt the thin metal handle in his clenched fist, held it tight. He screamed, a desperate barbaric yawp as over his body's protest he fought to lunge with the letter-opener with all his strength.

He pushed it into Mendes's side. Felt it slide in between two ribs. Pushed until it was to the hilt of his clenched fist.

Mendes's eyes went wide and he took a step back, then another. Let out a loud breath that might be his last.

Fox stared into Mendes's scary, empty eyes.

Fox still held the handle and he was off the desk now. He stood, and almost fell forward as his legs took his weight. His right hand was still on the letter opener; he put his left onto the opposite side of Mendes's body and pushed them together.

The blade had disappeared into Mendes, the full fifteen centimetres of metal.

Mendes collapsed onto the floor on his knees.

Fox slowly crouched down. The sound of gunfire echoed about the room. He looked Mendes in the eyes. Held his face up to his eye-line by a fistful of hair.

'Michael Rollins,' Fox said. 'Why did you kill him?'

The confused stare of Mendes was searching Fox's face.

'You're dying, pal,' Fox said, uneasily balanced, hand still tight on Mendes's hair. 'Even it up. Why'd you have Rollins killed?'

'Your mis— mistake . . .'

'My mistake?' Fox asked.

No answer. Mendes was fading and Fox had to get out of this room before more bad guys came filing in. He shook Mendes's head, watched his eyes roll around. 'You're dying. You're dying, man. Why'd you want us killed? Why'd Michael Rollins die?'

There was a glint in the man's eyes as he convulsed violently and died. The reason would be another secret that the career intelligence officer left the world with and would never reveal. He left with a final look on his face that read, *I know something you don't know . . .*

73

THE SITUATION ROOM, THE WHITE HOUSE

'Four dead Secret Service agents, thirteen injuries, being bussed out now,' O'Keeffe said.

'The terrorists?' McCorkell asked. On a screen in the room he watched the replayed image from Fox News, the surreal view of a headless corpse remaining upright on his knees with the White House's south portico as a backdrop.

'Two targets, both down,' O'Keeffe said. 'Each confirmed as our two suspects.'

McCorkell shared a look with the President.

'Do we think there's something else coming?' the President asked. 'I mean, that's all the suspects accounted for now?'

'All those we know of, Mr President,' McCorkell said. 'We'll know when we go through all the recovered data from the Key West site. With the death of Massoud, it might have forced their hand to fall back on what they know best. Suicide bombing.

They've gone for our seat of government in a highly visible way. This seems outside the scope of their cell's objective. This is a case of Mendes using these guys for his own objective to raise oil prices so as to have a higher bargaining position, and to divert our attention. Both actions worked. What he didn't fully realise is what would happen in going into business with terrorists.'

'You lie down with lions . . .' the President said.

'Mr President, the True Target element is on site,' Vanzet cut in. 'UAV air strike is five minutes out, our boys on the ground have called in the fire. We just need your say-so.'

74

LAGOS, NIGERIA

Lachlan Fox stood before Brutus Achebe.

He had his Glock pointed close at the Nigerian's head. Blood ran over his hand, down the pistol grip, and dripped onto the off-white carpet. His aim swayed, but at this range an inch to the left or right hardly mattered.

Achebe knelt on the ground, his face up at Fox. He had his wife and kids behind him. He shook his head, searched Fox's face, his eyes pleading, *No, not in front of my kids*.

Fox swayed, blinked into focus. Looked around the room. Bags were packed, they'd been ready to leave. There was a big case full of US cash on the bed – portable, ready to roll to the next safe house once it was zipped up. Serious amounts of US bills in there. Twenty, thirty kilos worth of Benjamin Franklin.

Fox coughed. Touched his lip – his fingers came away wet. He rubbed the bright red, foamy blood between his thumb and forefinger. Couldn't help but wince. He wiped his hand on the front of his Kevlar vest. The whole hand came away covered with thick, sticky blood. He blinked away the image of Rollins dying in his arms. Focused. Held the Glock up level with Achebe's forehead.

'Just tell me why,' Fox said. Matter-of-fact.

'Lach?'

Fox turned his head – saw Gammaldi enter the room. A US Army captain stood at the door.

The gunfire had died down from inside the house now. There was only the sporadic machine-gun fire from out front on the street.

Fox looked back down to Achebe. The Nigerian stared back at Fox, confused. Fox motioned that he expected an answer.

'I – I wanted power?' Achebe said, unsure what the answer was that Fox wanted to hear.

'Michael Rollins . . .' Fox said. His finger tightened in the Glock's trigger-guard. 'Why did you have Michael killed? Why'd you try to kill us?'

Fox waited for an answer. Took a step closer, the pistol point-blank to Achebe's face.

'Hellfire strike in three minutes!' Nix yelled into the room. He stood braced in the doorway, his M4 scanning for targets. 'Achebe stays. Friendlies evac now!'

Achebe shook his head at Fox. His eyes had that same gleam of wonder that Mendes had left with, mixed with some disbelief of everything that was happening to him.

'Last chance,' Fox said. In the background he saw the face of Achebe's young son looking up at him. He blocked it out, pressed the Glock hard against Achebe's forehead. 'Right-the-fuck-now, tell me: Why – did – you – have – him – killed?'

Achebe stood, to draw Fox's aim clear from his family. A protective father. Finally, this man had realised the value of life. Too late.

Fox fired into the air above him.

Achebe turned, said goodbye to his kids. Looked back at Fox, some measure or resolve there in his face.

The Glock touched against Achebe's forehead, seared it with the hot metal. Fox's arm was shaking. He knew this was the end. He had just moments left to live and this fuck was going down first.

'You are mistaken, Lachlan Fox,' Achebe said.

There was a pushing on Fox's leg. Achebe's son beat his little three-year-old fist against Fox's knee.

Fox still held the gun on Achebe.

'Lach, don't do it . . .' Gammaldi said.

'Get out of here, Al,' Fox replied. His eyes never left Achebe, who looked like a man resigned to his fate. Fox swayed a little; Gammaldi steadied him. He was standing right next to Fox, calmly by his side, as if they had all the time in the world.

'Two minutes!' Nix said. 'Let's move it out, people!' He entered the room, with total disregard for whatever Fox and Achebe had going on, picked up a kid under each arm and carried them out, Achebe's wife close behind him and her screaming kids.

'*Friendlies coming out the front door!*' Nix's words into his helmet mic echoed up the stairs into the bedroom.

'Take him in . . .' Gammaldi said to Fox. His voice was calm in his friend's ears. 'Lach, let's go. Bring this guy in.'

'Why? So he can hide behind a hundred lawyers?' Fox said. His Glock was real unsteady now, he almost didn't have the strength to hold it up any more. His voice quietened as he said to Achebe: 'What did you say about Rollins?'

'He said you were wrong,' a voice cut in.

Fox and Gammaldi turned their heads.

There was a guy in the open doorway that connected this bedroom to another. Dressed just in underpants and with bloodied bandages wrapped around his body. More an apparition than a real figure. Fox blinked to clear his vision.

It was Michael Rollins.

75

THE SITUATION ROOM, THE WHITE HOUSE

'Final code is in, both targets are in the building,' Vanzet said. 'UAV is in approach run.'

'Take them,' the President said. 'Take the shot.'

The image from the UAV's real-time camera showed the neighbourhood streets of Lagos flashing by underneath it.

'What's the situation with chalk one?' McCorkell asked. 'True Target personnel – are all friendlies accounted for?'

Vanzet had one ear to an open phone line to The Pentagon.

'They're leaving the site right now, waiting for final friendlies to evac,' Vanzet said. 'They've got Achebe's family out, wife and two kids.'

'There were kids in there?' the President asked, alarmed.

'They're out now, Mr President. Leaving the target area.'

They all watched the black and white image on the main screen.

'God be with them.'

76

LAGOS,
NIGERIA

Fox's feet hardly touched the ground as he was led outside with an arm over the shoulders of Gammaldi and Achebe.

Nix was at his Humvee, which was loaded tight with Achebe's family. There were still security contractors on the roof and down the street, engaged in sporadic fire. Nix made the slightest pause as Achebe stood in front of him. The Army captain looked back to the house, then into the vehicle at the Nigerian's family – no way did he have what it took to put a bullet in Achebe's head right there, in cold blood, in front of them. He pushed Achebe into the back seat, got in the front, and the two Humvees roared off.

Fox was helped into the back seat of a Range Rover, motionless as he sat next to Gammaldi. Gibbs was behind the wheel with Sefreid riding shotgun. Javens climbed awkwardly into the back and they tore off down the road as he closed his door.

With his head resting on the back seat, Fox looked out the rear window. His breaths were short and sharp, irregular, as he fought to focus his eyes. He saw the figure of Michael Rollins standing in the first-floor window. Fox's world was spinning, and that moment of time seemed to span hours, weeks. It was as if he were watching this very scene from afar, that he was no longer a player in the action. He, like Rollins, was being pulled from this earth. The figure of Rollins grew smaller, until he was a blur. In seconds he would pass into the unity of all things.

There was a sharp *whack-whack* of missile strikes followed instantly by a massive thunderclap of rolling explosions. Fox felt the concussion in his chest and somehow sensed that this was all that now beat in there.

'Lachlan!' Gammaldi shouted at him. 'Lach! You with me?'

Fox watched the plume of smoke reach into the sky, the safe house reduced to a pile of rubble and smoke that covered the street in their wake. He tilted his head to face his friend. He felt at peace; his face radiated what he saw in Gammaldi's. Despite his wounds, he felt no pain. He could not feel beyond his face. He smiled. He could feel his mouth form into a half-smile that spoke of the knowledge that comes with death.

'I'm with you, buddy,' Fox said. His journey here was done. All of a sudden, as if he had given up on his quest, he collapsed into himself with the strain of the bullet holes in him.

The sun began its departure as well.

EPILOGUE

THE WHITE HOUSE, THE NEXT DAY

McCorkell sat at the porch reading a book on the Iraq War. It was an embedded journalist's account and he was reading about some of the engagements that he had been involved in from afar. Already some of his legacy was apparent. It was interesting reading, although he wished there were less photographs. He looked forward to a day where he could look back with enough distance to be removed from immediate guilt. He wondered if he would have been a good soldier. He doubted it.

'Bill, walk with me,' the President said, exiting the garden door of his office and heading towards the Residence. The Secret Service agents kept their distance, although there were more of them than usual. McCorkell took stride next to the President, stopped for a moment as the Commander-in-Chief bummed a smoke from an agent, and they continued walking.

'The media are calling for blood over the attack here yesterday,' McCorkell said.

'So's most of congress and the senate,' the President said. 'Even some of the people I respect most are calling for revenge . . .'

They stopped and watched the gardeners attending the roses. Birds pecked at newly scattered lawn seed. Sunday traffic sounds were faint. Armed agents were silent.

'O'Keeffe told me that the FBI found the terrorist's safe house here in Washington,' the President said.

'Yes, Mr President,' McCorkell said. 'They recovered a courier van with a mortar set up in the back. They had planned to hit the White House, things could have been much worse. Seems Massoud took the location of his safe house with him.'

'The nurse, McFarland, he talked yet?' the President asked.

'Late last night. Never knew the real identity of his lover.'

'You believe him?'

'Love can be blind.'

'Romantic.'

They watched the gardeners prune and plant and snip and cut. The overflying air force jets were distant. McCorkell watched the President's gaze follow the slipstreams in the clear air. Calculating more than miles.

'You did good in there yesterday,' McCorkell said.

'I was all right. I've got a good team.'

'You're a man down now.' Not ten minutes ago, through the glass of the door of the Oval Office, McCorkell had seen Fullop pass the letter to the President.

'Plenty of good men around,' the President said. 'Although I do think it's time for a woman's touch.'

The President took a final drag and tossed the butt onto the grass by his feet. Ground it out. Picked it up. His chocolate Labrador, Tenzin, came from nowhere. Licked his hand. Went over and sniffed McCorkell, tail wagging as he received a scratch behind the ear.

'Oil prices have gone down a bit,' McCorkell said.

'Not enough. Not nearly enough.'

They continued to the Residence. Tenzin bumped in between them as they walked.

'We've all seen it rise and we'll watch it rise again,' the President said. 'One thing to come out of all of this: we gotta get away from oil.'

NEW YORK CITY, TWO WEEKS LATER

The BBC news anchor introduced the lead story of the hour:

'The ex-president of Nigeria, Hassan Ruma, appeared today before the International Court of Justice at The Hague. Mr Ruma pleaded guilty to all charges of gross corruption and human rights violations during his fifteen-year reign.'

The image on the screen showed Hassan Ruma surrounded by medical staff as he entered the Peace Palace. The cameras of the world's media flashed away.

'It is hoped that his admissions of guilt will set an example for other African leaders, a step already seen in the actions of fellow Nigerian, former Energy Minister Brutus Achebe. Achebe, who was recently involved in a failed coup against the sitting President, has today announced his intention to follow Mr Ruma's lead . . .'

At the very least, it was the first crack in what had long been an unspoken pact among such leaders to protect one another.

The ticker along the bottom of the screen read: *US military force in Nigeria secures peace in the Niger Delta. Local governments gain federal support in implementing sweeping reforms of the oil contracts in the region.*

'And you didn't want me to pick you up a seventy-inch screen,' Gammaldi said. He shook his head in mocking disbelief. 'Game or movie?'

Fox pointed to the movie.

'You're sure? I got you *Star Wars: The Force Unleashed* for the PS3 . . . all right.' Gammaldi clicked the news over to Apple TV, and started up a movie on the big Sony LCD.

Fox pressed the button to make the bed-head rise. It was a hospital-type trolley bed, brought into his apartment with him strapped to it two days earlier. A nurse came over and checked Fox's temperature.

'I'm actually feeling a little sick myself,' Gammaldi said. 'Would a sponge bath be out of the question?'

The nurse, used to his wise-cracks by now, gave him a stare reserved for the pathetic, and went and sat back down to read her magazine.

'*She is smoking!*' Gammaldi mouthed to Fox.

Lachlan shook his head.

'How's it going with you and what's-her-name?' Gammaldi asked.

'Jane? All right,' Fox said. His voice sounded tired. 'She visited last night.'

'Straight back into it, you dog you.'

'Shut up, Al, we're friends is all.'

'Yeah, right.'

'How about you and Emma Gibbs? She still around or have you scared her off with your skill at watching sports, eating pizza, snoring and farting all at the same time?'

Gammaldi didn't grace that with an answer. Just smiled and watched the movie's opening credits.

'Why would they call this *Quantum of Solace*?'

'Question is, why make another movie with the premise of bad guys planning to take over a country? Bit of a yawn if you ask me.'

'Stranger than fiction, hey?'

They laughed.

'So, what's next?'

'Next?' Fox asked. He could see what his friend was getting at. 'What's next . . . ? I think a trip to India is next.'

'What's in India?'

'Indians,' Fox said. Smiled. 'Water. Or, rather, a lack of it. Conflicts over it. I reckon there's a good story there, one that needs to be told.'

'Fresh water scarcity? That'll never fly, who cares about that?'

'Like, maybe about six and a half billion people,' Fox said. 'It's a big issue and it's happening right now. You seen *Chinatown*?'

Gammaldi shook his head.

'Well forget the Bond film,' Fox said. 'Put *Chinatown* on. Nicholson, Dunaway, Polanski at their best.'

The door buzzer sounded and Gammaldi went to get it. Came back with Tas Wallace.

'How's my favourite reporter holding up?' Wallace asked Fox.

'I bet you say that to all your staff when they get shot to shit,' Fox said.

Wallace shook Fox's hand with ceremony. He put a large envelope on the bed near Fox.

'That was a handshake from McCorkell, who in turn passed one on from the President,' Wallace said. 'Next time you two are in Washington, you've got an invite to the Oval Office.'

Gammaldi looked impressed. Fox was too exhausted to really appreciate it. He picked up the envelope. Plain manila, not labelled, heavier than it appeared. 'What's this?'

Wallace looked from Fox to the envelope.

'That's from McCorkell,' Wallace said. 'CIA transcripts of Michael Rollins, from his extraordinary rendition . . . experience.'

Fox considered the parcel. The weight of it. Took a minute to respond.

'You read it?' Fox asked.

His boss nodded.

'I think you should too,' Wallace said. 'It explains why Michael was picked up in the first place; his rendition wasn't exactly an error. Sure, he wasn't a terrorist, but he was something close.'

'How can that be?' Fox asked.

'This information was locked away in the files of the previous director of the CIA,' Wallace said. 'Turns out, Rollins was working a story that started in Russia and led him through New Europe and into Pakistan, investigating business oligarchs and their organised crime outfits, men connected by their old associations as former spies. For a while he passed as one of them, deep undercover. He was so convincing in the role that the CIA flagged him as a legit target and took him in. And what's more, it's now known that it was these friends of his on the outside who arranged the attack and break-out at the rendition camp.'

'And so why didn't these friends pick Rollins up from those guys we met in Afghanistan?' Gammaldi asked. 'I mean, he contacted us to come and pay a ransom for his release.'

'I guess he figured this brotherhood of ex-spooks would be more interested in silencing him than sending him off into the sunset with a pat on the back,' Fox said. 'And they would definitely have had some questions about what he'd talked about in those three months inside.'

Wallace nodded.

'Rollins would have told those Afghanis that he had a better pay cheque available for them,' Wallace said. 'From us.'

'Friends he knew he could trust . . .' Gammaldi said.

'Until we persuaded him to come to Nigeria . . .' Fox added. Beyond all the curiosity and numbness and fatigue, Fox now fully understood that death was not an adventure for those who faced it. Quite the opposite. True courage wasn't the ability to face death; it was the ability to face life. Rollins had taught him that. So whatever was in Rollins's file, whatever he'd done, whatever his connection with Mendes and how cloudy that might be, Fox wasn't ready to know that. Not yet. Not after setting out on the path he'd just taken when he'd thought his friend was dead. He had done what he'd done armed with the best information at the time. He'd taken his friend on face value. He couldn't second-guess himself or he knew he was as good as dead . . .

'Mendes was a part of this group?' Gammaldi asked, making the connection. 'He drew Rollins in when he realised who he was . . .'

'That's the conclusion I came to, but it is just the tip of a big iceberg,' Wallace said. 'I don't have any information beyond what's in that envelope. Although, if either of you were inclined to want to know more . . .'

'What?' Fox asked. He knew that look in his boss's eyes – work time.

'There's an FBI agent working on this who's very interested to hear if we are able to help out in any way,' Wallace said. He sat at the foot of Fox's bed. 'I said I'd see if I could find anyone willing.'

Fox and Gammaldi traded tired looks. Wallace signalled with raised hands of surrender that there was no rush.

'What are you going to tell his wife?' Fox asked. 'Will you tell Penny how her husband really died?'

'Do you think she should know?'

Fox sat up a little straighter. He put the envelope on the table next to his bed, among the masses of mail and newspapers and magazines. For a moment, the eyes of all three men stayed on that envelope.

'No,' Fox said. 'Let them keep their memories intact. They don't need this, this glimpse of a man unknown to them. The doubt, the second thoughts, the confused morality behind deception. I know I can't afford any more of that right now, either.'

There was a long silence broken only by Fox's uneven breathing and the beeping of the ICU machines hooked up to him.

'Are we any better than them?' Gammaldi asked finally. He was standing by the side of Fox's bed, staring down at his own hands. 'We – the West, the US, the Brits, Germans, French, Aussies, whoever . . . Do you ever think, when we take a life in the name of our cause, are we any better than these terrorists and criminals? Are we worse than them when we put a missile in through their window? When we call in air strikes. When we take a life to save one? To avenge one?'

'The saddest thing is,' Fox said, 'things far worse than that come too easily.'

Fox put his hand on his mate's, winced as he squeezed it. It was something that he needed to feel. Through that pain he knew he was alive, and there to fight another day. To continue on to whatever lay ahead.

GLOSSARY

AFRICOM	United States Africa Command
ANFO	Ammonium Nitrate Fuel Oil
APEC	Asia-Pacific Economic Cooperation
BCT	Brigade Combat Team
BCU	Battery Coolant Unit (Stinger Missile)
CAS	Close Air Support
CBD	Central Business District
CCTV	Closed-Circuit Television
CENTCOM	Central Command
CEO	Chief Executive Officer
CIA	Central Intelligence Agency
CO	Commanding Officer
CS	Chlorobenzalmalononitrile (Tear Gas)
CSL	Cooperative Security Location
DCIA	Director Central Intelligence Agency
DDCIA	Deputy Director Central Intelligence Agency

DEA	Drug Enforcement Administration
DEFCON	Defense Condition
DHS	Department of Homeland Security
DNI	Director of National Intelligence
EMT	Emergency Medical Technician
EOB	Executive Office Building
FBI	Federal Bureau of Investigation
FLOTUS	First Lady of the United States
FN	Fabrique Nationale
FOI	Freedom of Information
GSR	Global Syndicate of Reporters
HHT	Headquarters and Headquarters Troop
HRT	Hostage Rescue Team
HVT	High Value Target
IED	Improvised Explosive Device
IMU	Islamic Movement of Uzbekistan
JDAM	Joint Direct Attack Munition
JSOC	Joint Special Operations Command
KIA	Killed In Action
LCD	Liquid Crystal Display
LOOP	Louisiana Offshore Oil Port
LZ	Landing Zone
MEND	Movement for the Emancipation of the Niger Delta
MEU	Marine Expeditionary Unit
MOPOL	Nigerian Mobile Police
MRE	Meal, Ready-to-Eat
NASDAQ	National Association of Securities Dealers Automated Quotation System
NATO	North Atlantic Treaty Organisation

NIE	National Intelligence Estimate
NCO	Non-Commissioned Officer
NOC	Non-Official Cover
NRO	National Reconnaissance Office
NSA	National Security Agency
NSC	National Clandestine Service
NYMEX	New York Mercantile Exchange
NYSE	New York Stock Exchange
OLED	Organic Light-Emitting Diode
OPEC	Organisation of Petroleum Exporting Countries
PDB	President's Daily Brief
PFC	Private First Class
POTUS	President of the United States
PS3	Sony Play Station 3
PTSD	Post Traumatic Stress Disorder
ROE	Rules of Engagement
RPG	Rocket Propelled Grenade
RSTA	Reconnaissance, Surveillance and Target Acquisition
RTO	Radio Telephone Operator
SAC	Special Agent in Charge
SAM	Surface to Air Missile
SAS	Special Air Service
SAW	Squad Automatic Weapon
SEC	Securities and Exchange Commission
SIGINT	Signals Intelligence
SIPRNet	Secret Internet Protocol Router Network
SLR	Self-Loading Rifle
SOCOM	Special Operations Command

SPR	Strategic Petroleum Reserve
SUV	Sport Utility Vehicle
UAV	Unmanned Aerial Vehicle
UCP	Ultimate Combat Pistol
UKUSA	United Kingdom, United States, Canada, Australia, New Zealand signals intelligence community
UN	United Nations
WMD	Weapons of Mass Destruction

ACKNOWLEDGEMENTS

Novels are able to encompass all the disciplines and interests of humanity. It is an art where one tells lies to tell the truth. Getting that onto the page is hard, merciless work.

I'd long planned to write a thriller about morality set against an oil crisis and this book was written at breakneck pace. To help the story and I survive I am indebted to all my family and friends who supported and understood me in this insane endeavour. Eternal thanks goes to the creative genius of Malcolm Beasley, who was, again, my go-to guy to bounce ideas off and test scenes on. Tony Wallace, Tony Niemann and Emily McDonald were again my early pro-readers and this story is the better for it, and my mate Al Gammaldi chucked in his usual two cents worth (see Al, you got a girl in this book).

The staff of Hachette Livre Australia have done another beaut job in bringing a Lachlan Fox story to the masses. Getting a novel successfully produced and out there takes extraordinary effort and I'm keenly aware that I continue to work with the best team in the business. My editors Vanessa Radnidge and Sara Foster deserve accolades beyond words as they continue to make sense of my mess of thoughts and dreams on the page.

My agent Pippa Masson and the team at Curtis Brown Australia have dedicated another year to representing me beyond the ordinary. Third time around in this partnership and I couldn't be happier.

I owe Nicole Wallace a gratuity that knows no bounds. Suffice to say: thanks babe for continuing with me on this journey, you are my closest friend and truest love.

FIVE QUICK QUESTIONS WITH JAMES PHELAN

Fox has been through a lot in the past three books – will he ever get a rest?

The time line of FOX HUNT to BLOOD OIL spans about a year and a half, so Fox has been busy. The next novel, titled LIQUID GOLD, is set about six months after the events of BLOOD OIL, and Fox has been to India to cover the water crisis, picked up a Pulitzer, and is teaching writing at Columbia. This relatively quiet life comes to a crashing halt in the opening scene: set in a café on Lake Como, Fox is sitting across a table from a Russian crime boss, a sinister figure at the centre of his reportage of the water crisis. Fox is there to do a trade – stop investigating the story and give up a source, and in turn someone will get to live. That someone, Fox learns in this scene, is a person from his past . . . As a tip of the hat to Hitchcock, throughout this prologue we are aware that there is a bomb under Fox's table; even if he does the trade, he's not going to get out alive.

Does Fox take on the undercover work that Michael Rollins was doing?

In some ways, yes, he does. He doesn't go so far as to infiltrate the Umbra organisation as Rollins managed to do, but he is working closely with the FBI and CIA to bring these ex-spies to justice.

Much of the previous three novels have come to define who Fox is, so from the start of LIQUID GOLD we know he is equipped to handle pretty much anything that comes his way. Where the first three novels were a search for identity for Fox, dealing with themes of honour, redemption, friendship, loyalty, revenge and betrayal, this next novel will ultimately deal with faith and the myth of sacrifice for a greater good.

What kind of storylines will we see in LIQUID GOLD?

Well, he continues to have some kind of relationship with Jane Clay, who was introduced in BLOOD OIL. But of course it's not that simple! A past love comes back into his life and he's going to have to make a choice – not between these two women, but for something much more noble.

In terms of archetypal storylines LIQUID GOLD pretty much has it all: unhappy love, flight, passage, waiting, desire, the triumph of purity, the faithful servant, the love triangle, beauty and the beast, the enigmatic woman, the ambiguous adventurer and the redeemed drunkard – and, of course, some twists!

What kind of tone can we expect in LIQUID GOLD?

As with the first three Fox novels, it will have a three act plot.

Expect the next novel not to be as dark as this one. There is a great appetite in the world right now to look at anything cultural that's American, English and Australian and try to figure out who we are and who we have become in this War on Terror age. It is as if the war, and the social eruptions in its aftermath, unleashed demons that had been bottled up in the international psyche. BLOOD OIL kind of lived by the mantra 'Justice is about harmony. Revenge is about making yourself feel better' which I think was very reflective of the time of the book's writing. Now, I think we are entering a more hopeful era. So expect LIQUID GOLD to be a little less hard-boiled and neo-noir, and more a relentless thriller that's bigger than anything I've written before.

Who's Fox going to be up against?

Mendes was a good antagonist but the true counterforce for Fox is unfolding over the next couple of books in the form of

Umbra, a loose collection of ex-spooks and present-day terrorists. I think readers will be pleasantly surprised at the tentacles that stretch into the first three novels from Umbra. Again, Fox is on a quest to uncover the truth, although this time he's more aware of the cost that comes with that. Ultimately, he's up against himself: if BLOOD OIL was something of an awakening, this is the next step on his path of enlightenment, and he's going to show us, again, why we look to stories of heroes to show us the way.